Victoria Woodhull has done a work for women that none of us could have done. She has faced and dared men to call her the names that make women shudder, while she chucked principle, like medicine, down their throats. She has risked and realized the sort of ignominy that would have paralyzed any of us who have longer been called strong-minded.

Leaping into the brambles that were too high for us to see over them, she broke a path into their close and thorny interstices with a steadfast faith and glorious principle would triumph at last over conspicuous ignominy, although her life might be sacrificed. And when, with a meteor's dash, she sank into a dismal swamp, we could not lift her out of the mire or buoy her through the deadly waters. She will be as famous as she had been infamous, made so by benighted or cowardly men and women… In the annals of emancipation, the name… Victoria Woodhull will have its own place as a deliverer.

—Elizabeth Cady Stanton, 1876, before she and Susan B. Anthony wrote Victoria out of history…

THE RENEGADE
QUEEN

EVA FLYNN

OMEGA
PRESS

Ω Omega Press

© 2016 Eva Flynn   MAY 0 9 2017

Publisher: Omega Press
Author: Eva Flynn
Editors: Amanda L. Boyle, Sam Clapp
Cover design by Alan Clements

ISBN: 978-1-5196292-1-0

Social media connections:
Twitter: @Evaflyn
Facebook: Eva Flynn_author
Goodreads: Eva Flynn

Dedicated to every woman who has taken risks

Written with deep gratitude to Victoria Woodhull and Susan B. Anthony, who risked everything for equality

CONTENTS

1

GENESIS

1838

I was conceived in a whore's tent at a Methodist revival. I know this because my father recounted the story often and with some pride. In those days, a meeting was not in a big tent but rather in an empty field surrounded by small tents. Prostitutes, hawkers, and every unsavory fool who had something to sell to the downtrodden camped out in tents, perching themselves like hawks ready to scoop up feeble mice. The preacher man encouraged them to stay, wanting to turn each one into a tick mark indicating a saved soul. Mama, who would weep uncontrollably for the world's sins and dry her tears with the most stomach-churning stream of never-ending underworld profanity, begged Father to attend the revivals. Once Father realized that fancy ladies would be surrounding the meeting, Mama didn't have to beg no more. He always said both the preacher and the whores had a way of saving men. The preacher kept a tally in his Bible, and the whore kept a tally by counting the cash in her hand. Father, a smooth talker who could convince Saint Peter to open his gates for the devil, always made friends with the whores. Without the money to make a tent of their own, Father wormed his way into the whores' hearts, all the while keeping his eye on the prized dirty canvas. It didn't take long before a boyish wink won the tent, if only for an hour.

Revivals in those days were hours without end; the preacher man could fall down dead and another one would hop up to take his place. For three days, my parents would sing hymns, pray, and listen to sensational and impassioned speeches. Sometimes, the speeches were words they understood. Sometimes, they were indecipherable shouts of emotion. It was these shouts of emotion that moved Mama and Father so. Sometimes taking turns, sometimes both at the same time, they would roll in the mud begging the Holy Spirit to take them home. They chanted and danced, only to suddenly fall down like the dead and foam at the mouth. And they sang, nonstop singing. Songs about rocks, songs about hell, songs about nails, songs about heaven, and a few songs about sharing wealth, wealth no one had. On the third night during a hymn about sharing prosperity, Mama spoke in tongues. Her tongue speaking was so hypnotic and melodious that everyone around tried to imitate her. Among the nonsense would be an occasional "Hallelujah Amen" and a few "Dear Jesus I beseech thees." In the middle of a "Dear Jesus I beseech thee," my father, Buck Claflin, defied convention and crossed over to the women's section of the field to grab my mother, Anna, dragging her to the whore's tent. After a wink, the tent was vacated and a frenzy of spiritual and sexual ecstasy ensued. When they left the tent, no one asked any questions because, as Father said, "Folks were too busy drinking Jesus' blood and eating his body."

The interruption of a woman's higher power by a man's lower urges seems to be a theme that has followed me throughout my life, beginning with my conception. And yet I remind myself that even in the marriage of the holy and the earthly, a miracle can occur.

I was born in September, the sixth of ten children (counting the dead ones), and named after Queen Victoria, who was then in the first year of her reign. When folks asked Mama why her camp meeting baby was named after the British monarch, the answer was "Because one day she will be the Queen of England." When folks pointed out the obvious, namely that we were poor Americans and did not have a drop of British royal blood, Mama replied, "We pride ourselves on never letting minor details interfere with our grand plans."

2

THE HAUNTED

1850

"The Dead! Bring out your dead!" the wagon driver yells. Mama weeps over the body of tiny Hester, a baby brunette with soft skin, blue eyes, and a serene smile, taken from us before her first birthday. I long to give her one more kiss, to put my cheek next to hers, but I am told that I cannot. Odessa is in my arms, the little thing wailing. Mary, the neighbor girl who helps out Mama, has her hand on my shoulder and tries to me of some small comfort. Mary has seen hard times before, but this is my first hard time. My first really hard time. Tennessee, preferring to be oblivious to any sadness, sits in the corner pretending her cornhusk doll is getting married. Father is not here for he knew this moment would come swiftly, the moment when Hester's body is placed in a small pine box. The driver nails the wooden box shut. Bang! Bang! Bang!

The dead wagon comes daily now. Our home grows tense with every gallop, aching to know whether it is the dead wagon or simply a neighbor on a horse. I fail to understand why we should lose my sister, I do not know how Jesus could take her from us. Mama and Father try to explain. Yellow fever, Mama says, is God's way of punishing mankind for our wicked ways. But I do not know why Hester would have to suffer because of others. Father agrees and says this is a test to weed out the weak. If we survive it is because we were meant for greatness. I do not know how Jesus could tell if a baby was meant for greatness, but I pray that I am meant for greatness. I pray that Father is not.

I ask my sisters and brother to complete a circle promise. Tennessee is the only one who will agree, the rest having no energy to climb Williams Mound. The Injuns built Williams Mound. Some say the Injuns built it so they could see the enemy coming. For once on top of the mound we can see far and wide, crops dotting the farmland. Other folks say that Injuns built this mountain so they could climb it and turn themselves into birds and fly away from the white folks.

"Circle Oath," I say. Tennessee gets in front of me. At six she is shorter, but I bend down so we can press our foreheads together. Wordlessly, Tennessee grabs my arms and we move in a circle together.

"Death will not come for us," I say.

"Death will not come for us," Tennessee repeats.

"We were meant for greatness," I say.

"We were meant for greatness," Tennessee repeats.

"The circle will be unbroken," I say.

"The circle will be unbroken," Tennessee repeats.

"On all I hold sacred and dear," I say.

"On all I hold sacred and dear," Tennessee repeats.

I close my eyes tight and whisper, "Injuns, turn us into birds and let us fly and be free." Tennessee hears this and repeats it after I do. We say this over and over, but then we open our eyes and we are still standing, flightless. Tennessee looks at me with relief and says, "I was afraid only I would fly. And I don't want to be a bird without you."

Hugging and kissing Tennessee, I run my hand through her long hair. Her bewitching face gives me the most beautiful smile, and I know in that instant that we are more than sisters. We are soul mates.

AΩ

"Dead! Dead! Bring out your dead!" the wagon driver yells. Odessa this time. I silently curse her for not completing the circle oath, and I curse her again for not being meant for greatness. Mary holds my hand. Tennessee hides in the woods.

Father is missing. Mama is cursing the world for their sins. Her talk of ungrateful, odious bastards and damnation fills the air. Bang! Bang! Bang!

Our home, our shack, is an unpainted hovel, a mere twenty-five feet long. Inside, we have nothing except an old Bible. Our clothes are rags held together by pins and dirt. Mama spends her day helping us complete the chores and teaching us about our heavenly destiny. Father works all the time; although, I do not know what he is working for. He certainly does not earn enough money to bring anything home. I often wonder if he works for free. He owns and runs Homer's only grist mill, one of the nicest in Ohio. Beyond the mill, he delivers the mail daily to every Homer resident. And still we have nothing. We have nothing except each other, and some of them I could do without. Ten of us, now seven of us, in a small space. Two taken by the fever. One taken by a man.

"Bring out your dead! Bring out your dead!" the wagon driver yells. I run to the window and see a large pine box outside. "Mama!" I scream, "Mama!" And then I see a man place Mary, sweet neighbor Mary, in the wooden box. Bang! Bang! Bang!

AΩ

"Miss Victoria, Miss Victoria," Mrs. Taylor says, banging her hand on the chalkboard. "Do you want to share with the class what you and Billy are discussing?"

Mrs. Taylor is everything a teacher should be. Wearing her dress with its high neck of lace, she looks at me with a twinkle in her eye. We try to hide it, but I am her favorite. She always makes sure that I have something to read and something to eat. Mrs. Taylor even bought me a pair of shoes once. These shoes were made of the finest brown leather with the most intricate details. Wearing those shoes made me feel like I was someone. I wore them for two days before Father stole them in the night and sold them.

"I was telling Billy that the Fugitive Slave laws ain't right. If a man can run away from his owner, then he should be free. It's not right for one man to chase another all his life," I say.

"But Victoria," Billy says, "a Sambo is property, bought and paid for."

Mrs. Taylor bangs on the board again. "Miss Victoria, are you a fugitive slave?" she asks.

"No, ma'am," I say, "but if I was, I'd run, run, run, and keep on running until I was free."

"Since you're not, we shan't worry about it today," Mrs. Taylor says.

I nod. I look out the window and see my dead sisters with Mary. They are playing hopscotch. No longer ill, they have bright faces, rosy cheeks, and smiles. Their bodies have an otherworldly glow to them, and they look very much alive, not like ghosts that I could stick my arm through. I reach out to try to touch them and Mrs. Taylor comes by and hits my hand with a ruler.

"Stop daydreaming, Miss Victoria," Mrs. Taylor admonishes.

I steal glances out the window the rest of the day to see my sisters and sweet Mary. Every time I look, they are there. I rush outside at the end of the school day. They greet me at the door. We all walk home together.

"Are you angels?" I ask Mary.

"Spirits," Mary says, "here to guide you. You may see other spirit guides as well. You also have angels, a band of angels, to protect you."

"That is kind," I say, "but I think I can figure out things on my own."

"You will be tested," Mary says, "maybe not today, but soon, and many times. You were meant for greatness."

"I know that," I say, "for I am not dead yet."

Hester laughs and starts playing peek-a-book and the four of us spend the rest of the afternoon playing, running, and hiding. I am behind a tree when I hear Mama call for me, "Victoria!"

I run to Mama. Mama is in a blue and green plaid dress wringing her hands, strands of hair falling out of her brunette bun, making her look either crazy or overworked.

"Your chores. We need firewood, and the meal has to be cooked," Mama says.

"I was playing with Hester, Odessa, and Mary," I say.

Mama looks at me, clearly taken aback. "They are dead."

"They are alive in the spirit world. I can see them," I say.

Mama grabs my shoulders, "Don't lie to me, child."

"I'm not," I say. "You could see them too, but they are hiding right now."

Mama holds out her hands to the heavens, "Sweet Jesus, sweet baby Jesus!" She then rocks back and forth on her feet and begins speaking the nonsense tongue talk, "La-be-do-ba-da, La-be-do-ba-da, Zing-ca-domaina- Jesus!-Ma-boo-par-de-de-Hallelujah!"

I watch, entranced, wondering if this is what Mama did the night I was conceived. As Mama continues her righteous display, I start to collect the firewood. After the wood is all stacked, I clean the house. And still she stands outside, speaking in tongues. I make dinner for the family. And still she speaks in tongues. I look out the window and see Father walking up, and I leave the home to greet him. Father, a tall man, a handsome man, is covered in sweat and dirt, even dirtier than normal. I curse thinking about all the time it will take me to get those clothes clean.

"What is it woman?" Father asks while gently shaking Mother. Mama ends with a "Sweet Jesus, I beseech thee," and snaps out of it. When she comes to, she has a blank stare on her face.

"What is it, woman?" Father asks again.

Mama raises her shaking hand towards me, "Devil or angel, I know not, but she sees the dead."

I take two steps back.

Father turns to me, "What is this about, child?"

I look down at the earth, wishing I was part of the dirt.

I hesitate and stammer but Father only grows impatient, his hand finds my shoulder and he begins to squeeze until he is so rough that I nearly cry out with pain. I blurt, "I see Hester and Odessa... Mary too."

Father releases me with such force that I stumble backwards, he laughs a hearty laugh, and slaps his knees. He runs over to me, picks me up, and smiles at me as he holds me as high as he can. As he brings me down he kisses me on the forehead. His kindness to me in this moment is more than he has ever shown before.

"This is wonderful, child," Father says. "Have you ever heard of the Fox sisters?"

I shake my head.

"Three sisters in New York, blessed by the spirits. Talk to the dead, they do," he says. "People travel from miles around just to see them. And they charge five dollars a head, five dollars, Victoria. With you and Tennessee..."

"What was their message?" I ask.

"Message?" Father asks.

"The dead," I try to clarify. "What did the dead say?"

"Oh that, let's see... yes, the paper said they spelled out the following message: Spiritualism will work miracles in the cause of reform," Father says.

"Reform? What does that mean?" I ask.

Father shakes his head. "The message is unimportant, child, the money is what is important. Even if we charge half, at two-fifty a head, we'd make enough to—"

"Humbug people?" I ask.

"Humbugging?" Father crouches down so he can look me in the eye. "You have the gift."

AΩ

I hear Father's footsteps and the air around me changes. The room becomes electric, hot, and oppressive. Before I can even pull the cover around me, Father is next to me, having stumbled over the others. I start to raise my head up to ask him what he wants, but I know. I can tell by his smell, the mixture of sweat, desire, and alcohol. He throws the covers off and gets on top of me with only my thin nightgown and his pants between us. His chest rubs against my breasts as he reaches down to remove his pants.

"Father, you are in the wrong bed, I am not Mama."

"I don't want your mother, I want you," he says.

I start to scream and he places his hand on my mouth. "You will wake the others," he says. I look across the floor and Tennessee is watching us with a mixture of curiosity and horror. She then turns around and pretends to sleep.

With one hand on my mouth, Father's hand finds my bloomers and slides them down. His fingers then crawl inside me, stretching me, while he softly moans. Father then raises my nightgown to my neck and buries his head in my breasts for a moment before doing something, maybe peeing, inside me. The pain and discomfort nearly cause me to leap off the bed, but he holds me down.

"Do you see the spirits now?" he whispers in my ear.

I see nothing but blackness.

ΑΩ

"Take your time, child," Father says, holding my hands at the kitchen table. "What do the spirits tell you about my future?"

It is morning, and Father and I are the only ones awake. While I was to acquiesce to his needs last night in a silent way, Father is no longer concerned about waking anyone. I look into his eyes and I can see a smug familiarity in them. He knows my body now and he's proud of it. I guess he has always owned my body. He just waited until last night to stake his claim. But my soul is all mine.

"I see death all around you," I say.

"Damn," Father says, banging the table, "you cannot say that, child."

"Why not?" I ask.

"Because the people won't come back to hear that. They don't want tales of death. You have to tell them that they will be rich, meet the mate of their dreams, have long health," he says.

Father walks to Tennessee, sleeping on a mattress on the floor. He picks her up and brings her over to the table. Startled, she knows better than to protest.

"Tennessee," he says, "let's pretend that I'm going to give you two dollars to talk to the dead and ask them about my future. What do you say?"

Tennessee rubs her eyes. "For two dollars, I'd tell you whatever you want to hear."

Father laughs and pats Tennessee on the head. "That's it, Tennie, that's it."

Father stands up tall and pats us both on the head. "Folks say that something called delirium can cause a commune with the spirits. If we are going to do this thing right then we need to put you in delirium."

Tennessee and I look at each other, not knowing what Father is talking about.

"Don't fret," Father says, "it won't hurt."

ΑΩ

Delirium. The torment before death. Folks call delirium The Man with the Poker. People usually get a visit from the man by drinking too much, going from the cheerful glass to the solitary bottle. It is during these times when people see heaven and touch the face of God.

The Man with the Poker is staying with us. Father has denied us food for days on end. We are given as much opium as water to drink. Mother walks around us, speaking in tongues. Tennessee tries to charm The Man with the Poker just like she tries to charm every man with pretty words and soft giggles. But her charms do not work on this man and she curls up in a ball and cries. Her eyes curse me.

I get on my knees and crawl to Tennessee. She shuffles away when I touch her. I grab her tight and whisper in her ear,

"Say that gold awaits in a tent and people will line up for miles around. And tell him that Ben Miller will become deathly ill, but will recover in a week's time."

"How do you know this?" Tennessee asks.

"My spirit guides," I say. I know my spirit guides are real because I met them before The Man with the Poker. Hester, Odessa, and Mary are still there, but now a man has joined them. A white winged horse gave my spirit a ride to the heavens to meet him. His name is Demosthenes and he moved the ancient world with his speeches.

"And if they are wrong?" Tennessee asks.

"Spirit is never wrong," I say.

Father comes home and picks me up, sitting me down at the kitchen table. He grabs my hands. "Girl, what does Spirit tell you?"

I stay silent. Father squeezes my hands and says, "Take your time."

"Death is all around you, Father," I say. Father looks at me, turns red, and starts foaming at the mouth. He rushes outside. Mama screams, "Jesus, Sweet Jesus." Tennessee cries. My spirit is ready for what comes. I'm sitting in Demosthenes' lap and he tells me to be brave.

Father walks in with switches in his hand. He grabs me and pulls me outside. He rips my bloomers off and whips my legs, my thighs, my calves, my ankles. Any flesh the switches can find is seared. The pain is sharp, unrelenting. I feel the blood drain out, I look down at the little pools of blood in the dirt. Roses emerge and morph into hearts. Hester and Odessa appear. I try to talk to them but only can manage a smile before the blackness comes.

ΑΩ

The Man with the Poker comes and goes. I have lost track of time, not knowing if the blood roses were yesterday or weeks ago. Tennessee whispers to me of being right, of Ben Miller being ill, of Father looking for canvas for a tent, but I fail to respond. Most of me is in the spirit world. Complete peace and love are the only feelings in the spirit world. I look down on our hovel from the spiritual realm, and I wonder how so many people have so many things so wrong. I like being with Demosthenes. I am safe. And from the lap of Demosthenes, I can see that all of humanity is one. We are all part of one large soul, one experience. I talk to Demosthenes and plan for the future. Demosthenes tells me that I must fight action with action, and not words alone. He is right. The only action is to run away. There must be a place in this world for me, somewhere. And if there is not a place for me on earth, I will happily live with the spirits. All I must do is drink more than Father gives me. And then I will be free.

"Victoria!" Mama's scream brings me out of the shadowlands. Mama is running around like she has The Man with the Poker, picking up anything of value, carrying what she can on her back. The children are crying. Tennessee is shaking.

"Out now, run," Mama says. I get up and start to change into a clean dress, and Mama puts her hands over mine. "No time, child."

Walking outside, there are people with pitchforks and guns walking towards us, screaming obscenities. I grab Tennessee's hand and leave the other children to fend for themselves as we all follow Mama up the hill, running as fast as we can. I look behind me and see that the mob has set fire to our home. It cannot be saved.

"Mama," I ask, "what did Father do?"

"Run, girl," Mama says. "Run from those miserable sons of bitches who deserve to be screwed by the Devil up the ass for eternity."

My wounded, weak body has trouble dragging a crying, resistant Tennessee while keeping pace with the fleeing family. I briefly think that I should let them leave us behind. But then, where would we go?

We land in the dirt and I take a few seconds to stare at the last few purple beams of sunlight. Mama's face blocks my view and she pokes me with a stick and tells me to get up.

"Mama," I ask, "what did Father do?"

"A sin of man is not a sin of God," Mama says.

Jumping up, I grab her stick and raise it to her. "What happened?" I ask.

Mama looks at me straight in the eye and says, "The Homer grist mill, burned it to the ground he did. We need that insurance money for a tent. Your brave Father risks it all for his family. Those tarnation cocksucker bastards can go to the devil. "

"What about school" I ask.

"No school. Nothing you need to know can be found in books. You were meant for greater things," Mama says. "You were meant for miracles."

No wonder the townspeople want us all dead. We took away their only way to make bread and promised them miracles instead. Even with all the time I've spent on the laps of the spirits, I know that miracles are no substitute for bread.

3

THE ORACLE OF THE MIDWEST

1853

"Step right up! Step right up! Speak to the spirits and get healthy. Victoria, the mystical oracle, can speak to the dead and foretell your fate! This Sybil of the Midwest sees and knows all! And Tennessee has the miracle elixir! Every sore healed, every pain subdued! Two dollars to speak to the dead and seventy-five cents for the miracle potion!" Father is hawking our services to everyone, but he has a way of looking directly at the men. The men look at us up and down and smile like hungry wolves. They will want me to talk to their dead mothers and will implore the spirits to send money and women their way. They will then go from me to Tennessee and ask for her healing hands and magnets to alleviate their bad backs, their weak hands, the aches in their heads.

It is hot and humid and we are wearing threadbare dresses that cling tightly to our bodies. We crouch down to try to get our dresses to touch the ground, hiding our bare feet. Father does not believe in shoes. But showing men your ankles means you are a whore advertising your wares. I've begged Father for shoes, but he says it is good for business for men to see how poor we are. Tennessee and I have made a circle oath that we will steal shoes in a week's time if they don't come to us some other way.

A beast of a man covered in pimples, facial hair, and sweat holds up a dollar. He tells Father, "I want to be alone with the Sybil." Before the man can get to the word "be" Father has snatched the dollar out of the man's hand and pushed me to him.

Uneasiness gets the best of me. I show the man where our tent is. He goes inside. I interrupt Father by coming up behind him and grabbing his elbow. He pauses his advertisement momentarily. "Father, I do not know…" I say.

Father smiles and kisses my forehead. "Girl, your worth has never been known, but to the world it will be shown." This is what Father tells me when he wants me to do something I do not want to do. It somehow always works to charm me, and I nod and walk into the tent. Every day when I walk into this grimy tent, I wonder if it is my conception tent. The tent is old enough, has plenty of wear, was bartered for second-hand, and smells just like conception. Twenty-five tick marks are on one of the flaps and I imagine those represent the number of men the whore satisfied fourteen years ago before letting my parents borrow the tent for an hour.

"Do you want to talk to the dead?" I ask the man who follows me in as I make my way towards the small, flimsy table.

The man stands up and grabs my wrist. "A woman like you was meant for the living," he whispers in my ear. I break free of his grasp before his tongue gets all the way down my face.

"Leave at once," I say.

He laughs and grabs me by the waist. My blue plaid dress, held together with pins, starts to fray at the strain. I struggle against him. "The more you struggle, the more I like it," he says, as a few of my most strategically placed pins pop out. Grinning, he nestles his head in my bosom, kissing my breasts while he holds my body so close that I feel his manhood rub against my leg. Pausing in my fight, I allow his sweaty embrace so my hands can be free to pick up the chair behind him. I hit him in the back with the chair, not having the strength to hit him over the head.

Backing away, stunned, I pick up the chair and hold it out as a weapon, using it to push him out of the tent. He lands on his back in the dirt, and the other men laugh at him. Crawling in the dirt, I find all the pins that I had lost and hastily try to repair the damage done. Father runs up. "What is this?" he asks. Father watches me pin the top of my dress, smiling when he sees a glimpse of my breast. Frowning, he looks at the man and asks, "Did you humiliate my daughter?" The man gives a slight nod. I am anticipating Father whipping this man, the way he whips me.

"That costs ye an extra fifty cents," Father says. The man nods again and throws the coins at him. Father does not look at me. He just looks at the money in his hands gleaming in the sunlight, obviously pleased with his extra funds. Father comes over and kisses me on the cheek.

I turn around and take deep breaths as I begin setting up the chairs. I can never let them see me cry, Father always tells me that.   I hear Father bellow, "Step right up! Step right up! Speak to the spirits and get healthy. Victoria, the mystical oracle, can speak to the dead and foretell your fate! This Sybil of the Midwest sees and knows all! One dollar!"

The tent opens and an older handsome man walks in. Dressed in a vest, a jacket, a bow tie, and wearing a hat, he is the best-dressed man in these parts. His movements are full of grace, suggesting he is well-to-do. He does not walk like a farmer or a peddler. He smiles at me with a kindness that is so sweet that there is no word for it. Some would call it empathy, but it is more beautiful than empathy. Some would call it angelic, but the smile is not completely devoid of self-interest. Wiping the tears from my face, I smile back, "Do you want to speak to the spirits, sir?"

"You have beautiful eyes," the man says, "I've never seen such sky blue eyes before."

"Do you want to talk to the dead?" I ask, ignoring his compliment. I've learned that a man who compliments a girl on her looks before he knows her is trouble.

The blonde man with mesmerizing hazel eyes chuckles and shakes his head. "No, I want to speak to you."

"Me?" I ask. I move towards the chair and have it within my grasp should I need it. The man towers over me, but is aware enough to hunch a little so as not to loom so large.

"Ohio has an event, a celebration of sorts. The state fair," he says.

"A fair?" I ask. "One with tents?"

"Yes, but not just with tents. It has all kinds of animals and foods and goods," he says.

"You want us to set up a tent?" I ask. Of course this man would be here to ask me to work, many men do as we attract visitors from the far counties.

"I'd like you to accompany me, as my guest," he says.

Anger starts at my bare feet and crawls up my skin. As what? I want to ask. As your whore, your lover, your mistress, your pet? Instead I say, "Sir, that is a long trip. It is not without cost."

"This is true," he says.

"Sir, I must ask you. What are your expectations?" I ask.

"Expectations?" he asks, as if he is an innocent. I know he is not innocent for have never met a man past the age of nine who is.

"Forgive my language, as the situation warrants it to be unadorned and unvarnished with subtleties and niceties," I say.

"Yes, I understand blunt language," he says.

"What are your expectations, sir? For I will not become your mistress," I say.

The man smiles another kind smile. "I just want you to have a day of freedom. I've heard things about your father, and I've witnessed some of his behavior with my own eyes. This behavior does not please me in the least."

I turn my back on the man and look through the opening of the tent. I see Father drinking the opium and backslapping all the ogres who are forming a long line to be my future customers. Torn, I weigh the utter ruination of what little proper reputation I have against getting away from my jailer and tormenter, my father, for a day.

"If my father will permit it," I say, knowing he will permit anything for a price. "But I must know your name."

The man laughs, embarrassed that we had not been properly introduced before he made such an invitation. "Canning. Canning Woodhull. Dr. Canning Woodhull to be formal."

"A doctor?" I ask. This man is rich and good. All doctors are. Canning nods and smiles.

"I must warn you, sir, that association with me or my kin will harm your reputation and give you heartache," I say. "You should consider withdrawing your invitation."

Canning laughs and places his hand under my chin.

"I fear that I am quite capable of ruining my reputation without help from the Claflin clan. And as for heartache, I'll take my chances," Canning says before dropping my chin and walking out of the tent to confront Father.

Fearing a great row, I barely allow myself to peek out of the tent flap. After a muffled exchange outside of Tennessee's tent, Father says loudly, "No refunds." Some of the drunk men in line laugh as if Father had just told the bawdiest joke ever spoken.

"I request permission to take your daughter to the state fair," Canning says.

"No."

"No harm or ill repute will come to the girl," Canning says.

"Lose a day of wages? Do you expect me to starve while you play lift the petticoat?" Father asks.

Canning reaches in his pocket and gives Father ten dollars. Ten dollars! It is more money than I have ever seen one man give to God on Sundays. This man must really like me.

"Fifteen."

Inhaling, I try to make myself even smaller hoping that Canning's anger will not transfer to me. Father would tempt an angel to kill. Canning, however, somehow remains calm, and hands over the additional five dollars.

"She'll need shoes I 'spose, walking in cow shit and all," Father says.

Canning grows rigid before exhaling deeply. He walks towards me with great purpose in his stride and redness in his face. I back away and knock the chair down with my backside.

He opens the tent. "Shoes," he says, and he starts to hand me a bill. I shake my head.

"I'll find a way," I say.

AΩ

"Be honest, were they your apples or did you steal them?" Canning asks as he admires my new shoes. I sold apples for my new shoes, and I told Canning so, but he knows this is only a slice of the story. We cross over a long wooden bridge into the fair. I see more people than I have seen in all my years put together. And all kinds of people are here; rich, poor, farmers, city folks, and even a dwarf. Livestock corrals, wagons, and tents are plentiful. And the food! Every delicious delicacy one could ever imagine is here.

"Apples are God's gifts to us all," I say, "for no one really owns an apple tree, do they?" Canning lets out a little laugh and I take his arm. This is the first time I've walked on the arm of a good man. Even my clothes show a bit more pride, as I'm wearing mama's Sunday finest.

We stop by a tent, a large and clean tent, not a tent like the conception ones that I am used to. Canning offers me a chair and I sit and listen to the ceremony. A boy, one younger than myself, reads his essay called, "Improving the Soil." It is the last entry in an essay contest. The audience claps afterwards, and the boy clutches his ribbon and money. I leave the tent on Canning's arm.

"Five dollars for an essay?" I ask.

"Yes," Canning says.

"I could write fifty essays in a fortnight. And I should. Then I could be rich and free. Just think of it!" I say loudly enough so that others turn around and stare.

"What would you write about, pet?"

"The evils of slavery, that would be my first essay. But I can have an opinion on nearly everything," I say.

"And what would you say about slavery?" Canning asks.

"This country is falling short of its ideals and needs to further evolve so that all people, not just men, and not just white men, can pursue their own self-interests without interference," I say.

Canning nods. "How does a fourteen-year-old tent girl get such notions?"

"Don't tell Father, but sometimes I ask for newspapers instead of coins for payment. And I also talk to wise spirits, they show me the need for reform," I say.

"Why would the spirits care what we do now?" Canning asks.

"The dead do not want us to repeat their mistakes," I say.

Canning looks at me with skepticism, as if he wants to debate, but he instead asks, "and how would a girl change minds on such a serious matter of debate?"

"The truth moves mountains, regardless of who speaks it," I say.

Canning stops and looks at me for a long time before saying. "Victoria, you are either incredibly optimistic or a naïve child. Which is it?"

"Perhaps I'm just opportunistic. Five dollars! For an opinion! Just think of it," I say.

Canning laughs. We continue on our carefree exploration of the fair as the hours go by, looking at the animals, and eating treats. Canning tells me about his patients and medical adventures. Crossing back over the wooden bridge that brought us here, I feel the dread in my throat and the uneasiness in my stomach that comes from night times with Father.

"Did you enjoy the fair?" Canning asks.

"The best day of my life," I say as I squeeze his arm.

Canning picks me up and places me in the wagon, but I'm stuck. I look down in a mix of horror and aggravation to see that my petticoat is caught on a nail. My ankles and my calves are exposed. Men stop and stare. Canning gasps. I feel myself flush with shame. I'll never be thought of as a lady now. I reach down to free my petticoat to cover my legs and Canning's hand grabs mine.

"Please, pet, allow me to examine your legs," Canning says.

"I most certainly will not, and it is improper for you to even ask," I say. And then I see what he sees. Scars, bruises, and open wounds. Scars from Father's whippings and bruises from everyday living. And wounds from fighting off one of Father's best customers.

"Child, I am a doctor. I can assure you that I have seen many legs," Canning runs his fingers along my scars. My hands try to push him away.

"What happened?" Canning asks with some sympathy.

"They will heal," I ask.

"What happened!" Canning asks, this time with anger.

"Father," I say, "he wants me to be a good clairvoyant, he brings deliri… The Man with the Poker…"

"He whips you this hard?" Canning whispers it with a force in his voice that I have never heard from a man. I nod.

Canning turns around and curses, saying words that are not proper to say in front of a lady. I wiggle my petticoat and get it in front of the nail to cover my legs. Canning turns around and places his hand gently on my own.

"I will clean the sores and bandage them. Then I will have a word with your father," Canning says, getting a medical bag out of the back of the wagon. He opens it and pulls out different bottles and bandages.

"You will not," I say. "He will…"

"He will never hurt you again," Canning says.

ΑΩ

We pull up to the house and it is late, much later than any proper woman would be out with a gentleman. The only reason a woman would be away from her father's home at this time of night is because she has loose morals and is engaged in intercourse. I have a different reason, of course, but folks would never believe it. My legs might heal but my reputation is shredded. Or what is left of it. None of the Claflin clan have a reputation worth enough to even buy us a few shallow pleasant greetings from neighbors. I had always hoped I would be different and that people would one day greet me with kind words as they do the other folks.

Canning does not say a word to me during the entire trip. His touch was careful when he bandaged my legs, and he held my hand when he put the stinging liquid on them. In the wagon, however, he has nothing to say to me. He just looks ahead with determination.

We go into the house and I am ashamed that Canning sees this. He is the only one outside our family who has ever been in this home. Seven of us live in two rooms, full chamber pots, dirt and squalor in every corner. I can tell by Canning's expression that he is struggling with the sight. Father, in his stained long johns wet with sweat, nearly pounces on Canning. I stand between them to protect the kind doctor.

"I forbade you to have my daughter out past dark. Now I need to be compensated for her sullied reputation," Father says.

"I intend to marry your daughter. At once. Tomorrow. When the sun is up," Canning says. I feel the world tilt and I do not know if I can stay upright. Canning never breathed a word of his intentions to me. Not one word. He is too old, he must be thirty if he is a day. And I am too young. Even more unsettling, I'm not convinced that I like this man.

Tennessee starts crying and latches on to me. I try to comfort to her, but I am more preoccupied with getting out of this marriage.

"A doctor in the family!" Mama says before screaming, "thank you Jesus, thank you! Son of Mary, thank you!"

"You can sell the elixir to your patients," Father says to Canning, "they will trust you. Think of the money we could make together!"

"Well," Canning says as he is taken aback by this outpouring of praise to Jesus and talk of commerce, "I…I'm not sure about the elixir…I…"

"Canning!" I say as I step away from Tennessee and grab his arm in an effort to pull him away from this freak show, "Why are you doing this?"

Canning takes me outside, just a step away from the home.

"We have not courted," I say.

"No, there is no time for that," Canning says.

"Why?" I ask.

Canning sighs, "To protect you. You can be my bride or you can stay here and endure your father for years more."

Before I have a chance to answer, Father opens the door and nearly screams, "I demand a compensation for her loss."

Canning looks over at me for a split second. I stay silent, not in agreement but in a moment of confusion. My silence, however, is taken as an agreement. Canning reaches into his medical bag and hands over the amount of cash I generate in two months. Father snatches the bills out of his hands. The rest of the family crowds around the door. Tennessee is out in front, crying.

"You have bestowed a great honor on our family," Father says.

"Marriage?" I ask, finally finding my voice. "I am not ready. I will not commit."

Father takes a pause from counting the money and says, "Commit you will. Commit you have."

Father and Mama and my siblings go inside and shut the door. A closed door is in front of me and a wagon behind me. What started as the best day of my life ends up being the worst. I have been bought and sold like a cow. I start to cry. Canning holds me and tries to comfort me.

"Do you have anything you would like me to fetch from your home, pet?" Canning asks.

I shake my head knowing that I have the family's best dress on and my only pair of shoes. "I have nothing."

The door opens and Tennessee runs out. We grab each other and hold on tightly. Our tears are free flowing. I whisper in her ear, "Do not fight father when he comes to you for he will only hurt you more."

Tennessee nods and then says, "Circle Oath."

"Circle Oath," I say. I ask for a moment from Canning and he agrees. Tennessee and I run behind the house under an oak tree, the largest tree for miles. We put our foreheads together and start walking in a circle.

"Near or far," Tennessee says.

"Near or far," I repeat.

"We are never apart," Tennessee says.

"We are never apart," I say.

"For we are entwined in the heart," Tennessee says.

"For we are entwined in the heart," I say.

"On all I hold sacred and dear," Tennessee says.

"On all I hold sacred and dear," I say.

We hug and Tennessee whispers in my ear, "Come back for me, darling sister, come back. I will not survive without your tender care."

4

CHILD BRIDE

1853

Canning promised that he would not make me his mistress. He kept his promise. He made me his wife. Out of the two, I would much rather be a mistress. Mistresses come and go. Wives are stuck forever. But I have no say in my fate. Courts never grant divorces. The courts say that a husband is allowed to beat a wife, as long as a reasonable instrument is used. Wives are property to be treated as the man desires. A man pays for a wife like he pays for a cow, with a few kind words, a pat on the head, and a little amount of money. We wives are no better than cows, and wives must endure regular intercourse without complaint. Although from the looks of the men around here, some cows must endure the same.

Our wedding is small, just Preacher Taylor and my parents. Tennessee does not attend, nor do my other sisters. Canning gives me a plain band that he tells me is gold, but I know it to be brass. Father may not have taught me poetry or history, but he did teach me how to tell the difference between the metal of the beggar and the metal of a king. My finger is already starting to turn green, although I try to rub it off so as not to hurt Canning's pride.

Canning brings me to his home, our home. I walk around in wonder. It is a proper home with a kitchen, a parlor, an office for his patients, and a bedroom. Everything is nice and tidy. I turn around and give Canning a smile and a hug.

"Do you approve, my chick?" Canning asks.

"I have never been anywhere that is grander," I say.

Canning grabs my hand and leads me back to the bedroom. He kisses me and I respond. His tender kiss is quickly replaced by a rougher one. His hands move over the bodice of my dress as he picks me up and lays me on the bed. Although Canning is fumbling and awkward, some movement, some noise that he makes, reminds me of Father. I try to push Canning away, landing soft blows on his chest. Canning backs up and puts space between us.

"Victoria, child, I will not hurt you," Canning says.

"I am not ready," I say.

Canning nods. "The first time is…"

"My father made me a woman before my time," I say.

Canning swears and gets out of the bed. He turns his trembling back on me, and keeps walking, out of the bedroom, out of the house, off our property, further than my eyes can see. I begin to cry. I am a fool. No man wants to hear that his wife had relations with her father. Canning will never love me now. I am only 14. With any luck, I'll be dead by 35. Twenty-one years in a loveless marriage. I console myself with the thought that maybe I'll die in childbirth. After all, Canning will expect children.

The night drags on and Canning has not returned. I light my lantern and wrap myself in Canning's coat for I have no coat of my own. I walk to the center of town, getting kicked out of one bar after another, looking for my husband. I go into one last business. The sign outside says, "Miss Susie Mae's."

I walk in and notice all the fine curtains and rugs and lamps. A petite blonde with long curls walks out of another room and sees me. A whorehouse. I'm in a whorehouse and as soon as I realize this I start to leave, but this woman walks up to me with a kindly smile.

"Are you Susie Mae?" I ask.

"Yes," she replies.

"You have a beautiful establishment," I say.

"Child, what are you doing here?" she asks.

"I am looking for my husband, but I did not realize this was… I do not think he would be here…" I say, trying not to stammer.

Susie Mae laughs, a short cold laugh, "Husband?" she asks. "We have plenty of those."

"Canning Woodhull, Dr. Canning Woodhull," I say.

"Dr.!" Susie Mae throws her head back and laughs again. She places her manicured hand on my shoulder and says, "yes, honey."

The piece in my brain that keeps me calm and composed breaks, and all the anger I have ever felt, the anger at Mama, at Father, at Canning, and at God rushes through my body. I start running through the whorehouse.

"Second door on your left, honey," Susie Mae calls out. "Knock first, they might be playing doctor."

But I do not knock. I barrel through the door and see Canning on top of an ugly woman, a troll. I can still see his fluid on her leg. My body flushes with shame. Canning gets off the woman and angrily says my name, as if to curse me. He is drunk or drugged, or both.

"Marriage was your desire, now you must honor the commitment," I say as I pick up the clothes from the floor and throw them at him.

"And you must fulfill your part of the compact!" Canning says.

"Go home and take care of your child bride," the brunette troll with missing teeth and frizzy hair says, making no effort to cover up or even wipe my husband's saliva off her breasts.

I walk out of the room, furious. I walk ahead of Canning. Once we are out of Susie Mae's, I keep walking, faster and faster, until I am running. I cross a stream and I'm running through a small wooded area. Having left the lantern behind, I am moving by the light of the moon. Canning catches up with me easily, jumps in front of me, and grabs me by the shoulders.

"Get your hands off me," I say.

"No man would tolerate what I just did and not give you a good thrashing. I should give you one in the public square and embarrass you just as you have me," Canning says as his grip on my arms gets tighter and tighter, the alcohol on his breath reminding me of Father for the second time this day.

I look into Canning's eyes and say, "Do what you must, but I will never quake, I will never cower."

Canning softens his grip. "The temptation may be great, but I will never raise my hands against you."

I exhale, feeling relief.

"But I'll be damned if I fail to exercise my wedding night rights," Canning says as he pushes me to the ground and yanks up my dress to my stomach. He rips off my drawers, my stockings, tears them to shreds with his forceful hands.

"No, Canning," I say, "I'm not ready."

Canning does not kiss me this time. He does not fondle my breasts. He shows no tenderness. Placing his hands around my waist, Canning picks me up and lays me down, holds me down on the mud, the sticks, and the rocks. I feel one sharp rock tear a hole in the back of my dress as Canning thrusts inside me three times before moaning and rolling off.

Canning stands up and holds out his hand. I take his hand and stand up, not saying a word. We start walking home, and for some reason I keep his hand in mine as tears run down my face, and his liquid runs down my inner thighs, branding me.

Maybe I am pregnant now and will die in childbirth. Only one year in a loveless marriage.

5

Magic Elixir

1854

Some men are given everything and they throw it all away. Canning is one of those men. I, however, tightly clutch what I have, knowing that if I let go even less will come my way. Canning knows this, although he could never put it into words, but his soul knows this. He pushes me away and I stay. I push him away and he seeks comfort in whores and bottles.

When he is with his whores and bottles, I am with his books. Canning has the most impressive library, with medical books, books on great orations, Shakespeare, novels, and even books on history. Reading these pages is watching out the window and seeing a different world, a beautiful world, a world with honor. When Canning is sober, we discuss the books and it is in these moments, in these discussions, that I love him body and soul. Canning even, on occasion, holds me for a few hours at night and apologizes for his behavior on our wedding night. But every time he has me at the point of forgiveness, he stands up, and walks out to be with another. And my soft thoughts for Canning are erased.

I am reading *Taming of the Shrew* when Canning rushes into our home, panting and pacing. He is clutching a bottle. He sees me and stops for a moment, calmly asking, "What are you reading, pet?"

Taming of the Shrew, I reply.

"Ah," he says, "Katharina's last speech: Thy husband is thy lord, thy life, thy keeper."

"It is fiction," I say. Canning laughs and puts the bottle down. Something about the bottle catches my eye and I pick it up. I gasp. A picture of myself as a young girl is staring at me. This is Father's elixir. It used to be called Tennessee's Magic Elixir and it had an angelic drawing of five-year-old Tennie on the label. Now I'm on the label.

"Yes," Canning says, "these are all over. Popular with the ladies."

"Whores, you mean," I say as Canning gives me a look of disapproval. "Why?"

"I confronted your father today. If his blood were not your blood, I'd kill that bas—" Canning stops. He takes a breath, pulls up a chair next to me, and grabs my hands and kisses them. "I do not know the details, but your father says that with your likeness on the bottle and your name the elixir sells more. Tennessee has earned some sort of bad reputation in these parts. I told him that you are my charge and that we do not want your name or likeness used this way."

"What did he say?" I ask.

"Your father, he always has a price," Canning says. "He will stop using your picture and your name if he and your mother and Tennessee and Utica live with us."

I know I should consent. Tennessee needs my protection, especially now if her reputation has been sullied. I'm sure whatever she did was for survival for I am not there to protect her. But the thought of living with my father again makes my entire body want to explode. I head for the door, wanting to run outside and scream and scream. Canning places his arm around me and stops me, "I told him that as long as I am your husband, he is not to be within ten feet of you."

I manage to choke out a "Thank you" between sobs.

"But we still have the bottles," Canning says. He picks up the bottle and opens it. He smells it and takes a swig. He leans back in his chair and smiles. "I could buy all of them."

"You would be supporting my father and his mischief," I say.

"Yes," Canning acknowledges, "but your magical elixir is quite tasty. It is the right combination of sweet subtleness and bold flavors."

I walk over to Canning, get down on my knees, and take the bottle out of his hand. "You don't need this," I say, "when you can have this." I lean in and kiss Canning softly.

Canning pulls away, "The first kiss initiated by my wife, why? Was it the Shakespeare?" he asks.

"No," I say, "it was you. Your protection from Father fills me with gratitude." I pick up Canning's hand and lead him to the bedroom. I begin to unbutton my dress and Canning places his hand over mine. He kisses me passionately. His hands find my breast, making my entire body arch in response. He picks me up and lays me on the bed with care, stripping me bare by removing one piece of clothing at a time. Canning loses his clothes quickly, as in a race against the second hand of the clock, and he quickly thrusts in me a few times and it is all over. I manage a smile for Canning, but truth be told I could use less thrusting and more kissing.

And yet, for the first time since men have been having relations with me, I did not hate it. I did not enjoy it, but I did not hate it.

ΑΩ

The night of not-so-terrible intercourse has left me with child. In the unborn, I see hope. If my unborn is a girl, I will teach her to be strong, I will ensure she marries the right man, and I will see to it that she can work in any position she desires. If my unborn is a boy, I will teach him how to be a kind man, a compassionate man, and to see women as equal, worthy, creations of God. My fondest hope, should I be honest, is that I will have a son who will become a politician and change the laws. He will see to it that women will not be beaten or raped without consequence. He will see to it that women will be able to vote and run for office. All my wrongs will be made right. He will save the world.

Before my child saves the world, I hope he saves me, or Canning, or both. Every penny brought into this house disappears to elixir or women or charity. There is not one false sob story that fails to elicit a forgiveness of debt on the part of Canning. It would be endearing if I weren't starving, if our baby weren't starving. Yet even those who do pay would see their money go to whores and elixir if they followed the penny trail. And that is not endearing even if I am fed.

I walk into Canning's office and grab one of my miracle elixir bottles. Despite my admonishment to Canning to not support my father, he keeps buying these or accepting them as payment from a few of his patients. As this bottle is the only currency I have, I take it. I go to food stands, walking two miles in the sun, hoping to barter spirit tales for fruit. I work the first apple cart man I see.

"How much for three apples?" I ask.

"Seventy-five cents," the man says, giving me a look that tells me he has seen me before. I suppose everyone in this town has. Whereas I try to block out faces, my own face seems to make a mark on people.

"Would you barter?" I ask, holding the elixir.

"No ghost talkings," the man says.

"No, indeed," I say, "I can sense that you are blessed beyond your years with wisdom. But..."I shake my head in sadness.

"Pray tell, what is it?" the man asks.

"I am troubled to say—"

"Woman, speak it..."

I close my eyes and lean back, rocking back and forth, "My spirit guide shows me that ill health is a rock in your path," I say.

"What do you mean?" the man asks.

I close my eyes again and rock back and forth, I reach out to the sun with my left hand. "Yes, yes, I see. Thank you, Demosthenes."

"Demosthenes?" the man asks.

"My spirit guide," I say.

"What did you see?" he asks.

I place my hand on the man's heart and he jumps back a little. I remind myself that proper women are not so forward, but this message is of the utmost importance. "Heart troubles. You may not even notice any pain at first, but then, well, if they are not properly treated…"

"Death?" he asks.

"Most certain," I say. "Fortunately, I have a cure. And for three apples, it can be yours. My husband has used it to bring the dead back to life." I show him the bottle of the elixir, with my young face smiling at him from the label.

"Folks say your husband is not a real doctor," the man says.

"Just yesterday I saw Mrs. Smith surely draw her last breath. The body even started turning before my eyes, and when my husband administered this, she rose from the bed… a modern day Lazarus," I say.

The merchant shakes his head. "The apples are seventy-five cents, Mrs. Woodhull. If you do not have the money today, I suggest you come back when you do."

I start jumping up and down and waving. "Canning! Canning!" I yell.

The man looks in the direction I am waving and I grab two apples and place them in the top of my dress and hold one arm across my chest to make sure they don't fall loose. The man turns around and looks at the apples, and then me, and then at the apples.

"Dear Jesus," I say, "my eyesight is getting worse with every day of pregnancy for I cannot even recognize my own husband. Thank you for your time, dear sir, and I wish you good health." I leave, feeling the man's stare on me all the way home.

I open the door to find Canning slumped on the floor, next to a few empty bottles of the magic elixir. I take the apples out of my dress, and set them down on a table and go to Canning.

"Please, can you not stay sober for a day?" I beg Canning. "The child will be here…"

Canning looks up briefly from his stupor, drooling, needle marks in his arm. I push a clump of his hair away from his forehead and try to see the man that showed me kindness at the state fair. Opening his hand, I hand him an apple.

"Apples are God's bounty that belong to everyone," Canning says.

"You remember," I say.

Canning kisses me on the forehead, "It was a glorious day." He takes a few bites of the apple before his hands drop it. He passes out. I pick the apple up and eat the rest of it, crying, wondering why Canning has to be a hard rock when he could easily be a gem. Snuggling up to Canning, I kick my empty elixir bottles out of the way and fall asleep.

I wake up and Canning is gone. Sighing, I get on my coat and head for Susie Mae's. One day, I will be enough. A man will come in my life and I will be enough. No whores, no alcohol, no morphine, no hustling. Just me. I will be enough.

Crossing the familiar path to the whores' den, I feel the baby move, and then some pain, low, low, low in my body. The baby is coming. I hurry my steps. Trying to run, the baby rebels and the pain is more intense. Liquid oozes down my legs, wetting my dress.

I barrel through the door with such gusto that Susie Mae hastily rushes out of her bedroom, half dressed.

"Chickadee!" she admonishes.

"The baby is coming," I whisper before crumbling to the floor in a heap of calico and pain.

Doors open. Doors shut. Canning comes stumbling with his pants loose, carrying his medical bag. He picks me up and begins to carry me to a bedroom.

"Not in a whorehouse," I say.

"No time," Canning says.

"Outside," I say.

"I need light, and a bed, and access to water," Canning says.

With all the strength I can muster, I place my hands around Canning's throat and I squeeze as hard as I can, "Canning Woodhull, so help me God, I will slit your throat if your condemn our child's first moments to a whore's bed," I say.

Canning looks down at me with a mixture of concern and exasperation. He sighs and carries me out of the whorehouse, pausing only to grab two more lanterns to add to his load. He lays me down in the woods, next to the stream that I splashed in when I was running from him on our wedding night. Canning holds my head up and pours elixir down my throat to dampen the pain.

"Yell all you want," Canning says, before moving down my body and lifting my dress up, taking off my wet and stained bloomers.

"I see the baby's head," Canning says before placing his hands in my body. My body pushes on instinct, just a few times and the baby is delivered. I hold my breath until I hear the baby cry, and then I cry. My baby is alive. I'm alive. Canning works on me for a few minutes, cuts the umbilical cord, and bathes the baby in the stream. He then takes off his clothes so he can swaddle the baby in his undershirt.

"We have a son," Canning says, handing me our baby.

"Hello, Byron, this is Mama," I say as I kiss him on the forehead and lay him on my breast.

"Byron?" Canning asks.

"After your father," I say. "It is acceptable?"

Canning wipes tears from his eyes. "My soul is unworthy."

"The judge was a brilliant man, changing lives and making just rulings. People bowed down before him. That is what I want for our son," I say.

Canning kisses me on the forehead. "And I pray that he has his mother's strength."

6

SINS OF THE FATHER

1857

Byron is not well. It started when he was crawling. He would not coo like the other babies. I told myself he was just a late bloomer. Then he started walking and he would not babble. I told myself that he was deaf. But now he is three and all he can do is moan and hit himself. He makes the most wrenching noises, as if they are cries from another world that got garbled on their travel to earth. I feel so helpless when Byron tries to communicate and I do not know what he needs. I'm a failure. I go on long walks daily just so I can get away from my flawed creation, not knowing what to do. Canning remains loving towards the boy and says nothing to me about his condition. Instead he acts as if Byron is the most normal boy in the world. Doctors are excellent liars, but I have had enough of this game of pretend. I pick up Byron and burst into Canning's office. Canning has fallen asleep in his chair, his clothes in disarray. I shake him.

"What is wrong with him?" I ask Canning.

Canning awakes with a start and gives me a strange look. Perhaps it is a look of pity, or a look of love. I am uncertain. He grabs my hand and stands up. He lets my hand go and turns his back on me. "He is an imbecile, an idiot," Canning says.

I walk in front of Canning and slap him hard. I slap him again. I start to slap him a third time when he grabs my hand. "Well then do something! Cure him!" I yell.

Canning shakes his head. "I have talked to other doctors, I have read numerous books. There is no cure. He will be like this for the rest of his life. He will not be able to talk or read or reason or manage himself or…"

"How did this happen?" I ask.

Canning pulls out two papers. "Two new studies on idiocy. Each has a different theory. The first: '*The 1848 studies shows us that eight-tenths of the idiots are born of a wretched stock; of families which seem to have degenerated to the lowest degree of bodily and mental condition; whose blood is watery; whose humors are vitiated, and whose scrofulous tendency shows itself in eruptions, sores, and cutaneous and glandular disease.*'"

"My family?" I ask. I would agree that I am of wretched stock, but would this cause Byron to be an idiot?

Canning does not answer. Instead he picks up another paper, "*The vast amount of idiocy in our world is the direct violation of the physical and moral laws which govern our being; that often times the sins of the father are thus visited upon their children, and the parent, for the sake of a momentary gratification of his depraved appetite, inflicts upon his hapless offspring a life of utter vacuity.*"

"Sins of the father?" I ask. I look at the floor and see several empty elixir bottles, Victoria's miracle. I pick up a bottle and look at my own face. My innocent face.

"Because of this, this, poison?" I throw the bottle against the wall and it breaks. Byron cries. Canning moves away.

"Our son is an imbecile because you are an addict," I scream, throwing another bottle against the wall, and another, and another. Canning does not try to intervene. Instead, he leaves the room with Byron in his arms.

"Damn you," I say, throwing another bottle.

"Damn this," I say, throwing another bottle.

"Damn me," I say. Damn me for making my bed with Canning. Damn me for giving Byron an empty life, confining him to a physical and mental prison. I throw three more bottles. I collapse among the shards of glass and drops of brown liquid, sobbing, "Damn me, Damn me."

7

THE GREAT STRUGGLE

1860

The Great Struggle is coming. War. And I am pregnant. I do not know if I will survive either the war or this pregnancy. The papers say the Confederates will rape and murder all of us. At least I know how to flee. Father taught me that. If there is one refrain that I heard over and over from my father as a child it's that it's never too late to run.

Canning says we won't have to flee, that our men will protect us. Still, he's stocking up on guns and ammunition. I'm so grateful that at thirty-six, he is considered too old to serve in anyone's army. He will be one of the only able-bodied man left in this town. Now I'll have to compete with both the whores and the war widows for any affection from that man.

He paces at night. And drinks. Paces and drinks. And that's when he's here. I'm not sure what he does with the whores. Does he just fuck and drink, or does he fuck, drink, and pace, or does he talk to Susie Mae's maidens? And if they talk, what do they talk about? When I ask him, he tries to charm me by telling me that he spends all night talking of his love for me. If he loved me, he wouldn't be there.

This baby isn't mine by choice. Every woman knows if she were free, she would never bear an unwished-for child, nor think of murdering one before its birth. And I initially had those dark thoughts, thoughts of infanticide, thoughts of saving this child from Byron's prison. But then a ray of sunlight came through my soul and I realized what a privilege it is to carry a miracle. This baby is a miracle.

We're old parents. Old, old, old. Canning has never known a thirty-six year old to be a father to a baby. By his calculations, Canning will be dead by the time this child is ten. I'm old, too, at twenty-two. I should live until the child is twenty, unless I die in childbirth or the rebels get me. Dying in childbirth was my wish for quite some time, but I now know I cannot leave Byron. I can never leave Byron.

"What if this one is like Byron?" Canning asks one night during the paces.

"This baby is fine," I say. I sit in the chair, watching Canning, knitting.

"How do you know?" Canning asks.

"Spirit is never wrong," I say. "Besides, I will it so."

I put my knitting needles down and walk to Canning. I put my hand on his arm and he pauses in his pacing. "I am concerned about me," I say, "I had no ill effect from Byron, but I'm old now. If I should not make it, what will you do?"

Canning hugs me and whispers, "You will be fine."

"How do you know?" I ask.

"Because I will it so," Canning says and we kiss. I back slightly away from Canning. "My heart would rest easier if we could find Tennessee," I say, "she could help and become a second mother." I say this with confidence, not even knowing if Tennessee would ever agree to such an arrangement. Her anger at my marriage is deep. I should have done more to help her, to get her away from Father, but managing Canning and Byron were all I could do.

Canning nods. "I'll collect newspapers from all over the state tomorrow."

"How will that help?" I ask.

"Your family will be in the news for something," Canning says.

AΩ

Cincinnati Daily Press
October 15, 1860

*A **Wonderful Young Lady**. Miss Tennessee Claflin, A natural-born Clairvoyant and Healing Medium has located in Cincinnati at 371 Sixth Street where she can be consulted upon all matters pertaining to life and health. This young lady has been traveling through the United States for the past four years and visiting the most important cities in the States. She has traveled, and is now only 14 years of age.... She can see and point out the medicine to cure the most obstinate diseases including old sores, fever sores, cancers, rheumatism, sprains, weakness in the back and limbs and all forms of female complaints. Through the assistance of some superior power, is endowed with the healing art. Her mode of examination is with a clairvoyant eye, and she tells invalids of their disease and its location with great certainty and satisfaction. Price one dollar, exclusive of medicine.*

I put the paper down. Canning was right, my family always makes the papers. We must go to Cincinnati, "The Queen of the West."

AΩ

The Queen of the West is a hodgepodge of Irish, Germans, blacks, and Rebel sympathizers. The police fail to intervene in disputes, firemen fail to put out fires, and sanitation is non-existent. The stench of human waste and wasted humans greets us on our foray into the city. The smell, mixed with my pregnancy, causes me to lean over the side of the wagon and vomit several times. Canning hands me his handkerchief, stating again and again that I did not need to join him. I ignore the commentary, disliking being chastised more than disliking the morning sickness.

Changing topics, Canning tells me that the Queen is now the second largest manufacturing center in the country. The Irish, Germans, and blacks are cheap. They'd do anything for a penny and what's more, they'd do it 100 times over. And they do. They work hours and hours and hours, nearly killing themselves. Canning and I often talk of the need for reform for the working man. A man needs some time to himself and some time for his family and some time for God. But the cities swallow up these men whole until there is nothing left.

Abolitionists come here to speak and are often chased out with threats and stones. But the new immigrants, especially the Germans, love Lincoln. Lincoln stayed largely silent during the 1860 campaign while his opponent Stephen Douglass made a speech at every whistle stop and outhouse north of the Mason-Dixon line. Douglass kept saying that he was only trying to visit his mother but that the people kept stopping him, wanting to hear his brilliant oratory. I do not know if he ever found his mother. Regardless, motherless Lincoln stayed put and stayed quiet. And the German folk must appreciate silence, because now they worship the tall, quiet one.

Home to both the birth of *Uncle Tom's Cabin* and fervent states righters, the city has two papers, one for slavery and one against. Father uses both papers to sell Tennessee. His only cause is money.

Sixth Street is known as the market for the city where all the farmers, artisans, and butchers open up shop daily. It is on this street where Tennessee is practicing her powers, somewhere inside. We park the wagon and I start to grab Byron's hand and leap from the wagon, but Canning grabs me and sits me back down.

"You will wait for me," Canning says, lifting his jacket slightly to show me his pistol. I nod and watch Canning. He walks past the vendors to 371 6th Street. I see him knock at the door. The door opens. While I can't see Father, I can feel his presence, and I know I'm right when I see the look of restrained hate pass over Canning's face. I get out of the wagon with Byron and run to Canning, almost knocking him over. Canning puts his arm out and keeps us behind him.

"I demand to see Tennessee, Buck," Canning says while moving his jacket back to show his gun.

Father ignores the threat. "The Sibyl has returned," Father says. "You are a sight. Is that my grandson? Come in, come in."

We walk up the stairs to get inside and then walk up more stairs. Father finally leads us to a drab, smelly room and opens the door. A large room with rows of beds and hundreds of bottles of tonic.

"What is this?" Canning asks.

"Making money, opening a clinic to cure cancer and other ills, sophisticated folks would call it a large profit center," Father says excitedly clapping his hands. "Just think how many wounded people the war will bring us. We'll be millionaires before the war is over. We'll be to medicine what Vanderbilt is to the ships!"

I ignore these ramblings and start to ask where Tennessee is but Canning interrupts me, "Buck, you can't cure cancer. No one can. You are going to kill people. And then you're going to end up in jail or you'll be hanging from a rope with a broken neck. I don't object to these circumstances for you, but your daughter…"

"Tennessee has the healing hands and I have the tonic, and they'd be better off with us than doing nothing. Modern medicine does not have all the answers," Father says.

Canning grabs Father by the shoulders and shakes him, "If you have ever heard one word any man has ever uttered, hear this you fool, you cannot do this, you must not do this."

I nod, "Canning is right."

Father just backs up and laughs at us. He then turns to Byron and pats him on the head. Canning grabs Byron away from Father.

"Where is Tennessee?" I ask.

"You missed her," Father says. "Off to Chicago, getting married. She will return."

"Married?" I ask. "She is only fourteen years old."

"John is his name. Bartels. Gambler. Good one. Don't even get mad when the men have fun with Tennessee. Folks around here think she's a whore, I try to explain to them that she's a healer…"

Byron starts moaning and hitting himself. I run over to soothe him.

"He is not in an institution?" Father asks. Father walks closer. His scent reminds me of everything I want to forget.

"Never," I say. "He will be by my side until I'm in the ground."

"He is a goldmine, child," Father says, "Barnums pay a fortune for freaks. Father pats my belly, "Let's hope this one is an idiot too, with two freak children none of us would have to work again."

White hot anger courses through my veins, cutting off my breath, choking off all my thoughts. Canning, standing behind me, whispers, "Hit him, Victoria, hit him." I turn my head towards Canning's flushed face. Canning, rocking back and forth from the balls of his feet to his tiptoes, says, "If you want to be the man, you have to beat the man."

Father laughs.

I shake my head. I cannot. Canning says, "You once threatened to slit my throat, and I did not doubt your sincerity. Strike him and I will protect you from any retribution."

Father hears this, rolls his eyes. He presses on. "At least three dollars a day," Father says, "plus meals. That is all he is good for." Shards of anger from five thousand one hundred and ten days of torment all came together in my soul and work their way through my fist and I punch my father in the eye, relishing the moment when my flesh meets his in violence. Father, an old man now, staggers a bit but then bounces back.

"You ungrateful whore!" Father says, grabbing my arm. Canning pulls Father off of me and punches him in the jaw and then once in the stomach. Father falls to the floor. Looking his age, perhaps older than his age for the first time in memory, he moans as he lays there in a pool of sweat, blood, and embarrassment.

Canning lords over him. "I should kill you. Don't ever speak to my wife or my son again," he says. Canning puts his arm around my waist and I grab Byron's hand. We quickly run down the stairs. A young woman stands in front of our wagon and tries to sell us flowers on our way out. I cannot even spare a kind word.

I get into the wagon and I break down, thinking of my sister in this filth, thinking of her among the diseased and dying, thinking of the abuse she gets from Father. Canning puts his arm around me. While I have never loved Canning more than I do in this moment, I cannot find any kind words for him. I am only able to whisper my prayer of "Tennessee, Tennessee."

8

BLOOD OF THE INNOCENT

1861

Zulu Maud is here. War is here. Canning is gone. He has gotten worse since our visit to the Queen City. He stumbled in at four in the morning after I begged a neighbor to fetch him from the whores. Canning was completely under the spell of The Man with the Poker when Zulu Maud was being born. Canning's shakes led him to cut Zulu's cord too near the flesh. The he tied it so loose that the string came off. He left, claiming it will be many days before I see him again. Zulu is in a pool of blood—and my own hair is soaked in a little red stream oozing drop by drop from the cord that once connected us.

My bed and my country are soaked with blood of the innocent.

I pray we will survive. I pray my country survives. If not, may death be swift and painless.

9

LAND OF THE DEAD RABBITS

1862

We will move to New York. Ohio is a wishy-washy state in a black-and-white time, and if we stay then the Rebels may overtake us. Two training camps near Cincinnati house thousands of Confederate soldiers. This state is a prime target. The Queen city is even begging blacks to form a unit to protect us all. Negroes! We are so desperate for able bodied men that we're begging former slaves to protect us? And what would we do if the Rebels show up at my house with intent to rape, pillage, or kill? Canning can shoot straight if he is sober, but he never is sober. And he's never here. He has not spent one night at our house since Zulu was born. How am I going to kill all the Rebels myself with an idiot son hiding behind my skirt and a baby feeding at my breast?

Canning objects to the move, but he will come running when I hitch the wagon. He knows I'm his golden goose. He can no longer practice medicine. The Man with the Poker rarely leaves his side. All he can do is hawk my services, just like Father. Calling for people to hear the Oracle, Canning leaves once I have a long line of people wanting to speak to the spirits. He even sells my elixir now, with my label on it. The very stuff that angered him years ago is now his profit. First, he bought up what he could and charged twice what he paid. And when that ran out, he started making his own.

When I say I'm the golden goose, I put the emphasis on golden. Money is coming in faster than Canning can spend it, even with two or three whores a night. Since the start of the war, the Great Struggle as some folks call it, plenty of women want to speak to the dead. They want to know if poor Johnny will be safe or if dead old Ed is enjoying the afterlife or if nasty George is going to resume his daily wife beatings when he returns.

Canning says we're fools to leave when business is this good, this rich. I tell him New York has desperate people too. And New York is far away from my family. And we will blend in better. A psychic with a whoring, addict husband, an idiot, and a baby isn't such an unusual sight in a large city like New York.

But where in New York City is the question. The city has more neighborhoods than Ohio has towns. And I know nothing of the neighborhoods. After placing the children to bed, I sit in the corner and close my eyes, "Demosthenes, come to me, come to me Demosthenes," I say, breathing deeply in and out. After a few repetitions, the visions come. First apples, red and green, pass through my mind, then a naked Jesus on the cross with mother Mary weeping, and then Napoleon screaming for Josephine on his death bed, and then it comes, the address: 17 Great Jones Street.

AΩ

The landlord had given us the wrong key, so I break in to 17 Great Jones Street, a huge bare brownstone. I walk on inches of dust and make my way through cobwebs to the one piece of furniture in the entire place: a small round table in the parlor room. To my blood-chilling astonishment, I find a book, *The Great Orations of Demosthenes*, on the table. This is where I was meant to be.

Canning creates a sign proclaiming the new home of the Oracle of the Midwest before I even have the cobwebs cleared out. Byron runs up and down the stairs, completely enthralled and laughing at the experience.

"Byron, dear," I say, "please be careful." Byron ignores me and continue to runs throughout the house.

Canning walks in, holding his sign selling me for $1 a visit. I nod. The sign is good. "Don't speak to any Dead Rabbit people,

Vicky," Canning says, "and if you even think they are Dead Rabbits, come get me right away."

"Drinking already?" I ask.

Canning shakes his head, "Not a drop. A gentleman, a very fine one, just told me that there is a gang that hangs out around here called Dead Rabbit. Immigrants. And what they do to women is beastly. He offered protection, but I told him that I would protect us."

"So I've run from the Rebels into a dead rabbit?" I ask, "Canning, you better teach me to shoot."

Canning walks over and hugs me, kissing my head. "I will protect us," he says.

"You have to be here to protect us," I say.

Canning nods and kisses my head again, "Always, sweetheart."

AΩ

True to his word, Canning has stayed home and guarded the door with a loaded pistol for four days. No rabbits or rabbit people, dead or alive, have shown up. Canning has also been here during the days. Maybe New York has changed him.

The past four days, our introduction to the outcasts of New York, have been a whirlwind. I knew New York would have desperate people, but I didn't realize how desperate and how many. We have a never-ending line of destitute women, emancipated slaves, and immigrants. And the accents! The German and the Irish and I can't tell them apart by sound. More often than not I find myself saying, "No sprechen sie deutsch" and the Irish man responds, "I am speaking English!" I try to listen with empathy and comfort them. When that fails, I tell them that good fortune is around the corner and that they will thrive and prosper.

The sob stories of the immigrants, as horrible as they are—working continuously for pennies, living in slum conditions with others, facing prejudice—these stories don't bother me. I reckon that they have it better in New York than they would in their own country or they would not be here.

It is the stories of the women that keep me up at night. The outcast woman who is carrying a dead soldier's baby and feels that she has no alternative to prostitution. The young girl trying to earn money for her parents by working at the factory who is raped by four men after her shift. The newlywed whose husband started drinking and hitting her on her wedding night and has not stopped. And those are the healthy women. The diseases! Every sexual disease one can imagine lives among the women, the married women. And these virtuous women must show their privates to men doctors to be scorned, laughed at, ridiculed, and be told how impure they are. Some of these women do not even understand that their husbands gave them the disease after contracting it from whores. I have seen two women just this week who can never bear children because of what their husbands' whores transmitted to them. And then the husbands have the audacity to tell the women that it is their fault because they do not bathe often enough.

And then there are the brilliant women who break my heart in a different way. I see the teachers who make $3.25 a month while the men make $10.00. I see the women who want to be doctors, or lawyers, or bankers but are told that they will lose their gentile manners, or that they are not suited for the work, or that they cannot work side by side with men. Their role is to bear children and keep a clean house.

I've taken some of these women under my wing, and we have regular meetings and discuss ideas, politics, and the arts. These meetings do not fulfill their dreams, of course, but they at least have one outlet for conversation beyond idle gossip and discussion of the best pie baking methods. One of the women, Lucy, is from Ohio and she brings me the Ohio papers or *Harper's Weekly* when she can and I, in turn, give her free readings. New voices, new thoughts, new reading material is more valuable to me than money.

I do not even need to open the Ohio paper that Lucy brought me today, for the advertisement is on the very front page:

> *American King of Cancers—Dr. R. B. Claflin is stopping at Mr. M.D. Calkin's home in South Ottawa. He claims to be the King of Cancers and all kinds of chronic diseases, fever sores, bone diseases, scrofula, piles, sore eyes in the worst stages, heart and liver complaints, female weaknesses, consumption, inflammatory, rheumatism, asthma, neurologia, sick headache, dropsy in the chest, and fits in various forms. The doctor also guarantees a cure in all cases where patients live up to directions. The poor dealt with liberally. Cancers killed and extracted, root and branch in from 10 to 48 hours without instruments, pain, or the use of chloroform simply by applying a mild salve of the doctor's own make.*

I thank Lucy, hoping my eyes betray nothing. Once Lucy leaves, Canning comes back in the house, trembling. He trembles when he opens the bottle, stops when he starts drinking, and then trembles again before he drinks too much. He walks in the kitchen and I follow him. When he reaches for an Elixir bottle, I place my hand on his arm. I hold the newspaper in front of him.

Canning shakes his head and sighs. "I'll leave tomorrow."

"Leave?" I ask.

"To fetch Tennessee. If she stays there much longer she'll be facing murder," Canning says.

"We will all go," I say. "We can afford it."

"No," Canning says, "it is dangerous."

"I care not," I say, "Tennessee is my sister and…"

Canning shakes his head, turning his attention towards me fully. He grabs my arms. "I have made more allowances in this life with you than I ever thought wise. I allow you to read whatever you desire, to discuss ideas with others, to talk politics, to travel unaccompanied, to have a business. I allow you to spend time in the company of men, all sorts, without a chaperone. But Victoria, I am a man," Canning starts shaking me and yelling, "and you are not my master, despite this tyranny you have imposed. I will not have my wife and children accompany me to a potential war zone."

I nod. Canning lets me go and walks two steps away. With his back to me, he whispers, "Tennessee's charms pay your father's bills. I might have to pry her from his dead hands."

10

EMANCIPATION

1863

January 1, 1863

I t's a new year, a new world. The slaves are free thanks to the emancipation proclamation. Lincoln has acted like king and set the slaves free. If the negro is no longer property, perhaps there is hope for women. I want to be hopeful, but I have my doubts. No president is going to go to war for women or sign a proclamation for us. We women will have to free ourselves.

I read the news and pray that Canning can emancipate Tennessee from my father. I know that their long journey has just begun.

AΩ

The city is in mourning. Old Lyman Beecher is dead. Most New Yorkers had forgotten about this man until his son announced his death. And once we all are reminded of this man of God, there is great weeping and gnashing of the teeth. Only hushed tones are allowed when speaking about him.

Having thrown off the serious Puritan yoke of Calvinism, he introduced emotion into preaching and became evangelical. With his stirring and impassioned speeches spoken in perfect cadence, Lyman started the "Second Great Awakening" which was a countrywide religious revival designed to save souls. I don't know how many souls it saved, but it brought mine to earth. For it was during this awakening that I was conceived in the whore's tent.

Lyman's fame was only eclipsed by his daughter's for it was Harriet who wrote *Uncle Tom's Cabin*, which Lincoln stated was the reason for this great war. Old Lyman was not an abolitionist himself, preferring that the government send all the negroes to Africa on a luxury liner. People say he softened his stance in his later years after having a conversation about colonization with escaped slave Frederick Douglass.

Lyman was preoccupied with men in chains. He saw chains everywhere. Not only were the slaves in chain but so were the drunks. He spoke of the mythical man in chains often. I heard him speak once, I was disappointed. Having lived nearly 100 years and seen all sorts of progress and struggles, I was hoping to hear some insight from the saver of men. But Old Lyman only wanted to talk drunk white man being tortured by the brown bottle. I just quoted his speech two days ago during a reading. A young girl was crying, trying to understand why her injured soldier husband was a drunkard. I told her:

> *Wretched man, he has placed himself in the hands of a giant, who never pities, and never relaxes his iron grip. He may struggle, but he is in chains. He may cry for release, but it comes not; and lost! lost! may be inscribed upon the door posts of his dwelling.*

Poor Lyman started losing his mind a few years back. The paper quotes his son Henry as saying, "For about a year and a half his mental condition has been exceedingly feeble and child-like. He has been like a traveler who had packed his trunk in anticipation of a journey, and, expecting every moment to start, could not unpack it."

I put the obituary down and I look at Byron, my traveler without luggage. He holds himself, rocks back and forth, and makes guttural noises. Is this Byron? Did he too start to pack his trunk for the shadowlands? Did I bring him back with my love only to have him with one foot in eternity and one foot on

Earth? Is this why he is simple? Or is it, as I believe, because his father has been a wretched man, placed in the hands of a giant who never relaxes his iron grip?

I wear black for Lyman. I do not know why. I am not particularly mournful for a strict evangelical who lived longer than two men put together. I suppose I do it for my clients. They want to see that the psychic also respects tradition. Not that I have too many living visitors this week. With Canning gone, Zulu is wandering in and out of readings with wants, needs, songs, accidents, and tears. Spirit does not like being interrupted by a toddler. Demosthenes is barely tolerant and Napoleon is downright outraged.

When the Spirits are stubborn, I have little window into the future. I resort to what Father taught me. Listen. Respond with "Your future is bright, you will be well loved, and rich, and blessed beyond imagination. You are special."

Everyone believes me.

ΑΩ

Canning gets off the wagon, but no sign of Tennessee. The children and I run to him. Canning gives Byron a kiss on the cheek and picks up Zulu. Zulu squeals with happiness. "Where is she?" I ask.

Canning shakes his head and places Zulu down. He grabs my hand and leads me indoors. He motions for me to sit on the stairs. I walk up a few steps and sit down. Canning sits on the step below and holds my hand.

"Victoria…"Canning says before shaking his head. He gets out his handkerchief and blows his nose.

"Dear…" Canning begins again clutching his handkerchief, and then his entire body begins to shake.

"She's dead," I say.

"No, no, no…" Canning says. He takes a couple of deep breaths. "I found her. She and your father must have a dozen patients, all suffering from the cancer. People who gave their life savings for a cure… Victoria, I do not know how to tell…"

"Your wife is not as fragile as she looks," I say.

Canning nods and takes my other hand. Squeezing both of my hands, he starts speaking slowly, quietly, as if he is trying to calm a wild horse, "Took a while to find 'em. Moved from Ohio to Illinois. Ottawa. They are in the Fox River House. Must be making money. I expected to walk in to see a grand old hotel. But the smells hit me first. The dull, sour smell of death mixed with urine. I opened the doors to untold filth. I get there and your father does not want to let me in. I knock him down and push my way through. Your mother is there, dancing in circles, alternating between praises for Jesus and curses for men. Women, children, laying in their own feces and vomit in beds that have not been cleaned for weeks. Open sores oozing blood and pus. And the screams: men begging for their mothers, women begging for Jesus, and children begging for help. And what your father did to them… I saw him cut people's limbs off and he watched them bleed to death without concern. I bought morphine. They were suffering so… and I gave them double doses, there was no other way… I hope they are at peace…"

Canning starts weeping, sobbing, with more emotion than I have ever seen from this man. His tears bring on my tears. We sob and hug for minute after minute. I then push him back.

"Tennessee?"

Canning shakes his head. "She was there. Your father has some kind of powerful hold on her," Canning looks down and says softly. "I think she is in his bed now."

"No! She's married," I say.

"Was," Canning replies. "The gambler left after your father started offering her as teacher in some classes he calls 'the cult of love.' She met with the first group of gentlemen and left ten dollars richer after the meeting."

"Ten dollars? Do you think she…" I ask.

"I do not know," Canning says. "But she is divorced now. She will never be respectable again. And Victoria…"

"Yes," I say.

"Her skin, her legs, are full of scars and infection, just as yours once were. She allowed me to clean them..."

"Why didn't she come back with you?" I ask.

Canning starts crying again, this time only silent tears. "She said things would be worse for the patients without her, and she is particularly close to this one woman, Rebecca. Tennessee thinks she has some ability to help the patients. But Victoria... they are all going to die. Your father's cure is going to kill them."

11

TOTAL WAR

"Where is your husband?" Lucy asks as she twirls her rich brunette hair while admiring her beautiful green taffeta dress in my hallway mirror. The fabric alone for the dress must have cost her husband several weeks' salary.

"I sent him to the butcher," I lie. It is easier to lie than to try to explain that my husband has started spending all his nights with hookers who hook Canning to The Man with the Poker. Canning is no longer concerned that the Dead Rabbit will chase me. He is more concerned with chasing the images of the dying children out of his mind. For all of his talk of being a man and my tyrannical reign, he really is quite fragile. He has failed to learn the fine art of locking evil doings away in a secret room of the mind and throwing the key away.

We move to the parlor room where I conduct all of my business. "Zulu is down for her nap. We will not be interrupted today," I say as a way of apologizing for our last visit, when Zulu came in having just had an accident.

I sit down and motion for Lucy to do so as well. I hold her hands and start taking deep breaths. I silently call on Demosthenes and Napoleon. The first image in my mind is a burning bed.

"Your husband, is there another woman in his life?" I ask.

Lucy nods and starts crying. I hand her a handkerchief and grab her hand. "Tell me," I say.

"He says he cannot get aroused with a mother, he does not think mothers should be… carnal… is what he calls it," Lucy continues to cry. "And Victoria, I've always done everything he wanted from me in bed. And I mean everything." I squeeze her hand and nod in understanding. Lucy continues, "Now he does not come home at night and when he does, he refuses his place in my bed."

"You should find another."

"Divorce?

"The courts will never let you divorce, unless you can bribe a judge? Go to Indiana? They have liberal divorce laws…" I look at Lucy. She shakes her head. She does not have the money for a bribe.

Lucy wipes her face with the handkerchief. "Victoria, I know I am a mother. And in two-months time, I'll be thirty. I should not feel this way, but I cannot face the rest of my life being celibate."

"Nor should you," I say, "find another. Have an affair."

"My husband will kill me," Lucy says.

"Do not tell him. You can be discreet. Find a man who can be discreet as well," I say.

"How would I find a man who would want to…" Lucy says.

I laugh. "That's the easy part, child. Every man in this city, save your husband, would eagerly bed you. Go to the docks and you'd have a hundred Irish men in a minute. Men are easy to catch, just hard to train. Young men are full of passion and romantic ideals. If you find yourself with one of these, use a fake name and do not let him follow you home. Otherwise he may have some notion about fighting for your honor. Older men will have no such notions. However, they are not always satisfying in bed. Avoid angry men, for they will eventually hurt you. Drunk men the same."

"What if I fall in love?" Lucy asks.

"Don't," I say. "Your husband sounds like he would fight you for the children, and he would win. The courts always side with the man. Can you possibly love someone more than your children?"

Lucy shakes her head.

"In that case, you would have two choices. Convince your husband to have an open marriage and hope that in the course of this freedom he does not change his mind. Or say goodbye to your lover. I believe saying goodbye is the easiest course," I say.

"I cannot separate love from sexual relations," Lucy says.

"Men do it all the time," I say. "Learn from them."

Lucy nods and starts crying. I get up and walk around the desk, placing my arm around her shoulders, comforting her. "Spirit tells me," I say, "that brighter days are ahead. All will be well."

Lucy stands up and gives me a hug. She starts to open her purse. I place my hand on hers, indicating that this session is free. She nods in appreciation, and begins to walk out before turning back.

"I have something for you," Lucy says, handing me a copy of *Harper's Weekly*. I grab it like a starving child would grab a piece of bread. I immediately start flipping through the January 31 issue. The first page I turn to is a story on old Lyman Beecher. The words, "Of his son, Henry, Dr. Beecher was peculiarly fond and proud" turn red and leap off the page. The paper starts getting hot, too hot for me to handle. Spirit is trying to tell me something. Henry Ward Beecher will be part of my destiny.

I drop the paper. Lucy looks at me with confusion. She picks up the paper and somehow flips to the same page. She points to the story next to the engraving of Lyman Beecher, "You should read about this Battle of Vicksburg. It's a thrilling read. A Colonel, a Colonel Blood, showed incredible bravery. He kept advancing in the face of danger."

Lucy hands me the *Weekly* and I smile, "That is what we all must do, Lucy. Keep advancing in the face of danger."

ΑΩ

"Vicky! Vicky! Victoria!" Canning screams and runs through the halls interrupting my commune with Napoleon. I say nothing and still he finds me. I hear him in front of me and keep my eyes closed, staying seated on the floor.

"Is it not the time for you to be with your ladies?" I ask. I open my eyes and Canning is white, shaking, holding a gun. I jump up and grab his arms, "What is it?"

"They drew my name, my name... off to war," he says.

"No," I say, "you must be mistaken. You are too old..."

Canning starts running around, locking every door, shutting every window, barricading the doors with furniture. I follow him.

"It does not matter, every man between the ages of eighteen and forty-five is in the drawing," Canning says. Canning is thirty-nine.

"After Gettysburg? After Lee's retreat?" I ask. "You must be mistaken. They do not need any more troops."

Canning runs up the stairs and grabs the children, bringing them downstairs. We all head to the kitchen.

"Woman, are you listening to me? They drew my name. They drew other names. People are rioting, looting, killing, setting every building on fire. They beat the nuns and are burning the orphanage. Every black-owned business, gone, James Smith's pharmacy..."

Canning opens the cupboards where he keeps all weapons of war and starts to load another gun. He hands it to me. Byron, sensing that something is terribly wrong, stays quiet. Zulu grabs Byron's hand and holds it.

"Are you talking about the Colored Asylum?" I ask.

Canning nods. Less than two miles away from us. Mayhem, murder, looting and arson are rampant only two miles from us and yet everything is eerily silent here.

"Do you remember how to shoot?" he asks.

"I'm no good," I say.

"Quantity, not quality," Canning says.

"Do you really think we are in danger?" I ask.

"The mob is close. And if they find out that I paid the commutation fee for a substitute," Canning says.

Three-hundred dollars. Canning paid three-hundred dollars. My three-hundred dollars.

"You could not discuss this with me?" I ask.

Canning gives me a hateful look, "Do you want me to go to war, woman? Leave you and the children to be shot dead by some Rebel scum?"

"Of course not," I say, although I briefly wonder if I would rather be the unhappy wife of a whoring addict or a respectable war widow. "I am just in shock, Canning."

Canning nods. He closes the door to the kitchen and we sit with our backs to the door. We want to be low to the ground in case the bullets start flying. The children curl up to me. Zulu lays her head on my lap.

"Canning..." I start.

"Yes, Vicky," he says, grabbing my hand.

"At this perilous moment I believe that nothing between us should be left unsaid," I say.

Canning stays silent. I take a deep breath. "Thank you," I whisper, overcome with emotion, "thank you for rescuing me from my father, from that life. Thank you for my two children. Byron has taught me the meaning of unconditional love, the importance of treasuring each moment is awe inspiring. Zulu is a revelation, a marvel, and I see the best kindnesses of you in her."

Canning leans over and kisses me on the forehead. "When I told your father that we were to be married, I thought I was being the hero, doing my duty. I thought I was getting a devoted little girl who would do what I wanted without question, a woman who would give me freedom but always be in my bed with open arms when I returned."

"I can't just be..." I start. Canning puts his fingers on my lips to quiet me.

"But what I got was a woman with dreams of her own. And ideas of her own! And a woman who makes more money with words of comfort and dreams of Napoleon than I make with my medical training. It's true, part of my soul admires you. But living with someone and loving someone ain't the same. Here I live in tyranny, but when I go uptown, I am the king there.

And I when I take a drink, the feelings of shame, the shame I have for relying on a woman's money, wash away and I feel like everything will be fine, everything will work out. I even believe for those few moments that you love me…"

"Canning, I do…" I start.

Canning shakes his head, "Not the way a woman should love a man. And I've never loved you enough to let you go, to let you find your own happiness."

I kiss Canning on the cheek and remain silent. We both sit in silence for hours. Even Byron eventually falls asleep. Heavy rain and thunderstorms start. Canning and I agree that this will disperse the rioters. Wordlessly, I put the children to bed.

Canning opens the door to leave for his whores and all kinds of rain and wind blow in, getting us both wet. I place a hand on his arm, stopping him, saying, "Not tonight." Canning closes the door. I hold his hand and we walk to the bedroom together. And tonight, just for this one night, I'll be the obedient woman he wants.

ΑΩ

Lincoln has a new general. A man named Grant who they say is arm in arm with The Man with the Poker every night. Sober abolitionists and ladies are critical of this, but I hold my tongue. If I had to send young men and fathers to their certain death night after night, The Man with the Poker would be my best friend as well.

But a drunk Grant is preferred over a sober General Butler, at least in the eyes of the public. Butler, partial to the negro, is so hated that the Rebels paint his face at the bottom of chamber pots. It is not only his love for the darkie that gets his face beneath shit, he also has a reputation for treating ladies poorly. In New Orleans he issued Order 28:

> *As the officers and soldiers of the United States have been subject to repeated insults from the women (calling themselves ladies) of New*

Orleans in return for the most scrupulous non-interference and courtesy on our part, it is ordered that hereafter when any female should by word, gesture, or movement insult or show contempt for any officer or soldier of the United States she shall be regarded and held liable to be treated as a woman of the town plying her avocation.

Once Butler issued this order, the outcry was great. Even the British House of Lords convened to decry it as a "most heinous proclamation." The *New York Times* reprinted an editorial in the London Review which called him a cruel savage, worse than a Red Indian, and a barbarian who never should have gotten hold of an Anglo-Saxon name. There were even rumors that Butler's wife wrote the order because she was rejected from New Orleans high society events when she joined her husband during the war.

The Southern gentlemen say this means the women can be groped, beaten, or raped with impunity. The Beast, as they call him, denies this and says it is all a matter of interpretation and that he only meant for the offending women "whose hearts have been captured by the devil" should be ignored.

My opinion is uncertain, but usually if a man is hated by the public then he is doing something right. And if an American is hated by the British, then he is definitely on the right side of history. But Butler is not winning battles, and winning is all that matters in war.

Lincoln says this is a new phase in the war, and now we will engage in total war. I must confess that I had failed to realize that hundreds of thousands of dead boys is indicative of a half war.

12

OUTLAWS

1864

As luck would have it, one of Canning's whores is a milkmaid from Ottawa. Canning gives Rose enough of my money for her services that she has the local papers sent to her to ease her homesickness. Evidently in a moment of shared passion, Canning looks down at the floor mid-thrust and sees the *Ottawa Republican* staring at him with Tennessee's name in the headline. He finishes quickly with the plump Rose, gets on the floor and scoops up the paper. He also snatches two later issues that were under the bed, leaves an extra tip, and races home to show me.

Ottawa Republican
June 4, 1864

To Whom It May Concern—Miss Tennessee Claflin, having published a card addressed to the public, touching her treatment of myself for cancer, which statement was prepared by Miss Claflin herself, and which is in many respects false and untrue and calculated, as I believe to mislead the public and may result, if uncontradicted, in wrong and injury to others to the same extent that I myself have suffered. I deem it but an act of duty to say that I have been imposed upon by her statements which have proved to be wholly false and untrue. I am not only not cured. I am much worse than I was when I first submitted to her treatment. Every step of her treatment has been accompanied by extreme pain and aggravation of all the symptoms, and I have grown worse day by day. I make this statement realizing the fact that I have but a short time to live, and that it is my wish to prevent, as far as I am able, the injury which might otherwise be inflicted upon innocent sufferers, who might be induced by the statement purporting to have come from me, to apply to Miss Claflin, whom I believe to be an imposter, and more, and wholly unfit for the confidence of the community.—Signed Rebecca Howe

The next week Tennessee is charged with murder. The court case reads, in part:

… then and there being diverse quantities of deleterious and caustic drugs to the jury aforesaid unknown, then and there feloniously and wilfully did apply and place by means a large amount of flesh upon the right side of the breast of her, they said Rebecca Howe was wholly eaten away… consumed and destroyed… mortally sick, sore, and distempered in her body…. Rebecca Howe did languish and live on until death… the jurors say Tennessee Claflin did kill and slay Rebecca Howe….

I read this aloud to Canning and turn to him, "You were right." My body trembles and Canning places his arm around me and says, "I didn't need Napoleon to tell me that this would be the outcome."

"What will Tennessee do?" I ask.

"Run. If there is anything you Claflins are good at, it's running. Like your father says, 'it's never too late to run.'"

AΩ

Ottawa Republican
June 18, 1864

Sudden disappearance of Tennessee Claflin. Miss Tennessee Claflin, clairvoyant, doctress, etc. whose ability to perform miracles in the way of wonderful cures, has been somewhat largely advertised in the local press hereabouts for the last six months, and who has opened a magnetic infirmary at the Old Fox House in Ottawa Center, suddenly disappeared about a week ago. There are said to have been some fifteen patients in her "infirmary" two weeks ago, all of whom she had 'paroled' except four who were too sick to leave. These were cancer cases, and were literally deserted, having no notice of her intentions to leave them. They were in the most horrible condition and were taken charge of by humane persons in the vicinity....

13

Exclusive Privileges

1865

April 7, 1865

Lee Surrenders! The Rebellion Ends! Ghosts and skeletons flood the city. I stand outside and search all of their faces hoping for a glimpse of Tennessee, but her face never appears. All I see are sad young men and immigrant families with a mixture of hope and despair painted on their faces.

April 15, 1865

Lincoln is assassinated. While many are in shock, I am not. Total war is total.

July 7, 1865

Hypocrites. Nothing burns my soul more than a hypocrite. And politicians are hypocrites, all of them. They hide behind elections and call themselves nice names like Democrats and Republicans, but they are not. They are tyrannical despots, imposing their will, their laws, on blacks and women. And now blacks get some relief and women get none. Where the hell is my Emancipation Proclamation? Instead of having one king, we have hundreds who buy and steal elections by giving favors to their cronies. I have half a mind to lead a revolution all the way to Washington D.C. and storm Congress.

Case in point, a Mr. Charles Walters raped, beat, and stabbed his twenty-year-old mistress to death before setting her body on fire. He was to hang, but made a deal with someone. Today's *Tribune*:

> *We think Gov. Fenton has done the right thing in commuting into prisonment for life the punishment of Charles H. Walters, who was to be hanged for the murder of his mistress. Walters, we learn, seems thoroughly penitent and deeply religious. There certainly must be better use for Christian men than hanging them.*

I do not know if Mr. Walters found sweet Jesus before the rape, during the rape, or while he was watching his lover's body burn like a burning bush.

And yet Mary Surrat will hang today. Mary was found guilty of merely renting a room to Lincoln's assassin, John Wilkes Booth. When President Johnson was asked to spare her life he said that Mary "kept the nest that hatched the egg." What was poor Mary to do? Was she supposed to have foreseen that one of her boarders was plotting to kill the president? And if she had, and went to the authorities, would anyone have believed her? And women always keep the nest, Mr. President. You do not allow us to do anything else.

Jake Rittersbach, who was at Ford's theater during the assassination, tried to chase after Booth, but one Ned Spangler hit him in the face and said, "Don't say which way he went." And ole Ned gets six years while Mary gets death.

One of the Wilkes prosecutors believes women are equal to men in terms of hanging, but not equal in terms of owning property, marriage rights, or voting. He's a real horse's ass, and he's from my state of Ohio. I do not know when John Bingham had this epiphany that women should be in the noose, but the *Tribune* agrees:

> *We do not concur with those who deem it particularly revolting to hang a woman. It seems to use horrible that a woman should murder; but if she does so, she should fare neither better nor worse than other murderers. Let there be no exclusive privileges, even at the gallows.*

Exclusive privileges. Women do not even have non-exclusive privileges and now we are accused of asking for special treatment. Mr. Walters can rape, beat, stab, and burn his woman and escape the noose, but poor old Mary takes some money from a stranger for a night's lodging and she hangs.

Exclusive privileges.

14

FOUL SMELL

1866

Tennessee is back in the papers. Like any clever outlaw, she moves to a nearby city and advertises. Tennessee is betting that Ottawa lawmen don't read the Chicago newspapers. She may be right. As foolish as we Claflins may be, our enemies are always bigger fools.

I wait until the children are in bed, but before Canning leaves for the whores. I show him Tennessee's advertisement as he is getting on his boots in the parlor.

"Where did you get this?" Canning asks, drinking the last half of his bottle of elixir.

"One of your whores," I say. "Do you not remember?"

Canning shrugs his shoulders and continues to drink. "Chicago?" Canning asks. I nod.

"Filthy Fenian cesspool," Canning says, talking about the Irish. "I bet they have Dead Rabbit gangs there too."

"Canning," I say, "you have been talking about these Dead Rabbit people since we moved here and I have yet to see one man walking around with a dead rabbit on his head."

"And they have no values. They allow divorce and…" Canning says.

"Yes," I say, "the scandal of the century. Illinois allowed one couple out of thousands to divorce. A woman begged the courts to divorce a man who married her for her money and then proceeded to have relations with her niece. And the jury voted that she would be allowed this. How progressive."

"It's not right," Canning says. "It's not right."

"Better for women to be miserable for the rest of their lives?" I ask.

Canning eyes me suspiciously, "Maybe if a woman is miserable then she just needs to be a better wife. A good cook makes a good husband. An obedient wife makes a good husband. A woman who does not question her husband, a woman who is always willing in bed…"

Canning grabs me by the waist and throws me on the stairs. I cry out in shock and pain as he gets on top of me, his bad breath and his rough hands caressing my face. He then smiles as his shaky hands fumble and grope their way to my cotton drawers.

"Take it off," Canning says, "all of it."

"No," I say.

"Behave," he says as one of his hands moves up and squeezes my arm.

"Go to your whores," I say.

"It's you I want," Canning takes off my drawers and tosses them aside. "Now take the rest off. I want to see your body, all of it."

"I will not comply," I say. Canning stands back for a short moment, and in that moment I'm able to wiggle away, run a few short steps, and grab my dagger from my hope chest in the parlor. Even though Canning is not sober, he is still strong. He grabs me once I leave the parlor and easily wrenches the knife out of my hands and pushes me back on the stairs. He tosses the knife beside him and it makes a clanking noise that I hope does not wake up the children.

"Take them off," I say. "If you want to see me naked then you'll have to strip me yourself."

With a body full of fury and rough movements to match, Canning takes off my dress with his trembling hands. He gets down to my black, silk corset and he hesitates. It is not something that can be yanked off with shaky hands regardless of how many swear words accompany the fingers.

"Take it off," Canning says.

"No."

Canning picks up the knife he had wrenched out of my hand. "I'll cut it off," Canning says.

"Do it," I say.

I feel the cold metal trace a path down my neck to the top of my breasts. Canning starts to cut the very top of the bodice, his hands shaking. Two inches of this material yield to the dagger without incident. Then I feel a sharp poke and blood oozes out of my left breast onto Canning's hand. Canning gasps and throws the dagger down. He gets off of me. I start to stand up. He pushes me down and says, "Stay there." He grabs his medicinal bag and gets bandages out. He tears a small bandage off and places it on the puncture wound on my breast. I place my hand over his.

"Why do you make me hurt you?" Canning asks, looking straight in my eyes. "I never want to hurt you. When we married, I…." Panting and sweating, Canning looks at the floor and rubs the blood off his hands onto my dress and asks, "Do you want me to go with you to Chicago so you can divorce me?"

"This is only about Tennessee," I say, not allowing myself to show any emotion." And I do not want you to go at all. If you and the children can manage without me…"

"Ridiculous," Canning says. "You know a woman cannot travel unaccompanied. Your reputation will be ruined. I cannot bear to think of the names you will be called. And not only your reputation will be harmed. Think of all the places where disaster can occur on a long trip. On the train, in the hotel, on the street…"

I start putting my dress back on. "Go if you must," I say, "tomorrow."

Canning puts away his medicinal bag and picks up the dagger. He places it back in the hope chest.

"Do you know what Chicago means?" Canning asks.

I shake my head.

"It's an old Indian word for foul smell."

AΩ

Foul smell is right. As soon as we step off the train, the smell covers me like some sort of diseased blanket. Chicago is the only city I have ever visited that smells like unwashed genitals and rotting meat. Do these poor immigrants not know how to bathe or what to bathe? In addition to being unclean, the immigrants walk around with sausage under their armpits. I do not know why they cannot carry their meat with their hands. Chicago is even dirtier than Cincinnati, home to both Irish and Rebel scum. But Chicago is bigger too. This foul smelling city is second only to New York in size. But New York smells better. New Yorkers know how to wash their genitals. And carry their meat.

Tennessee advertises from Michigan Avenue, not far from our train stop, but it takes several minutes for us to make it through the crowd. Everyone seems interested in us as curiosities. The lower-class men, the poor, the immigrants, the outcasts, stop and leer at me. The upper-class men stop and stare at Byron, who is moaning and mumbling. Canning alternates between glaring at the men and winking at the women.

We arrive at a brownstone and I start to climb the steps, children in hand. Canning pulls me back.

"Stay here," he says.

"Canning…" I start to protest.

"When it comes to your sister, we never know what or who we're going to find," Canning says. "And if your father is there, he…"

"Yes," I say, "my father would hurt me."

Canning nods and runs up the stairs. The children manage to take a seat on the steps without complaint. How different their childhood is among the tall buildings and concrete than mine was among the trees and the hills. Even still, they have a better life than I did. And I can thank Canning for that.

I hear commotion and turn around to see the door burst open and a negro man trying to hold up his falling-down pants running down the steps with Canning chasing after him. I grab Canning when he reaches me.

"Was it forced?" I ask.

Canning shakes his head, "Bought."

I take a deep breath and nod, "Then give up your chasing."

Canning is bent over, taking deep breaths, out of wind. I place my arms around him and help him sit down on the stoops. I then take a seat next to him. I pick up his hand and kiss it.

"Go to her," he says. "She is alone."

I walk up the steps. Once inside the door, the signs that proclaim "Tennessee's Magnetic Healing and Miracle Elixir" point the way to her door. I reach the door and it is ajar. I push it slowly open. Tennessee is standing with her back to me in her corset and drawers, hastily trying to put on a dress.

"Hello sister," I say.

Tennessee turns to me and I am reminded of what all the men see in her. Her unusual beauty is bewitching, hypnotic. Our eyes are the same, sky blue and entrancing. Her delicate features are accompanied by thick, dark chestnut hair. Her breasts are so large that they threaten to split the seam of her clothes. Every inch of her body is ample and soft all over. It is no wonder men want to bury themselves in her.

And yet there is a hardness in her eyes. A hardness that I had not seen before. I walk to her to embrace her and she backs up. I back off. Years ago, she would have run to me with an embrace and words of love, and now she looks at me as if I am a ghost, or an unpleasant reminder of who she is.

"How did you find me?" Tennessee asks.

"I read the papers, and you can bet the lawmen do too. It's not smart for a woman who is wanted for manslaughter to advertise," I say.

"Women may remember my face, men remember my body, and everyone remembers how I make them feel, but no one remembers my name," Tennessee says.

"Be that as it may," I say, "I would like you to come to New York with us. We can change your name and…"

Tennessee shakes her head, "I'm not going to hide who I am."

I nod, admiring my sister. "As you like it," I say. "The Ottawa lawmen are less likely to chase you eight-hundred miles to New York than they are to chase you eighty miles to Chicago."

Tennessee says nothing and just stares at me. "Tennessee," I say, "what happened?"

Tennessee walks close to me, so close our foreheads are touching. "Circle Oath?" Tennessee asks.

"Circle Oath," I agree.

Tennessee places her forehead against mine and we clasp hands, walking in a circle as we did many times many years ago.

"Words you must never utter," Tennessee says.

"Words I must never utter," I say.

"Questions you must not ask," Tennessee says.

"Questions I must not ask," I say.

"Silence forever," Tennessee says.

"Silence forever," I say.

"On everything you hold dear," Tennessee says.

"On everything I hold dear," I agree, not knowing what I hold dear.

"A soldier came to me," Tennessee says, "and he had a real bad headache. I rubbed his shoulders and his temples and it went away. He paid me, paid me well, and left. A few days later, he sends Rebecca to me. Rebecca did not have a headache. She had a lump in her breast. I tried everything. I tried to massage it away. I tried magnetic healing. I tried the miracle elixir. I bought some herbs from a doctor and applied them. I prayed and prayed. We even implored the spirits. But sister, I do not have your gift. The spirits did not talk back to us. They did not listen. Daddy was there the whole time, taking money and offering his reassurances in his kind way. You know how charming Daddy can be. But he just wanted his money. Against Daddy's counsel, I went to see a doctor, a real doctor. He said to try the mustard plasters. I used my own money and bought everything and mixed the mustard plaster and I let it sit a while. I came back and applied it and it wasn't much time before Rebecca was talking in nonsense and screaming…"

"Screaming?" I ask.

Tennessee imitates Rebecca's anxious and scared voice repeating her words "Why did you do this to me? Why did you do this to me? Mother of God, Jesus, Mary, why?" Tears stream down Tennessee's face, "I took the plaster off and her breast was gone. Ate away. Only blood and bone left. That's when I knew that Daddy either in a moment of drunken delirium or in a moment of intentional cruelty, and we know he suffers from both kinds of moments, had mixed lye in with the mustard."

I gasped. Tennessee lets go of my hands and backs away from me. The circle is broken.

"What did you do?" I ask.

"I ran. I've been running ever since," Tennessee says before whispering, "I'm afraid if I stop I'll fall into a well so deep that I won't be able to climb out,"

"Canning and I went looking for you. Twice," I say. "You were not there either time. The last time I broke Father's nose."

Tennessee looks at me with wide eyes, "That was you? Daddy said he fell. Not a word of your presence was spoken." Tennessee starts sobbing. She allows me to embrace her.

"I died a little every day waiting for you," Tennessee says. "You can't imagine what horrors I have endured."

I take a step back and take the sight of her in again. "Tennessee," I say softly, "The men. Why the men? You can make money humbugging, you do not have to…"

Tennessee sits on the filthy bed with blankets covered with dirt, blood, and all sorts of undecipherable stains. I sit next to her and grab her hand. Tennessee takes a deep breath and says, "There is a moment with every man when he makes a low, guttural moan of pleasure. And in that moment I hold all the power. These moments of power are the only power I have in my life."

"That is not real power," I say.

"We're women," Tennessee says. "It is the only power we will ever know."

We will have to change that, I think to myself silently. I point to Tennessee's bag, "Let's gather your things. Canning and the children are waiting."

"What should we do about all of these?" Tennessee asks and she pulls back a curtain to reveal stacks of Elixir bottles. All of them have my face on them, or what was my face. My face from years ago continues to haunt me.

"Destroy them," I say. "Byron was born an idiot because his father was addicted to that poison, and I don't want my face or my name associated with this opium, this sin of our father's."

"Destroy them!" Tennessee says. "This is my income, my future. I will not throw these away, sister."

"You will find another way," I say. "I have clients, and you can practice your magnetic healing…"

"No," Tennessee says, "I will not cut my profit in half because Lady Misfortune visited your child. If I come to New York, I'm coming with my miracles."

"Sister, the only emotion that trumps my love for you is my disgust that my face and name are being used to sell the very drug that has ruined my life. Canning is a mess. He would sell us all down to the river for a bottle. Byron is a daily reminder of my sins, the sins I will have the burden of for the rest of my life. I have to work day and night to keep a roof over our heads, and it's all because of 'my miracle.' My miracle has ruined us all."

"None of this is the elixir's fault," Tennessee says. "It is your fault. You chose to marry Canning, you chose to leave me with daddy, and you chose to start a family with a man you did not love. The universe is simply rewarding your bad choices."

"Tennessee, I never wanted to leave…"

"Besides," Tennessee says, interrupting, "you are a tyrant. Daddy told me that you do not even know how to be a woman. If Canning drinks it is to get away from your controlling, withholding ways."

I slap Tennessee. She looks at me with stunned, hurt eyes, "Mother always said she named you Victoria because she wants you to be queen. Daddy always said you were named Victoria because even in the womb you acted as if you were queen. Still the same Victoria, always demanding, we are all to bend to your will and wants."

I walk out, slamming the door behind me, not knowing if I will ever see Tennessee again.

15

MEDIOCRITY'S FOE AND THE UGLY VIRGIN

1867

The papers call George Francis Train an enemy of dullness and a foe to mediocrity. The same papers refer to Susan B. Anthony as an ugly, virgin spinster. Mediocrity's foe and the ugly virgin have joined forces to give the woman the right to vote. Other reformers want the negro man to have the right to vote first, and woman last. The Foe/Virgin ticket want women first, and they have travelled up and down Kansas to win the referendum for the women and lose the referendum for the negro. In the end, they lost both. Some say woman's cause was lost already on the account of Eve's mistake in Eden that we must all bear for eternity. Some say that the foe being a Copperhead, an Irish Democrat who was not concerned with the end of slavery, hurt the cause. Still others say that if the virgin had been less audacious and kinder to the negro, perhaps they would have won. Whatever the reason, the foe and the virgin lost their fight, but they can't let each other go and they continue on.

I make my way through the stench and darkness to reach 71 East 14th Street, and I walk into Steinway Hall, the grandest building I have ever graced. Gorgeous pianos made out of ivory, ebony, and every kind of wood that you can imagine shine and glimmer under the lights. The auditorium has room for thousands. And yet, it is nearly empty of people but full of a curious energy. I join forty-five men, twelve women, and a handful of boys and wait patiently for several minutes for a glimpse of mediocrity's foe. I am not too interested in the virgin. I've seen women reformers before. But I've never seen a man who supports women with time, energy, and money as this man has. And a rich man at that, the clipper ship king now constructing the Union Pacific railroad.

A drum roll sounds and a suave, handsome man with a head of dark curls, wearing a three-piece double-breasted dark blue suit with copper buttons runs out on stage to tepid applause and some sneers of "Copperhead." He bows and for the first time I see his silk, lavender gloves. Without an introduction, he launches into his speech:

"Right, truth, justice is bound to win. Men made laws, disfranchising idiots, lunatics, paupers, minors, and added women as junior partner in the firm," Train who was standing center stage skips all the way to the right and says, "The wedge once inserted in Kansas we will populate the nation with three millions voting women." Train then does two cartwheels to the left. The audience laughs, most of us have never seen a grown man do cartwheels, especially one dressed in Sundays' finest with lavender gloves. He stands up, takes a bow to guffaws and applause and then says, "Nebraska already allows women to vote in School Committee. If women can rule monarchies they should vote in republics. Woman first, and negro last, is my program; yet I am willing that intelligence should be the test, although some men have more brains in their hands than others in their heads."

The tepid audience claps more this time, starting to warm up to this charismatic self-made man. I fall in line as well, becoming entranced, imagining being in love with him, daydreaming of riding in the finest train compartment with him on the Union-Pacific, speaking to adoring crowds at every stop. Train continues, "I am an egotist, and as I, before talking about women, shall talk about myself, suppose we explain what egotism is. It is not properly understood. I think that humility is a swindle—rank cowardice. I believe in egotism, and for this reason: Men can't get above their level in this world. There are certain natural laws that keep us in our positions. Moral courage is not purchasable. Physical courage you can purchase for thirteen dollars, a month in the army… I have made the introductory remarks just to break the ice. I want you to know me, and I want to know you. For it is hard work for these ladies to commence breaking the ice until they get votes, and then they will break ice over the country. Now you may remember Miss Anthony, the abolitionist. When she started campaigning, she was four-fifths negro and one-fifth woman, and now she is four-fifths woman and one-fifth negro."

The applause is less this time, presumably because they are not too keen on having this dandy replaced with an ugly, virgin spinster. A few moments of silence and then she appears. In all black with her hair in a severe bun and wearing spectacles, Susan B. Anthony appears. I have heard that this woman always wears black, but I do not know why she is always in mourning. Susan was once brave enough to wear pantaloons, but was told by men that by showing the definition of her legs she was at risk for losing her status as a lady. The virgin tried to explain that it was easier to ride a bicycle with pantaloons, but the men thought that her very riding of this new vehicle might hurt her status as a lady as well. Some men even argued that riding a bicycle would take away woman's virginity as it requires a woman to place something hard between her legs. After the public outcry, Susan apologized and agreed that society was not ready for these fashion changes yet, nor was the world ready for a woman to transport herself unaccompanied. If she had asked me what to do, I would have said, "Ride Susan, Ride."

Train gets down on his knees and pretends he is washing clothes in a washtub. He speaks in a high-pitched voice, "Oh husband, I need money to feed your five children."

Susan speaks in a low voice and says, "They will make due. I must go to the tavern, and drink, and see the prostitutes."

Train pretends to cry and gets on his knees and grabs Anthony's hand and begs "Husband to stay." The crowd laughs.

I scan the interaction between Train and Susan and look for sexual tension, chemistry, or some evidence of shared carnal knowledge between the two. I see none. Susan is indeed unsexed.

As for Train, he has children, but he does not seem preoccupied with sex as so many of his kind are.

Anthony picks up the imaginary washtub and throws it on Train's head before saying, "Stupid woman."

Train sobs and asks in a high-pitched voice, "What will I do now?"

The audience claps slowly, as if unsure if the timing of the clapping is proper.

Train stands up, dusts himself off, and loudly asks, "How is it that man can break all social laws and remain respected while if woman commits the slightest fault she is damned, driven from town, and ruined? Because man can vote and woman can't. Give her a vote and she will protect herself. We shall then have fewer divorces and better morals. Drunkards in the cabinet. Drunkards in the Senate. Drunkards in the House of Representatives. Drunkards in the army. Drunkards in the pulpit. Drunkards in Wall Street, and drunkards among mothers, wives, and daughters of the land. Give women power—give them votes, and this will cease in both sexes. What is this poor woman's choice? Divorce! Starvation! Or prostitution!"

Susan nods and says, "Any man who votes against female suffrage is a blockhead. How can the muscle, color, and wool of the blacks deserve a vote, but not virtue, beauty, and brains?"

A man from the audience yells, "Why ain't you married?"

"Because there's not one man in a thousand worth marrying," Susan says, "I'd be happy to marry a man, but most women who think they are marrying men end up married to whiskey bottles. No thank you, sir. No thank you."

She's right. He's right. But the foe and the virgin won't win this way. You can't tell the audience that you want the vote before the negros—you alienate the true reformers. And you can't tell the audience that you want fewer drunkards—that alienates everybody. What man is going to allow women to vote against their right to enjoy whiskey?

Another man shouts out to Train, " Mr. Train, would you drag our fair women down to the Bowery to be polluted by coming in contact with the drunken orgies of a contested election?"

"Most certainly not, sir. I would have the Bowery throw away its pipe and whiskey bottle, and dress itself in its Sunday clothes, and vote in the lady's parlor. The uneducated is more gentlemanly in a lady's presence than the so-called gentleman. Men who become debased in the society of men, become elevated in the society of women," Train says to some applause.

Susan steps forward and says, "We believe the ballot will secure for women equal place and equal wages in the world of work; that it will open to her schools, colleges, professions and all the opportunities and advantages of life; that in her hand it will be a moral power to stem the tide of crime and misery on every side."

Train makes a motion to the orchestra pit and the drum beats start. Yelling over the drums, Train asks, "Do you want to reform our system of government?"

Train and Anthony respond, "Vote for women!"

Train asks, "Do you want the people to rule instead of politicians?"

Train and Anthony respond, "Vote for women!"

Train asks, "Do you want 'charity for all, malice for none,' instead of malice for all, charity for none; your creed?"

Train and Anthony respond, "Vote for women!"

Train asks, "Do you want beauty, virtue, and intelligence, instead of vice and ignorance to have the ballot?"

Train and Anthony respond, "Vote for women!"

Train asks, "Do you want temperance, sobriety, morality in Kansas, instead of drunkenness and licentiousness to be in the ascendant?"

Train and Anthony respond, "Vote for women!"

A stunned silence overcomes the crowd. After a few moments, there is some applause, but most people leave without showing their customary gratitude. Two newspaper reporters walk to the stage. I recognize one of them as Horace Greeley,

Radical Republican, hater of President Johnson, editor of the *Tribune*.

"Go west, young man, go west," is what Greeley is known for by many, but he is more than an advocate for the great wild west. He is called both fickle and pragmatic. Greeley once wrote to President Lincoln, "If I could save the Union without freeing any slaves, I would do it—if I could save it by freeing all the slaves, I would do it—and if I could do it by freeing some and leaving others alone, I would also do that." After some complaints by his inner circle, Lincoln is reported as having retorted, "Uncle Horace agrees with me pretty often after all; I reckon he is with us at least four days out of seven."

Indirectly, I can thank Greeley for my whippings, starvations, and introduction to The Man with the Poker. He was the chief proponent of the Fox sisters, vouching for them, giving them their lucrative career of tapping and knocking, pretending it was the dead who were making all that noise. He even took one of the sisters in and raised her as his daughter after his son died. People say neither the wife nor the Fox girl were happy about the arrangement.

Greeley also tentatively agrees that women's rights are a natural right. Although he has also said that such "Donna Quixotes" are misguided. "So long as she shall consider it dangerous or unbecoming to walk half a mile alone at night—I cannot see how the woman's rights will be anything more than an abstraction."

With his top hat, dark suit, and white hair both on the back of his head and under his chin, he walks up to Susan B. Anthony and bows. Susan rolls her eyes in response.

"Yes, Mr. Greeley," Susan says, "what would you like to debate today?"

Greeley gestures to Train. "Do you really think aligning yourself with a traitor Copperhead ignoramus is the right path? What about the abolitionists that you worked with for years?"

Susan takes a deep breath. "Mr. Greeley. Since turning our faces eastward from Kansas we have been asked many times why we affiliated with the Democrats there, and why Mr. Train was on our platform. Mr. Train is there for the same reason, that when invited by the 'Women's Suffrage Association' of St. Louis, he went to Kansas, because he believes in the enfranchisement of woman, not as a sentimental theory, a mere utopia for smooth speech and golden age, but a practical idea, to be pushed and realized today. Mr. Train is a business man, builds houses, hotels, railroads, cities and accomplishes whatever he undertakes… Though many of the leading minds of this country have advocated woman's enfranchisement for the last twenty years, it has been more as an intellectual theory than a fact of life, hence none of our many friends were ready to help in the practical work of the last few months, neither in Kansas or the Constitutional Convention of New York. So far from giving us a helping hand, Republicans and Abolitionists, by their false philosophy—that the safety of the nation demand ignorance rather than education at the polls—have paralyzed the women themselves."

Greeley, unimpressed, turns to Train again, "Are you not, dear sir, hoping to get the women's vote for your next presidential election? Is this not why you are campaigning so tirelessly for women?"

Before Train can answer, Susan steps in front of him and says, "Mr. Greeley, you are the perennial candidate, blooming every time there is an election. Perhaps courting women is a strategy you should employ yourself. Because it may not be today, it may not be tomorrow, but one day soon women will unite and devastate the men who stand in our way and we will do it again and again."

Ride Susan, Ride.

16

THE TENDERLOIN

1868

New York was supposed to be different. Today was supposed to be different. Canning promised with kind whispers and warm embraces. And yet it is time to sleep and I cannot find my husband. Just like all the days before. I feel my anger start as a low hum and then it compounds and grows until I can no longer hear my own thoughts. To hell with it. Somehow forgetting that I'm dressed only in a nightgown and robe, I get Byron out of bed. He starts moaning, looking at me with all the understanding of a wild animal. I open Zulu's bedroom door. She is awake, waiting for Canning to open the door and blow her a kiss for I do not permit Canning to go any further into Zulu's room when he is drunk. I hold onto Byron, grab Zulu, and grab my purse next to the door.

We walk down the steps and out into the city street. The air is damp with humidity and stinks of manure and soot. I hold Byron's hand tight, fearing his hate of the dark will lead him to run. Even I am tempted to run. I am not accustomed to walking without light. For the first time since coming to New York, I am grateful that we live close to The Tenderloin, the long row of whorehouses. We pass Union Square and the penniless Irish immigrants who live there. They approach me, looking for money or food, but we walk too quickly for them to touch us. One man calls out, "Looking for Madame Restell? Two brats too many?" He speaks of the New York abortionist who advertises in the *Times*, boasting of the number of wombs plundered.

We make it into The Tenderloin. Dozens of whorehouses line the streets, and I do not know how to choose one. Canning seeks variation and is not at the same brothel every night. And I simply cannot bang on all the doors. I start to shake and cry when I remember reading a dog-eared review of the whorehouse of 106 in *The Gentleman's Companion*, "*A second class establishment. It is asserted that her landlady and her servants are as sour as her wine.*" Of course, he also dog-eared the review of 111, "*Hattie Taylor keeps a third class house where may be found the lowest class of courtesans. It is patronized by roughs and rowdies, and gentlemen who turn their shirts wrong side out when the other side is dirty.*"

I must visit both. I first find 106. It is a narrow, three-story, brick building with a plain façade. I drag my children up six steps and see the nameplate: 106 Miss Dow. I knock on the door. "Ahh," Byron moans and then slaps himself. Zulu asks, "What are you doing, mother?"

The door opens and I do not wait for an invitation. Holding Byron's hand in my left hand and Zulu's hand in my right hand, we rush in. The room is covered in smoke, red velvet, and a layer of white gooey filth. Gas lamps with hazy shades give the room a soft glow. Two spittoons full of tobacco juice in the parlor are on either side of me as I walk in. A scantily clad woman walks by and we all catch a sight of her near-naked breast.

"Hands over eyes! Hands over eyes!" I immediately move my arms so both children have their eyes covered by my arms. I curse myself for bringing my children here. I did not realize naked women would just be walking around. Shouldn't someone have to pay before they see that? Aren't they giving themselves away for free? Or are they trying to work up a man's appetite?

"Sally! Get these children out of here!" the half-naked fancy lady screams. A door slams. A woman, this one dressed in a beautiful blue velvet frock, marches up to me. She looks at me up and down and reaches out to touch my nightgown. She pulls her hand away as if she had touched a stove and shakes her head.

"Honey, we're not hiring. And even if we were, never bring your children to a performance," she says.

"I'm looking for my husband," I reply.

She sighs. "Which one?"

"Canning. Dr. Canning Woodhull."

The madam gives me the most startled look, as if I had just told her that my uterus had fallen out on the way over here. She shakes her head and leaves for a moment. Two more doors slam. Laughter erupts in the back of the house; I'm sure they are laughing at me. Half-pushing, half-prodding Canning, three fancy ladies plus sour Sally manage to get my husband to me. In his long johns, and clearly not in his right mind, Canning can only manage a stumble. I think back to when we first met and how virile and manly he was. Now he's been reduced to an infantile old man. He is carrying two half empty bottles of the miracle elixir. He can hold on to his opium, but he has lost his clothes in the process.

"Where are his clothes?" I ask.

"Clothes, pocket watch, ours till he pays," Sally says without a trace of humanity in her voice.

"You don't expect me to?" I ask. I take out the little money I have in my purse and hand it to her.

"Two nights," she says.

"He has only been here for one," I reply, my anger nearly blinding me.

"He was here yesterday afternoon. More than an hour and we count it as a night."

I give more money to the whore. Sally responds by throwing his clothes on top of my head. The whores start laughing at me. Byron responds by clapping. Zulu starts to cry. The whore then tosses the pocket watch, and I get on my knees and crawl to pick it up. I grab it, pausing to look at my reflection in the time piece. I see the reflection of a poor, crazy old hag looking back at me. How did I come to this?

We stumble down the stairs, the enraged clairvoyant, the drunk in his long johns clutching his miracle, the idiot hitting himself, and the bewildered child with pigtail curls. If father were here, he'd set up a tent and charge admission. I quickly help

Canning dress. I hold onto Byron. Zulu holds onto Canning. Canning holds onto the elixir. We are all silent, making our way quickly past Union Square. My anger is so deep and wide that I start imagining slitting Canning's throat and pushing him into the East River. When my mind is not slitting his throat, it's putting a bullet in his brain. I recognize my own insanity, but do not try to exert control over my thoughts. The whore's laughter still rings in my ears, the weight of Canning's pants still rests on my head, the ugly old hag is still staring back at me in the pocket watch.

We are almost home. Almost. Just a few steps. We pass The Old House at Home Bar. Its light is the only light shining on the sidewalk, providing some relief from the darkness. The light, however, casts a shadow, a shadow of a perfect pyramid. I investigate the pyramid and see a display of miracle elixir, my miracle elixir, in the window.

We, the freak show, barge in. The rowdy laughter dies down upon our entrance. The piano, which was playing a tune of love and loss, stops immediately. I hear calls of "whore," "honey," and "idiot" but I choose not to respond. The bartender, a short, fat young man in suspenders and a bow tie, runs over. He looks us up and down. He sees Byron hit himself and he jumps back.

"Gentleman only! Gentleman only!" The bartender points to a sign with the chalk proclamation, "Good Ale, Raw Onions, and No Ladies."

I respond my raising my eyebrows. Why should I follow their silly rules?

"Leave at once!"

The patrons start making noises, a threatening hum that increases in intensity with every second. The tiny hairs on the back of my neck stand up, telling me that I should run. I push Canning and the children outside, telling Zulu to make sure they all stay put. I then walk back to the bartender.

"Where did you get that elixir?" I ask.

"I throws you out meself," the bartender dries his hands on his apron and takes it off. He comes closer to me but is still behind the bar.

"How did you come by these?" I must know.

The barkeeper makes an hourglass motion with his hands to indicate a curvy woman. I swear under her breath and mutter "Tennessee." I reach in my purse and hand him my calling card. The Oracle of the Midwest.

"When you see her," I say.

"Leave at once!" he says with a harsh loudness as he grabs my card and places it next to the large bottle of bourbon on the bar. The bartender's directive has attracted a crowd. Men start to form a circle around me. I try to look each and every one of them square in the eyes to show them I'm not afraid. A half-second of taut silence occurs when I feel the crowd sizing me up. To my right, there is a tall, handsome man with a mustache and a goatee sitting on a barstool who has been watching everything unfold, silently. He stands up. I look him too straight in the eye to show him that I am unafraid, and instead of giving me a look of malice as the other men have, he gives me a little smile. He walks in front of me and shifts his jacket slightly so everyone sees the gun holstered around his waist. He places his hand on the gun, not saying a word. The men back up. I hear whispers of "war" and "hero" but I dismiss them, knowing I have precious few seconds to conduct my business.

"Ten cents a bottle," I say.

"Twenty," the bartender says.

"You are charging the men fifteen. My price is fair. I'll buy all of them," I reply. "I'll give you half now and half…"

The bartender shakes his head and jabs his finger on the bar, "Twenty cents. Cash on the barrel."

"It is my face on these bottles, and I do not wish they be sold!"

The barkeeper looks at me with a mixture of surprise and disbelief. He walks over to the pyramid display and picks up a bottle. He studies the face on it, looks at me, and studies the face on the bottle again. He slowly shakes his head.

"No, madam, this is a beautiful, young virgin," the bartender says matter-of-factly without a trace of cruelty in his voice.

The men behind me erupt in laughter. I hear shouts of "hag" and "ain't no virgin." While they are laughing and shouting, they are also pushing, squeezing. The handsome man tries to hold them back, but flesh is being pressed against me. I reach to my right and grab the handsome man's half-empty glass of bourbon.

I leave, walking outside, with shouts of "hag" and "streetwalker" following me. Other men shout graphic descriptions of just the type of sexual treatment I deserve for interrupting their drunken fellowship.

I look at the glass in my hand. I look at the pyramid of elixir. I throw the bourbon through the window and knock down the first two tiers of the miracle elixir. I hear a collective gasp as the glass breaks and the elixir spills onto the floor. The patrons run towards the liquid, dipping their fingers in it and licking it while the barkeep tries to shoo them away. The handsome man smiles at me and gives me a slight nod. Canning is now sitting on the corner. I run to him and try to lift him. He's passed out. Byron slaps Canning. Canning does not stir. Zulu cries.

The bartender runs out and yells "Whore! Police!"

I grab the children's hands and start walking briskly, leaving Canning behind to fend for himself. I hear footsteps behind me and I do not need to turn around to know that the men are chasing me. I pick up Zulu and carry her with my left arm while still holding Byron's hand in my right. We run. Shards of glass from the broken windows fall off my clothes, leaving a trail. A gunshot. The heavy footsteps become silent. I look over my shoulder and can make out the handsome man holding his gun in the air.

ΑΩ

Not many hours elapse between my escape from The Old House at Home Bar and the sunrise, but sleep is not an option.

I must earn money. And find my husband. While my husband would usually be my priority, I am bereft of the energy it would take to retrace my steps to whores at The Tenderloin. At the moment, I'm thinking sour landlady Sally can keep him, or maybe that bartender can put him to work and make him clean up the mess I left. Zulu wakes, full of sunshine as if yesterday was a normal part of a great day. Byron wakes and I help him button his shirt. I get out my sign that proclaims "The Great Oracle of the Midwest" and hand it to Zulu. Both children go outside, trying to attract attention from strangers who want to talk to the dead. I watch them with heavy regret. I never wanted my children to spend their youth working, as I have. My only consolation is that I'm not selling their bodies as father sold mine. And Zulu and Byron have never faced an angry parent or wanted for food. On the whole, they have a better life than I did. If it is true that lives improve with every generation, then Zulu's children will be carefree.

I prepare myself for the dead by communing with my spirit guides. I walk into my parlor and open the hope chest and grab my book on Demosthenes. I begin rereading his speeches:

> *No man who is not willing to help himself has any*
> *right to apply to his friends, or the gods.*

"You found her!" I am brought out of my meditation by the sound of my husband's voice. I run and open the front door. The handsome man, dressed in very fine clothes, is helping Canning sit next to Zulu. Canning has on fresh clothes that hang off his scrawny frame. He kisses and hugs Zulu. I smile. His affection toward our children always touches me. Standing next to Canning, the handsome man is holding elixir bottles in his hand. The handsome man sees me. I take a step back and he starts walking towards me. Canning halts his progress by jumping up and grabbing a bottle of elixir.

"Bless you. One taste of her miracle and you cannot stop," Canning says. I shake my head. The handsome man smiles and walks up my steps.

"You found me?" I ask, knowing that Canning is in no shape to provide our address.

"Madam," he says, taking off his brown bowler, "if I may offer you some advice. Next time you commit a crime, don't leave a calling card."

Damn. I back up, as the implications of my calling card in that bar dawn on me. The bartender knows my address.

"Am I to be arrested?" I ask.

The handsome man ignores my question, but bows and says, "James Blood, Esquire." I hold out my hand to shake his, like a man would, but he flips it and kisses it. It has been a long time, probably since I first met Canning, that a man has treated me with such care.

"Am I to be arrested?" I ask again.

"No," James says.

"The bartender…" I begin

"He will not be here," James says.

"How can you know?" I ask.

"I know."

I nod and ask no more, so confident and strong he is in his answer. I fear that if I know the details, I will owe this man more than I can repay. I jerk my head towards my husband, "How is he?"

"A bath and a new set of clothes did not lead to sobriety, I'm afraid," James said. He then holds up the miracle elixir and says, "The last of them."

"Sir, why did you do this?" I ask.

"May we call it a goodwill gesture?" James gives me a smile full of promise and want.

"And to what end?" I ask.

"A mother running around half-naked among the whores in the middle of night, breaking saloon windows to destroy her own intoxicating miracle… I guess I figure that is a woman worth knowing." James still has his hands full with elixir bottles and I remember my manners. I give a slight nod and open the door to the house. I point down to the floor and James leaves the bottles there. Walking into the parlor, James follows me. I take coins out of my hope chest and hand them to him.

"Come by next week for the rest."

James puts his hand on mine as if we are more familiar with one another than we are. He pushes my hand back close to my chest.

"A free reading, then. You can talk to the dead," I say. I start walking towards my chair and table, moving my book of Greek speeches aside.

"I only want to talk to you," James says. He disappears around the corner for a half-second, coming back with the bottle of elixir. Perhaps he wants it as payment. He holds the bottle up in the air. "Why?"

Why indeed. How to explain to this man that the girl on the bottle is not the woman standing beside him? Would he understand that my father forced me to sell that poison? Would he understand that my miracle ruined Canning, ruined my only son? And why explain such things to a stranger?

"Who are you?" he asks, breaking into my thoughts.

"Victoria Woodhull," I reply.

"Yes, Victoria, I know your name. But who are you… really?" he asks. Is this man asking about the state of my soul?

"If you do not want a reading, sir, kindly leave," I start to walk past James. He lifts up his pants leg.

"What are you doing, sir?"

"Showing you who I am," James points to an ugly round scar. "The first bullet made me a soldier." James straightens up and removes his coat. A man is never supposed to remove his coat in the presence of a lady. Does he think I'm a common whore? After last night, I'm sure he does. My skin becomes hot and flushed. I do my best to stare at the ground despite my eager curiosity to take in the sight of his rippling physique.

"Are you a Dead Rabbit?" I ask, backing up.

James laughs, "No, I'm a live man."

"My husband says there are Dead Rabbit people who don't treat ladies like ladies. And you are removing your coat," I say.

"Only to reveal who I am," James says. "You have already revealed so much to me."

I blush, not sure of this man's meaning. I instead plead, "Please remember that you are in the presence of a lady."

"Ladies do not break windows," he replies. "Be assured that is why I am here. I have no yearning for ladies. They are boring and predictable. And then I saw you, and I knew you would not bore me." James begins to slowly unbutton his white cotton shirt. My gaze starts at his waist, where I see his fingers deftly unbutton the tail end of his shirt. His fingers work their way up his chest. I quickly glance at his mouth and he smiles at me as if we are already lovers. I move to the window. I knock on it to get Canning's attention. Canning may not be much of a husband, but he won't let another man hurt me. I knock again. No response. Canning does not even move. Passed out again.

James unbuttons the tip-top button and shrugs off the shirt. It lands on my feet. Nothing good has ever come from a half-naked man standing this close to me. I keep my eyes averted. James stretches out his arm, but I do not dare look up.

"The second bullet made me a half-anarchist and half-socialist" he says. A half-anarchist? How can you believe in only half anarchy? Anarchy on Mondays, Wednesdays, and Fridays? Government on Tuesdays, Thursdays, Saturdays and Sundays? Who is this shirtless man standing before me in my parlor? Half-socialist/half-anarchist. As if the two could peacefully coexist. Hate the government. Love the government.

James takes off his undershirt. I've never seen such a hard, taut chest. Not an inch of scrawniness like the young boys and not an inch of fat like the old boys. He turns around and I raise my eyes to see all of his muscles. I size him up, comparing his strength to mine. Even if I use my teeth and bite really hard, I know that my own feminine weak body would not be able to fight him off. With his back still turned, I walk to the hope chest and pull out my dagger. I stab the air a few times for practice. Unaware, James places his hand on another bullet scar on his back, "The third bullet made me a mystic."

James turns around to the dagger pointed at his heart. He arches his eyebrows, and then relaxes and smiles. He takes two steps towards me and grabs the dagger from my hands too quickly for me to react. James tosses the dagger down with one hand, making a loud clink sound. He holds my wrist in his other hand. I gasp and my one gasp turns into another until I start to hyperventilate. With his hand encircling my wrist he leans in and whispers in my ear, "I will never hurt you."

My breathing starts to steady and James drops my wrist, taking two steps back. Pointing to his chest he says, "The fourth bullet made me a free lover."

"Free love?" I ask.

"The belief that we should be equally free to love who we want without any social or legal constraints," James says.

"Like animals, you mean… we should all mate like animals? Is that what we should do every day or only during the part of the week when we are practicing anarchy?" I ask.

James laughs. "Not exactly… Those who believe in free love believe that any forced affection is a crime and should be punished as such," James says.

"The courts do not agree. The husbands have rights… bedroom rights," I say.

"That is because the courts see you as property. I do not. I see you as a woman. As flesh and blood," James reaches out and tucks a wayward strand of hair behind my ear. "You are a child of God with inherent rights to liberty, happiness, to use your body as you wish and under no one else's command." I allow James a genuine smile for the first time since we've met. My body relaxes and I move closer to him. I commit a grave sin, a serious infraction for a proper lady as I place my fingers over a fifth bullet wound next to his left rib cage. He is slightly startled at my touch. He places his hand over mine.

"The fifth bullet?" I ask.

James looks down, having forgotten the wound. "The fifth bullet... yes... the fifth one made me The Hero of Vicksburg."

"The Hero of Vicksburg?" I ask. Not waiting for an answer, I open my hope chest.

"That's what the papers call me," he says.

I grab the faded newspaper out of the hope chest and begin unfolding it. "You took three bullets and kept advancing," I say from memory.

James shrugs and looks out the window, "Survival is not the same as heroics."

"The picture given below illustrates one of the most daring feats of arms ever attempted in the progress of the war, and not surpassed by anything in the annals of warfare," I read out loud. I look at James, who does not glance my way. I skip to the end of the article and continue reading, "During the whole time the regiment was crossing... it was exposed to a heavy crossfire, which threatened it with annihilation; but it never faltered or hesitated."

"You have kept that account for many years now," James says.

"Not on your account, Colonel Blood..."

He shakes his head, "James."

"Not on your account, James. I kept it because of Beecher," I say.

"Beecher?"

I step close to James and show him the folded up page 77 from the January 31, 1863 issue of *Harper's Weekly*. In the center of the page is an illustration of the late Reverend Lyman Beecher. The surrounding text is an obituary of sorts.

"When my customers cannot pay me in coins, I ask for newspapers or books. In 1863, a customer gave me this page *Harper's Weekly*. When I came to this page, my hands turned hot. I started to read about the late Reverend and his son's name, Henry Ward Beecher, jumped out at me in huge letter type. My vision became blurred and I collapsed. And I knew at that moment that my destiny would be linked with this man. But now you are here…" I say.

"I am here," James says.

"You are on the right of this page and Henry Ward Beecher is on the left. Perhaps my spirit guide was wrong. You may be my destiny," I say.

James leans in to kiss me. I hold up my hands and push him back. James steps back and smiles, "May I see you tomorrow?"

"You are not angry?" I ask. "After all you have done for me, you are not demanding…"

"You are under no obligation to yield to me," James says. "I do not demand or force affection."

"I'm married," I say.

"Yes," James says, "I've met your husband. Quite charming."

"I cannot just…" I say.

James reaches for my hand, I give it to him. "Victoria, there are laws of man and laws of God. The law of man says that you must stay in servitude to your husband until your last breath, regardless of who he is or how he treats you. The law of God wants you to be happy. One mistake with an old man when you were evidently quite young does not mean that you must be miserable the rest of your life."

"What about duty? Honor?"

"Yes," James says, "duty and honor. I saw many a boy die for those Sunday school words. We use those words when souls hesitate."

"You can scoff at honor," I say, "as honor seems assigned willy-nilly to those least deserving. But duty, duty is real and should govern our conduct."

"The only duty you have is to live life to your fullest potential and to contribute to the betterment of society. And you can scarcely do this when you are in chains," James says. I look down and feel a few tears slip down my face. James lifts my chin with his finger and kisses the tears away. "I apologize," James says, "I have upset you. I never meant to."

"You should go," I say. "Too many moments in your presence and I will forget who I belong to."

James kisses my forehead and whispers, "You belong to no one."

James turns and walks away. I watch him walk down the steps, hand candy to Zulu and Byron, and pick up the empty elixir bottles that have littered the street.

17

THE HERO OF VICKSBURG

Sometimes God throws pebbles at you. When the pebbles fail to gain your attention, God hits you over the head with a brick. James is my brick.

"If you want to fight patriarchy," James says, "you have to break the rules." James, after telling Canning that he wants a clairvoyant reading from the Oracle of the Midwest, makes himself comfortable in my parlor. It has only been a fortnight since we parted with a chaste kiss, and my eyes have been searching for his face in the crowd ever since. And now he is here. We have been talking for several minutes, politics, religion, art, and children. I have never before had a man seek my opinion on any issue of any importance.

"Are you confident you do not want to speak to the spirits?" I ask.

"I do not want the dead, I want you," James says. "And if it is a revolution you want, you must prepare."

"I will do what I must," I say, knowing that with this man's support I can do anything.

James stands up and walks over to the window. He watches Zulu and Byron play on the sidewalk.

"You will need money," James says.

"I will find a way," I say.

"It will not be easy," James says.

"No," I agree. I walk behind him to see what he sees. "You will help me, will you not?" I ask.

James turns around, startled. "I want to," he says, "but to be in your presence knowing that we cannot be together... I..."

I place my finger on his lips. "I will find a way," I say and James grabs me around the waist, moves me over, away from the window, and kisses me. Feeling lost in his arms, I grab his shoulders to steady myself. He takes his lips off mine and I manage to say, "I did not know a kiss could be like that." His lips then find my ear lobes, and he nibbles my ears, his lips leaving a string of kisses down my neck. My entire body responds in a way it has never responded before. For the first time I feel complete, I feel all woman, and I want to spend the rest of my moments with this man and give him all of me.

"I want you," James whispers. "All of you."

I nod and James kisses me again. This kiss is the most intimate kiss I have ever known. It is as if in that one moment we are betrothed by the powers in the air. He unbuttons the top button of my blue dress, kisses my collarbone, unbuttons the next button, and kisses the top of my left breast, unbuttons—

"Humping, Bumping, Jesus!" I open my eyes to see Tennessee staring at us. James straightens up and moves in front of me as if to protect me.

"Destroying private property and adultery. Two laws broken in less than twenty-four hours. These family traditions of ours are glorious," Tennessee says with mischief written all over her face. I move past James, hug Tennessee, and kiss her. I push Tennessee back and stoke her impish face covered with a mass of brown curls. She has aged in her eyes only, her complexion and her figure remain guarded against time.

"How did you find me?" I ask.

"You left your address at the scene of the crime. I guess we Claflins are good at leaving a trail, are we not? You know, Jerry is my best customer and he is not happy," Tennessee says. "Still," she says, "I have been looking for you for the past months and now I have found you. I knew there was a reason to keep your face on those elixir bottles. Even if it only served to anger you."

AΩ

I hand Tennessee and James cups of tea. Tennessee pulls an elixir bottle out of her bag and mixes in the opium.

"Throw that out!" I say. "That poison ruined Canning."

Tennessee laughs, "He was no good before."

"I'm divorcing him," I say.

"And bring shame on the family?" Tennessee asks.

"Says the divorcee wanted for manslaughter," I say. Tennessee glares at me and I immediately regret my words. James gives me a quizzical look but stays silent.

"He left me," Te ays. "I never filed. And if the courts allowed every woman to divorce their whore-loving addict husband, then we would not have any marriages left."

"When Byron was diagnosed and I knew he would never be complete," I say. "I made a sacred vow to him and to Zulu."

"What kind of vow?" Tennessee takes another sip of her tea.

"That no child would ever be born into a troubled marriage. Byron is the way he is because his father was an addict when he was conceived. No woman should be forced into marriage like I was. We need a revolution. We must cure the world of its ills, so no woman has to be forced to enter or remain in a marriage fraught with misery."

"Vicky…" Tennessee begins, pouring another shot of elixir in her tea.

I continue, "Every child will be born into a perfect union based on mutual love and respect. Women will not be raped inside or outside of marriage."

Tennessee continues to drink. I stand up and start to pace, "Women will have the right to earn their own money, buy their own property, and conduct commerce freely without the interference of a man."

Tennessee rolls her eyes and puts down the tea. She picks up the elixir bottle and drinks straight from it.

"You are talking treason," Tennessee says before letting out a belch.

"And women will vote. For President, for mayor, for undertaker," I say.

"We just finished one war," Tennessee says.

"Join me," I say.

"Me?" Tennessee asks. "Blow against the winds of history?"

I stop and give Tennessee a stern stare. She snaps to attention. "You can either sit by and criticize, or you can join me and prosper."

"Yes, Queen Victoria," Tennessee says with anger, "first you abandon me to a wretched life and now I am to serve you." I ignore her.

"First, we will make money, then we buy power, and then we build a new world order."

Tennessee shakes the bottle of elixir. It is empty.

"Money? How much?" Tennessee asks.

"At least a million," I say.

Tennessee drops the bottle. Glass breaks everywhere. "Are you mad?" She asks as I get down and pick up the pieces of glass. James gets down off the chair and slaps my hand gently. "You'll cut yourself," he says. James grabs a napkin and starts picking up the glass with his hand protected by the napkin.

"Spirit Napoleon has assured me," I say.

"Never take advice from a short man," Tennessee says. I point out another piece of glass and James picks it up.

"Vicky, this is not healing the lame, this is a grand scam," Tennessee says.

"No, no, an honest endeavor," I agree.

"Conceived in a canvas brothel at a Methodist revival, born to a horse thief and a crazed simpleton, a humbug sold into marriage, an adulteress mother with a halfwit. And to think you can compete with a Vanderbilt…" Tennessee says.

"Vanderbilt!" James says and stands up. "That's it. I will introduce you."

"How?" I ask.

James cuts his thumb on a piece of glass. He mutters, "Damn," and puts his thumb in his mouth.

"Don't forget," James says with his thumb still in his mouth, "I'm the hero of Vicksburg."

18

THE COMMODORE

"The Commodore wants to communicate with the dead. Preferably his mother or his soldier son George Washington Vanderbilt. But really any dead will do. Just not his dead wife," James says as we model our new fine dresses. I denied Canning his whoring money for a week to pay for the silk. Tennessee requested that her dress be extra tight in the bust. The poor white haired seamstress was scandalized. James says nothing about our dresses, but nods his approval. When he looks at me, I know he is picturing my dress crumpled on the floor, discarded as we make love.

The three of us get in the carriage, James will ride with us until we get to the Vanderbilt home, then he will wait in the carriage. James tells us, "The Commodore is defeated. He lost control of the Erie Railroad. His enemies Fisk and Gould printed additional shares and diluted his stock."

I heard something about this, but I did not know the details. Cornelius Vanderbilt, known as the Commodore, is nothing if not shrewd, even in his old age, and I'm positive that any man beating him at anything eats at his soul. At seventy-five years old, he has outlived most of his rivals and continues to impress. Despite his age, he changes with the new technology. He sold off his ships and put every penny into railroads. The sole owner of New York Central Railroad, he is the sole owner of all train service in and out of Manhattan. And now he is building a house for his train. The papers call it Grand Central.

The carriage pulls up to 10 Washington Place, a stately three-story brick townhouse. It is impressive, but not what one would expect from a man who is worth more than the U.S. treasury.

Tennessee and I start to get out and James grabs Tennessee's arm, "Vanderbilt loves cursing, ample women, food, and tobacco. In that order."

Tennessee acknowledges the insight with a nod and the carriage drives off. We walk along the long brick pathway to the front door and knock. We hear quite a commotion behind the door, steps, muffled voices, and a hint of exasperation. The door opens and we are greeted by a black servant. He nods and we walk in. We stand in the foyer when we hear a noise from upstairs. Commodore Vanderbilt, with stark white hair and dressed in a black suit, follows another negro servant and says, "... Either goddamn prostitutes or whoring charlatans, but I never know who is going to bring me an original idea."

Vanderbilt stops in his tracks when he catches us out of the corner of his eye. He looks us up and down, and focuses on Tennessee's extra big bust. The scowl on his face is replaced by a broad grin. "Ladies!" he says as he practically runs down the steps, "I was not expecting such beauty to grace my humble home."

Vanderbilt walks down the staircase, practically running. Ignoring me, he takes Tennessee's hand and kisses it.

"You must be Tennessee, the healer," he says. Tennessee smiles and curtseys.

Without looking at me, Vanderbilt says, "And you must be Mrs. Woodhull, the clairvoyant." I nod and Commodore takes my hand, seemingly out of obligation, and kisses it. I curtsey as well. Vanderbilt studies me for a moment and says, "Colonel Blood said you have communicated with my dear mother."

"Yes," I say, "and I bring advice on the matter of your enemies."

Vanderbilt turns red, looking like a beaten man who is ready to beat another man. "Let us speak without delay," he says.

The Commodore shows me into his parlor room. I see a portrait of his mother immediately. Off to the side is a portrait of a man in a Union uniform. It must be his son, George Washington. The family resemblance between the dead and living is strong. Anyone would know they all fell from the same tree.

"Your son, he was handsome," I say. "Like his father before him."

"All my hopes, my future, my legacy," Vanderbilt says. "He was carrying the Vanderbilt flag."

"You have other children," I say, "other sons…"

"None like him," Vanderbilt says, walking over to his mother's portrait. "Right, mother? None like him."

Vanderbilt's face is one of vulnerability. This man who used to physically beat his competitors, this cruel capitalist titan who has an armed blockade on the bridge into New York so his competitor's trains cannot enter the city, looks like a lost little boy. Manipulating him will not be nearly as difficult as anticipated.

He points to a beautiful cherry table. I take a seat. A little bust of Napoleon is staring at me. I know this is a message from my spirit guide. I am in the right place.

"What does mama say?" Vanderbilt asks.

"May I contact her so you can speak to her directly?"

Vanderbilt nods. I take several deep breaths and relax, wiping my head clean of any thoughts and allowing the spirit world in. I feel the spirits wash over me, one after another like a series of soft blankets, one being laid on top of me after the other. All kinds of disconnected thoughts wash over me. Potatoes, chamber pots, bloody bandages, burning beds, breastfeeding babes, and flightless birds all occupy my mind briefly until I begin to feel heavy with a spirit. Spirit speaks through me, but does not sound like me, a deep, shaky, loud voice appears, saying, "Son, it is mama."

Cornelius grabs Mama's hand and kisses it, "Mother, dear Mother," he says. "What should I do?"

"People see you as a lamb," Spirit says, "but you are a lion. Show your claws. Roar."

Vanderbilt gets up and begins to pace the floor. He places his hands on his hips and takes in several short breaths. "Goddamn sons of bitches. Fisk and Gould. I won't sue, the law is too slow. I'll ruin them."

"You will," says Spirit, "this medium will help you."

"How can she help me?" Vanderbilt asks.

Spirit leaves and I open my eyes. "I will find a way," I say.

I get up to leave, and as I walk past Vanderbilt he grabs my arm. "What trickery is this woman?" he asks.

"I do not know what you speak of," I say.

"You even smell like her," Vanderbilt says. "How?"

I hand Vanderbilt my business card as Tennessee is walking in. "Her spirit lives through me," I say. Even as I say this, I know Vanderbilt's ears are closed to me as his eyes are open to Tennessee. Looking her up and down like a wolf sizing up its prey, Vanderbilt asks, "My pretty sparrow, can you possibly heal this old man?"

I pause long enough, just long enough to watch Tennessee work her magic. The art of seduction has always eluded me and yet comes so easily to my sister. I did not ask Tennessee to seduce this man, but I would not need to. Tennessee seduces everyone, even the poor men with nothing to offer.

Vanderbilt has everything to offer, so I imagine she will put a bit of extra effort into her performance. With a blatantly flirtatious smile, Tennessee pushes Vanderbilt into a large, overstuffed chair. She gets behind the chair and places her right hand on his balding head.

"My right hand is the North Pole. This hand helps the blind to see," Tennessee says as she moves to the side, leans over the Commodore, and presses her breasts against him while placing her left hand on his inner thigh.

"My left hand is the South Pole. This hand helps the lame to rise." Tennessee massages the old man's head and inner thigh at the same time while pressing her breasts against his cheek.

"Do you feel the magic of the opposite polarities?" Tennessee asks before clarifying, "the healing magic?"

Vanderbilt gives out a moan of pleasure and grabs Tennessee's waist. Tennessee loses her balance and ends up in the old man's lap, laughing. The old man gives her a kiss and Tennessee returns it with fervor.

I leave. I have seen enough.

AΩ

Canning's association with whores has finally paid off. Brothel after brothel, the madams are willing to answer my questions. They recognize me from all of my late night quests. If I were to be honest, I would go as far as to say that some do pity me. After consulting Canning's copy of *The Gentleman's Companion*, I target the establishments that appeal to the "legends of the city" and the "gentlemen of the most refined taste." Once I narrowed down the list, I gathered the Thomas Nast caricatures of Fisk and Gould from the *Harper's Weekly* and I search for two particular whores. I say two, I know not how large an appetite these men have. It could be ten whores. Inquiry after inquiry ends with a "never seen 'em" and the closing of the door, but I know that every no is leading to a yes.

I knock on the door of the finest home in The Tenderloin. From *Gentleman's Companion*:

> *This elegant parlor house is furnished in the most elaborate and magnificent style. The landlady and lively young ladies are a very pleasant set, full of fun, love, and fond of amusement. The carpets, mirrors, furniture, and paintings are of the latest and most costly designs. Everything is here arranged in the first style, while the bewitching smiles of the fairy-like creatures who devote themselves to the services of Cupid are unrivalled by any of the fine ladies who walk Broadway in silks and satins new.*

This townhome not only looks distinctly regal, it smells better too. The proprietor must punish men who try to relieve themselves on her steps. The door opens and I am ushered into the grandest parlor room in all of New York. All the furniture looks to be gold and fine velvet and it feels like silky clouds to the touch. The ceilings have cherubs looking down and smiling. One of the little angels is playing a harp. The plaster and crown molding are intricate and ornate. The cost of it all must be immense. The madam must oversee at least a thousand orgasms , and that is just to pay the rent. Who knows how many orgasms she needs to keep the place clean or keep the whores fed.

Struggling for words, partly because I've been saying the same thing for hours and my mouth is exhausted, and partly because I am overwhelmed by this whorehouse's interiors, I just point to the cartoonish Fisk and Gould.

"Which one is your husband, honey?" Annie Wood, the madam, asks me. She looks to be only twenty years old or so. I can tell that she is kind, but guarded. Annie does not have the big busts that most women have, and I can tell that she pulls her corset extra tight to exaggerate what she does have. She is the kind of woman that men would be split on. Some would call her plain, some would call her beautiful, but all would agree that she wears her clothes well and carries herself with an appealing sort of dignity.

"What?" I ask. I start looking for Canning. He better not be paying the high rent of these whores.

"Is it Mr. Fisk or Mr. Gould?" she asks.

"I am Victoria Woodhull. Neither is my husband," I say. "I want to meet Fisk and Gould's ladies." Annie gives me a questioning look and so I continue, "A great injustice has been done, and I want to correct it."

Annie starts walking me back to the front door. "I'm not in business to right wrongs," she says.

Annie opens the door and I close it quickly. "You are in business to make money," I say. I reach into my purse and give Annie three gold coins, after Canning's weekly drinking and whoring spree, it is all the money I have left.

Annie grabs the coins from my hand with such eagerness that one would think she is a hungry beggar child grabbing the last bit of bread, and still she says, "This will not buy you much."

"This is the first," I say. "Regular payments. Weekly."

"No one can know or I will be harmed," Annie says.

"I am clairvoyant. All information comes to me from my spirit guide," I say.

Annie smiles and slowly circles me like a shark sizing up its prey. "Your plan?" she asks.

"The plan is unimportant," I say, "The goal is equality. Women's equality."

Annie looks at me as if I am mad, but still she motions for me to follow her up a grand staircase. After a couple of twists and turns, we enter into a small parlor room. The door opens and I see a plump brunette with a huge head of hair piled high, who is dressed extravagantly and sharing secrets with a thin blonde who has long, straight hair dressed equally extravagantly. I am introduced to the brunette. Josie Mansfield. The blonde is Emma Smith.

"Ladies," I say, "you and I are going to change the world."

AΩ

"Stay with the whores?" Canning asks. After walking home from The Tenderloin, I went inside to cool off and found Canning napping. I woke him up and asked him not to come back when he leaves tonight.

"You already spend more of your nights there than you do here. You're welcome to come back and see the children during the day. They love you so," I say.

Canning stands up and moves towards me, getting so close that our arms touch. I hold my ground. "You are my wife," Canning says. "This is my home."

"In due time I will seek a divorce," I say, starting to tremble but still holding my ground, "I understand it may be difficult to obtain, but Indiana has liberal divorce laws now and we can travel and…"

Canning grabs my arms, "You promised God that you would honor, love, and obey me until the day I place you in a pine box."

I look up, into his eyes, and nod, "Tis true. You made the same promise. While I kept my promise for seventeen years, you broke yours on our wedding night."

Canning lets go of me with a little push, saying softly, "What changed Vicky?"

"I've made a decision to be happy," I say. "I do not believe in divorce, but I also do not believe I must be miserable for the rest of my years because of a decision I made when I was fourteen."

Canning sits down on the sofa and puts his head in his hands, shaking, close to weeping. "I always knew you had dreams, Vicky," Canning says. "I just hoped that one day they would include me."

I take a seat next to Canning and hold his hand. Canning kisses my hand. "Can you not love me?" Canning asks.

"I can," I say. "I do. But as you once told me loving someone and living with them are two wholly distinct propositions. I cannot and will not fetch you from whores every night. I cannot and will not stand by while I watch you destroy yourself with drink. Nor can I abide you refusing to contribute anything to society when you have so many talents to share."

Canning stands up and moves away from me, looking at me as if I had just whipped him. He nearly screams, "Sharpen your knife, Queen Victoria. You who is without sin. You would not even be here without me. You'd be dead, wanted for manslaughter like your sister, or pregnant with your father's fourth child. I saved you, I made you. I followed you on odyssey after odyssey. I protected you from your father. I chased after your unscrupulous, crazy sister. I gave you two children. And now you want me gone? All it takes is a wink and a few soft words from a barfly to make you forget?"

"Canning," I whisper. I am out of energy and out of emotion. I walk towards my husband, take a deep breath and whisper, "I am forever grateful, but my gratitude can no longer serve as my chains."

"Chains?" Canning asks. "That is what you think of our marriage, isn't it? I have you trapped like some poor, dumb field negro?"

I stay silent.

"If it is true that we are chained together, then we always will be, throughout generations to come. Our love lives through Byron and Zulu and our story is never ending. Do not force a false conclusion." Canning holds me to him, and for the first time today I smell the drink on his breath. Canning bends down and kisses me. I allow the first kiss. He ends the kiss and tries again and I start to push on him.

"Let me go, Canning," I say.

"Never," he says.

Canning pushes me down on the sofa and I realize that he wants our last night to be like our first night together. I struggle against Canning, but we both know that my struggles are useless, merely registering a silent protest in both of our memories. I hear a knock at the door and I try to wiggle away from under Canning's weight to get the door. Footsteps and a door opening tell me that Zulu has allowed someone into our home. I again push against Canning and say, "Let me go." I'm halfway off the sofa when Canning grabs my arms and forcefully throws me back down on the sofa. Again I say, "Let me go."

And somehow, magically, Canning is lifted off me. I sit up to see James gritting his teeth, holding his emotions in check while keeping Canning trapped.

"I believe your wife asked you to let her be," James says.

Canning shakes free of James and sizes him up. He slumps his shoulders knowing that he cannot physically defeat James. Looking James up and down, Canning says, "She's your tyrant now."

The door slams and James sits next to me on the sofa, his hands shaking. I pick up one of his trembling hands and squeeze it into stillness.

"I was ready to kill that son-of-a-bitch," James says before deeply exhaling. He turns to me, and whispers, "Are you hurt?"

"Yes," I say. James starts examining my arms, my neck, and my face for cuts or bruises.

"No," I say, "not in that way."

James kisses my forehead and holds me. "Part of Victoria," I say, "thinks Canning is right. I am ungrateful, worthless low-class scum who broke her vows and deserves contempt. Perhaps I was born this way. Men always treat me this way, so I must deserve it. It is as if all my life I've emitted a smell that is like to blood to sharks, and the sharks are always here, circling me, ready to attack."

James lets me go and searches my face, "what about the other part of Victoria?"

"The other part of Victoria is full of rage from a million atrocities both large and small committed over the centuries not only to her but to all the women before her. This rage is wide, strong, and deep. I know I must channel it into social change or it will destroy me, powerful as it is."

"Rage is a useful tool," James says, "I used it myself many a time on the battlefield, for you cannot kill without it. But then rage runs out and you need more. You need reasons for doing what you do, reasons other than retribution. You need a cohesive ideology that is rational and sound, one that can change men's minds and soften their hearts."

I nod. A cohesive ideology. Equality…free love….

James pats my arm, breaking into my thoughts, I look at him and he whispers, "you still have not told me what happened here."

"I demanded a divorce, kicked him out," I say, "why did you intervene?"

"Why did I intervene?" James asks as if it is the stupidest question uttered since apes could talk, "I am not going to stand idly by and let a man destroy you."

I lock my hand with James and admire his long, elegant fingers. "James," I say, "nothing Canning could do would destroy me. I'm a survivor."

James picks up my hand and kisses it, "Why did you ask for a divorce?"

"I would like to be with you," I say, "but if that is not to be then at least I will be without him."

James wraps his arms around me and kisses me slow and deeply. "My darling," he says, "I have been marching towards you, towards this moment, my entire life. Before there was you, there was the promise of you. You are my alpha and my omega."

AΩ

The flag was in the whorehouse window. All thirty-seven stars. All thirteen stripes. The flag, my calling, my signal, my cue to act. I run along to the side street and up to the fruit stand. Annie is judging the strawberries.

"What beautiful strawberries," I say.

"Five cents a quart," says the young boy behind the fruit stand. He has shaggy hair, a dirty shirt, and dirtier fingernails. For a moment I long to take him home and give him a good bath, and then I snap out of my short daydream.

"A scheme is afoot," Annie says, paying the boy for the strawberries.

I hold up two fingers to indicate to the boy that I would like two quarts. Byron will eat the first quart before I can wash and cut the second quart.

"Gold fixing," Annie says.

I pay the boy and smile. I even add in a couple of cents extra. "When?" I ask.

"Hard to say. Watch the door," Annie says.

I press two gold coins into Annie's palm.

"Anything else?" I ask.

"Oil," Annie says. "John D. is buying his competitors."

AΩ

Vanderbilt, completely disheveled, walks down the stairs towards me. I search his face to see if there is evidence of tragedy, as anyone who knows Vanderbilt knows there is never a hair out of place unless it is a time of tragedy or trial. He gives me a broad grin, and I instantly dismiss any concern.

"My dear Mrs. Woodhull," Vanderbilt says as he nods, "I was not expecting to see you so soon."

I nod in kind. "Forgive me, sir. The spirits have spoken and we must act right away."

The Commodore nods again and he rather roughly turns me around and walks me into the parlor. I hear a giggle, a belch, a bit of a commotion, and another giggle. I do not even have to turn around to know it is Tennessee, but turn around I do. Tennessee had fallen down a few steps and is struggling to get up.

"Tennessee!" I say.

Vanderbilt, red-faced, uses his body to block my view of Tennessee. He hastily pushes some of his hair back in place. "I can assure you, Mrs. Woodhull, that my intentions are honorable."

"I certainly hope not," I say.

"Excuse me?" Vanderbilt says, arching his white eyebrows.

"Nothing brings two people more misery than honorable intentions when all they want to do is be dishonorable," I say.

"Goddamnit! You women is my kind of people," Vanderbilt says bending down to slap his knee. He then gives me my first genuine smile and puts his arm around me as if we were old compatriots celebrating a victory.

Tennessee laughs and Vanderbilt motions to his servants. Instead of leading me to the parlor, he leads us to the dining room. Tennessee walks beside me and whispers in my ear, "My old goat is twice as naughty as me. He has had one thousand women, and I have had only half as many men." I try to silence her but she continues to giggle.

In the large dining room that could easily sit a dozen is a beautiful long cherry table decked out with every kind of breakfast food imaginable. I try to hide my shock, my lack of sophistication, but I know my face betrays me. Enough food for two fortnights is not a sight I have ever seen. The servants pull out chairs for us. We sit down and I carefully look at all the pastries, fruits, and meats to determine what I want first.

Tennessee chooses three pieces of bacon and a doughnut. I choose an apple. Vanderbilt chooses everything.

"What is this business?" Vanderbilt asks, chewing with his mouth open so bits of sausage fall back onto his plate.

"I need a guarantee first," I say, taking a bite out of my apple.

"What type of guarantee?" Vanderbilt asks.

"Ten percent of all profits for my advice," I say. This is fair, I know it to be fair, but Vanderbilt is clearly caught off guard, for he stops shoveling food into his mouth.

"I have never struck a business deal with a woman," Vanderbilt says.

"I am forthright as any man," I say.

"Five percent," he says.

"No, ten," I say.

"Eight."

"Ten."

"Why should I give you ten?" Vanderbilt asks.

"Because I can sell this information to Fisk and Gould for twenty," I say.

"And what if your information is wrong? Are you going to cover my losses?" Vanderbilt asks.

"Wrong?" I say. "Unlike the living, the dead never lie."

Vanderbilt leans back in his chair and pushes his plate away. He takes a sip of his coffee and rubs his chin a few times. He looks at me, then at Tennessee. Tennessee returns his gaze by giving him the best adoring puppy dog face I have ever witnessed. Vanderbilt pulls back up to the table and starts eating again.

"What the hell. Ten percent," he says.

"Payable within a week of the trade."

"Yes," Vanderbilt says again.

"One more stipulation," I say.

Vanderbilt throws down his fork and it makes a loud clinging sound, "Jesus, woman, has no one ever teached you that business deals must be simple."

"You must invest your servants' wages and give them their profit," I say.

"Risk their income? And if you are wrong?"

I bang the table and all the plates jump up and crash down. Vanderbilt is startled. "Spirit is never wrong," I say.

Vanderbilt nods silently.

"Good," I say. "Buy Central Pacific stock. Buy today."

Vanderbilt nods and starts eating another platter. Tennessee walks over and gets on her knees, places her hand on one of his knees and says, "Darling, you would feel better if you ate less. Can you try that? For me?"

Vanderbilt laughs. "You sisters is going to keep me healthy and wise."

"And wealthy," I add.

AΩ

I did it. Annie did it. Tennessee did it. Vanderbilt did it. James did it. Even old Fisk and Gould did it. Their whores too. We all did it. We all made Vanderbilt even wealthier than he was. Central Pacific was trading at $130 at the very moment Vanderbilt bought, and it was trading at $160 when he sold. Thousands and thousands of shares.

"We must celebrate, Victoria, you won your first battle," James says while rubbing my shoulders while sitting on my bed.

"Should we go to Dan Tucker's for dinner?" I ask.

"That was not the kind of celebration I had in mind, I was thinking about something a bit more private."

I lean over and kiss James. His passion is larger than my own. He begins caressing my hair, my face, he unbuttons my dress. I allow him to see and kiss the top of my breasts and then I cover up.

"You may touch me," I say, "but under the covers." I take my dress and underthings off and throw them in a heap next to the bed.

"Victoria, I want to see you when I'm kissing you, when I'm pleasing you…"

I curl next to James and kiss him on the neck, eliciting soft moans from my war hero. I whisper, "My darling, my body is not young. I have borne children. I have borne… many things," I say.

"I want a woman, not a child. You bore two children and survived. Celebrate your body. You have nourished life. The body is a temple to God, and I only want to worship at the temple," James says. His eyes are kind. I hesitate for a couple of moments and then remove the blanket, uncurling my body to lay straight next to his. James exhales. "You're beautiful."

James starts at my head and kisses my crown, working his way down my face, pausing at the lips for a few kisses, moving down my arm. He stops at a scar below my shoulder. His breathing quickens. He moves away.

"Did your husband do this?" he asks.

I shake my head. "Canning never whipped me," I say.

"Who?" James asks.

"Most of them healed and you cannot see them now, but that one…" I say.

"Most of them! Who did this to you Victoria?" James asks.

"It is of no consequence," I say.

James lays down next to me and pulls me to him. I feel his mustache on my forehead. He kisses my hair and places his hand on my shoulder, squeezing it gently. "What happened?" he whispers.

"Father," I say, forcing myself to betray little emotion, "he whipped us for days trying to put us in a state of delirium so we would be better clairvoyants. Tied to a bed, given no food. Tennie too. I protected Tennie from what I could… but I could not protect her from that. That is why she has moments when she looks at me with hate, because I escaped and Tennie continued to endure."

James moves away again and sits on the edge of the bed. He looks away from me and starts taking deep breaths. He is rejecting me. James will leave, just like Canning did on our wedding night. Why can I not keep these secrets? I start crying. James remains unmoved, not caring of my emotion. My crying quickly turns into sobs. "You are angry," I say.

"Anger is too tame a word," James says. "Closer to murderous fury."

"Forgive me," I say. "I offer my deepest regrets. I should never have…"

James is beside me in an instant, holding me, rocking me, kissing my tears. "Not angry with you, sweetheart, never with you. Your father. If I ever meet him… well… it would be a serious situation."

I dry my face with my hands and kiss James on the cheek.

"Victoria," James says, "I hope you know in your heart, mind, and soul that you did nothing wrong, nothing to deserve this treatment. Your father's mistreatment of you was criminal, insane, cruel, and it cannot be explained on earth or in heaven or even in hell."

"He was going to take Byron once," I say, crying again at the memory of it, "and sell him to the circus." I sit up, trying to control my breathing. I feel on the verge of a panic attack. Deep breaths. In. Out. In.

James places his hand on my shoulder. "What happened?"

"Canning beat him," I whisper, still gasping for air.

"More than deserved," James says.

"Me too. I broke his nose," I say.

"He is lucky you didn't kill him, he deserved no less," James says.

I turn to James, taking another deep breath.

"James," I say, "this is why, I know we have money now, but I do not want to use it to buy things, I want to…"

James interrupts me by placing a finger on my lips, "Victoria, that money is yours, I claim no right to it."

"But you are the man of the house, so to speak, and…" I say.

"We are equals. You keep your money and I keep mine. What kind of man would I be if I took your money?"

"You did introduce me to Vanderbilt," I say.

"Not every act of kindness has a monetary cost, Victoria," James says. "The money is yours and yours alone."

I push the blanket on the floor and I begin to undress James. I start with his shirt. I undo the first button and kiss his neck, his jaw line, his mustache, his ear. My lips find his lips and his hands find my breasts as I unbutton the rest of his shirt. James sits up and takes off his undershirt. Placing my fingers on his bullet wounds, I whisper, "I wish I could take these away."

James leans me back in the bed, kissing me, and whispers, "All my wounds point to you. I had to fight through the war to find you, and I would happily do it all again just to spend one moment in your presence. *Put me as a sign on your heart, as a sign on your arm. Love is strong as death; its coals are the coals of fire.*"

James kisses my lips, my breasts, and pauses only to remove the rest of his clothes. His naked body is the closest thing I have seen to Greek perfection. The marriage of his strength with his gentleness takes my breath away.

"You have the perfect body for a solider," I say. "You were made for battle."

James leans down and kisses my knees, working his way up to my thighs. "We were both made for battle," James says, "and now we fight together."

His lips move up my leg and he finds me. I want to tell him to stop, for people say this will make us both ill, but the pleasure takes my breath away and I cannot find any words. His tongue, his lips intimately caress me, leaving me gasping. I grab his shoulders. James stops.

"Did I hurt you? Do you want me to stop?" he asks, his eyes full of concern.

I shake my head. "Don't stop," I whisper.

James smiles and kisses my forehead. His fingers find me again, "Do not fear, it is only your pent up aching river, my love." A few more caresses and the dam breaks. My head is whirling, spinning out of control, my body arching uncontrollably, begging for more, my breathing erratic. I struggle to regain composure. James holds me and whispers, "Shh. Relax. Do not fight it, just enjoy it."

"I did not know," I say, "I never knew."

James kisses me on the lips, caresses my hair, nibbles on my earlobe. After a few minutes, James whispers, "Victoria, I want us to become one, is that all right, sweetheart?"

I whisper, "Promise you will not hold me down."

James kisses my forehead and looks into my eyes, "Victoria, I will never hold you down."

I nod and we kiss, his tongue moving deeply in my mouth, his lips move to my ears and he whispers:

"*Hark close, and still, what I now whisper to you.*"

His moves his mouth to my breasts, still whispering:

"*I love you—Oh you entirely possess me.*"

He takes my left breast in his mouth, circling my nipple with his tongue. His right hand plays in my pent up aching river, pushing deep inside.

I'm gasping, unable to think. James lifts his head up and whispers:

"*Oh, I wish that you and I escape from the rest, and go utterly off— Oh free and lawless, Two hawks in the air—two fishes swimming in the sea not more lawless than we—.*"

James takes my right breast in his mouth, his tongue teasing my nipple. I instinctively arch my body so he is close to all of me. James takes my legs and wraps them around his waist, he kisses me long and deep before whispering.

"*The furious storm through me careering; the oath of the two inseparableness of two together—of the woman that loves me, and whom I love more than life.*"

He plunges in me, whispering:

"*Oh I willingly stake all for you.*"

James moves in and out and I match my rhythm to his. My body contracts and I wrap my legs and my arm tight around him, whispering, "I love you James, I love only you." James makes a low, guttural primal moan and I feel not only connected to him physically, but our souls become entangled, one, our beings no longer having any discrete boundaries. Another moan is made, and I am not sure if it is James or myself, but we both release more of our pent up aching rivers. James whispers:

"*O let me be lost, if it all must be so.*"

James gives me one deep more kiss before release. I turn to him and stroke his face.

"Are you mine?" I ask.

James kisses me on the forehead, "You know I am a free lover."

"Yes," I say, "are there others?"

"Call me a hypocrite, as other men would. I believe in the tenet of free love, but my love for you is in such excess that there could be no other."

I kiss James.

"Why did the gods bless me so? That you would be waiting for me, having no other?" I ask.

James turns away from me, and says, "I had another. I was married."

"And you speak to me of this now? At this moment? Not before?" I ask.

James shrugs, still looking away, "Another life. Another James."

"What transpired?" I ask.

James turns back to me and moves so he hovers over me, intent for me to understand. "The war," James says. "Fighting and dying changes a man. I left Missouri a conventional politician. I was delegate to the state, an auditor, and I had power and influence. I had a good job, with a nice home, and a pretty lady as my wife. I had everything a man is supposed to have for happiness. I had followed all of society's grand plans. And then this country asked me to go to war. And I did. And even then,

I did what I was supposed to do. I led men into the line of fire in an impossible situation. I had men, my own men, die in my arms. I shot unsuspecting teenage boys dead, and I could not figure out why I did that except that they were wearing grey instead of blue. And then I got home and people were calling me a hero and nothing, nothing made sense anymore. I didn't know my wife, I didn't know myself, I didn't know my life. And that is when I realized that what we want, is not really want we want. We run around to create some order, some hierarchy, in the world. We care about status or money or right or wrong, but we don't care about people, about respect, about the dignity of the individual."

"What did you do?" I ask.

"Mary Ann, my wife, my ex-wife, understood. We divorced. She wanted a conventional life. I want one of change, I want to instill a new world order," James turns to me and caresses me. "Do you understand that? We have a limited number of days and we must use them for progress, and not fritter them away on anything less than a more perfect union."

"I would argue that the war was fought for a more perfect union, for the freedom of the negro," I say.

James shakes his head. "Revisionist history. It was a land grab by Lincoln, and he wanted their cotton too. He wanted to send all negroes to Africa or Central America. We can paint the war with a romantic brush and pretend he was a noble liberator, but it was capitalism. We only made it noble after the fact. What man, any man, even the cruelest most vile, evil, ignorant son of a bitch would watch 500,000 men get slaughtered for anything less than this country's fiscal interests. You think Lincoln would sacrifice that many men for slaves?"

"I never know why any man does the things he does," I say, "even you are a mystery to me."

We kiss. "That sound you made," I say, "when we were making love."

James kisses my hair and murmurs.

"A low guttural moan," I say, thinking back to what Tennessee told me about men.

James continues to kiss my hair.

"It means you are coming back, you are coming back to me," I say.

"Coming back?" James asks. "I'm never leaving."

AΩ

"The queen being too good refused to receive us," says Vanderbilt before slurping his soup at Dan Tucker's, "and so I told my wife, piss on her. We have enough money to buy her from England and sell her to the goddamned French."

Tennessee laughs and takes a napkin and wipes the soup off his chin. Vanderbilt grabs her hand and kisses it. James squeezes my hand under the table.

"Who believes in that divine right poppycock anyway?" Vanderbilt asks. Divine right. If any man in this country was to be king, it would not be the one in front of me. He is too coarse and vulgar. He is also a miracle. He fought his way out of his mother's womb to be born into squalor, and then he kept fighting until he had more than a million men combined. Along with embracing new technology at an old age, he also embraces newcomers and new thoughts. I'd like to think we are of the same tribe.

"What do you believe, Mr. Vanderbilt?" I ask.

Vanderbilt looks deep into my eyes for the first time since we have met. His left fist curls up in a ball. "I believe in strength," Vanderbilt says. "I believe in strength. A man must fight and take what is his, and not allow himself to be brought down by the weak."

A scuffle outside spills inside. Two are men fighting, one slender man is getting badly pummeled. The other man, husky and twice the size of his victim, is shouting, "Worthless swindler." James stands up. I place my hand on his elbow. No need to get involved.

"Your son," James says.

Vanderbilt sighs and nods, "My one regret. Corneil."

James begins to walk over to the fight and Vanderbilt grabs his arm, saying, "Do not intervene on my account."

James shakes off the Commodore's grip and walks swiftly to the fight. With two quick moves, he lifts the husky man off Corneil and tosses him out. Corneil struggles to get up and I can see cuts and scratches around his eye and his nose is bleeding. Dan of Dan Tucker's starts to flap about and make noise and James hands him a fistful of dollars. Tennessee runs up and begins to tend to Corneil's abrasions.

"It is my fault," Vanderbilt says nearly choking on his words. "His dead mother was my first cousin. He was born into this world physically ill, and now he is mentally weak. A gambler, drinker, spendthrift. Can't even win a fight against a man half his size."

I grab Vanderbilt's hand. "Do not blame yourself," I say. "Mothers bear responsibility for their children by making sure that the union they enter into is a healthy one. I escaped my cruel home by marrying an addict. I gave birth to an imbecile," I start crying, thinking of my dear, sweet Byron and all he will never know. "Byron," I say, "He pays the price for my sins. "

Vanderbilt holds up two for the waiter and two shots of a yellow liquid are brought. Vanderbilt is surprised when I down it quickly. My throat burns and I immediately feel a little woozy. Vanderbilt slowly downs his shot, turns over the glass and pulls his chair close to me. He places his hand on my shoulder, an intimate touch that is reserved for married couples. The other diners stare at us, but I block them out and focus on the Commodore.

"My dear…" Vanderbilt says, "Most women are kind hearted because they are fragile and they do not know any other way to be. But you, you my dear, are kind and strong."

19

BLACK FRIDAY

1869

A carriage door closes. Annie Wood walks towards my steps. I motion for Mabel, our new negro servant, to open the door quickly. Annie and I exchange information in excited whispers. We both leave, running down the steps into separate carriages.

I knock on the Commodore's door, and Tennessee answers in her nightgown. The servants are behind her admonishing her and clucking their tongues in disapproval for they say they are certain this will cause the greatest scandal New York city has ever seen. I wordlessly push past my sister and walk into Vanderbilt's bedroom just as he is waking up. Tennessee follows, three steps behind.

"Damn it, woman," Vanderbilt says when he sees me. "Let me get dressed."

I walk over to his bed and rip off the covers, exposing Vanderbilt in his underwear. I walk to the wardrobe, pick out one of three identical black suits and toss it on the bed. Vanderbilt sighs, hops up, and begins to put on his pants, although he does struggle a bit with them. Tennessee plants herself in a corner of the room and watches silently except with the occasional nervous giggle.

"The day of reckoning is here," I say.

"Whose?" Vanderbilt asks, finishing with his pants, and placing his left arm in his shirtsleeve.

"Fisk and Gould," I say.

Vanderbilt nods. "Tell me," he says. Done with his shirt, he now puts his jacket on.

"Buy gold now. Sell at $150," I say.

"A thirty percent increase?" he asks.

"A scheme. They have made friends of Grant's sister," I say.

"That foolish drunken bastard Grant, can't even see..." Vanderbilt shakes his head. He walks over to the window under the enormous portrait of a naked Venus and takes in the sight of his colorful garden. "As a patriotic American," Vanderbilt says, "it is my duty to warn the president that the financial health of the Union is being tinkered with."

"When?" I ask.

"After gold passes $150."

"A sell-off will create a panic," I say.

Vanderbilt, smiling, walks over to me and places his hand under my chin and stares into my eyes.

"The Commodore will steer the ship through rough waters," Vanderbilt says. I nod, knowing what he will do. A knock and then an entrance. A tall, well-built man walks in with a look of horror on his face.

"I don't believe you have met William," Vanderbilt says.

"What are you doing in my father's bedroom?" William asks.

Vanderbilt laughs, "Excuse my son, he bears the curse of his mother's refinement." Tennessee laughs and William sees her for the first time. He looks Tennessee up and down, takes note of her state of undress, and his horror grows. No doubt he is counting the pennies he thinks we will squeeze out of the old man's will.

"Use every penny we have and buy gold," Vanderbilt says.

"Father?" William asks.

I nod. "It is not prudent to invest it all," I say.

Vanderbilt places his hand on my shoulder. "My dear, for this, you will receive half of my profits."

I look William squarely in the eye and say, "Every penny."

AΩ

"$125, madam," the mop-head messenger boy in suspenders says. I hand him a coin from my carriage window. I wish women were allowed in the gold room so I could watch the price change myself. Women are not allowed near the stock exchange or the gold room. I don't know if the men are afraid we will steal just as they do or if we will force them to be honest. I expect the latter. I close my eyes and I can hear the sound of the chalk being erased and the price continuing to inch up. A few minutes later another boy runs up. Another coin into another hand.

"$130, madam."

First boy is back again. A third coin out of my purse.

"$140, madam."

Spirits, don't fail me now. We're almost there. Second boy gets his second coin.

"$150, madam."

I smile and nod until the boy is out of sight. And then I yell and sit back, stunned. I sewed an invisible thread between the spirits, corrupt business men, whores, an old tycoon, a Civil War hero, a madam, and my sister, and made a quilt of money.

After many minutes pass, William Vanderbilt, in a dashing custom grey suit, gets in the carriage and tips his hat. I am surprised his is willing to risk being seen with me. "You are a rich woman now, Mrs. Woodhull."

I nod and smile, saying nothing.

"$700,000 is your share," William says.

I try to hide my shock. The average New Yorker makes three-hundred dollars a year. In one day, I've made more than what twenty-three thousand New Yorkers make in a year. No wonder women are not allowed on Wall Street, if women can be this successful and earn their own fortunes then there would be widespread divorce.

"What will you do now?" William asks, his expression kind and patient as compared to his expression of shock and horror at our last meeting.

"Make more money," I say.

"How? By consulting the spirits?" William asks.

I look out the window and smile. "Wall Street will have a great sale. And there is nothing a woman likes more than a sale," I say.

William smiles, nods, and gets out of the carriage. William starts to leave, but comes back and pokes his head through the window. "Father is right," William says, "you are a bold operator." William tips his hat and leaves the carriage. I watch William and admire how he carries himself, with none of the sniveling entitlement that most rich men's children have. William is a man I could be friends with, if his status did not prevent such relations with women. Men like that are only allowed to bed women or marry them. Platonic is improper.

As I watch William leave, I see him pass James on the sidewalk. They nod to each other. James gets in the carriage with a brown bag. "I thought my queen of finance could use something to eat," James says. He unwraps some white paper and presents me with a cheese sandwich. I kiss James on the cheek and take the sandwich.

"We're rich," I say, before taking a bite.

"You're rich," James corrects. "No more humbugging."

I shrug my shoulders and swallow. "I'm not making any promises," I say.

James wipes the crumbs off my face as I quickly eat the rest of the sandwich. Once I'm done he opens the carriage door, "You need to walk, you have been sitting all day."

I get out of the carriage and take James's arm.

"You now have enough money to buy the world, Victoria," James says, "What shall you purchase first? Diamonds? A new coach? A pony for Zulu?"

We walk past the stock exchange and I pause and stare at the building that is the key to my immediate future.

"Things are not what I desire," I say.

"Revolution?" James asks.

Before the word "revolution" is out of my mouth, the air around us grows tense and heavy. A thousand angels, the same ones I saw when I was a child, circle around James and I and form a protective sphere of white light. Men surround us, yelling, throwing punches, wailing, and crying. One man urinates on himself. Another man, a short man who looks to be forty or so, takes his spectacles off and strokes his thin mustache. Looking at me, he says, "I am ruined." He then takes a gun out. James immediately shields me with his body and I hear the loud boom of the bullet. Blood splatters in my hair, on my dress collar, and on my glove. I grab James and turn him around. He is covered in blood, but he is not hurt. The banker lies dead in front of us, blood flowing down the pristine, white steps.

"The Revolution has begun," I say.

James grabs me and hustles me, picking me up and running to the carriage. We get in and he starts to tell Thomas, our carriage driver, to leave, fast. I put my hand over his mouth, we are staying put or at least I am.

"Boy," I scream out my window, "fetch me the price of Erie." I had him a coin, pausing to wipe off the blood that came from my right glove with my left hand.

"Madam," the boy says, "the market is collapsing."

"Hurry!" I say.

The boy runs off and James stares at me. Whatever he is thinking, it is not complimentary.

"You have enough money," James says.

"Revolutions are expensive," I say.

ΑΩ

Four days of sitting in the same blood-splattered clothes and I remain unmoved. I've bought so many stocks that I cannot even tell you what I own, it seems to be everything from railroads to furniture makers. But I know I will be far wealthier even than I was four days ago. At the first morning light, I look out my window and I see a familiar carriage. It is Vanderbilt. He sees me and nods. I nod back. I knock on the carriage roof. Thomas takes me home. Black Friday is over.

20

THE QUEENS OF FINANCE

1869

"Failure is predetermined," Vanderbilt says, pacing in his pristine and regal parlor. He occasionally stops to adjust his jacket or pat the Napoleon bust on the head, but he avoids looking at me, preferring to look out onto the roses in his garden. His parlor has stayed the same through his enormous coup on Black Friday. My parlor, on the other hand, went from bare to splendid. Adding wealth makes no material difference to the Commodore for he has so much already. He told me that money is his way of keeping score and seeking revenge.

"Yes, it certainly seems so," I say, "but I will find a way." I stay seated, trying to play the prim and proper student, for when it comes to finance, I am a mere novice.

"In all of the world, there is no woman banker," Vanderbilt says. "Fewer than 100 women in this country own stocks, even penny stocks."

"Change has to begin at some point in history, and it might as well begin with me," I say.

"No woman is allowed on the exchange floor or in the gold room. Who will do your bidding?" Vanderbilt asks.

"James. Messenger boys," I say.

"The wolves will destroy you, my dear. And my little sparrow. They will call you humbugs, charlatans, whores. They will destroy your character, destroy your spirit, and they will eventually ruin you," Vanderbilt says. "Even after I had millions, the mercantile agency publicly denounced me as illiterate, boorish, very austere, and offensive." Vanderbilt slams his hand on the table for effect,

"And that was about a Vanderbilt, a man with great power. I cannot imagine what they will say about you."

"I will swallow any recriminations with a silent smile," I say, "as long as change occurs."

Vanderbilt smiles and says, "You have enough money now. Why do this?

"I look at Byron and I am ashamed of the world I have given him. I look at Zulu and I think of the world I will leave her," I say. "Will her life be better than mine? Will she have any opportunities that I do not have? And what of all the other women, forced into loveless marriages? What about all the women who work but are not allowed to? What about the women who want to have a say in government who are not allowed to vote?" I pat the bust of Napoleon and say, "I have spoken to our friend Napoleon. He has told me that I have a duty, a sacred obligation to change the world."

"Woman…" Vanderbilt begins, "that's one hell of a task, more than Napoleon could do."

"And I cannot do it without you. The first step in our social revolution is to make an audacious statement about women. I need to prove to the world that women can hold their own with the bulls and bears. Labor must be honorable for all. Women must have new avenues for aspiration and ambition. If women start proving that we are equal to men in the sphere of business, then Congress has to grant us the right to vote. The states have to grant us the right to own property. Divorce laws could be liberalized. Businesses will employ women. Women can become lawyers or doctors, or anything they want."

Vanderbilt nods, "I didn't get nigh the satisfaction out of the two millions I made in the Harlem corner that I did out of stepping into my own periauger, hoisting my own sail and putting my hand onto my own tiller. Yes, that was the biggest day I ever had. Never taking a salary, being my own boss." Vanderbilt pauses before whispering, "I admit at times that I thought about Sophie and all the thirteen children she gave me, did she have other dreams? Would she have been happier if she had something to occupy her mind other than children?"

I say nothing.

Vanderbilt turns to me, "Do you know why I respect you, Mrs. Woodhull?"

"Because I added to your wealth?" I ask.

Vanderbilt laughs, "So did Missy. Won the purse last week, beat all the stronger nags." He shakes his head, "No, I respect you because I look at you and anticipate fragility and yet all I see is strength."

I smile and lock eyes with Vanderbilt and for a brief moment, our souls touch. I know he feels it too, for I see an expression of peace and satisfaction cover his face, it is unlike anything I've ever seen from this man. Vanderbilt walks to his front door and I follow. He opens it and turns to me.

"Do it."

AΩ

Our carriage arrives, and we, the twin queens of finance in our matching blue velvet and taffeta dresses with large feather hats, step out with an air of regal authority that serves to set the tone of refinement in the rough and smelly financial district. Thousands of men—naysayers, oglers, curiosity seekers, reporters, progressives, and politicians—have all lined up to see us. The first man is lined up at our front door. The line curves around the block. The last man in the line has his back to the back of the last woman who is the woman's line which stretches up to the back door of our establishment. Under counsel, we were told it was wise to have two separate entrances so the sexes do not mingle, and so the prostitutes and servile housewives can hide their money without attracting notice.

Tennessee precedes me, nearly marching down the street. I cannot see her face, but I imagine she is winking to all the good looking gents, and the guffaws from the men confirm this. As for me, I'm all business and keep my head down. I look no one in the eye, but I can hear their whispers.

"A humbug. A crook. A schemer....all prerequisites for bankers."

"She and that old goat Vanderbilt, why else would he…"

"She made a fortune on Black Friday."

"They say there is two men in her bed."

"The dead tell her what to do."

We reach the front door and open it. Tennessee walks around behind me and opens the back door. I hang Vanderbilt's portrait and under it I place a sign that reads, "Men must state their business and retire at once." The first man walks in, short and stout and afflicted with huge warts and perhaps color blindness, judging from his navy jacket paired with his brown pants. He tells me that he is Elmer, and Elmer starts shaking his finger at me, "What do you, a gentle maiden, know about the market?"

"I know not to panic," I say.

"What is your business plan?" Elmer asks.

"Teach women how to invest so they can protect their future," I say.

"But my wife's money is mine," Elmer says.

"Not if we teach her how to hide it," I say to Elmer.

The twenty other men crowded into the small office exchange looks of amusement and horror. A couple of men laugh. A man dressed in a cheap dark suit pushes to the front of the line.

"Ma'am, I'm here from the *Herald*. This is quite a turnout. I stopped counting at 800 men, but not everyone is here today and we want to help our readers. What financial advice can you give?"

Tennessee, always able to overhear anyone from the press, is immediately by my side like a dog hearing a bell that promises a treat.

"Have gold and plenty of it, because then you can tell everyone to go straight to the devil," Tennessee says. I gently stomp on her foot. We cannot be having such talk, especially on our first day. We are supposed to be refined and elegant.

The men laugh at Tennessee's advice and the reporter pushes on. "Miss Tennessee," he says, "if I may say so, you sure know how to fill out a blouse."

"I studied law for six years," Tennessee says. "You should be intrigued by my brains and not my blouse."

The reporter, red-faced, nods and leaves. I take Tennessee by the arm and pull her into a private corridor.

"Law for six years?" I ask.

"But it's true, sister, I had to study it to get around it," she says.

Disgusted, I release her arm. Lying to the press. Tennessee thinks her words are of no consequence. I cannot wait for the article that exposes Tennessee, and by implication, me, as liars. Studying the law. Indeed. We return to the front and the *Herald* reporter who no doubt would prefer to investigate Tennessee under more intimate circumstances turns to me instead.

"Ma'am, what advice would you give to our lady readers?" he asks.

"Every woman is welcome here, and we are happy to advise. We want to help all women secure their financial future and independence," I say.

Tennessee speaks up, "But we'll take money from anyone, even you."

Everyone laughs and there is some great commotion as more men walk in to gawk at me. Boss Tweed is here, as are the Vanderbilt-fighting duo Fisk and Gould. I begin to speak to them when suddenly everyone is silent. All the men take off their hats. It's not for me or for Tennessee, so it must be for someone they deem worthy of the title "lady." I turn around and see Tennessee usher in Susan B. Anthony, Elizabeth Cady Stanton, and Isabella Beecher Hooker. My face turns crimson thinking of these women waiting in line with the whores. But what could I do? This building does not have three entrances. Maybe, I think to myself, it is good for refined women to mingle with the working ones. I excuse myself and run to the back entrance.

Susan B. Anthony is dressed in the same austere outfit and spectacles that she wore when I saw her all those years ago. She must buy black fabric by the bolt, for she has never known a day away from the imaginary mourning since she gave up her pantaloons and bicycle. Elizabeth Cady Stanton, plump from years of what she calls "voluntary motherhood," with a head of white hair, is decidedly more feminine. In a light blue dress with a matching bonnet, no one would see her as alluring due to her age, but she makes a pretty picture. A mother of eight, one can see a mother's empathy in her eyes, whereas Anthony's eyes are cold coffee brown. I recognize Isabella Beecher Hooker from the many biographies of her father, Lyman Beecher, that were printed in the papers after his death, during a period of prolonged mourning. The youngest of the ladies, Isabella covers her curly locks with a light lace bonnet that allows her chestnut curls to shine through. Her dress is a conservative blue but has lace frills that hint at mischief.

We usher the ladies into the back parlor. I turn around and say, nearly stumbling over my words in my excitement, "Miss Anthony, it is an honor, I have been an admirer for years. I saw you and George Francis Train years ago around the time of the Kansas referendum."

"Men say," Susan says, "that I should not have aligned myself with the Copperhead. And yet, he is the one who gave us support. He financed Kansas and he is our benefactor for *The Revolution*."

"Perhaps," I say, "he should not have been so hard on the negro."

"Mrs. Woodhull," Susan begins, "a far greater crime than enslavement is disfranchisement. No class having the ballot in their hands could possibly have been enslaved. Not only did we help the anti-slavery movement, we were elected leaders of it. And we were told that once the black man was free, our rights would be secure. But when the war came to a close, our abolition friends were unwilling to help us. They said "before the women seek for enfranchisement we must obtain enfranchisement for the negro." And we say "if you are going to ask for the ballot for the black man, demand it for the woman."

Isabella Beecher Hooker, seeming a little exasperated, steps closer to Susan and puts her arm on Susan's shoulder. Without turning around, Susan says to Isabella, "And your brother is the biggest offender. He says privately that he wants women to have the right to vote, but then he stays silent and lifts not one finger for the cause. After all we have sacrificed in his company for the freedom of the negro. It is shameful."

Elizabeth sways back and forth on her feet, red in the face with anger, "For years we were told that black men were dogs, the lowest of the creatures, and then these same men give black men the vote before us. What does that say about their feelings towards women? Our friends say it is the negros' hour. When is it our hour? Even Susan's good friend Frederick Douglass voted for our rights in '48 and then abandoned us when we wanted to join forces for the 15th Amendment."

"An incredible betrayal," Susan says, "that I will never forgive. After we worked so many years together to free his people, he stayed in our home, he ate our food, we were always working on strategy, and then...."

"He is a realist," I say, "he knows we are right but he knew that the 15th amendment would not pass if it allowed women to vote. He did not want to sink his ship with our anchor. Our hour had not arrived, but times change swiftly in this new world of fast movement, fast thought. Now is our hour. This very moment. Look around! We have a woman on Wall Street."

Susan looks around seemingly unsure of what she should see. "Do you not find consorting with the bulls and bears a little... unseemly?" Susan asks.

"Look at this office!" Tennie says. "Is it not better than sewing drawers at ten cents a pair? Or teaching music at ten dollars a quarter? And the men with influence have received us with the greatest possible kindness."

I instantly regret that Tennessee mentioned music lessons. I know Susan taught piano for years and put all of her money into the cause of the abolition. I can feel Susan rearing back as if an insult has been hurled. Susan B. Anthony circled the two of us twice, slowly, looking us up and down. "How can this be?" she asks. "You have no idea the abuse, the scorn, I have earned."

I nod, knowing the names Susan has been called. Ungainly hermaphrodite, ugly face, leader of the delirium of unreason. I struggle to find words to comfort her, to inspire her, but Tennessee breaks into my thoughts.

"There are a few of the 'small potatoes' sort of men," Tennessee says, "who never mention the name of any woman, not even their own mother, with respect; who sneer, and try to get off their poor jokes on us, but it doesn't hurt us. We shall soon be part of the regular machinery."

Elizabeth walks forward and says, "Please forgive me, I have forgotten my manners. May I introduce Isabella Beecher Hooker, fellow suffragist."

We nod to each other and I walk to the desk in the parlor room and pull out the newspaper that has the obituary of Lyman Beecher next to the story of my beloved James. I show it to Isabella.

"Why did you keep this after all these years?" Isabella asks.

"The spirits told me this was important to my future. The story here is about my James, the Hero of Vicksburg," I say.

"Is James your husband?" Susan asks.

"Our souls are betrothed in spirit," I say.

Susan shakes her head in disgust and turns to leave. I block her exit. "You state in *The Revolution* that you are the Moses of my sex," I say.

"Like Moses, she is leading us to the promised land: complete political emancipation," Isabella says.

"The time is coming. One day we will be able to vote, put food in our mouths, and money in our pockets without asking men's permission," Susan says.

"With regards to the emancipation of women, I assure you that our souls are one, united," I say. I take a breath before remarking, "You need money for the promised land, Moses."

"And people," Susan says.

"People always follow money," Tennessee says.

"We need more ads," Elizabeth says. "We refuse medicinal ads and this does hurt us. I advise against this policy but…"

"Morphine and alcohol contribute to the ills of society, Elizabeth," Susan says. "All the money in the world will not purchase a cup of ice water in Hell."

"We would be honored to be part of *The Revolution*," I say, "I'm happy to sit for an interview with you."

"An interview?" Susan asks with a skepticism in her voice.

"And we can advertise," Tennessee offers.

"Advertise in my paper? I am unsure, a brokerage firm will not be viewed as respectable…"

Tennessee opens the drawer of the desk and pulls out a few gold coins. "Moses," she says, walking towards Susan, "here is some free financial advice." She picks up Susan's hand and places the coins in her hand, "Take it where you can get it."

ΑΩ

"My little sparrow," Commodore Vanderbilt says, standing beneath his portrait, calling around the office for Tennessee. He is our last customer, or, more precisely, last onlooker for our first day. Tennessee comes running, giggling out of the back office and grabs Vanderbilt's hand. Vanderbilt leads Tennessee back down the hall to the back office. Tennessee starts to close the door, but Vanderbilt stops her and he leaves it open. I watch from a distance as Vanderbilt sits in a chair and pulls Tennessee into his lap.

"How was today?" Vanderbilt asks.

"Oh, it was wonderful," Tennessee says. "We must have had two thousand men here and three thousand women. And all the women just gazed at your handsome portrait, and I could tell that each one of them was feeling a bit of love for you in their hearts."

Vanderbilt laughs a little and pats Tennessee on the head. "I have something to tell you, my little sparrow… I would like to marry you, but my family is against it."

"Since when have you…" Tennessee begins. Commodore silences her by placing two fingers on her lips. "I am marrying my cousin, Frank. She is a good Christian woman and will offer me some company."

"What?" Tennessee asks.

"But I can still see you as I wish," Vanderbilt says, "for you and your sister, you are my spiritual advisors."

Tennessee nods, breathing in several minutes of silence before asking, "How old is Frank?"

"About your age," Vanderbilt says. "She will keep me young."

I stop spying, unable to bear Tennessee's disappointment, which I feel even from this distance. Busying myself, I stay out of sight until I hear the front door close. I then peek around the corner and see Tennessee staring at Vanderbilt's portrait, getting teary eyed. I move in and place my hand on her shoulder.

"I almost had everything," Tennessee says.

"You have what you need," I say. "You have his portrait. You have his endorsement. You have his friendship."

"Why is it not enough?" Tennessee asks.

I hug Tennessee and offer her the promise of a warm dinner, "Let's get some soup."

AΩ

After a long day of fancy ladies, bears, and bulls, Tennessee and I take a carriage to Dan Tucker's. As we get out of the carriage, we notice Mr. Smith, the manager, yelling at a drunk, dirty vagrant.

"And take a bath," Mr. Smith says. "You smell like a dead mule!"

Tennessee and I walk into the restaurant, trying to avoid staring at the man, as there is no sense in adding to his public embarrassment. Before we can sit down, Mr. Smith runs over.

"Good evening, Mr. Smith," Tennessee says. Mr. Smith runs his hands through his hair and paces a bit.

"Soup for two," I say.

"Is Mr. Van… der… Vander… Vanderbilt joining you tonight?" Mr. Smith says with a peculiar smile on his face.

I shake my head.

"Colonel Blood?" Mr. Smith asks.

I point to Tennessee and to myself and hold up two fingers.

"My dear Mrs. Woodhull, my dear Miss Claflin, you are aware that I cannot possibly serve two women unaccompanied by a man at night," Mr. Smith says.

"Please tell me why, Mr. Smith," I say.

"But you know why," Mr. Smith says. "You have not changed all the rules, Mrs. Woodhull."

"We want to hear you say it," Tennessee says.

Mr. Smith sighs and holds up his hands, "The law… my place will be a house of ill repute."

I nod and leave Tennessee and Mr. Smith for one moment. As I'm walking away, I hear Tennessee saying, "A whore house? Who's fucking? I just want some goddamn soup. After all the money we have spent here?"

After a moment outside, I walk back with the smelly bum on my arm. We are given a reception of stares and jeers as his unfortunate odor fills the tiny establishment.

"Mr. Smith," I say, "soup for three."

ΑΩ

After finishing my tasty onion soup with my sister and smelly Harold, it is difficult for us to leave Dan Tucker's, for every creature, sexed or unsexed, married or unmarried, human or snake, wrapped themselves around us, blocking our exit with their bodies and harsh words that were designed for quick seduction. While I often find myself marveling at my sister's talents with men, my admiration of her grace was never greater than at this moment. Somehow, with a smile, a few kind words, and several sweet laughs, Tennessee can make every man think that they have already engaged in the most intimate of ways that left them both more than adequately satiated. And while she weaves this mind spell over them, she is politely refusing their advances, even without making false promises of later interludes.

Part of Tennessee's magic is that she has no fear and no anger towards these creatures. I, on the other hand, stew that despite my accomplishments, these men only see me a piece of meat to chew up and spit out. A mere plaything I am, not one with hope, ideas, or dreams. I'm not even worthy of their respect as a human being. At one point an ape of a man corners us and puts his hand into mine, interlocking our fingers as if we were secret lovers from centuries back, I spit out, "Let me get you a bowl of peaches and you can have your way with the fruit, for it will be sweeter to you than I could ever be."

This man, to his credit, does not hurt me as I feared he would, but he does say, "Missy, if you want to be unsexed, then you must look unsexed." I ask him what he means, fearful that he will tell me to wear black all my days left into my coffin. Instead, he fingers my long light brown tresses, and says, "If you want to be treated as a man, look the part."

Tennessee, seeing me cornered, comes over and plucks me out by complimenting the ape, and we are able to finally make it to the carriage without sacrificing any affection. Perhaps Mr. Smith has a point about women dining alone. Society will always assume you're a whore if a man isn't there to wipe the dribble off your chin. I think about Mr. Smith, the ape man, Harold the smelly bum, and Tennessee's grace all the way home, not even answering any of Tennessee's silly chatter with contributions of my own.

A weariness so deep that it pierces the core of my bones sets in as I slowly walk up the stairs to my home. Tennessee, dragging behind me, remains strangely silent. The door opens before I reach the first step and James comes out, his head down.

"First day of your reign," James says. Tennessee gives me a smile and walks past him and goes inside.

"Where were you?" I ask.

James lifts his head and in the moonlight I can see a large bruise on his cheek.

"What happened?" I ask.

"It is of no importance," James says. "Besides, I won the fight." James takes a seat on the step. I follow his lead and sit next to him.

"What fight?" I ask.

"I could not be there because the men would think that I am the one operating the firm," James says before grabbing my hand. "Please know that I do support you completely."

"What fight?" I ask again.

James kisses me on the cheek. "It is nothing," he says. "Sore men that lost their savings on Black Friday. They think me a bought man."

I reach for James's hand and I squeeze it on the dimly lit steps. I reach up to tenderly caress the bruise. "I do not always consider the price others pay for me," I say. "I never want you to suffer for my words or deeds."

James grabs me and kisses me, his body melting into mine, his lips full of promise.

"I will gladly take a bullet for a just cause… and you are my cause… my only cause."

I kiss James and hold him tight, silently thanking the spirits for bringing us together. Thinking about the men at Dan Tucker's, I walk inside and grab a butcher knife and lamp, carrying the items upstairs. I sit in front of the mirror and measure out my long tresses, taking a knife to the hair that rests below my shoulder. James watches me silently. I turn to him.

"You do not mind?" I ask.

"Looks like we were both in fights today," James says. I smile, he nods, and I saw through my hair with the butcher knife, cutting slowly as to not cut my fingers. I watch as thousands of strands fall to the ground.

I look in the mirror and see an unfamiliar imp staring back at me. My lips start to tremble as I realize that I have erased part of me, the part that gets smiles of desire from strangers. James walks up behind me, resting his hands on my shoulders, but I cannot look at him. "Victoria," he says, "you are still beautiful. Some women can never hide it."

AΩ

"Sister," Tennessee whispers in my ear as I try to sleep despite snores coming from James. Following Tennessee into her bedroom, I am greeted by two outlandish French shepherdess ball gowns in the style of the court of Louis XV. Two satin masks were tossed on Tennessee's bed. The blue gown is for me. The pink one is for Tennessee.

"No one will know we are there," Tennessee says, "while we spy and see how the rich party." While I take some time getting into this ridiculous get up that Tennessee borrowed from Annie's girls, Tennessee explains that we are attending the New York French ball organized by the Société des Bals d'Artistes. She had to go to great lengths to get us invitations. Thousands will be there, lawyers, Wall Street investors, politicians, and other king makers. I want to tell James, but Tennessee insists it must be our secret. James is too protective. And James has to stay with the children.

We arrive at the Academy of Music on the corner of 14th and Irving Place and I immediately understand why Tennessee is so curious about tonight. This imposing brick building with its plush velvet interior and private boxes is the musical sanctuary of a closed society—the oldest, most refined, and wealthy families. The Astors are welcome here. The Vanderbilts are not. The trustees deny entrance to the vulgar nouveaux riche—the Vanderbilts, the Morgans, the Rockefellers, and the Goulds. The Commodore is so incensed at being told that his money is not welcome here that he is aligning himself with rivals to build a new opera house even though he has no fondness for any music that is not in English. He wants to call this new theatre the Met, short for Metropolitan.

Shunning the nouveaux riche is in the normal course of business. And a ball is not the normal course of business. A French ball is much more welcoming to all sorts.

We get out of our carriage and see thousands of men who wear no masks as they hoot, yell, and whistle at all the masked women. Several women are wearing similar ballerina costumes with very little left to the imagination. I look at the policemen to see if they are going to arrest these nudists, but the policemen are too busy dancing and groping the women, their hands inside the top and the bottom of the pink tutus.

Once inside, we see women with even less clothing. Women, who shelter their identities with masks, have their nipples covered but nothing more. The seats, the stage, the floor, the boxes are illuminated with thousands of gaslights in crystal chandeliers. A band is playing some vulgar melody with a loud drumbeat as people laugh, scream, moan, and seduce each other. I feel physically ill at seeing breasts, vaginas, labia all compressed in a writhing mass as they grind against well-dressed hooligans. We make our way to a plush velvet box. The box next to us is full of whores and Wall Street investors. One young investor picks up the whore and throws her to the crowd below. The crowd catches her, rips her clothes off, and then tosses her up in the air while laughing and spraying her with champagne. The same man then picks up a heavy, big whore and tosses her into the crowd. No one catches her and she lands with a thud. I do not know if she is alive or dead. The nonchalant crowd does not even pause as four policemen carry her body out, making their way through two different orgies.

"I hope the Astors like semen on their theater seats," Tennessee says pointing to the Astor box across from us where a prostitute is spread eagle on the velvet lounge either being raped by three men or is voluntarily making three times her hourly rate.

"This is where the debauched come to get debauched," I say, "and the trustees know this very well. And they are too good for the likes of Vanderbilt? For the likes of us?"

Tennessee shakes her head and we talk of our shock at what we are seeing when we hear some scuffle below. We look down on the stage and a man is covered in blood. I grab her hand with urgency and we start to leave. As we are leaving, we run into another Wall Street investor, Luther Challis. Young and handsome, Luther is the stupidest son-of-a-bitch on Wall Street. And that is saying something. Luther is from a playboy family and would invest in anything. Anything. I could tell him that I invented a machine that turns cow shit into gold and he would give me thousands sight unseen. He would then get confused and brag to his friends that he invested in a machine that turns gold into cow shit. Then poor, stupid Luther would take everyone out and celebrate with champagne and truffles and talk about how cow shit is going to change the world. Luther's family has a box here, for he and they are the right kind of people for the trustees.

Luther is with a young, petite, blonde who looks to be a painted virgin—a silly teenager, fifteen if she is a day, who escaped her parents to see what a ball looks like. Wearing a tasteful tutu, Luther has her leaning against him and his hands are in the bodice of her tutu, groping her breasts. The girl is drunk. I can tell not only by her demeanor, but also because she is holding an empty bottle of champagne.

"Luther," Tennessee says, "let her be. She is an innocent. Plenty of experienced woman…."

Luther holds up his finger and it is covered in blood. He laughs and says, "I got one maiden tonight, gonna get me two."

Tennessee then lunges for the girl and grabs her, saying, "you are coming with me." The girl does not stir. Tennessee has her in her grasp when Luther grabs the girl back and snaps, "Let her be!"

I throw my mask down and grab the girl, Tennessee helps me pry her tutu-clothed limp body from the dumb scoundrel. We start walking with her, nearly carrying her, when Luther and his other friends push us down and grab her, running away. As a last attempt to free this young girl, I grab Luther's ankles but he slips out of my grasp.

Sitting on the floor of this elite theatre box in these huge blue and pink ball gowns, our hair is in disarray, and our gowns are ripped. Tennessee starts to cry.

"You did all you could," I say, trying to comfort her.

"It could have been me," Tennessee says, "It could have been me." Tennessee starts to cry and I put my arm around her and kiss her on her forehead.

"Women are merely property for men's amusement," I say softly, "even here. Look at all these well-respected men and how they behave."

"One day," Tennessee says, wiping her tears, "the world shall know the wrongs these women suffer and the men who inflict them."

21

THE VICTORIA LEAGUE

Finally, *The Revolution* is here. I have been waiting for more than a fortnight for Anthony's paper to announce our arrival on Wall Street, even writing the article myself and reading it over and over hoping my words would make it into Anthony's quill. That was during the day. At night I have dreamt of autographing copies for young, inspired women. As Horace Greeley's *New York Tribune* has been kind to us, I imagine Anthony's paper will be triumphant. I greedily grab the paper out of Mabel's hands. Too nervous to read it, I run into the dining room and hand it to James, who is having breakfast with the children. Tennessee jumps up and reads it over his shoulder.

"The first page is all Anna Dickinson," Tennessee says.

"Anna Dickinson," I say without hiding the disgust in my voice. This abolitionist has been crusading since she escaped her mother's womb and has not stopped. She never goes away, always in the paper. How many years must I hear about this woman? "Slavery has already been abolished!" I say, "We are the new cause."

"And I even gave gold," Tennessee says. "You know how I hate to depart with my gold."

James begins reading, "The popular feeling against them, was not so much because women embark on the business of stock brokerage, but because of their antecedents."

"Our family?" I say, feeling something snap in my brain.

"These women are accused of having humbugged the public as clairvoyant physicians," James says.

Zulu finishes her oatmeal and I grab her bowl. I throw the bowl against the wall and yell, "Moses just spit on me," feeling the injustices of thousands of years within the span of a few seconds. I get no satisfaction when the bowl breaks into many pieces with leftover oatmeal covering the wall looking as if someone had vomited on it. Mabel ushers the children out of the room.

"What else?" I ask.

"Victoria…" James says.

"Read it," I demand.

"I should not fancy the business of stock brokerage nor relish the associations one must have, but they have a right to do so," James reads.

I turn to Tennessee, "Moses is too good for business."

Tennessee nods before saying, "Just like when men say women are too good for politics."

"Quite the revolution," I say, "read the rest."

James takes a deep breath, probably waiting for another thrown dish, "No additional words on the matter. Miss Anthony had a jubilee, people came from every corner to praise her and give her gifts, gold, silver, and pearls."

"I have the perfect present for Moses myself," I say.

"What?" Tennessee whispers.

"We will have our own paper," I say.

"Victoria," James says before letting out a little sigh. "We know nothing of the paper business."

"If an old Quaker spinster full of vinegar can write a paper that people read, so can I," Tennessee says, "after all, my stories are infinitely more interesting."

"Readers will be the Victoria League," I say.

"The Victoria League?" James asks.

"They will campaign for us," I say.

"Campaign? James asks.

"She can be Moses," I say. "I'm going to be President of the United States."

James looks at me, no doubt wondering which institution he should commit me too. Tennessee reaches under her petticoat and grabs the elixir and drinks a shot, saying, "Bumping, humping, Jesus, Victoria! Women can't even vote."

Tennessee pours me a shot and I down it.

"They will," I say. "I will find a way."

AΩ

"President of the United States!" Benjamin Butler enthusiastically exclaims, standing in the front of my line of gentlemen investors on an early morning in my brokerage firm. A balding humpback with a lazy eye, Representative Butler is considered the ugliest man to have ever served Congress. And that is saying something, for there have been all kinds of gnomes, trolls, and short monsters roaming those sacred halls. Ugliness aside, his disposition never earned him any loyalty from his congressmen, but it did earn loyalty from his soldiers when he commanded them during the War.

Butler unfolds the *New York Tribune* and reads my announcement:

> *While others of my sex devoted themselves to a crusade against the laws that shackle the women of the country, I asserted my individual independence; while others prayed for the good time coming, I worked for it; while others argued the equality of woman with man, I proved it by engaging in business. I boldly entered the arena of politics and business, and exercised the rights I already possessed. This is why I'm announcing my candidacy for...*

"I want you as Vice President," I say, interrupting Representative Butler.

Butler raises his eyebrows and laughs, "Lincoln asked me to be his Vice President. I asked him what sins I committed that would damn me to preside over the Senate and spend my days listening to arguments that are more or less stupid."

"Then what happened?" I ask.

"I agreed to accept only if he would guarantee his death within three months of the election. He would not. And the rest is history. So I will not try to extract the same promise from you, as it seems to be deadly," Butler says.

James and Tennessee walk in. I knew Tennessee would be late. I'm surprised to see James at all. My lover and my sister exchange brief glances of surprise at Butler's appearance at my door.

"Representative Butler," James says.

Butler nods. I place my hand on Tennessee's back and move her closer to Butler.

"My sister, Tennessee…" I say.

"You look familiar…" Tennessee says, interrupting my introduction.

"Representative Butler was a Union general during the war," I say. "He was the one who freed the negros by calling them contraband."

"Yes, I remember now," Tennessee says. "I used to shit on your face."

Humiliated, I give Tennessee a stern look that I ask Demosthenes to force the ground to open and swallow her up. Tennessee responds by smiling angelically.

"The chamber pots," Tennessee says.

"The Butler chamber pot," Butler agrees. "The Southerners made more money on those chamber pots than I am to have allegedly stolen from New Orleans." Butler, who looks to be struggling to hide his annoyance, looks at me, "I incite strong emotions, of this I have no doubt, but I believe in your cause."

Butler starts to put his hand on my shoulder, but James swiftly steps in and creates a barrier between us, "Thank you, but we have all the support…"

"We need the vote," I say, pushing James out of the way so I can once again stand nose-to-nose with Butler.

"Pardon?" Butler says.

"You freed the negro, now free us," I say, "You want to help, get us the vote."

Butler shakes his head and smiles, "My legal argument for the slaves was that they were war contraband. I can hardly classify women…"

"Taxation without representation…" I offer.

Butler shrugs his shoulders, indicating this argument is not strong enough. He would know, as he is the finest legal mind in this country. His fellow lawmakers, however, are ruled by emotion. One of these bastards was just quoted today, as he has been before, as saying that a woman is more beautiful with a baby in her hands than a ballot. "You must find legal justification for the vote and press the case," Butler says.

"How?" I ask.

"Study all the laws, every document, every Supreme Court opinion, every legal precedent of any kind and find a loophole," Butler says.

"And when I do?" I ask.

"Come to me," Butler says, causing James to go rigid with annoyance.

"Lady Broker," my next customer says, "I just need to buy gold."

Benjamin looks behind him and sees the long line of customers. He tips his hat and leaves. James pulls me to the private parlor and Tennessee entertains the men. I hope she is not giving gold away or stealing from her customers. One must watch her like a hawk, for I have already found dollar bills of unknown origin stuffed in her bodice along with slips about trades she never made.

"You know what he did during the war," James asks.

"He freed the slaves," I say, allowing irritation to creep in my voice. He is a national hero. Of course I know what he did.

"He encouraged Union soldiers to rape Southern women. They called him the Beast. And he looted New Orleans. For that, they called him Spoons," James says.

I grab James's hands. "James, I am thirty-two. I will likely be dead in ten years. Byron is lost to me. Zulu's potential will be smothered. Ten years to change the world. If I need to use a Butler or a 'Spoons' or a 'Beast' to gain equality, then I will."

James grabs my shoulders and holds me tightly. "This country just spent the blood of five-hundred thousand to buy freedom for the slaves. And this battle may be larger."

"This battle won't cost a single man," I say.

"It will cost one fine woman in body and soul," James says.

I stroke James's cheek. "Travel this path I must, but only if you travel with me."

James hesitates and then gives a slight nod before kissing me, pausing between kisses to whisper, "Where you go I go."

AΩ

"Glory Be! Hallelujah!" I have found the word that will change the course of history. Citizens! I've done it, I've done it. I've done it. James is asleep, his head resting on legal papers I asked him to read. My legal books and papers, stacks and stacks of them, are on the kitchen table. Tingling and nauseated at the same time, I throw a coat over my nightgown, grab a sack of donuts, and go out into the dark city street.

I knock repeatedly on the door, banging loud enough to wake everyone east of the great Mississippi. Curse words are muttered and Representative Butler opens the door. He is in his red pajamas and matching robe. He looks at me, blinks, and looks again. I hand him the bag of donuts, push him back, and walk in his home.

"Dear Lord, woman," Butler says. "Are you intent on ruining both of our reputations?"

I keep walking into the parlor, forgetting any etiquette I have ever known. Butler sighs and pours himself bourbon. I grab the glass out of his hand and take a sip and hand it back to him. Butler shakes his head, but then downs the rest of the whiskey quickly that it is a wonder it does not burn his throat.

"14th Amendment," I say. "All persons born or naturalized in the United States are citizens."

Benjamin takes a donut out of the bag and eats it, oblivious to crumbs falling everywhere.

"Yes, yes," he says.

"15th Amendment. The right of citizens of the United States to vote shall not be denied or abridged by the United States or by any State on account or race, color, or previous condition of servitude," I say.

Wiping a donut crumb from his face, Butler says, "My dear, you just figured out what more learned men have not. The Constitution already gives women the right to vote. I could have told you myself, but I wanted to see how serious you are."

"What do we do?" I ask.

Benjamin pours himself whiskey and starts to drink. "You may submit your memorial to the House Judiciary Committee in written form, where it…"

"No," I say.

Butler grimaces then downs his drink.

"I refuse to submit a written legal argument that can be tossed in the spittoons with no reply. I will deliver it myself, and I will debate the naysayers," I say.

"I will have to open the judiciary committee for you," Butler says, wiping his head as if he is sweating, even though he is not.

"Is it difficult?" I ask.

"It is rather… unusual," Butler says.

"I will personally lobby…" I say.

"Allow me a few days to reflect," Butler replies.

Butler starts to open the door, but I take a seat. I grab a copy of *The Revolution*, which is sitting on his parlor sofa. I begin to page through it.

"Why help me?" I ask.

Butler looks down on me and smiles. "My dear, God made me only one way. I must always be with the underdog in the fight. I can't help it; I can't change it; and on the whole, I don't want to."

I hold up *The Revolution*.

"Why *me*?" I ask again. "Anthony has been laboring for years, paying her dues."

"Only a fool aids his rivals," says Butler with a bit of venom in his voice.

I let out a little laugh, "Moses would never run for Congress."

Butler smiles at the thought, "Not political rival. Romantic. We love the same woman."

The same woman? The same woman? Surely not his wife. Sarah Hildreth Butler is known as a fiercely independent woman who has been ill for some time, confined to a bed, no longer able to do much of anything. It is rumored that during the war, she crossed enemy lines and visited Butler on the battlefield, begging to stay by his side for the entire war. Butler convinced her to leave him be, telling her that their children deserved a lot better in life than to be left orphans.

The same woman? I pick up *The Revolution* and see again the first-page article. Is this why Susan gave an abolitionist so much ink? I hold it up. "Anna Dickinson," I say, "abolitionist."

Butler nods. "Sharp mind, engaging presence, beautiful soul."

"Who does she love?" I ask.

"Some days it is me, some days it is not. And yet I do not care how many flowers bloom in Anna's garden, as long as I am one of them. But I fear the Black-eyed Susan may crowd me out."

"You limit Susan's victories to diminish her," I say.

"Without hurting the cause," Butler says.

I get up and get down on my knees in front of Butler, grabbing both of his hands in mine. "My sacred vow to you, Mr. Butler. Open the judiciary committee for me and any victories will be mine and mine alone."

ΑΩ

"Months!" James asks, pacing up and down. James still has the red creases on his face from laying his head on the books. Just waking up at my urging, he is not quite comprehending what

I am saying to him. I'm still in my gown and overcoat. James is kind enough to not ask about my judgment in chasing after Beast Spoons in the darkness of the night, not even properly dressed. Tennessee, hearing the ruckus, joins us in the kitchen. Scantily clad in a nightgown, Tennessee is mixing orange juice and elixir. I wish she had the good sense to cover up in front of my lover, but it is not a fight I can pick tonight.

"It is too dangerous, Victoria," James paces and runs fingers through his hair, as he always does when he is nervous. "You do not know what you are up against," James says, "Revolutions are bloody affairs."

"I must accompany you," James says.

I shake my head.

"Be reasonable, Victoria," James says.

"I need you to take care of the children and the business," I say. It is the truth, but I also know that as a man he would be assigned the victory should he accompany me. This is the woman's hour. This is my hour.

James lightly grabs my shoulders. "Victoria, I've never begged for anything, but I'm begging you not to do this."

"If you must leave, go," I say, my mind and heart committed. "But this is a battle I must fight, if not for Zulu then for the unborn."

James paces for several minutes, sighing, cursing, shaking his head, and muttering to himself. He then stops and looks at Tennessee. Tennessee smiles at him and pours him a shot. He takes it.

"Then take Tennessee with you," James says.

Sensing the history and gravity of the moment, Tennessee lets out a big belch and laughs.

"This must be a dignified affair," I say, conscious that I'm rolling my eyes at Tennessee's antics.

"Dignity will get you nowhere with Congress!" James exclaims, putting his arm around Tennessee. "You shall convince the Congressmen by using your brain, but Tennessee will convince by using her body."

"James!" I say. I have never heard him talk this way before.

"One sometimes has to bend their morals to change the world," he says.

Now it is my turn to start pacing, I rub my temples. I can just see this turning into some disaster, a farce, a jail term. Tennessee suddenly gets serious and grabs me by the arm to try to reassure me.

"Vicky, do you remember when you would protect me?"

I nod, remembering the whippings and rapes I took in her stead. Perhaps if I had done it more often or for more years, Tennessee would not be the trouble seeker she is or constantly seek comfort in the arms of strangers.

"Allow me to help you this time," Tennessee says, kissing me on the cheek. My body relaxes and I nod. I cannot deny my sister.

A drawer opens and closes and James walks towards us with a gun.

"Take this. Men can be violent when their authority is threatened," James says.

I shake my head.

"Not you, Tennessee," James says. James hands Tennessee the gun. Tennessee twirls it around as if it's a toy. James sighs, grabs it out of her hands and places it on the table. "It makes my head spin to think how quickly this one could charm her way out of jail. And Tennessee, don't go mixing drinking with shooting, or you will shoot off your own foot."

Tennessee gives James a slow bedroom smile that makes me question my judgment in taking her to Washington, but also makes me breathe a sigh of relief she will not be here alone with James. No man is immune to her tempting ways. She then makes a mock salute towards our Hero of Vicksburg and leaves. I shake my head and give James a kiss.

"The children…" I say.

"We will manage…" James says with complete confidence.

"My longing for you will be dreadful," I say. I place my hand over my heart. James leans in and clasps my hand with his.

"We will always be under the same sun, the same moon, the same stars. When you think of me, place your hand over your heart and allow your spirit to touch mine. And I will do the same," James says.

"James, whatever may pass between us, I want you to know that I will always be indebted to you. My love for you in this moment will never be dimmed," I say, conscious of the tears streaming down my face. How can I leave this man?

James gets on his knees and reaches into his pocket. "I was going to wait until Christmas, but…" James grabs my hand. He has a plain gold band in his hands.

"But you don't believe in marriage," I say.

"All my beliefs fall away with you," James says.

Speechless and crying, all I can manage is a nod. My heart searches for poetry or at least something romantic from the Greeks, but I cannot find any words meaningful enough.

James stands up, and holds me, whispering, "Victoria, every man has an alpha and an omega, a beginning and an end. You are my alpha. You are my omega. Not just in this life, but in lives past, in lives future."

James wipes my tears and kisses my cheeks. He then places his hand under my chin, forcing me to look into his eyes.

"Come back," James says. "Promise me."

"Always," I say.

22

VOLUBLE CHARMERS

The Evening Star:

Mrs. Victoria C. Woodhull, alias Victoria Blood, and Mrs. Tennessee C. Claflin, together with the husband of Mrs. Woodhull, compose the firm in question, and they are a very bad lot indeed, as they certainly must be if the tenth part of what has all along been said about them to be true. At any rate, the public men in and around Washington and elsewhere in the world would do well to be a little watchful of their relationship to the voluble charmers.

"We have not even opened our mouths yet," I tell Tennessee as I fold the newspaper under my arm as we walk around the capital city, taking in the sights and avoiding the smells. "And we have threatened all the men in the world."

"We are a bad lot, dear sister," Tennessee says. "Voluble charmers."

"Perhaps Greeley was right," I say. I try to avoid the manure as we walk in front of the Capitol. I'm not sure if the shit comes from the horses' asses or out of our politicians' mouths.

"Greeley?" Tennessee asks.

"Hopeless Donna Quixotes fighting the windmills," I say.

"Our windmills have penises," Tennessee says linking her arm in mine, "and that makes all the difference in the world."

AΩ

In a scandalous move that adds extra whispers everywhere we go, Benjamin Butler has asked us to eat every dinner with him. These mealtime visits are under the guise of plotting strategy to win political converts to the cause of equality. And I know, and I think we all know, that Mr. Butler wants to enhance his reputation as a desirable man, and dining with two beautiful "voluble charmers" certainly does that. I cannot blame the man. If I was known as the ugliest man ever to serve Congress, I am sure I would surround myself will all kinds of pretty creatures in hopes that my title might fall away.

Representative Butler boldly declares that he cares not what mere mortals think of him for he answers to a higher power. Not only does he answer to the higher power but the higher power has already reassured Representative Butler that he has made the right choice in every instance. And yet, he recounts every slight from the mere mortals and refutes them nightly at the dinner table. On this occasion, he is fighting against the newspaper that refers to him as "the hideous front of hell's blackest imp; total depravity personified."

"You do not have a coat of arms," Butler says answering a reporter's earlier insult and spooning mashed potatoes in his mouth before saying with a full mouth, "we may not have the coat, but we have the arms." Butler then waives his arm in the direction of the swords hanging on his wall, each from a different skirmish that either he or one of his ancestors was in.

"You were too hard on the prisoners, the fine gentleman from Maryland says," Butler says, picking his chicken off the bone. He then slams his fist down, "This is war! The army isn't a town meeting. We are not governed by civil law, we are governed my martial law."

"But what about poor Colonel Smith?" Butler asks, mocking his critics. "They say you nearly starved him to death." Butler places more chicken in his mouth and answers, "I know not this Colonel Smith, they are all xs, ys, or zs, in an algebraic equation that I manipulate for the greater good. This is what you do in war. People are not people, not flesh and blood, they are tools to be used for winning."

"Am I an x, y, or a z?" Tennessee asks.

Butler looks around confused, "Pardon me?"

"We are all algebraic variables and you are placing us in line to achieve what you want. Am I the x or the y or the z?" Tennessee asks.

Butler smiles, almost tenderly, and says, "My dear, you are the entire equation. You are the variables and you are the solution."

Tennessee smiles with her flirty eyes and she and Butler share a moment. He then looks at me and a sour look comes across his face again. The moment of lightness is gone. Butler pounds the table again, "And I'm not a good general? It is true, General Grant relieved me of my command, but that was engineered by my enemies. Did we win? Did we win?"

"Why do you concern yourself with such fools?" I ask. "They did not face your choices or the consequences and yet you expend your energy refuting them. Not only here in private, but in public, and now you are working on your memoirs. You must have three-hundred pages already written. You detail every battle, every man's position, and your entire thought process. If you care not, why do you spend your time in this manner?"

Butler places his chicken down and wipes the grease from his mouth. He then stares into my eyes, still furious and defiant. I want to lower my gaze out of discomfort but do not. "My dear," Butler grinds out as if he is holding himself back from choking me, "having lived through and taken part in a war, the greatest of many centuries, and carried on by armies rivaling in numbers the fabled hosts of Xerxes, and having been personally conversant with almost all, if not all, the distinguished personages having charge and direction of the battles fought, and with the political management which has established the American Republic in power, prosperity, glory, and stability unequalled by any nation of the earth, I owe it to history to shed light on these events."

"History?" I say. We will all be dead by then.

"If you do not take the steps to define yourself, then others will readily and greedily write the history, and they will have the power to make you the bungling fool, or even worse, write you out altogether," Butler says.

"We have too much to do to worry about what future historians will think," I say. "As long as we get the vote, the historians can cast me as the very devil and my spirit would be undisturbed."

"You say that now because you are at the very beginning of your public journey," Butler says. "Suffer through years of vicious attacks, personal setbacks, and financial woes all in the name of righteousness and liberation, and you will begin to pick up that pen and write your truth."

ΑΩ

Lobbying is an activity that ladies do not engage in, for a lobbyist is the most loathsome individual, worse than a whore and the moral equivalent to the filth on the streets. But if I act like a lady, then I will have nothing except the kindnesses afforded a lady. I'll gladly forego kind words and soft gestures from strangers in exchange for my rights.

Tennessee and I trudge through the manure-laden snow. Even with thick boots on, we get smelly black water trickling down our ankles, freezing our toes. We walk up the steps of the Capitol, slowly. The men walking down the steps look at us and whisper, no doubt wondering if we are a new crop of prostitutes from the downtrodden Southern states or if we are the voluble charmers that the newspapers mention. Tennessee winks and giggles at each man, no doubt cementing the impression that we could be either.

Our first target is Ulysses Mercur. In his early 50s, Representative Mercur hails from Pennsylvania, where he was the Chief Justice of the Supreme Court of Pennsylvania. As a young judge, he was known to beat unethical lawyers right in his courtroom, squeezing their throats until they turned purple. His votes in Congress have labeled him as a radical plunderer, a thief.

Not only did he vote for the present policies of Reconstruction for the South, but he also voted for the continuance of the Freedman's Bureau to feed, clothe, and educate the negroes of the South. His opponents see this as stealing money from the hard working Northerner and giving it to the lazy, dumb negroes. His enemies call him a socialist, a believer in the redistribution of wealth. Mercur's response to his critics is the rather cryptic and pugilistic, "If you do not respect the stars, then I will make you feel the stripes."

We walk in Mercur's bare and neat office, and I'm ready for anything. Representative Mercur immediately stands as we walk in and looks at us with curiosity as I stare back. He is tall, pale, and thin, with his facial hair styled after dead President Lincoln. Tennessee smiles, giggles, and flirts. I immediately regret bringing Tennessee to meet such a serious man.

"Representative Mercur," I say without introduction, for he knows who we are. "I am being taxed without representation."

"You have a representative, Mrs. Woodhull," Mercur replies. "You have one from New York and I even hear you have the able Mr. Butler in your pocket. I'd say you have two representatives."

"I do have a representative," I say, ignoring the insinuation about Butler, "One that I cannot vote for or against. Women constitute a majority of the people—they hold vast portions of the nation's wealth and pay a proportionate share of the taxes. Why not give us equality at the ballot box?"

"That is for the states to decide," Mercur says, shrugging his shoulders.

"If States did not have the right to decide the slavery question, how can they decide my fate? Am I worth less than a negro?" I ask. This man is a friend of the negro. He should understand.

"Is it true that you share a bed with a man who is not your husband?" Representative Mercur asks.

"My personal affairs have no bearing…" I begin, grasping for words in my state of shock that this serious man would inquire about affairs that do not concern him.

Representative Mercur perches on the end of his desk, "And you expect me to listen to a legal argument from one who is morally suspect?'"

"Sir, if I may use plain talk," I begin. Representative Mercur nods and I continue, "Whether the truth comes from a whore or from a virgin, it is still the truth."

Representative Mercur arches his eyebrows, shrugs, and says, "Perhaps the courts can help you."

I begin to leave, knowing that I could not lose more than I have already lost in this conversation. I turn around and motion to Tennessee. "Perhaps my sister, Tennessee, can help you," I say.

Tennessee opens her purse and grabs a cigar and two shot glasses and a flask. Mercur's expression goes from shock to mischievous.

"Let's celebrate," Tennessee says.

"Miss Claflin, what are we celebrating?" Mercur asks.

Tennessee pours two shots and hands him one. "Women, darling, women."

I close the door to the sound of giggles and snorts.

AΩ

Day after day, time after time, Tennessee and I perform the same routine. I appeal to their minds, and Tennessee appeals to their brains, which on men are anatomically located considerably lower than women's brains are. I use logic, and Tennessee uses liquor, flirts, kisses, and bedroom promises. In truth, I am uncertain as to how far Tennessee has gone to procure the vote and I do not want to ask. Tennessee feels, however, that she is having some effect on the men. As for me, I know that seducing the Virgin Mary would have been a much easier task.

Our lobbying, or more aptly, our begging for our American birthright has paused. It is Christmas and Representative Butler has been kind enough to open his home to the voluble charmers, no doubt hoping Anna will read of this in the papers and come rushing into his arms. While he entertains Tennessee with his grand war stories, I sit blankly, ruminating only on my impending failure and all I have lost. Days. I've lost days with Zulu, Byron, and James. Weeks. I've lost weeks with Zulu, Byron, and James. Time that I cannot buy back. I hope one day Zulu understands why we are separated. Byron will never understand. James understands, for he has been to battle, alienated from home.

"I have something for you," Butler says, kneeling down and touching my hand. I was so lost, thinking about my loves, that I had not even noticed my host talking to me. I look down at my red velvet dress and place my hand on his. Any other man would take this simple gesture as an invitation to fornicate, but Butler understands our relationship well enough not to read anything into this gentleness. Butler smiles and stands up and motions for me to follow him.

Butler's office is a temple to knowledge. With books lining the walls to the ceiling, so high that one must use a step-ladder to reach several rows of them, he has accented the corners with four busts. One is of Alexander the Great, one is of Alexander Hamilton, and one is of Thomas Jefferson.

"Hamilton and Jefferson?" I ask.

"As to the powers and duties of the government of the United States, I am a Hamilton Federalist. As to the rights and privileges of the citizen, I am a Jeffersonian Democrat," Butler says, taking a seat in an oversized leather chair and motioning for me to sit on the other end of his desk in a smaller, wooden chair.

"Who is the ugly one?" I ask nodding to the east corner of the room. Staring at this bust, I think Butler has finally found someone homelier than he is.

Butler turns around to look and lets out a little laugh. "Rufus Choate, deceased Congressman, First Attorney General of Massachusetts. I tried a case against him, I represented a sailor with scurvy, and he represented the East India Company. Rufus asked me to resign, saying I had little experience and that I would embarrass myself."

"What happened?" I ask.

"I won a verdict of three-thousand, plus interest," Butler says. "I keep Rufus around to remind me that I should not listen to my critics, not that I often need a reminder." I smile at Butler and we share another moment, one full of admiration.

"My dear," Butler begins. "I have fought for many causes. None dearer to my heart than the preservation of the Union." Butler pauses and starts fidgeting. "And yet, I was a terrible general."

I start to protest and Butler silences me by holding up his hand.

"It's true. I deemed the life of my men too valuable. I could not confide in a man at night and send him to his death in the morning. And then there was Newmarket... I deliberately exposed my men to the loss of greater numbers than I believed the capture was worth," Butler says.

"Why?" I ask.

"Because they were negro troops," Butler says, holding my gaze steady.

I gasp.

"It was for a great purpose on behalf of their race. The negro had no opportunity to prove his valor. Soldiers and politicians cried that the negroes never struck a good blow for their own freedom. I never saw such bravery... One soldier, Christian, carried the flag through fire and death, even rallying his men." Butler shakes his head, trying to contain his emotion, but his eyes fill with tears. He bows his head and wipes his tears away, reaching into his desk drawer and pulling out a long leather box.

Butler opens the leather box to show a silver medal suspended by a ribbon of red, white, and blue with a strong pin at the top in the shape of an oak leaf engraved with the words, "Army of the James."

"And for every act of bravery which number nearly 200, I commissioned a medal be made. I had done for the negro soldiers what the government has never done for its white soldiers—I had a medal struck of like size, weight, quality, fabrication, and intrinsic value which those which Queen Victoria gave with her own hand to her distinguished private soldiers of the Crimea,"

Butler says. He pulls the medal out of its case and hands it to me. The front is inscribed, "*Ferro iis libertas pervenient.*" Freedom by the sword. The back says, "Distinguished for Courage."

The front of the medal is engraved with a negro solider fighting alongside a white soldier. They both have rifles. The back has laurel leaves. The silver of the medal is very fine, turning it on its back, I can see the mark of Tiffany and Company. Oh, how I love this man, such a generous and considerate soul. I place the medal back in the box, not wanting to smudge the silver. I keep the box in my hand, admiring it.

"I asked Christian how he rallied his fellow men," Butler says, still struggling to keep his composure. "He said "I told them if we took a bullet, they can never again deny that we are men."

I take a deep breath and wipe a few tears from my face.

"And while this is an unusual Christmas gift, I give this Butler medal to you for inspiration, and for warning," Butler says. "In one week you will testify, and you may have to take a bullet for your cause."

AΩ

A hand comes from out of a doorway and grabs my arm. I gasp and stop. Tennessee, walking so fast behind me, bumps into me due to my sudden stop.

"Who is next?" Benjamin Butler asks. Our days are limited now. The committee meeting has been set. January 11th.

"Bingham," I say.

Butler squeezes my arm, "Be careful with Bingham. The man thinks he is Aristotle, but the only victim of the gentleman's intellectual prowess was an innocent woman hung upon the scaffold." I nod. I remember the bastard. His reputation does not bode well for any woman. Tennessee laughs and lifts her skirt to show Butler that she has a gun in her ankle holster. Butler releases my arm and shakes his head, whether in amusement or frustration I cannot be certain.

AΩ

"Representative Bingham," I say, "we both hail from Ohio." I manage a small smile for the gray-haired, ghastly pale, woman-hating bastard. Bingham is staying seated in his large, unkempt, but beautifully furnished office. He sits while I stand, a blatant sign of disrespect reserved for the Irish and the whores.

"Yes," Bingham says, "but you come from a long line of scoundrels, liars, drunkards, and humbugs."

"Unfortunately none of them were able to parlay these skills into a political career," I say.

Bingham jumps up, "So you chose agitation as a career."

"We have it in our power to begin the world over again," I say.

"Your legal justification is the 14th Amendment."

"Yes."

Bingham bangs the cluttered oak desk with his fist, "You are subverting it."

"I'm glorifying it!" I say, nearly yelling.

"The states have always possessed, and still possess, the power to regulate suffrage," Bingham says.

"All persons born in the United States are citizens," I say.

"Damn it woman, I wrote the Fourteenth Amendment," Bingham says, his voice rising in volume as mine had.

"Perhaps you wrote it," I hiss, "but you definitely don't understand it."

Bingham motions for me to leave. "I refuse to be lectured to by a woman with a second grade education."

I nod. "Before I leave, Representative Bingham, I must thank you."

"Thank me? Why?"

"When you ordered Mary Surrat's death for merely owning the boarding house where John Wilkes Booth slept, you argued for equality then, saying both men and women had the equal right to hang. It helps me sleep at night knowing that I have an equal chance of being executed by a government I have no say in."

I slam his office door on my way out. I do not even bother to send Tennessee in.

AΩ

Moses is knocks at my door, and the thuds sound like she is throwing her full body against the wood. Butler told me this moment would come. I had expected it to be sooner than the eve of my speech, the eve of the singular most important day of my life. But then again, Moses never possessed a sense for opportune timing. If she had we would already be in the land of milk and honey. Although unseen by me, Moses has been taking copious notes of all of our actions for the past two weeks. Two days ago, she asked her one and only ally in Congress, Representative William Loughbridge, what to do about the charlatan sisters who hail from a long line of scandal. Butler has reported that Loughbridge told Moses that women must band together to get what they want, and that if we stopped the Founding Fathers from fighting based on their ancestry that we would not have a country.

I nod to Tennessee. She opens the door to a stern-looking ever-mourning Moses and Isabella Beecher Hooker, looking more feminine but no less stern.

"What are you doing here?" Susan asks, marching past Tennessee without using any of the nice empty phrases that are the hallmark of a lady. Isabella follows behind.

"Helping Victoria lobby before her testimony," Tennessee says.

Moses goes from pale white to fire engine red quicker than I can snap my fingers. "I have been lobbying Congress for the past twenty years and I have never had a hearing."

Tennessee places a hand on Susan's arm and waves with her other arm in a grand, sweeping gesture to the line of flasks we have on the table in the parlor room. Susan, being a Quaker temperance leader, was scandalized. Isabella shakes her head in disapproval.

"Why, Miss Anthony," Tennessee says, "we have secret weapons at our disposal." Susan, pale and horrified once again, takes a seat on the sofa, and glares at Tennessee. Tennessee looks down at her own breasts and says, "Not all of our weapons are secret."

"We need to know who sent you," Isabella says, "and we need to know at once."

"I am present on my own accord," I say.

"This cannot be," Susan says. "One of your men friends must have sent you to annihilate the cause."

"I do not have men friends who are not in accordance with our cause, Miss Anthony," I say, trying to keep myself calm.

"I see men lining up to see you every day, Mrs. Woodhull. If they are not your friends then they are your lovers?" Isabella asks.

"You know very well those are my customers," I say. "I run two businesses now. I rely on men to invest with me and to buy my papers."

"Which bull put this idea into your head?" Susan asks.

"You," I say.

Susan looks ill and I sit down next to Susan and grab her hand. "Miss Anthony, I was moved by you years ago. I watched you and George Francis Train take the stage in Carnegie Hall after the Kansas referendum. If any one person placed this idea in my head, it was you."

"Mrs. Woodhull, I would be pleased if you would never indicate that I inspire your behavior in any way," Susan says.

"Why don't you join us in chambers tomorrow," I say, "and then you will understand."

I walk to the door to show Susan and Isabella out, and Susan grabs my arm. "I need to understand, now, today, this precise moment, the legal justification..." she says.

"Susan," Tennessee says, patting Ms. Anthony's back in an overly familiar way, "you are sweating like a whore on nickel night. Do not fret my dear, you will enjoy Victoria's show."

For the third time during this conversation, Susan is scandalized as both she and Isabella look like they were just kicked by a horse. My embarrassment leads me to quickly change the topics and let Susan in on our battle plans.

"The Fourteenth Amendment..." I begin.

Susan interrupts me, "Not the Fourteenth Amendment, woman, that gives the negro the vote. I have been campaigning against this very Amendment. Why should wooly hair and muscles vote before us? They are considered by society to be the lowest of the species, and now they vote before we do, after so many of us fought for their freedom!"

"The Fourteenth Amendment declares I am a citizen. Fifteenth Amendment. Section 1. The right of citizens of the United States to vote shall not be denied or abridged by the United States or by any State on account of race, color, or previous condition of servitude," I say. Susan drops her jaw and her eyes grow into the size of pancakes. Isabella cocks her head and scrunches her ears as if remembering what I said and listening to it over and over again.

Susan looks at me and whispers, "I will be there tomorrow." Isabella shakes her head. They both leave.

23

CORONATION

Washington D.C. January 2, 1871

B utler leads our parade up the Capitol steps. Me, Moses, Tennessee, and Isabella are all following the "the hideous front of hell's blackest imp; total depravity personified." And yet I've never been prouder than at this moment. Reporters are lining the steps, asking us questions, scratching their heads at our procession.

"Is it true that Victoria Woodhull came to you at night and you agreed to open the committee in exchange for an opportunity to feast upon her naked person?" a reporter from *The Evening Star* asks.

"Half-truths kill," Butler says, without glancing back at me. I let out a little laugh. Susan and Isabella cluck and sigh, and Susan even mentions something about fainting. They vehemently disapprove of me, my family, my profession, and even my stationary. Nothing meets with their approval. And yet they need me. And they hate it.

Susan, Isabella, and Tennessee walk into the chambers. Seats are quickly filling up and the reporters quickly realize that they must stand against the walls if they want to witness history. I do not step in yet, I need a moment to calm my nerves. I begin to doubt what I am doing here. Susan, Isabella, and the other women are refined ladies with proper schooling and upbringing. Who am I? Butler stands next to me and then he walks in front of me. Using his one good eye to stare straight in my eyes, he says, "The trouble with these women is that they are ladies. You have no such encumbrances. Do not request. Demand."

I nod.

John Bingham struts in and takes Butler's attention away from me. I struggle to hear and yet I hear nothing until Butler's voice booms, "If you do her any injustice, I shall be as prompt to punish a wrong done to her as one done to myself."

Bingham mutters something about "the Beast being in love" and walks off into the chambers. A little man comes out after Bingham and ushers everyone else in. I pause at the door to look at the immense room, the heart of democracy, and think of all the history that has occurred here. War plans made. Slavery ended. President impeached.

"Victoria," Butler says from his seat, jerking his head. It is my time. I walk into the Congressional hall and find my place behind a long, rectangular table. I look down at the men and hear nothing but disapproving clucks and gasps. Dour faces. I shake. I sweat. I panic. I take out my notes and begin reading, trying not to stutter.

"I was born in Ohio. I live in New York. I am a citizen of the United States. Since the adoption of the Fifteenth Amendment to the Constitution, no State nor any Territory, has passed any law to abridge the right of any citizen of the United States to vote, neither on account of sex or otherwise," I say. I can tell my voice is too faint by the way the men are cupping their hands next to their ears. I take a deep breath, and begin to speak loudly.

"That, nevertheless, the right to vote is denied to women citizens of the United States by the operation of election laws in the several States and Territories, which laws were enacted prior to the adoption of the said Fifteenth article, and which are inconsistent with the Constitution as amended, and therefore are void and of no effect, but which, being still enforced by the States and Territories, render the Constitution inoperative as regards the right of women citizens to vote," I take a pause and look at Moses. She has been making checkmarks in the air with her finger since I began speaking.

"And whereas article six, section two, declares 'That this Constitution and the laws of the United States which shall be made in pursuance thereof, and all treaties made or which shall be made under the authority of the United States, shall be the supreme law of the land; and all judges in every State shall be bound thereby, anything in the Constitution and laws of any State to the contrary notwithstanding.' And whereas no distinction between citizens is made in the Constitution of the United States on account of sex, but the fourteenth article of amendments to it provides that 'no State shall make or enforce any law which shall abridge the privileges and immunities of citizens of the United States,' 'nor deny to any person within its jurisdiction the equal protection of the laws.' To deny the vote is a grievance to your memorialist and to thousands of others, citizens must be able to vote, without regard to sex. And your memorialist will ever pray."

I bow my head, expecting applause or some sort of signal that lets me know my efforts are appreciated. The only signal I get is the sound of Susan crying. And that is more than I need.

"How can we trust women to vote?" Representative Hotchkiss asks. With a receding hairline and receding gumline, Hotchkiss wears a stiff upturned collar that is being strangled by a black bowtie that touches his long goatee.

"Women are entrusted with the most holy duties and the most vital responsibilities of society; they bear, rear and educate men; they inspire the noblest impulses in men; they are the best secret counselors, the best advisors, the most devoted aids in the most trying periods of men's lives, and yet when women propose to carry a slip of paper with a name on it, they fear them," I say. I get winks from the women and eyerolls from the men.

Representative Cook speaks up, "If Eve never would have consorted with the snake, we would not be in this shameful place. You get man kicked out of Eden and now you want more power. God made a hierarchy: God, man, women, and animals. That's how it should be. Men rule women."

Susan jumps up and with a booming voice that I did not know she possessed says, "I distrust those who know what God wants, because it always coincides with their own desires. No man is good enough to govern any woman, any citizen, without consent."

Murmurs and grumbles ripple through the legislators. Reporters laugh and smile. They know conflict makes a good issue; Moses against the law makes a best- selling morning edition.

Representative Peters, the only handsome man out of the lot, and the youngest, clears his throat and with a sly smile says, "Mrs. Woodhull. You are a beautiful woman, with your pretty eyes and your silken hair, and you are the epitome of a woman who would look better carrying a baby than a ballot."

Tennessee speaks up from the back of the room, "And you sir, would make a better nursemaid than a legislator." The room erupts into boisterous laughter and Tennessee nods to me.

Representative Peters, red from embarrassment, pounds the table in the midst of the laughter, "You are not a citizen, you are a woman."

I look at Butler and he mouths, "Demand."

"Then why hold me to your laws? Stop taxing me. I am taxed in every conceivable way. For publishing a paper, I must pay. For engaging in banking, I must pay. For tea, coffee, or sugar, I must pay to maintain a government in which I have no voice. If you do not hear me now, I have no recourse other than to start anew," I say, my voice echoing loudly.

"Anew?" he asks.

I take a deep breath and with a loudness and intention that I did not know I possess I say, "We mean treason. We mean secession, and on a thousand times grander scale than was that of the South. We are plotting revolution; we will overthrow this bogus republic and plant a government of righteousness in its stead, which shall not only profess to derive its power from consent of the government, but shall do so in reality."

AΩ

I left the House chambers in a state of chaos. After my grand talk of revolution and secession, the male representatives stood up and started yelling and all the women banded together and walked out. Before Tennessee and I walk down the Capitol steps, Moses puts her arm on me. I turn around.

"I am aware," I say, "that I lost my temper." I brace myself for a litany of criticisms both true and petty.

"Women everywhere owe you a great debt of gratitude," Susan says.

"What?" I ask.

"I saw it in their eyes," Susan says. "Having been asking men for the vote for decades, I finally saw the logic enter the heads and shine through their eyes. I predict by Saturday we will all have the right that we never should have had to beg for. And all because of you."

"You think so?" I ask.

"Yes," Susan beams, "and my soul has never soared higher than at this moment. Thank you."

"Any victory I have is because of you," I say. "You paved the way with your sacrifice, determination, and eloquence. I may have walked down the road, but you laid the bricks."

Susan hugs me. "My dear sister," she says, "will you address the women's rights convention at Lincoln Hall today?" I look at Tennessee and she nods to me. I, in turn, nod to Susan.

ΑΩ

"You speak," Tennessee says. "I'll seduce." Tennessee is sitting in Butler's chair in his office at the Capitol. We both take a breather before the start of the convention. She twirls one of his cigars, imagining the power that would come if that chair were legitimately hers.

"What?" I ask.

"Moses is overconfident. Even if many of the men agreed with us in the chamber, men quickly forget reason. I need to get the vote for the vote. Let me work on Peters first," Tennessee says. I admire her wisdom in starting with the most handsome one of the bunch.

"If Eve hadn't consorted with the snake…" I begin, mocking Cook's comments.

"What he doesn't know," Tennessee says, propping her feet on the table. "Is that now I'm the snake, and I intend to drive all Eves out of Eden."

ΑΩ

Lincoln Hall is overflowing with excited women. As if by magic, my testimony earlier was somehow transported like a siren call through all the elite D.C. neighborhoods and women rushed to the convention, looking for me. The registration table has been turned over by the crush of people rushing into the auditorium and there is much buzz in the air. I am able to walk in unnoticed, but everyone is talking about me. I'm glad they do not know what I look like or I would be mobbed.

"What about her scandalous ways?" I hear one woman ask the crowd. "A woman on Wall Street cannot be pure."

An elderly woman in a fur coat and a huge hat with a flower hears this and barges in the crowd. I recognize her as Josephine Griffing, a brave abolitionist and die-hard suffragette. "This is not about one woman, this is about simple justice before the law," she says. "Mrs. Woodhull has elevated the argument to a Constitutional one and I welcome her with every ounce of being in my soul. We must band together if we are to be victorious."

I continue walking until I see Susan. She grabs both my hands and pulls me down the aisle, pausing to ask the women to make way for us. We then walk to the stage together. I take a seat in the chair on stage and Susan starts whistling loudly to get all the women's attention. A few men snap to alert too, but I believe they are reporters, not supporters.

"Months ago," Susan begins, "I heard a tale of two women on Wall Street. I, with the thousands of others, who out of curiosity went to see these daring maidens, went to their Wall Street office to ascertain for myself their chances among the motley crew that operates on change. I found two bright, vivacious creatures, full of energy, perseverance, intellect, and pluck, and I said to myself, here are the elements of success."

The audience waves their white handkerchiefs in a sign of approval and Susan nods, continuing, "And when I arrived to attend this convention, I found that one of them, a poor lone woman, without consultation even with any of those who had labored for years in the great cause of female suffrage, had already presented her petition to Congress, asking them to pass a declaratory act that would define the rights of our sex under the Fourteenth Amendment. This was something we had not expected. We, who had labored for so long, had expected to labor on in the old way for five, ten, fifteen, or perhaps twenty years to come, to secure the passage of another amendment to the Constitution, known as the Sixteenth Amendment, but we were too slow for the times. In this age of rapid thought and action, of telegraphs and railways, the old stage coach won't do, and to Victoria C. Woodhull, as well as to her partner, perhaps Tennie C. Claflin, who caught up in the spirit of the age, and made this advance movement, we owe the advancement of our cause by as many years at least as it would take to engineer through the various ramifications of an amendment to the Constitution."

More white handkerchiefs go in the air. Susan motions for me to come up. I hesitate. My moment has arrived and I am a fraud. I look at Josephine Griffing, I look at Elizabeth Cady Stanton, I look at Moses and I know that it is they who deserve the proclamations, the applause, the glory. Josephine has aided thousands of negroes, risking arrest for allowing the use of her home in the underground railroad. And then she used her influence to form the American Equal Rights Association. Elizabeth Cady Stanton has put her marriage under considerable strain and left her children to travel throughout the nation to give speeches and has donated every penny towards abolition and suffrage. And Moses has endured all imaginable slurs about her appearance, her manliness, and her very demeanor every time she speaks. For thirty years she has spent her way to poverty trying to get equality for women. And what have I done? What have I endured? And yet these women want me, they clamor for me. They see a light in me that the others do not possess.

Susan walks over to me, leans over, and whispers, "Repeat your Memorial."

I nod and walk to the front of the stage. "I was born in Ohio, I live in New York, I am a citizen." I stammer the words out but gain confidence as I see more the wave of the white handkerchiefs. Taking deep breaths and several pauses throughout, I am able to make my way through the complete memorial as Susan stands next to me, moving her finger to make check marks in the air throughout just as she had done before. Once I am done, I bow my head and look at my feet. When I look up, I see thousands of women standing, waving their handkerchiefs and whistling for me. For me.

Susan takes the stage again and says, "I believe this is a good time to raise money for the cause. I personally pledge all that I have, for running *The Revolution* denies me any creature comfort. I pledge two-hundred dollars."

A murmur sweeps the audience. One woman stands up and says "Ten dollars." Another woman stands up and says "Fifty dollars." A third woman stands up and says "Twenty dollars."

Ten dollars, fifty dollars, twenty dollars? We will never get anywhere with such pennies from peasants. I stand up and yell, "Ten thousand dollars."

The entire audience staggers back as if I had delivered a death blow. After stunned silence, applause and handkerchief flying commences.

AΩ

"Catherine Beecher?" I yell at her sister, Isabella Beecher Hooker. Isabella motions for me to lower my voice. I imagine wrapping my hands around her scrawny neck and....I try to calm myself by looking at the petition again.

"Harriet Beecher Stowe? Another sister?" I yell, "the instigator of the Great War? Can you not get your people in line?"

"We are a family divided," Isabella Beecher Hooker says, shaking her head. Standing in front of Butler's congressional office, I hold a petition to the House of Representatives against holding a public meeting on my memorial. Tennessee, knowing that I am about to throw something, moves Lincoln's bust away from me. Susan closes the door.

"Over one thousand Judases in petticoats," I say. I read from the petition, "t*he majority of women in this country believe Holy Scripture inculcates for women a sphere higher than and apart from that of public life; because as women they find a full measure of duties, cares and responsibilities and are unwilling to bear additional burdens unsuited to their physical organization.*"

"We must redouble our efforts," Susan says.

"Redouble our efforts?" I ask. "Only two committee members voted in support and only forty-two House members voted to hold a public meeting on the topic."

"I had more representatives in hand," Tennessee says, "until their wives signed that Biblical declaration of helplessness." Tennessee shakes her head and says, "Goddamn wives. Looks like I'm going to have to seduce them too."

Susan mercifully ignores Tennessee's blasphemy and turns to me, "What we have is a silent majority. Our organization numbers ten thousand and the one thing, the only thing, the ladies agree on is the vote. But they are not loud enough to drown out the calls of these one thousand sirens."

"What should we do, Susan?" Isabella asks, biting her lip nervously.

"I must leave to tend to *The Revolution*, but I will arrange for Victoria to speak at Lincoln Hall in one week's time. She will rally the troops," Susan says.

"But Susan," Isabella says, "aligning ourselves so closely with a creature of Wall Street, I mean, our reputation…"

Tennessee laughs out of anger. The hypocrisy! For once, I keep my mouth shut despite being incensed at the suggestion that possessing the talent to make money means that I am not good enough for a group of ladies who spend their days at fancy teas.

"Cautious, careful people, always casting about to preserve their reputation and social standing, never can bring about a reform, Isabella. Those who are really in earnest must be willing to be anything or nothing in the world's estimation," Susan says.

"I do not have the eloquence you do," I say.

Susan walks up to me and places her hands on my shoulders in a too familiar way. "What you have, Mrs. Woodhull, is passion, and passion is contagious. That is your gift. The flaw in passion is that it leads to recklessness. You must guard against crossing the border of reason into the devil's land of chaos."

ΑΩ

"You should be pleased," Butler says, chewing with his mouth open, as is his custom. "Dare I even say proud that the *New York Herald* agrees that your legal reasoning is sound and women do have the right to vote even if unintended."

I manage a weak smile, but this small victory is meaningless. A newspaperman agrees with me; that is worth nothing. I look at the beautiful dinner in front of me and I push my plate away. I'm angry, depressed, and anxious. I need my James.

"What do the papers say about me?" Tennie asks, grabbing my plate as she greedily gobbled all her food, practically before she was seated in the oak dining chair.

Butler smiles and reads: "*Tennessee is young, pretty, interesting and quick as a bird in both movement and speech. The contour of her face is like a boy's, and her hair being cut short and surmounted with a distinctively boyish hat, gives her the appearance of a frisky lad, ready for mischief of any kind. But there is a peculiar smooth tone to her voice. She lends to conversation a positive charm and gives to her speech that which makes her irresistible.*"

"Irresistible!" Tennessee exclaims, laughing. Butler smiles back in response.

"If only the cause were irresistible," I say.

"Now the *Evening Star*, Victoria," Butler says, opening up the very newspaper that warned men to stay away from us, "says that not all is lost. The editors write: *at the same time the Committee grants that it is undoubtedly the right of the people of the several States to reform their constitution and laws as to secure the equal exercise of the right of suffrage, it is not to be doubted that whenever, in any State, the people are of opinion that such a reform is advisable, it will be made. Thus leaves the matter in a more favorable condition than even its warmest advocate claimed for it only a few months ago.*"

"If we can't convince a committee of twelve then how can we convince politicians from thirty-seven states?" I ask.

"I tend to agree, my dear," Butler says before pausing to wipe his mouth, "but you have your paper, your candidacy, money, time, and eloquence. You have all the advantages on your side. You may have lost this battle, but you must refocus and plot your strategy for the rest of the war." Butler downs his bourbon and pours me one. I take a sip, choking on the bitter. "The only time I was successful in war," Butler says, "was when I dismissed all the naysayers and I relied solely on my convictions. Now you must rely on yours."

24

QUEEN VICTORIA

"What think you, enslaved people, of the great, the free, the exalted government of a country which professes so much and grants you nothing?" I ask with outstretch arms, just like a preacher at a Methodist camp meeting. My voice booms, my sermon pours forth like a song with crescendos and rhythm. The audience, standing room only, leans forth, mesmerized by my newfound strength. Even my detractors, who consider me nothing more than a literate whore, have made themselves present for the show, my last speech in D.C. Thousands are here, and I know that this will be my last great chance to convince the politically powerful and their wives that our divine rights must be restored by the earthly body.

"I am subject to tyranny! I am taxed in every conceivable way. I pay so that men's government may be maintained, a government in the administration of which I am denied a voice, and from its edicts there is no appeal. To be compelled to submit to these extortions that such ends may be gained, upon any pretext or under any circumstances, is bad enough; but to be compelled to submit to them and also denied the right to cast my vote against them, is a tyranny more odious than that which, being rebelled against, gave this country independence." I look to the side stage and Tennessee winks and blows me a kiss. I look at Butler and he makes a fist and shakes it at me, encouraging me to be bold.

"There is one alternative left, and we have resolved on that," I take a breath so I can distinctly yell my strongest words to date. "We mean treason! We mean secession! And on a thousand times grander scale than was that of the South. We are plotting revolution; we will overthrow this bogus republic and plant a government of righteousness in its stead, which shall not only profess to derive its power from consent of the governed, but shall do so in reality."

I take a deep breath and I am blinded by the sea of white handkerchiefs waving in the air in approval. One woman shouts, "Revolution," and then the crowd joins, chanting, "Rev-o-lu-tion, Rev-o-lu-tion, Rev-o-lu-tion!"

A plump woman with the most beautiful blue bonnet stands up and yells, "Queen Victoria!" and the chants change from "Rev-o-lu-tion" to "Queen Victoria! Queen Victoria!"

I motion for the crowd to quiet and then say, "There is a Queen Victoria on the other side of the Atlantic in a country where women can rule but cannot vote."

The crowd laughs, jeers, and claps.

"Perhaps we need a twin sisterhood between the two nations," I say to loud applause, "Each nation with a Victoria. I have often thought that there is something providential and prophetic in the fact that my parents were prompted to confer on me a name which forbids the very thought of failure; and as the great Napoleon believed in the star of his destiny, you will at least excuse me, and charge it to the credulity of the woman, if I believe also in fatality of triumph as somehow inhering in my name."

The crowd starts chanting "Queen, Queen, Queen" and I motion them again to quiet down.

"England has royals, chosen by God" I say, "America has Renegades chosen by man. And so help me, WOMEN! And if you choose me as your President, together we will change the very fabric of our society!"

I walk off the stage to loud applause and adulation. I am fulfilling my destiny.

AΩ

The train pulls into the station and I jump off with Tennessee trailing behind. Before I even see him, I am immediately embraced by James. How I have longed for his familiar scent, his smooth skin against mine, his enchanting smile.

"Never again," James says. We kiss and I know that I am home. I quickly look over James, making sure he looks fit, and he does. He is dashing as always in his brown and cream suit, although I can tell he has lost some weight.

I'm vaguely aware of reporters circling, but I ignore them as I kiss Byron and Zulu. Byron claps to show his happiness and Zulu holds tight, asking me to never go away again. Both children look well, and I am relieved and grateful to have James in my life. I know I could have never left the children with their father. Tennessee joins us and hugs the children, and nods towards James.

A reporter that I recognize form the *Tribune* walks in front of us as we walk to retrieve our luggage.

"Is it true that you offered intercourse in exchange for votes?" The reporter asks and I cover Zulu's ears. James tenses up and I can see him make fists with both hands, though he keeps his hands by his side.

"No!" I say, before adding, "as if it were any of your concern if it were true."

"Let us be!" Tennessee says.

James collects the luggage and we walk to the carriage. The children and Tennessee get in the carriage and I stay outside, my hand on James' arm.

"Is the Hero of Vicksburg refusing to come to my defense?" I ask, disappointed that he did not punch the reporter for his filthy insinuation.

James pauses for three long beats and then says, "I've never known a woman more capable of her own defense. Besides, I cannot always be there."

Not entirely satisfied with his answer, I get in the carriage, and I sit across from my children, grabbing their hands.

"Mamma," Zulu says, "what was it like?

"What, sweetheart?" I ask

"Having thousands listen to your speech?" She asks.

"It was… glorious" I say.

"Even the *Herald* agrees with your mamma," James says, quoting from the paper. "Her legal reasoning is sound and the Amendments give women the right to vote, even if the authors never intended to."

James then places a thick document in my lap.

"What is this?" I ask.

"I seek your counsel," James says.

I pick it up and see the name "Karl Marx." I recognize the name, he is a reporter of sorts. He sends in stories from London. I begin reading aloud, "Karl Marx, *The Communist Manifesto. We declare that our ends can be attained only by the forcible overthrow of all existing conditions, including the abolition of private property.*"

"Marxism will change the world," James says.

25

MY WIFE AND I

"Reading it for the twelfth time, my dear?" James asks as I unfold Susan's letter to read one more time by candlelight before I go to bed.

> *Dear Woodhull,*
> *I just read your speech of the 16th. It is ahead of anything, said or written—bless you dear soul for all you are doing to help strike the chains from the woman's spirit. —Susan B.*

I carefully fold the note and place it on the nightstand. Before blowing out the candle, I tell James, "Those two sentences... they validate my life." James and I kiss, the kiss of a pent up thousand years of passion, but before our joy of rediscovery is complete, someone bangs on the front door, calling my name. James and I jump up. I throw on my robe, and we run downstairs.

Once downstairs I see Tennessee barely dressed with her nipples clearly showing through her nightgown holding out her hands to a policeman. She is purring, "Arrest me, handsome. I've broken all kinds of laws."

The police office, a young dashing man with a mustache, and a perfectly muscled body, stammers out, "Mrs. Wood... Woodhull... her hus... husband... is ask... asking for... her."

"Canning?" Tennessee asks, "Jesus, what has the bloody bugger done now?"

AΩ

"Live with us?" James asks, his voice a mixture of wonder, doubt, and perhaps anger. James had found Canning at Sally's, hitting customers and screaming for me. Out of money, Sally had not fed him for three days. An empty stomach full of opium certainly caused the delirium. By the time James brought Canning to me, he was nearly unconscious, mustering only a weak smile for me. Mabel is feeding him soup. I hope he manages to keep it down.

"Live with us?" James asks again.

"When I was 14, he gave me a name. When I was 15, he gave me a home. When I was 16, he gave me a son. When I was 18, he gave me a daughter," I say.

James grabs my shoulders and shakes me gently so that my head is looking up at him, "He forced you."

I think of the alternative: Canning sick and homeless, being spat upon strangers, not having any warmth or food. I begin crying and I look deep into James's eyes, pleading with him to understand what may be incomprehensible, "Canning has nothing, and I know what it's like to have nothing."

"You were a virgin child bride and he…" James begins. I place my fingers on James's lips and try to take two steps back, but James won't release me from his grip.

"My father made me a woman… before my time… before Canning," I say. James exhales and lets me go, he pushes me away with such strength that I nearly fall down before I can regain my balance.

James, head in his hands, whispers, "You never told…"

"And he sold me to other men, my father did…" I say, desperately needing for James to understand, "Canning protected me… from… that…"

James turns around and yells, punching the wall. The plaster breaks, cutting his hand. His hand, his arm are covered in dust and blood. The blood trickles down and turns his white nightshirt red. Seemingly unaware, he turns around and walks towards me. I hold up my arms to protect my head, unsure of what James will punch next.

"I would never hurt you, Victoria," James says, planting his feet, not advancing towards me.

"Hurting me would be very easy for you," I say.

"Hurting you would be the most difficult task I could ever undertake," James says. "I love you and would never, ever hurt you."

"You are angry," I say.

"Not at you," James says, "Never at you, my love."

My back hits the wall. I have backed up as far as I can go. I drop my hands and say, "Leave me. Your disappointment must be great. You will have no recriminations from me."

James sighs and a few tears stream down his face. He gets on his knees and crawls to me. His bloody hand, covered in plaster dust, grabs mine and he presses my hand to his lips.

"Dear heart. My deepest desire is to turn… turn back time and spare you what you have endured. But then you would not have your strength," James says before grabbing my other hand as well. "My love for you is steadfast."

"No need to explain," I say. "You may leave."

"Victoria," James says. "I'm not leaving. If I ever say goodbye to you it will be in words only. Our souls are one, and they cannot be separated in this life or the next."

I nod, tears streaming down my face as well. Oh how I love this man! James stands up and kisses me deeply, holding me tenderly. He pauses, steps back, strokes my cheeks and kisses me again with all the passion that the man has. I begin to unbutton his nightshirt as I plant tiny kisses on his neck, on his chest.

"Two men under one roof… they will say…" James begins.

I kiss James's neck and whisper in his ear, "Say what they must. They don't have to live with my choices."

ΑΩ

Officer Gorgeous wasted no time in selling recent events to the newspaper, as evidenced by the dozen reporters outside my door. I asked the *Tribune* how much Greeley paid for the information, and the reporter told me two dollars. I would have paid Officer Gorgeous three times that to keep his mouth shut.

"Woodhull," Jack, the young, sandy-haired reporter from the *Tribune*, asks as I make my way to the carriage, "is it true you share your bed with two men?"

"I will issue a statement in my weekly," I say. "After all, I have newspapers to sell, too."

The carriage takes me to the offices of *Woodhull and Claflin's Weekly*. I can see James working through the window. Byron is by his side. I stay in my carriage watching him, taking the sight of James in. I knew I was in love before last night, but now I realize that this is the kind of love one never recovers from. My love for James has stripped me of my power that comes from indifference. I am vulnerable now. This man could hurt me. He could hurt me more than anyone ever has. I must be careful. I get out of the carriage and walk into our brick office and the smell of ink hits me immediately.

"You left home early," I say, eying James as he sets up type. Byron walks up and I bend at my knees and outstretch my arms. I hold him in my arms and kiss him on his head on his face, and breathe in his beauty. I whisper to him, "You're perfect."

Without turning around, James says, "I had trouble sleeping, so I came where I could be of some use."

"Is that the front page?" I ask.

"Yes," James says.

"Do not set it. I will release a statement on our current living arrangements," I say.

James quickly turns around, "What!"

"The *Tribune* already knows," I say, "and if anyone is going to profit from my choices it is going to be me."

James runs his hands through his hair a couple of times before smiling and says, "Try as I might, I cannot find a way to fault your logic, my dear."

I smile back, grateful for the understanding. I sit down and start working on the statement when there is a knock at the door. Byron opens the door to a sour-faced woman wearing spectacles dressed all in gray. Her white hair is styled in soft rolls pinned to her head.

"Yes," I say.

"Are you Mrs. Woodhull?" the woman asks, with disapproval already registering in her voice.

"Yes."

"I am Catherine Beecher," the woman says.

Catherine Beecher. Signer of the women-are-too-pure-for-politics statement. Sister to Isabella. Sister to Henry Ward. Sister to Harriet. Daughter of Lyman.

"What can I do for you, Miss Beecher?" I ask.

"I request your company in the carriage," she says. "We must take a ride together and get to know each other."

I look at James and nod to him and grab my cloak.

Catherine and I get in her carriage and a tense silence comes between us and it lasts for several minutes.

"Your efforts to deploy teachers to the frontier are quite remarkable," I say, trying to be polite before telling her that her God, he who does not want women to vote, is a false one.

"Women must be taught the beauty in keeping a tidy, warm home, in supporting their husbands, and in obeying God," Catherine says, "We teach that the principle of subordination is the great bond of union and harmony through the universe."

"Subordination?" I say, "You mean like the slaves that your sister and your brother sought to free?"

Catherine ignores the comment. "I take it you never had that kind of education," she says.

"All women have been educated in subordination, regardless of the formality of the schooling," I say.

"Pity that you were taught, but never learned," Catherine says, "and now you are inflicting your sin on everyone. Look at your own boy. He is the outwardly manifestation of your inward sinful life. If you had been pure and obedient to God, he would not have been born so broken. And your selfishness keeps him with you instead of an institution where he would thrive."

"You do not have the right or the privilege to lecture me on my children," I say. "Nor do you have any understanding of the real world, as you have been an acidic, barren hag all of your life." I knock on the carriage door for the carriage to stop. I am willing to walk miles to get away from this woman.

As I start to leave, Catherine pulls me down, "Isabella has always been a helpless, innocent tool of the guilty and the bold. Pure and intelligent women can be deceived and misled by the baser sort, and we both know that you are the baser sort. You need to leave my family alone."

"Isabella is more than competent enough to choose her own friends," I say.

"You seek out money, you seek out fame, and now you threaten to take all women down with you to the most base of existences," Catherine says smoothly before barking our in a harsh whisper, "I would like to shoot you."

"I ask only that you shoot me in the chest so I can see what kind of shot a well-bred Christian lady is, for I suspect that you are wildly inaccurate," I say. I get up again and leave the carriage. Catherine shoves a newspaper in my hand and says, "From my sister. Goodbye Audacia, I hope this kills your reputation… what little you have."

AΩ

> *"Keep your distance, sir," said Audacia, giving him a slight box on his ear. "I prefer to do my own courting. I have been trying to show your friend here how little he knows of the true equality of women, and of the good time coming, when we shall have our rights, and do just as we darn please, as you do. I'll bet now there ain't one of those Van Arsdel girls that would dare to do as I'm doing. But we're opening the way sir, we're opening the way. The time will come when all women will be just as free to life, liberty, and the pursuit of happiness, as men."*
>
> *"Good heavens!" said I, under my breath.*
>
> *"My beloved Audacia," said Jim, "allow me to remark one little thing, and that is, that men also*

must be left free to the pursuit of happiness, and also, as the Scripture says, new wine must not be put into old bottles. Now my friend Hal—begging his pardon—is an old bottle, and I think you have already put as much new wine into him as his constitution will bear.

I hand Henry Ward Beecher's rag, *The Christian Union*, to James. The front page is an ad for Steinway & Sons, proudly proclaiming, "One Piano Every Working Hour! Ten Pianos a Day!" I tell him to turn to page three, middle column.

"*My Wife and I, Harriet Beecher Stowe*," James says, reading the headline.

"Yes, it must be the Beecher family sport to come after me," I say. "I'm being serialized as the character of Audacia Dangyereyes. This week I'm trying to fill up an old wine bottle with too much new wine, and I am simply on edge pondering what I will do next week."

James laughs, "I did not realize that the little lady responsible for starting the Great War was another windmill."

"Yes," I say, "A windmill. The shabbiest and ugliest of the windmill kind."

James shakes his head. I pull out a piece of paper and dip my pen in ink:

Because I am a woman, and because I conscientiously hold opinions somewhat different from the self-elected orthodoxy which men find their profit supporting; and because I think it my bounden duty and my absolute right to put forward my opinions to advocate them with my whole strength, self-elected orthodoxy assails me, vilifies me, and endeavors to cover my life with ridicule and dishonor.
One of the charges made against me is that I live in the same house with my former husband, Dr.

> Woodhull, and my present husband, Colonel
> Blood. The fact is a fact. Dr. Woodhull being
> sick, ailing and incapable of self-support, I felt it
> in my duty to myself and human nature that he
> should be cared for, although his incapacity is in
> no way attributable to me. My present husband,
> Colonel Blood, not only approves of this charity
> but cooperates in it. I esteem it as one of the most
> virtuous acts of my life.

AΩ

"I will not introduce you," Moses tells me the moment I walk backstage of Steinway Hall. Elizabeth Cady Stanton and Isabella Beecher Hooker are making their way to our conversation, but are out of earshot. Elizabeth, dressed in a light pink taffeta dress, is especially pretty this night. Isabella is dressed in navy and looks as regal as ever. For some unknown reason, Tennessee chose to dress like a man tonight. In royal blue pants with a matching coat and a collar, one could be forgiven for thinking she is a hermaphrodite.

"Why not?" Tennessee asks.

Susan looks Tennessee up and down and asks, "Are you two intent on destroying all support we have?"

"On the contrary, dear Susan," Tennessee says, "maybe when they see that I can dress like a man then they will understand that I can also vote like a man."

Before Susan replies, I ask, "why will you not introduce me?"

"This business with your two husbands," Susan says, "why do you not change your last name to Blood?"

"I changed my name for one man and I will not change it again."

"Yes," Susan says, "you call yourself a Woodhull, you make your bed with a Blood, but you really are just a Claflin, right?"

Elizabeth, having been just in earshot for the conversation, forces herself in our circle of conversation and asks, "Susan, what is this about?"

"Our group is fragile. Any disagreement, any whiff of scandal, will tear us apart. We must stay united for the vote."

"A fortnight ago I was striking the chains of woman's enslavement, and now you cannot spare a kind word?" I ask, turning crimson with hot rage, rage that has been building for lifetimes.

"Susan, pray tell, who has been advising you?" Elizabeth asks. Elizabeth was clearly irritated, as she is the one who advises Susan. Could Moses be seeking out new counsel?

"Anna said…" Susan begins.

"Anna Dickinson, who never thought enough of our movement to make a speech on our platform even though you have made it clear that her celebrity would be most desirable, questions the wisdom of us welcoming others into our ranks?" Elizabeth asks.

"Elizabeth…" Susan says.

Elizabeth nudges me to the side so she is standing directly in front of Susan, getting as close to her as would be polite. Elizabeth harshly whispers, "We have had women enough sacrificed to this sentimental, hypocritical prating about purity. This is one of man's most effective engines for our division and subjugation. He creates the public sentiment, builds the gallows, and then makes us executioners. Women have crucified the Mary Wollstonecrafts, the Fanny Wrights, the George Sands, the Fanny Kembles of all ages. And now men mock us with the face and say we are ever cruel to each other. Let us end this ignoble record and henceforth stand by womanhood. If Victoria Woodhull must be crucified, let men drive the spikes and weave the crown of thorns."

Susan take a step back and asks Elizabeth, "Did you see the papers today?"

Audacia Dangeryeyes. I'm sure that's what Susan is referring to. I speak up and say to both women, "James will introduce me."

My comment is heard, but ignored. Elizabeth shakes her head in response to Susan's question. I back up and try to appear as though I am not listening. Tennessee runs down and plucks James out of the audience and tells him to get onstage.

"You need not," Susan says, "I have it memorized. *Victoria Woodhull is the front of the movement now, having pushed aside Susan B. Anthony, Cady Stanton, and the others, who never manage to stir up public enthusiasm and enlist prominent politicians like Ben Butler in the cause as Mrs. Woodhull has done.*"

"Susan," Elizabeth says, reaching out to squeeze her shoulder in a comforting gesture.

"After all we have sacrificed?" Susan says quietly, before raising her voice loudly, "Working like plantation negroes on behalf of the cause to be pushed aside by that… courtesan, that charlatan."

Isabella Beecher Hooker grimaces and walks up to me, "Now, remember, be a lady. Did you get my note about your stationery?"

I nod before peeking out of the curtains. Standing room only. And the crowd is boisterous with their collective conversation roaring in my ears.

"Your stationery is too manly. Take away the third eye and add flowers," Isabella says. She then too takes a peek through the curtain.

Tennessee whispers in my ear, "Yes, sister, to be a lady you must be covered in pansies."

"Henry made it," Isabella says. Susan and Elizabeth join our conversation, neither one looking happy.

"Preacher man?" Tennessee asks.

"He's more than that, Tennessee, he is one of the most powerful men in the city," Susan says.

My mind ponders the different attitudes among this queer Beecher family. It seems that the only thing they can agree on is the existence of the sun. And even then, Catherine would rail against its sinful rays.

"Which Beecher faction is he?" I ask wondering if he only printed the Audacia story out of loyalty to his sister or for the money, "Is he sympathetic to women?"

"Is he?" Susan says. "If you got all of his mistresses to vote for you, you'd win the presidency."

Elizabeth laughs at Susan's rare moment of gossip sharing and Isabella is outraged, stomping her feet and walking off.

James starts introducing me. He talks of my Congressional Memorial, my brokerage firm, my newspaper, my presidential candidacy. I begin to walk on stage to loud cheers when Susan holds me back.

"Be careful," Susan says. "Do not give Henry any fodder for Sunday sermons. And apologize for your actions, admit the unseemliness."

I break free of Susan's grasp and walk on stage. The noise is unlike anything I have ever heard. Many are clapping, some are pounding the wooden floor with their shoes, white handkerchiefs are being thrown in the air, some people are standing. The love and generosity from the audience moves me so that I must take deep breaths to center myself.

"When I look at Democrats," I begin, "I see a party that wanted to keep the negro man in chains. When I look at the Republicans, I see a party full of corruption, keeping the common man down. So why not me? Women cannot possibly foul up government more than the men have!"

The crowd becomes boisterous, clapping and stomping on the floors. I hear quite a few whistles and a few "Hallelujahs."

"Women deserve the right to vote!" I yell. The audience enthusiastically responds with a loud "yes." I look at James and place my hand over my heart.

"Women have a right to say yes or no to marriage!" I yell. The crowd responds with a weak "yes," about half the "yes" I received a moment ago.

"Women have a right to say yes or no to intercourse, without penalty!" I yell. The audience goes silent and the whispers start. I look to my right and I see Susan B. Anthony on all fours and it looks like she is vomiting.

"I have a better right to speak as one having authority in this manner," I say, "than most of you have, since it has been my province to study it all in its various lights and shades. When I practiced clairvoyance, hundreds, aye, thousands of desolate, heartbroken men as well as women, came to me for advice. And they were from all walks of life, from the humblest daily laborer to the haughtiest dame of wealth. The tales of horror, of wrongs inflicted and endured, which were poured into my ears, first awakened me to a realization of the hollowness and rottenness of society, and compelled me to consider whether the laws which were prolific of so much crime and misery as I found to exist should be continued. What can be more terrible than for a delicate, sensitively organized woman to be compelled to endure the presence of a beast in the shape of a man, who knows nothing beyond the blind passion with which he is filled, and to which is often the delirium of intoxication? You do not need to be informed that there are many persons, who, during the acquaintance preceding marriage, preserve that delicacy, tenderness and regard for womanly sensitiveness and modest refinement which are characteristics of true women, thus winning and drawing out their love nature to their extreme, but who, when the decree has been pronounced which makes them indissolubly theirs, cast all these aside and reveal themselves in their true character. Women have the right to leave such circumstances without harm, physical or financial. And women can choose another."

More whispers of condemnation fill the air, along with a few too many "for shames." Henry Ward Beecher grabs his walking cane and places his hat back on. After giving me the evil eye for one never-ending minute, he stands up and leave. Others follow.

"I know esteemed public teachers who decry free love in public but practice it in private," I say, speaking to the back of Beecher, "Contemplate this, and then denounce me for advocating freedom if you can, and I will bear your curse with bitter resignation."

The crowd goes completely silent and I walk offstage.

Moses greets me by grabbing me hard by the arms. A trickle of vomit is still on her face, next to her lips. Tennessee hands me my purse and I hand Moses a handkerchief and she wipes her mouth.

"Woodhull!" Moses says, "Free love is the most odious epithet you could apply to a woman and now our entire movement will be known as a bunch of lustful free lovers. You have set the movement back by decades!"

"On the contrary," I say, "I've set it on a path for the new century."

Elizabeth walks up to me and says, "Woodhull! I support you. You are forging a path of light in the darkness. This is what we needed."

"Elizabeth!" Moses shrieks, "How could you?"

"Susan!" Elizabeth says, taking the same tone that Moses did. "How could you not?"

AΩ

New York Tribune, May 12, 1871; Editorial by Horace Greeley

For ourselves, we toss up our hats in air for Woodhull. **She** *has the courage of her opinions!* **She** *means business.* **She** *intends to head a new rebellion, form a new constitution, begin a revolution beside which the late war will seem but a bagatelle, if within exactly one year from this day and hour of grace her demands are not granted out of hand. There is a spirit to respect, perhaps to fear, certainly not to be laughed at. Would that the rest of those who burden themselves with the enfranchisement of one half our whole population, now lying in chains and slavery, but had her sagacious courage.*

New York Tribune, May 12, 1871; Letter to the Editor, Mrs. G.C.M

> *Sir: How can any pure wife and mother read the infamous speech published in yesterday's paper and not enter their protest? I blush to think I am a woman. How long, in the name of common sense, are we to permit the vampires to suck out our very heart's blood before we rise in our might and force the vile, slimy things back where they belong? If every good, and true woman, would but come forward and give her verdict against such foul libels, it could not help but have a good effect. Why won't they do it?*

I put the papers down, wishing to read no more. Every comment, whether positive or negative, bears the screaming headline of "Free Love," as if a woman's right to say no to a man is akin to wanting to mate with every ape that roams this earth. Why do men misinterpret me so? It must be because they are the apes and they want to mate with me. On the other hand, if I were to mate with every ape, what business is it of theirs? And why should I be condemned for behavior that has been the hallmark of man since the beginning of time?

I should go into the office today and complete my reading of Marx. Marx would understand that women are not private property. Besides, Marx does not believe in any sort of property at all. Maybe Marx can be my great ally in this fight. We need more men. I pick up Marx's *Manifesto* again when James and Tennessee come rushing in as if some great tragedy just occurred.

"What is it?" I ask James, who is red in the face and sweaty. He shakes a newspaper at me, I can't tell if it is the *Herald* or the *Times*. I shrug my shoulders in response and he opens to the editorial on page one.

> *The Woman Suffrage Movement cannot afford to carry this woman her load of vicious thieves. She has associated herself in business and seeks to*

introduce into society, a sister who exceeds her in indecencies."

Tennessee interrupts, "I am pretty fucking indecent." She then lifts up her skirt and grabs her flask and drinks.

James rolls his eyes and continues, "*Mrs. Woodhull is nothing but a common courtesan.*"

"James," I say.

"No, Victoria, no. I cannot bear this. I have half a mind to…" James starts walking towards the locked cabinet that contains his Civil War rifle. I place my body in between his and the cabinet and put my hand on his chest.

"What happened to laughing at the ignorance of our enemies? We do not need to go down this road of malice," I say.

"Calling you a courtesan is no laughing matter," James says.

"Only the most significant battles require protracted struggle," I say. "We are in a war, fighting for the very fabric of society to be sewn anew."

James nods and kisses me on the head, holding me tight. "How can you stay so calm amidst these unfair, malicious daggers?"

"Two blessings from all I have suffered," I say. "One is that I am immune to words."

"The second?" James asks.

"My path of toil and snares has led me to this moment, standing in front of you. And I would not change that for anything."

James kisses me, holding me tight, and then whispers in my ear, "They will crucify you. Crucify you."

I kiss him on the cheek but otherwise ignore his remark. Desperately searching for something to bring him cheer, I say, "*Communist Manifesto.*"

"Not Marx," Tennessee says loudly from the stairs where she has planted herself and her flask. "We talked about this."

"Print it," I say.

"Vanderbilt protégé, first woman on Wall Street, rich capitalist, prints first English edition of *The Communist Manifesto*. Bumping, humping, Jesus!" Tennessee says, shaking her head and drinking.

James gives me a large smile, nods enthusiastically, and runs out to the carriage to the newspaper office. I know him. He will stay up all night to set the type, for Marx has captured his imagination.

AΩ

I feel the apples at the fruit stand for bruises when I hear an earth-shattering boom followed by a great scream that ripples through the city. It is coming from the docks. Boat explosion. I throw my carrots back and have the carriage take me down to the water. Once we get closer and I see the complete chaos, I have Thomas park out of the way so the emergency trollies can get through.

I run towards the dock to see how I can help. I quickly gather from the distraught crowd that the Staten Island ferryboat *Westfield* somehow blew itself apart while passengers were boarding. As I get closer, I see dead men, women, and children. I trip over a child's dismembered leg. Bloody and burnt people are screaming, and the entire scene smells like a battlefield. I do my best to ignore those who were hurt but not seriously injured, and I try not to look at the dead. I search for those in between life and death, hoping to make a difference.

A young woman in a blood-soaked dress with black soot all over her face is weeping hysterically over the body of a girl, who looks to be about three-years-old. The toddler has passed out, her left leg badly injured, almost separated at the knee. She is bleeding heavily, all the meat of the muscle is exposed and her bones are poking out. I sit down and rip my skirt into strips of fabric for a tourniquet. For the first time in my life, I wish I had a bottle of my miracle elixir to help calm this screaming woman.

"Emma is going to die," the woman says to me while I am putting pressure on the leg, trying to stop the bleeding.

"We do not know that," I say, "no reason to borrow trouble. New York has the finest doctors in the world."

The woman continues to sob and mutters, "it was her first boat ride. Why? Why? Boats should be safe."

I want to comfort the mother but I must focus on the child. The little girl reminds me of Zulu at that age and I say a silent prayer of gratitude that Zulu has never been harmed. The mother keeps questioning how or why this could happen. I do not have the energy to tell her why. The ferry operators are not concerned about the safety of their customers. They ferry people just like they would ferry flour. Marx is right, we are all cogs. I get the bleeding to stop. Two men place the child in an emergency trolley for the hospital. I hug the mother and whisper, "I will be praying for her. Go with her." The mother nods and gets in the trolley as well, having to climb over the dead and dying to hold her daughter's hand.

I turn my back on the rest of the injured and try to avoid the bloody dismembered fingers and toes, but some still crunch under my shoes. My conscience and my Christ tell me I should stay and tend to the wounded, but I cannot. I cannot. In slow, measured movements I get into the carriage. Thomas, noting my ripped, bloody clothes gives me a look of concern. I give him a nod, silently telling him that I am unharmed. He nods in return and I climb in the carriage. Where Thomas is taking me I know not. I care not.

Thomas pulls up in front of the newspaper office. He brought me to James. I get out of the carriage and ignore the stares of passersby as I make my way to the door. I open the door, unnoticed. Tennessee and James are throwing around words and innuendo, either in argument or flirtation. I can never tell with those two.

"We cannot say that," Tennessee says. "The ferry owner is Jacob Vanderbilt, the Commodore's brother."

"If he were a poor man, you would make it the front page, Tennessee!" James says. "This is exactly the kind of inequity that Marx discusses."

"Tennessee, James," I say, and they both turn around to look at me. Tennessee gasps and places her hand over her mouth, and walks backwards while muttering something about fainting. James rushes to me and starts looking my over for bullet wounds, shrapnel wounds, broken bones.

"The blood is not mine," I reassure James, "it belongs to that of a child, a child who will probably lose her leg."

"What happened?" Tennessee asks.

"I can guarantee you that it was not a stuck valve or a rusty plate, sister," I reply. "The cause is that passengers are mere freight, goods to move from one end to the other, pawns in the game of commerce."

"You do not know what happened, sister," Tennessee spits out, her eyes shooting daggers at me, "just because you saw the aftermath does not give you the right to speculate on the cause."

"Mothers are dead. Fathers are dead. Children are dead. A Vanderbilt must pay," I say.

"I am sure they will make financial amends," Tennessee says, shrugging as if loss of life is a mere annoyance.

"Your old goose's brother needs jail time," I say, "A petty theft of a pound of steak would subject the miserable, hungry offender to months of imprisonment; the infamous dereliction of the most solemn civil duty perpetrated by men of intelligence and position in the pursuit of wealth will leave Vanderbilt intact except for some nominal financial penalties."

Tennessee leaves, unhappy, no doubt thinking that I am a hypocrite for taking Vanderbilt's counsel and endorsement one day and then condemning the rich bourgeoisie the next day. Perhaps she is right, but I have no time to consider that now. James interrupts my thoughts, reading from his newly penned editorial, "As human life is esteemed by such men of less value than dollars, their dollars should not save them from the punishment they merit."

26

DENIAL OF PETER

Mabel, our servant, has outdone herself tonight. She is arranging plate upon plate of food for the Victoria League. Finger sandwiches, cookies, fresh fruit, pies, cakes, and exotic cheeses all fill the room with delicious smells in a dizzying array of colors.

"Your third meeting," Mabel says as she puts strawberries on top of the white cake, "and I did not have enough food the last two meetings. I learned. Them people kept comin' and comin'. This one will be different."

"Mabel," I say, not sure how to say what I want to say. Although I should be thinking about my campaign, my thoughts have been about Frederick Douglass all day. White supremacists burned down his home in Rochester. His family is safe, thank God, but everything he owns is gone. Elizabeth tells me that he was almost done with his book about political struggles and nearly all his work is gone. Douglass found one handwritten note that survived the fire, he picked it up among the ruins and read in his own handwriting, "*If there is no struggle, there is no progress.*"

"Yes…"Mabel starts.

"My struggle may seem strange to you," I say.

"Ma'am?"

"I'm wealthy. I'm living the life I want to live. I'm not in chains like your people were, I need not be afraid…"

Mabel wipes her hands on her white apron and takes the liberty of placing her arms on mine. In other households she would be smacked for touching the madam of the house in such familiar ways. I, however, welcome the human touch. "You're in invisible chains," Mabel says. "I am too. Folks can't see them, so they don't remove them. But you, you see them…"

A knock at the door. Tennessee, dressed in a new and expensive light blue frock, a courtesy of the Commodore before the ferry article, opens the door. I start to follow Tennessee when Mabel says at my back, "I was born negro. I was born woman. The greater curse is woman."

I turn around and squeeze Mabel's hand and give her an empathetic nod. I look at the door and Tennessee is pointing to a black man and says, "Annie Wood's driver has requested our presence in her carriage."

I nod, thankful that Tennessee is here and still speaking to me. I was afraid the Westfield explosion would explode our relationship. And yet, here she is, ever faithful. Tennessee and I both put on our coats while the driver waits for us with an umbrella to shield us from the downpour. The last thing I want to do tonight is walk out in the rain, but I would walk through a hurricane to reach Annie. And by the time I sit my derriere in her carriage, I feel like I have walked through a hurricane. Soaked despite all of our precautions, I am shivering as I greet Annie.

Annie, dressed all in red velvet, looks down and speaks rapidly, "With regrets, I can no longer be seen in your company."

"Why?" Tennessee asks.

"Preacher Beecher. Calling you Mrs. Satan," Annie says.

"Mrs. Wood," Tennessee says, "You and your clientele obviously believe in free love."

"My men," Annie says, "believe they are free to love anyone at any hour of their choosing, but their wives must retain their fidelity under any circumstance."

Tennessee swears under her breath as if this is news. This is not news. This is as old as Adam.

"Protect yourself," I say to Annie. "Your economic prosperity and your safety is worth more than your support."

Annie smiles and we get back out in the hurricane with our soaking wet coats but minus the driver's umbrella. Annie drives off and Mabel, who was watching the entire time, opens the door for us at once.

Tennessee dries off and pours me a shot. I grab the shot glass and cut myself a big piece of white cake with strawberries on top. No one can bake like Mabel.

"Victoria," Mabel admonishes, "those are for the guests."

"I regret to inform you, Mabel," I say, "that there will not be any guests tonight, as none of them want to be seen in Hell dancing with the devil."

Mabel arches her eyes as I cut a piece of cake and spoon extra strawberries on the plate before handing it to her.

"More food for us," Mabel says. Tennessee and I clink our shot glasses together, down the elixir, and we each get our own slice of cake.

"You need to be careful," Mabel says as we all sit at the kitchen table, "first they hail you and then they nail you. And they have stopped hailing ya."

"I'm too scandalous for whores," I say, knowing that if Annie cannot be seen with us, none of our supporters will have the courage to either. My other supporters do not even have the courage to deny me to my face. I wipe some stray white icing off my face and brush crumbs off my green velvet frock.

"It is the Denial of Peter," Mabel says.

"What?" I asked.

"Madam Wood denying you is just like the three acts of denial of Jesus by Apostle Peter. Jesus told Peter, you will deny me three times before the Rooster crows, and Peter did," Mabel says.

"Yes, yes," I say, "I understand now."

"And what is next Miss Victoria, you remember…"Mabel says.

"Nails," I say.

"Nails," Mabel agrees, "you must start protecting yourself."

Tennessee pours us all a shot. I did not think Mabel would drink, but she downed it quicker than either of us, even earning a look of admiration from Tennessee. I started wondering what other talents Mabel has.

"The only way for us to protect ourselves, sister," Tennessee says, " is to take Beecher down."

"Don't go fighting a preacher man," Mabel says, "they may look and speak like children, but they have power."

Another round. Another win for Mabel in the category of speed. Having left the Man with a Poker decades ago back in my childhood home, I feel the effect nearly instantly, feeling as if I could fall over if I tried to walk. I eat another piece of cake and let out a big belch. Tennessee looks at me as if I'm some odd attraction and laughs. Mabel pours us all another shot and I grab it. "To the three of us," I say. "We escaped Eden and now rule Hell." Tennessee and I clink shot glasses and down the drinks.

"At least in hell you can have an orgasm," Tennessee says, "after all, Adam did not know what he was doing." Mabel and I burst out laughing. I get up to get another piece of cake when there is a knock on the door. In my drunken exuberance, I run to the door, nearly falling over, and open it, shouting loudly, "Welcome to Hell!"

I take a step back and a swallow a big gulp when a dignified man, a handsome man, my kind of man, walks in.

"Do you know who I am?" he asks he removes his hat.

"Newspaper man," I say, "and Reverend Beecher's best friend."

"Theodore Tilton," he says before removing his hat and shaking the excess water off, "and I am here to help."

ΑΩ

"A campaign biography," I say as James undoes the top button of my green velvet frock and kisses my neck, licks my neck, and kisses it again.

"He has another rea…pur…mo… motive," I say, slightly slurring my words still feeling light from the effects of alcohol. James undoes the next three buttons and kisses my left breast while his hand caresses the right one.

I let out a little moan and James looks up at me, "He is in love with you."

James goes back to kissing, caressing, and loving my body and I manage to say, "No, no," James stops immediately, thinking I am giving him a directive. "No, him," I say. "This is part of a grand scheme."

James kisses me on the lips deeply and says, "Why can't you believe that a man can fall in love with you just as I have?"

James lips move from my lips to my chin to my collarbone to my breasts.

"I must find out," I say, "if Beecher sent him."

James moves his hands under my dress up my leg and I let out a few soft moans.

"I may have to manign....mari... manipulate him," I say.

James pauses and places his hands on my cheeks, looking me directly in my eyes, "Give him your body if you must, but your heart and soul belong to me."

James removes the rest of my clothes, tossing my green frock on the floor. If he could have ripped my bodice off, he would have, so anxious he was. I reach up to take his shirt off, but I am too fumbling for he brushes my hand away and disposes of his clothes in a matter of seconds. After another deep kiss, he comes inside me and I dig my nails into his back. I say his name softly, wanting to scream it but showing restraint so the others will not hear. He leans down and kisses my neck. His lips move up to my earlobes and he sucks them while I whimper.

"In truth," James whispers, "it is I who belongs to you. You are my country, you are my cause."

AΩ

Election Day. New York City elections and I am voting. Tennie and I registered two days ago without complaint. This pleased me so. I am a registered voter. No one stopped me. No one threw away my form. I then gathered three more women to register. They too were registered without complaint. The five of us gathered in my parlor room with thirty other supporters that we managed to find, the thirty that will not deny us, or do not really know us. Tennie read my Congressional memorial three times to cheers and handkerchief waiving. I then got in front of the crowd and asked them all to take the following oath: "I will cast my vote proudly and loudly despite any Democratic denunciations or Republican sneers, for it is my God given right."

The five of us get to the polls to face a crowd, a crowd that is there to see us break the law. I get out of the carriage and walk to the back of the line, but the men in front of me either out of chivalry or a desire to see the judicial crisis play out quickly hustle me to the front of the line. I walk past three negroes, five immigrants, and ten native New Yorkers. I smile to the Republican Inspector, a middle-aged man dressed in fine clothes, and hand him my ballot. To my elation, he accepts it. I turned around to leave as the Democratic Inspector, dressed in laborer's clothes and chewing tobacco, comes rushing up as if to catch me in the middle of a criminal act.

"You cannot receive her vote," the Democrat says.

"You refuse to take my vote?" I ask.

"We cannot."

"Take it," the Republican says.

"By what right and on whose authority do you refuse to accept the vote of a citizen of the United States?" I ask.

"Constitution," the Democrat says. I grab the little grubby book out of his hand and notice that it does not have the Fourteenth and Fifteenth Amendments. I reach into my purse and hand him the updated Constitution. I then read the 14th and 15th Amendments to him.

"This Constitution completely kills the first and is now the law of the land, my good man," I say.

"I cannot hear you," he says.

"Can you give me a reason?" I ask.

"No further information will be released on the subject," the Democrat says before spitting his tobacco juice on my shoe. I hide my disgust.

A well-dressed man in spectacles, three people back, yells, "Let her vote. Are you aware that you are liable to a penalty of $500 for not allowing a citizen to vote?" The man is quoting the law passed for the negro man, I do not have the stomach to tell him that it does not apply to me.

"I know nothing about it," the inspector says.

"Listen here you incompetent, tyrannical puppet," I begin to dress down the inspector when one of our crew, Mrs. Miller, comes barreling past me with her ballot in hand.

"You'll accept my vote," she says. "It is for Boss Tweed."

"Yes ma'am," the Democratic Inspector says, grabbing the ballot and stuffing it in the wooden ballot box, and the rest of the men laugh as we are all hustled out.

27

MRS. SATAN

"I fear the news is grim," impeccably dressed Theodore Tilton says as he strides in my parlor room with an air of confidence and ownership.

"Who died?" I ask.

"Your reputation," Theodore slams down the latest issue of *The Christian Union* and an issue of *Harper's Weekly*.

"You men," I say, as I open the curtains, "you are given to fits of dramatic hyperbole. If you lived for one year as woman you could distinguish tragedy from mere annoyances."

Theodore picks up the *Christian Union* and reads, "*I found Audacia's newspaper to be an exposition of all of the wildest principles of modern French communism. It consisted of attacks directed equally against Christianity, marriage, the family state, and all human laws and standing order, whatsoever. The principal difference between Audacia and those of the French illuminati, was that the French prototypes were men and women of elegance, culture, and education; whereas their American imitators, though not wanting in certain vigor and cleverness, were both coarse in expression, narrow in education, and wholly devoid of common decency in their manner of putting things. It was a paper that a man could scarcely read alone in his own apartment without blushing with indignation and vexation.*"

"Yes, yes," I say, "I've read it. Is that the best that self-proclaimed firebrand can do? I'm hardly the first uneducated, uncultured American woman who makes men blush."

"You are not upset," Theodore says as if he cannot believe it.

"Theodore," I say as I look out the window, seeing curious onlookers gather in front of my home, "I know who I am. I know I'm not part of high society and I have never wanted to be. I know I am uneducated, at least in the traditional sense. And I know that my opinions are extreme. I harbor no illusions," I say.

Theodore arches his eyebrows and then picks up the *Harper's Weekly*. He turns to a page and hands it to me. At first glance, it is just another Thomas Nast-y drawing. Thomas Nast has been spending his time going after the corrupt Boss Tweed with cartoon after cartoon depicting Tweed buying votes, stealing gold, getting drunk on power. Town gossip tells me that Tweed offered Nast a fortune to stop illustrating him, arguing that his voters cannot read but they can understand Nast doodles.

Once I look closer, I see that Nast's pen is now aimed at me. With horns and dragon wings, I am holding a sign that says, "Be saved by Free Love." The first part of the caption reads, "Get Thee Behind Me, (Mrs.) Satan!" In the background is a woman who is holding one baby in her arms, has one on her back, and is also carrying a drunken husband on her back. This is, no doubt, in reference to my years with Canning. The second part of the caption reads, "I'd rather travel the hardest part of matrimony than follow your footsteps."

Tears of anger sting my eyes. How dare this man tell me I should stay married to a drunkard and that my love for James, or even my beliefs, makes me Satan? I throw the paper down and Theodore comes up behind me, putting his hands on my arms in a familiar and inappropriate way. I wiggle out of his arms and turn to face him.

"A new… possibly fatal… weapon in the war against women," I say.

Theodore looks down and says, "You mean the war against a woman."

"No," I say, "this is about all of us. Take me down, intimidate the others, and the sisters will have no one."

"What can I do to help?" Theodore asks.

"Can you draw a picture of Beecher having sex with a negro male while his sister watches?" I ask, before bursting out laughing at the thought.

Theodore turns red and backs away from me as if I was a witch who just threatened to slay him.

"Have some humor, dear," I say. "It may be your only protection during this association with me."

Relaxing, Theodore takes a seat on the sofa in the parlor. "I've never heard a woman speak like that," he says. I nod and Theodore continues, "But then I have never met a woman like you. That is why I am here. I saw you talk of free love and was enraptured with your courage… and I could not stop thinking about you."

"Thank you," I whisper, bowing my head feeling an odd sort of embarrassment.

Theodore moves to my desk and takes out a pen and paper.

"Tell me about your family," he says, "for your biography."

"Poor. Harsh. Devouring," I say.

Theodore puts his pen down, "Victoria," he begins, "I need details. Start from the beginning. If we are to have people understand you, we must show them every step you have made and why."

I begin to open my mouth when the front door opens and shuts loudly. Zulu, beautiful Zulu with her hair in curls and her bonny blue dress rushes in, crying. Once she sees Theodore, she backs up and motions for me to follow her. I get up immediately and run to her side. I take her head in my face and kiss away her tears.

"What is it?" I ask in a soft voice.

"I have been asked to leave school," she says.

"Why?" I ask.

"You," she says. "I try to defend you, to explain…" Zulu begins.

I nod and hold her head to my breast and whisper comforting words. I kiss her hair and ask for her to wait for me upstairs. I walk back to the parlor room and refuse to answer Theodore's questioning eyes.

"Where were we?" I ask.

Before Theodore can answer, a crowd forms outside the window, with one man yelling, "Huckster." Theodore springs from his chair and draws the curtains immediately.

"It's dreadful you are subject to this kind of treatment," Theodore says. "Shall I go out and confront them?"

I shake my head and place my hand on his arm, "If there were not great prejudice to overcome, our battle would not be so arduous." I drop my hand and back up, "Besides," I say, "If you go around defending me, I am afraid you will find that it is a lifetime pursuit."

Theodore reaches out and puts his hands around my waist, drawing me close to him. He leans his head down, brushing my lips, and says, "Maybe that is the pursuit I want." He presses me close to him, as close as two bodies can be, and we kiss. His kiss is tentative at first but grows hungry, desperate, and for the first time I want a man other than James.

"Free lover whore!" the crowd screams, waking me up to my senses. I push Theodore away, not knowing what to say. Theodore starts to reach for me again.

"I was the green leaf, and they were the devouring caterpillars," I say.

"Who?" Theodore asks, confused.

"My family," I say.

"Humbug! Whore! Huckster!" The crowd grows louder. A beating of the door. Theodore motions for me to stay back, whispering I should hide. Theodore opens the door and I hear, "Mayor Hall."

Oakey Hall, unpopular mayor who hates the Irish, walks in as if he owns the home. A full head of hair and a full well-trimmed beard makes him handsome which is unusual for a New York politician. In a three-piece suit with a bowtie, a cane, and a monocle, his fastidious appearance has earned him the nickname of "Elegant Oakey" from Thomas Nast. Nast does not like Oakey, claiming him corrupt, but Nast never drew him as the devil.

Oakey Hall says, "Mr. Tilton, I must speak to the man of the house at once. Or the men of the house. Or are you the man of the house for the present?" I move away from the parlor room towards the front door.

"Speak to me," I command, walking behind Theodore, using his body to partially shield my face from the angry mob. I'll be damned if these two make decisions for me.

"Madam, your house is under siege," says the Mayor, whose knack for pointing out the obvious has bought him a long and prosperous political career.

"What protection is the city offering?" I ask.

"None," says the Mayor. "You must leave at once."

"Leave?" I ask.

Theodore puts his hand on the Mayor's chest, "Come, man, this is outrageous! This is her home."

The mayor swiftly removes Theodore's hand from his chest and says, "The city demands you leave tonight."

"Tonight?" I ask.

"Be reasonable, sir," Theodore says.

"Mr. Tilton, if you want to help, get your friend Beecher to stop inciting hatred against Mrs. Woodhull," Mayor Oakey says, walking down a few steps before turning back. "Leave your possessions. Return when tempers are calm."

In an instant, I am a little girl again being raped my father, feeling so powerless and out of control. I collapse on the floor and start sobbing, real sobs that I have not felt since Canning told me that Byron would never understand anything. Theodore is on the floor with me, holding me, caressing my back. He takes out a handkerchief and hands it to me, whispering kind words that I cannot hear for the volume of my cries. Once my sobs subside a bit, Theodore shakes me to attention.

"What I'm telling you has not been spoken to another. Use the knowledge as you will," he says.

I rub my eyes and try to concentrate.

"Beecher had relations with my wife."

His wife? They are best friends. Beecher married the Tiltons. I try to swallow my surprise and I ask, "Are you quite certain?"

Without averting his eyes from mine, Theodore nodded and then whispers, "A baby was born and died."

Suddenly a brick comes through the window, shattering glass and spreading it everywhere, Theodore knocks me on my back and gets on top, protecting my body from any shards. Once the moment is over, he sits up and picks glass out of his hair. He looks at me and rubs his right hand along my hair, searching for glass. He finds none, as he has borne the brunt of the shrapnel. He then examines his left hand and sees that he has a few cuts on it, all of them bleeding. I jump up and run to the kitchen for bandages. Wordlessly, I take his hand into mine and wrap the cloth around it.

"You must leave at once," Theodore says.

"Where should I go? What should I do?" I ask him.

"Henry's secret is gold. Spend it."

AΩ

In another life. In another life. In another life, I think I would be friends with Henry Ward Beecher. This thought plagues me as I make my way to his church, Plymouth Church, the church with the largest organ in all of the country. Everything about Henry is large. Large church organ, large reputation, large body, and from what Tennessee tells me, he has his own large organ. Not that Tennessee has seen it (yet). But she has talked to a moderate percentage of his many mistresses.

His infidelity aside, I could be friends with this man. In another life. He is, after all, a fellow newspaper publisher. He fought hard for abolition. He never cowered from disagreeing with his father whose shadow has loomed large. And he supports Ben Butler, even having nominated him for president during the War. But he broke with Moses over the Fifteenth Amendment. He is happy, thrilled, elated to see the negro man get the vote before woman. Even after years of working with Moses side-by-side to end slavery, he thinks she wants the vote too quickly.

He pushes her aside on charges of racism and makes himself the head of the woman's organization. A man, the head of the American Woman Suffrage Association? Never such an arrogant, bombastic, and disgusting political move have I seen. Tennessee's theory, and one that I am starting to agree with, is that he is making himself sympathetic to women in order to seduce them in greater numbers. Even Butler says it's general knowledge that every Sunday Beecher preaches to eight of his mistresses.

Still, I could be friends with this man. In another life. I open the church door, the church that looks like a barn, and make my way to the sanctuary. I stop to see the framed paper from *Harper's Weekly* that I lent (but evidently I gave) Isabella, the obituary of Lyman next to the article of James on the wall. I run my finger over the glass.

The organ starts to greet me with its harmonic melodies accompanied by booming Beecher's voice singing, "Love to God and our neighbor makes our purest happiness." Beecher, with his hair falling in front of his eyes, bends over to write down a few musical notes.

"A new hymn?" I ask.

Beecher, growing pale, gets down from the organ bench and walks towards me until he is directly in front of me. He towers over me.

"Mrs. Satan," Beecher says almost conspiratorially, as if he has personally paid Thomas to draw the Nast-y cartoon.

I stare at Beecher, this egomaniacal self-styled hypocritical free lover in Puritan garb. He stares back. Not comfortable with silence, as few men of the cloth are, he speaks first.

"Why do you visit God's house?" Beecher bellows.

I do my best to look meek and helpless, even hunching down a bit to make myself appear shorter and smaller, hoping to ignite some sort of male-protect-female instinct in Beecher, and say, "I am visiting you at my most desperate hour."

"You have had many desperate hours," Beecher shoots back. I ignore the innuendo, unsure if it was meant to be sexual or meant to refer to my trials with my family.

"Your supporters have forced me from my home," I say. "I have a daughter, a sick boy, and a sick man to tend to."

"I can help you," Beecher says, nodding to himself and mumbling indecipherable nothings under his breath as he circles me, "but you must denounce your sinful ways, in public. Here. Sunday. Be baptized. I will pour the water."

"Reverend Beecher," I say, "I know you and I are the same in our hearts."

Beecher stops his circling of me and asks, "What makes you think I am a free lover?"

"Because you live as one," I say.

Beecher, stunned, opens and closes his mouth several times before grabbing me by the arms and shaking me, saying loudly, even nearly yelling, "Tilton was to spy on you, not fall in love with you."

"His wife is not your only mistress," I say as I wriggle out of his grasp. Henry turns his back on me and runs his fingers through his thinning gray-white hair, his rotund belly heaving up and down as if trying to digest something unpleasant. He then takes a sigh and holds his body stiff and ramrod straight. Abruptly turning around, he looks at me in the eyes, towering over me both in body, spirit, from some unseen imagined moral precipice.

"Perhaps I am a flawed, loathsome, vile sinner. My conduct aside, public acceptance of free love would rip our society apart. Children without fathers. Sexual diseases. Abortions. Women abandoned, penniless. I may be a sinner, but I will not take part in the destruction of the family. I must answer to my Savior. How will you answer to God?"

Returning the religious zealot's steady gaze, I ask in a whisper, "Would your God deny divorce to wives beaten by their husbands? Shall they stay in a violent home until they are dead?"

Beecher's stern face changes color and texture as his soul climbs off the imagined moral precipice. I know in the instant that his face starts to change to putty that he is either undergoing some unique and soul-wrenching metamorphosis in an instant, whereas such a change customarily takes years, or that he is trying another tactic to manipulate me.

Getting on his knees, he grabs my hand and says in anguished tones, "Oh how I should sink through the floor. I am a moral coward on the subject, and I know it, and I am not fit to stand by you, who speak what you know to be the truth."

In an instant I see through his game. He is trying to manipulate me as he does all the other women in his life. I am even more disgusted by his insincerity than his misogyny.

"Get up!" I snarl. Beecher remains holding my hand, caressing my palm with his thumb, turning his cold eyes into puppy-dog like saucers of emotion.

"Get up!" I yell. The ferocity in my yelling triggers Beecher to jump up. For a moment, I think he is going to salute me in his sick desire to please me so.

"Either you support me and call off your rabid congregation," I say, "or I expose you."

The shock of my yell having worn off, Beecher stands close to me, too close, and begins caressing my cheeks, a few tears coming to his eyes.

"Please," he says, "I cannot. I cannot. Please. Be merciful. For my family. For God's family. For future generations of both believers and unbelievers. I cannot. I cannot."

I grab his hands and throw them off my face and walk away. In another life… but not this one.

"Mrs. Woodhull," Henry says to my back as I continue walking, "if it must come, let me know of it twenty-four hours in advance, that I may take my own life."

I keep walking but answer, "Then this is your warning. Twenty-four hours starts now."

"I shall try to work up my courage," Henry says as I am walking out of earshot. "I shall try."

I get back to the framed page of Lyman Beecher and my James and I rip it off the wall, damaging the plaster. This possession of mine has been in Henry's hands long enough.

28

Tit for Tat

Seething rage. White hot madness. Blinding turmoil. First Moses spits on me, then she denies me, and now she vomits hatred on my family. Intolerable. From the time it takes me to walk from Beecher's Pilgrims to fetch my family, I hear all sorts of rumors started not by Beecher, but by my supporters. My enemies and my supporters have joined forces to destroy me. I tried to give Susan allowances for all her sacrifices, but I can no longer stand by and play the role of the meek. The meek shall inherit the earth, but I don't give one damn about inheriting the earth. It is vengeance I want and vengeance I will get. Moses and her followers have nothing better to do than to sit around and swap stories about my alleged sexual sins. I have not heard all the stories, for this I am certain, but the ones I have heard are false. And if every detail was faithful to the truth, what place is it of theirs to pass judgment and to tear me down? How can these ladies, these great and noble reformers, justify taking breaks from the women's movement to tear down one woman? One woman who has done more for their movement in months than they have in their combined century of efforts.

Moses is saying that I slept with Butler; her friend Laura is saying that I slept with Theodore. And somehow, in my abundant spare time, I also led a socialist orgy with my spiritualist friends. From the sounds of it, I even lifted my skirt for Boss Tweed and his ragtag group of elected criminals. In fact, there may be no one in all of New York that has not been in my bed.

And I am not the only victim of Moses, for she is also declaring that Tennessee has broken up four marriages in a matter of months. I must admit, this may be true. Accounting for every minute of Tennessee's whereabouts is a task that only the gods are capable of. I have tried to determine how many men she has pleasured, but this complex equation depends on how many minutes the average encounter is. She claims it is ten minutes, but I do not know if that includes the flirting. I do not think it does. I will add another ten minutes for flirting, and then five minutes at the end to get dressed and say goodbye. Twenty-five minutes per romp. Add in the travel time and make it thirty minutes per romp. Two per hour. 16 hours per day. 32 men per day (although some men double dip) for 365 days, 364, she takes Christmas off. Perhaps Tennessee has slept with all of New York. But it is of no matter. Whether Tennessee beds all the men north of the Mason Dixon or lives as a nun, who is Moses to comment?

I admire the idea of Moses, but I grieve the reality. A bright woman with every privilege and advantage that God affords only to a select few of our sex, Moses uses these gifts to destroy me. A woman who has never known a day of rain in her life, powerful, worshipped by the elite, and she strikes me down. It is she, not the men, but it is the one who leads us to the promised land who would sooner sell me down the river than accept me advancing the cause. Was she sold into marriage? Was she raped by her father? Was she raped by her husband? Did she work until she fainted with exhaustion to support her husband's addiction and whores? Does she have a child who is so damaged that he leads a half life? She who says no to these questions has no right to judge me. She strikes the cruelest blow. Women will never advance with leaders like these.

I will strike back. I will strike back for me. I will strike back for Tennessee. I will strike back on the behalf of every woman who was made to feel as if they were too inferior or coarse to fight for their rights. How dare the woman's movement be only for the rich socialites! These women are no better than the men who hold us back—in fact they are worse. Moses is Judas.

One could argue that I am to blame for this predicament. For it is I and I alone who put my faith in the golden promises of false prophets. But, alas, the veil has been lifted from my eyes and I see clearly now. Susan B. Anthony does not head a movement for women. She heads the movement for Susan B. Anthony.

Tit for tat. I sit down and hurriedly write one tit-for-tat article for each woman who besmirches my character or that of my sister. Each article dictates the hypocritical lives of these angelic maidens. I am at an advantage because they underestimate my knowledge of their carnal lives, but I know where each of them spend their nights when their husbands are away. I will send out the tit for tats at once and if they buy silence then I will expend no ink, no oak, on profiteering from their sexual escapades. If their silence is not bought, then their bedroom antics will be front page news.

"Defend yourself woman," Napoleon tells me, "by any means necessary."

AΩ

The home of Moses is solid and without any external flaws. It is a bit plain, just like its owner. Built before the war, it is a two-story brick home with an ornamental wood porch. As Susan has given all of her money to abolition and suffrage, this home was built with money her family gave to her. Her siblings are constantly providing her sources of financial support. Susan is flying the American flag. She does this to ward off her critics who accuse her of undermining the country. Wasting no more time considering architecture, I knock tentatively, like a scared schoolgirl. I then knock again, this time rapidly, loudly, and I start yelling, "Susan! Susan! Susan!"

The door opens and this woman who looks more like a man than most men is staring back at me. She has short, dark hair parted straight down the middle and lying flat on either side. Her big forehead and nose detract from her freakishly small lips. My eyes travel down her neck, and I see that several buttons are open and the ones that are not are married to the wrong holes. That's when I know who is staring at me. Anna Dickinson.

Anna holds up one finger, disappears, and comes back with the Nast-y cartoon in her hand.

"Mrs. Satan," she says with a smirk, as if she has just caught goody two-shoes Santy Clause stealing presents from an orphan boy. Before I can tell her the truth about Satan and all of his glories, Moses herself shows up in a robe, just like one the real Moses would have worn in ancient times. But instead, this robe was put on hastily, not a garment worn every day. Before seeing me, Moses called out to "darling Dickey" but stopped abruptly when she saw me. Trying to hide her scantily clad body behind Anna's boy-man body, Susan looks at me with a mixture of disgust and embarrassment.

"Susan," I say, "the city has evicted us. We have no place to go. I have two children and a sick man to tend to. May we spend the night here?"

"Certainly not," Susan says.

"After all I have given?" I ask.

Susan steps out from behind Anna and points her finger in my face, "Given?" she bellows, "Taken! You have taken the helm of the movement away from me! And I shall regain control!"

"Mrs. Woodhull," Anna says sternly, "We are ladies with a reputation. We cannot be associated with free lovers."

"But free love is what you varietists practice," I say, with anger starting at my feet and travelling through my veins to the top of my head. Hypocrites. Nothing I hate more.

"Victoria!" Susan says with shock and contempt in her voice. I can tell by her reaction that no one has pointed out the obvious to her before, namely that she is not a heterosexual. I don't think she even realized it herself, or at least, never gave it a name.

"Miss Dickinson," I say, "does our mutual friend Benjamin Butler know you are here?" Jesus, I hate to think of Butler with this woman. I can see why Susan is attracted to her, after all, Susan is still a woman, unsexed though she may be. And Anna looks like a man. That makes sense to me. But Butler? Is he trying to find someone homelier than he is so he no longer has to take home the ugly prize from every dinner party he attends?

At the mention of Butler, Anna shrinks away, walking backward onto Susan's feet. Susan yelps a little and Anna keeps walking.

"Victoria…" Susan begins. I cut her off.

"I would be happy to tell him. He would want to pay his respects," I say.

Susan grabs my by the elbow and pulls me into the parlor, shutting the door. The parlor looks just like you would imagine a Moses parlor would. A Bible. Chairs covered in fabric, with needle pointed flowers on them. Drab walls are accentuated by paintings from some grand European coot depicting chubby women in ample dresses eating apples under trees while their curly-haired blonde children frolic in velvet.

"Now Victoria," Susan says, "I'm going to speak plainly so even you understand. Every penny Anna had was spent fighting slavery. Her only means of financial support is Mr. Butler."

"I understand, Susan. Thank you for providing clarity to an otherwise murky situation. It seems that Mr. Butler would not be so generous if he knew his offer of marriage was being mocked by you two in between your lovemaking sessions," I say.

"Are you threatening us?" Susan asks.

I hesitate for a moment, my mind thinking through all that Moses has done for the movement. She sacrificed for slaves. She sacrificed for our sex. But then I think about living on the streets with two children and two husbands.

"I deserve an answer," Susan says, interrupting my complex calculation. "Are you threatening us?"

"Yes," I say. I reach into my purse and hand her the tit for tat article that details her relationship with Anna.

Susan opens it, reads it, and burns holes in me with her eyes. She then opens the door, pushing for me to leave.

"You are not going to help?" I ask.

"Free advice, Mrs. Woodhull," Susan says. "Find a new cause."

The door slams.

29

SHADOWLANDS

After much cajoling, flirting, and a lifting of her skirt so the old man could feast on white ankles, Tennessee managed to get herself and the children rooms at the Commodore's home. I did not even ask to be included in Vanderbilt's generosity, for he had already done so much for me. Vanderbilt paved my path and now I'm embarking on a detour that he would not approve of. I can only hope that he understands it. As for Canning, I paid sour Sally to host him another night at her brothel. It wasn't the first time I paid for Canning to be with a whore. But this time I know Canning will not be indulging in any of their services, for he is only strong enough to lay in bed and stare at the walls.

As for James and I, we have the floor of the brokerage firm. James takes off his jacket and rolls it into a pillow for me, lifting my head up and placing it gently back.

"I miss the children," I say.

"As do I," James says, sitting on his knees and giving me a half-smile. "I cannot count the number of days that I wished they were my children. Not only so I could be their true father, but so there could be something tangible that would link us together for eternity. Even in name we are not linked."

"Hold me," I say.

James gets on the dusty floor and puts his arms around me, and I breathe in his musky scent. "When you put your arms around me," I say, "and I put my arms around you, we form a circle. And that circle will never be broken."

James kisses me on the lips, then he allows his kisses to travel down my neck.

"I'm sorry, love," I say, not able to enjoy his lovemaking, as delicious as it is.

"Why?"

"We are here on a dusty floor. After all the money I've made, and all the powerful friends I have made, I have somehow squandered it all," I say.

"Sweetheart," James says, "this is what revolution is about. Sacrifice for the greater good. Your sacrifices today will pave the way for women throughout generations, throughout the entirety of history."

"I would like to be able to sacrifice without forcing my husband to sleep on a dusty floor with no blankets, no pillows," I say. "Can we not affect change and still be comfortable?"

James laughs, "I have been in war, woman, why do you forget this? I have slept in mud next to dead bodies, with my bare feet covered in all types of nasty bugs, worms, and fungus. I've been covered in every bodily fluid one can imagine. There were times I was so hungry and weak that I prayed for death."

"When you got shot, what was it like?" I ask.

"What do you mean?" James replies.

"Was it like a beating, or a stabbing or…"

"It's more powerful and concentrated than a beating. It's messier than a stabbing, deeper and more blood. First you're in shock and you have this tingly, warm and light feeling, as if you could soar over all the earth. Then the pain is burning, intense. And then you get to a place of peace with one foot on the earth and one foot in the shadowlands," James says.

I shift and kiss James on the cheek.

"Why do you ask me these questions?"

"I'm preparing myself," I say. "We both know that if I were a man, I would be shot already."

"Victoria," James says, "you know I will kill for you."

"You cannot be by my side every minute of every day."

James pulls me close and I lay my head on his chest, listening to the soothing pattern of his heartbeat. James whispers in my ear, "If you fear for your safety, then it is time for retreat."

"Never," I say. "I have come too far. Besides, the world will never let me retreat."

"Zulu and Byron cannot live out their days without their mother," James says.

"Nor can they live out their days in an unjust and cruel world. Think of the trials Zulu will face," I say.

"And I cannot live without you," James says.

"We'll find each other. We always do," I kiss James and we spend the night in each other's embrace.

AΩ

A former Paris radical was executed by gun in France. He was only a true communist for nine days, but even a second of membership buys you death. Louis Rossel, one Frenchman wrote, was "a man whose hand we grasp even when we shot him." I'm leading the march to protest Rossel's death and to make the case for the fundamental tenets of Marxism. Tilton is joining us as well. Still dusty from sleeping on the floor, we travel to Cooper Union and see the thousands of unwashed masses with broken souls and trampled lives. Immigrants, radicals, negroes, socialists and women are here in mass. These victims of this country's desire for homogeneity gather to fight back. They know if the French can start executing its citizens for having different ideas, so can the Americans.

A carriage with six gray horses draped in black is painted with the words, "Honor to the Martyrs of the Universal Republic." I am offered a seat by the driver, but I instead march with my banner that reads, "Complete Political and Social Equality for Both Sexes." Tennie, dressed in red and carrying a banner that reads, "Social Freedom" comes up to me with a red carnation in her hand. She points out where the children are sitting.

"I properly thanked the old goose for taking us in last night," Tennie says as she pins the carnation on me. "I told the Commodore goodbye this morning. My last goodbye."

"Why?" I ask as I grasp her hand.

"Even I know that I can't be in bed with both a Vanderbilt and a Marx," Tennessee says, giving me a look of disapproval.

"Vanderbilt understands that I need a new constituency. The reformers have turned on us," I say.

Tennessee shakes her head and I pick up my banner, ready to march. Tennessee tugs on my sleeve. I turn around to see Tennessee crying. It has been a long time since I have seen her cry.

"I loved him," Tennessee says. I drop the banner and wrap my arms around Tennessee, whispering that all will be well while trying to hide my surprise that Tennessee has a notion of what love is.

I grab Tennessee's hand and pull my blue chinchilla coat tight around me and we try to make our way to the front, but the crowd stops us. In a fit of otherworldly adulation, men and women take turns trying to kiss and grope us. James and Theodore bust their way through the crowd as only two muscular, determined men can do, and they pull people off of us, sheltering us from repeat visits. Some of the young boys then climb the lampposts to get a glimpse of Audacia Dangyereyes-Satan and her buxom sister. Others simply go inside the surrounding brownstones, climb the stairs, and poke their heads out the windows. James hands me my banner that got tossed about in the mayhem, protected by our men, Tennessee and I make our way through the crowds, ending up in the front, and leading the march.

After a few minutes, the crowd yells, "Speak, Victoria, speak!"

I look at Tennessee and she nods, pointing to some steps on a residence. I climb to the top and the crowd forms around me.

"We are swindled every day and are too blind to see it," I say. "A Vanderbilt sits in his office and manipulates stocks and make millions. But if a half-starved child were to take a loaf of bread to prevent starvation, it's off to the Tombs!"

The crowd yells in agreement. A couple of men are struggling to get closer and James and Theodore both break a sweat holding them back.

"The privileged hate me," I continue, "And I am glad they do. I am a friend not only of freedom but also for equality and justice as well. I want people to have what is their right! Social and political equality amongst all! I want revolution! The despots will yield!"

The crowd yells in agreement again. Men and women tear off the carnations from their lapels and throw them at my feet.

AΩ

James and I make our way to sour Sally's to check on Canning. I try to brush all the yellow pollen from the red carnations off my blue coat. The fine dust sticks and will not let go. After getting our fair share of stares from the hangers-about in the Tenderloin, we finally knock on Sally's door.

"Thank God you're here," Sally says as she opens the door.

"You know you will get your money," I say as I push past James and past Sally into the smelly, dusty brothel that has pillows stained by every bodily fluid I can imagine and some bodily fluids that I'm blissfully unaware of. Like that brown stuff in the shape of an elephant on the cream pillow. What is that?

"Your husband," Sally says. "He is dying."

I snap out of my analysis of the stains and look at Sally, "I know he is ill…"

"I've been around dying men before," Sally says. "He is dying, child."

Sally says this with such kindness and empathy that I know she is speaking the truth. I exchange glances with James and rush back to the third door on the left, the bedroom of Canning's milkmaid from Ottawa. I open the door and I see Canning struggling to breathe. His breaths are coming in short gasps. He sees me and uses all of his energy to quiet his grasping and give me a smile. I sit beside him and hold his hand.

"Vicki," Canning says. "Remember that day at the fair?"

I nod, tears threatening to come down my face. "Happiest day of my life," I say.

"I search my mind, time after time, not knowing how such a sweet beginning went so wrong," Canning says.

"Hush now," I say, stroking his cheek. "You gave me a home, you gave me a name, you gave me two children and they are the very reason I breathe. You gave me everything."

"I loved you as much as I could, but I never loved you enough to let you go," Canning says. Crying, I bend over and kiss Canning on the forehead.

"Take care of the children and tell them that I love them," Canning says.

"Every day," I say.

"And Vicki," Canning says, gasping for breath. "Do what you must, but no regrets. Regrets will pick at your soul until you have nothing."

AΩ

Canning's obituary in the *Woodhull and Claflin's Weekly*:

> *On Sunday, April 6th [sic], as the shades of evening were gathering, our former husband and later friend and brother, Canning H. Woodhull, 46, escaped, after a week's painful struggle, from his confinement in a material form, to the freedom of Spirit Life. This transition, though somewhat sudden, was not wholly unanticipated, either by him or us. Certain unhappy habits of life, with peculiarities of constitution, placed a not indefinite tenure upon the extension of his physical life. Some ten years ago he remarked, "I cannot expect to live longer than till 1875." This prophecy was shortened by only three years, expiring in 1872 instead.*

> *There are various circumstances connected with his life, and ours, some of which, having been snatched from us by the public, sometimes in an unmerciful manner, and at others by duplicity and*

treachery have placed us in an unfavorable light in the judgment of those who have had no means of justifying their opinions by personal acquaintance. To such, we now have no recriminations to offer, nor any unkind words to say. We leave them all to their consciences and their God, simply remarking that he has taken a departure, called hence by the uncontrollable powers of nature, which they would have had us hasten by leaving him, at the expense of our own sense of right, to abandon himself to his unfortunate habits.

It will scarcely be maintained by any, that all people are ushered into physical being, equally endowed with the germs of greatness and goodness, or their opposites. In other words, people are born to be what they are. There are those who are possessed of peculiarities, which they can never overcome. Even confirmed habits either for good or for ill are not always merely acquired; but usually grow out of inherent tendencies. Some people are constitutionally drunkards; while others, though as fully accustomed to drink, never become drunkards. In either case, there is neither merit nor dismerit, since both are alike the result of circumstances and causes beyond individual control; and the former is only to be remedied by a better understanding of the laws of life and generation and the application in general experience.

It is in this sense that we regard the life of the deceased who has just left us. Our acquaintance with him began while yet we were quite young and very unpleasantly situated. Years of unremitting, wifely devotion, tried by every possible species of worldly temptation, and testified to by him upon every occasion, terminated a condition which became unendurable. When he found us inexorable in the determination to separate from him, he made no objection. He permitted us to depart in peace, and never from that day did he either upbraid or complain of us; but on the contrary often wondered that we had not left him before. And we knew that he, though he felt the change severely, was just enough to rejoice in knowing that the changed conditions opened a wider field of usefulness and happiness to us, and in all our movements none were more gratified at our success, or more regretful for our seeming defeats than he. But with the cessation of our marital relation there were others who could not be so easily sundered as this had been. We had our children; for whom he had as warm a love as his nature could know. It was not in our heart to banish him entirely from them. Besides we owed him personally a duty, higher than that which any law can formulate or enforce. It was impossible for us to be indifferent to the needs and necessities of him to whom we had given so many years of our life, and though the world demanded that we should abandon him to all the exigencies of his unfortunate weakness, we thank Heaven that we had the courage to brave its judgments and to perform that which was no more our duty than it was our pleasure to perform. He has always had a home with us whenever he has desired to occupy it.

We must confess, however, that this condition was one which, for a long time, we shrank from letting the public know, and it became the rod in the hands of unscrupulous persons, held in terror over our heads to compel us to do their bidding, and most cruelly and unrelentlessly did they make use of it. At length patience and forbearance ceased to be a virtue with us. The sequence has been heralded world-wide and used against us in every possible shape, until, in the minds of those who have had no means of correcting their judgment, we are held as little better than veritable demons. We trust the vindictiveness of the authors of all this, now that the stumbling-block is removed from their way, will cease, and the desperate energy they have devoted to affect our condemnation will be transferred to a nobler purpose.

30

NOMINATION

"I'll break in and fetch you a change of clothes," Tennessee says of my home that is now the gathering place for religious zealots and other protestors who see me as instigator of the apocalypse. "No lady should be walking around in the same dress for two days."

I look down at my dusty dress still dotted with pollen from the communist carnations. My eyes wander over to the floor of the newspaper office where we have been sleeping. The outlines of our bodies are clear and dust-free. I pick up an issue of *The New York Times* that James has fetched and read: "*Mrs. Victoria C. Woodhull has been married rather more extensively than most American matrons, and hence it might be deemed inappropriate to style her a foolish virgin; yet the characteristics which have made the foolish virgins of the parable famous for nearly nineteen centuries were mental rather than physical and in her inconsequential methods of reasoning, Mrs. Woodhull closely resembles them...*"

The door opens. In walks Moses. I nearly knock Tennessee down, trying to greet her. I've had some regret since our last meeting.

"Your heart has changed," I say. "I apologize for the harsh words I spoke, the pressure... I would never print that, but the rumors about me and my family have to stop."

Moses holds up her hand as if she is parting the Red Sea. "You are not welcome at the Suffrage Convention. We will not hear you," Susan says.

Tennessee makes a fighting sound, a combination of a ghastly intake of breath and a grunt, and gets in Susan's face, "Victoria is the only reason people are going!"

"I have worked tirelessly to build a coalition, Susan. Our economic, educational, and social reform agenda…" I begin.

"Suffrage is the pivotal right," Susan cuts me off. "We will not discuss…"

I stomp my feet and yell, "No! Equality is the issue! Equality under the law in every sphere!"

Susan grabs me by the shoulders and shakes me, "Moses spent forty years wandering in the desert and died within sight of the Promised Land. I will not allow your free love, Marxist, utopian views to keep me in the desert."

"A woman who is on her deathbed because she just gave birth to her twelfth child in as many years? A woman denied the right to earn her own money? These women do not care if they can vote," I say.

Susan searches my face and then releases me, "When women help make laws and elect lawmakers, these things will change."

"There is not a man in this country I would walk across the street to vote for," Tennessee says.

"Elizabeth is telling everyone to vote for me," I say.

"Yes, she is," Moses admits. "Our friendship was never strained until you came into our lives. Now it is at a breaking point, but one day she will see you for who you are."

"Maybe," I say, "you are afraid that she will see you for who you are, a domineering, narrow-minded, half-measure, self-centered reformer." I look at Moses, deep into her eyes, and I warn her, "You will fail."

"Failure is impossible," Susan says, turning to leave. Before she reaches for the doorknob, she takes a couple of coins out of her purse. She walks back to me.

"I've heard that the *Weekly* now spends more than it takes in," Susan says. I look down and nod, embarrassed. "My advice?" Susan asks. Susan then grabs my hand and places three gold coins in it. "Take it where you can get it."

I say nothing and Susan leaves. Tennessee, shaking her head and rolling her eyes, takes out her flask and retrieves a previously hidden shot glass. She pours herself a shot and slams it. She pours another shot and I grab it out of her hand, drinking the strong, burning, horrific liquid myself.

"What are we to do?" Tennessee asks.

"We are going to have a party, and we're inviting every Marxist, spiritualist, utopian, free lover, immigrant, anarchist, and negro we can find."

"Hot damn," Tennessee says, pouring herself another shot. "My kind of party."

AΩ

Annie Wood allows me to quickly change my dirty communist rags for a whore's dress. Thankfully, Annie's whores know how to dress with taste and modesty when they are about town. The plain green velvet and silk dress does not give any hint that it is ripped off and tossed on the floor more often than not. And Theodore gives James a change of clothes. Tennessee won't tell me how she is in fresh clothes daily, but I suspect it is the Commodore looking after his little sparrow.

Tennessee, James, and I make our way to Steinway Hall, against the wishes of Moses. Moses can say what she wants, but she cannot stop me from attending a public meeting, nor can she stop me from having one of my own. We stop at George Bunnell's wax display. George Bunnell made his fortune by showcasing freaks. Once a close collaborator of P.T. Barnum's, George argued with P.T. about the price of admission and went his own way. George then got on a train to New York and started working on "Dante's Inferno," also known as Hell to the uneducated. Hell is infused with effigies, Jay Gould (Vanderbilt's nemesis), Boss Tweed, and me. Hell would not be complete without Mrs. Satan.

"Men are always putting me on display," I say, thinking back to my young years, when father would make me hold a sign and charge folks admission to see the Oracle of the Midwest, "whether I consent to it or not."

"Not this time," James says as he tackles my wax statue and tears it apart with his hands. Red-faced, panting, and working up a sweat, I stop James from taking off my wax head.

"It is of no importance," I say.

James jumps up and grabs my shoulders with his waxy hands, "It is of the utmost importance. It is everything. It is about respect."

"Melt it today," Tennessee says, pausing to take a drink from her flask, "they will make another one tomorrow."

Tennessee bends down and gently pries James from me. She uses her dress to wipe the wax from his fingers and gives him a smile. Tennessee could calm any beast down, she has that gift, that special touch, that infinite understanding of the human condition. It is as if I can see their souls embrace as James smiles and all is well again.

We walk the rest of the way in silence. We open to doors to Steinway Hall and here Elizabeth's exasperated voice boom, "Sir, Sir! Mr. Steinway has lent the hall with the understanding that there will be no political discussions."

I walk further into the hall and I see Moses, Isabella, and Elizabeth on stage. The triumvirate looks quite agitated. A man in a brown suit shakes his hands and shouts, "What is the purpose of this meeting?"

Moses, in her customary funeral attire, stands up and slowly says, "Our only resolution is that we will work and vote with the great national party that shall acknowledge the political equality of women."

The audience murmurs, boos, and hisses.

A beautiful woman, no older than twenty-five and in a fine lilac dress, stands up and says, "I have travelled four hundred miles to attend a human rights meeting, but there is no discussion of human rights."

"We are here for woman, woman alone, and her enfranchisement," Susan says.

The crowd starts to get unruly. Men get up to leave. I look at Tennessee and James, and they give me their nod of approval. I begin walking down the middle aisle. The audience claps. People who were leaving sit back down. I take the stage. Moses tries to push me off, but I hold my ground. I surround myself with a white light, I pray to Demosthenes, and I plant my feet firmly. I am immovable. The clapping gets louder and louder with shouts of "Victoria! Victoria!" These are my people.

I hold up my hand to signal for quiet. When the crowd calms down, I yell, "If you are here to discuss true political, social, and economic reform, follow me!"

The audience applauds. I jump off the stage and lead the procession out of Steinway Hall.

I lead the procession across the street into the old Gilsey's Apollo Hall. Now they call it St. James. The auditorium was bare a few hours ago, but dear Theodore plastered it with large banners reading "Government Protection and Provision from the Cradle to the Grave" and "The Unemployed Demand Work of Government." Over the stage a banner reads "Equal Rights Party."

I take Tennessee's arm in mine and we walk with linked arms down the aisle. Shouts of "Victoria!" and "Tennessee" greet us all the way down the aisle. Men and women alike swarm us, kissing us on the cheeks, making us offers of marriage. Tennessee flirts with each and every person with winks and a return of kisses. I demure. The only one I want kisses from is James.

I take the stage and I catch a glimpse of Moses sneaking in the back. She thinks I cannot see her, but I know she is watching like a hawk, an envious hawk. Foregoing an introduction, I yell, "All men and women are born free and equal, entitled to natural rights which no government can take away!"

The crowd yells and applauds. I look down at James and place my hand over my heart, silently telling him that he is my foundation, my love.

"You applaud, but not everyone agrees my friends. My detractors created a wax version of Hell and in this Hell is an effigy of me, and they call me Mrs. Satan."

"No! No!" The crowd yells.

I raise my hands like a camp meeting preacher and yell with a biblical cadence, "I tell you now, I'd rather be a free woman in Hell than in chains in America!"

"Victoria! Victoria! Victoria!"

"I nominate Victoria C. Woodhull for President of the United States!" yells a supporter who I recognize as Judge Howe from Kentucky. The crowd roars in approval, stamping their feet, throwing their handkerchiefs, clapping, and some of women are even weeping. Moses is still there. In the back. Watching. Waiting.

"I second it," says Theodore.

"All who say aye?" the Kentucky judge asks.

"Aye! Aye! Aye!"

"All who say nay?" the Kentucky judge asks.

The crowd is silent.

"Thank you friends. We ended slavery of the negro. Now we must end our own! And if we should fail…"

The crowd is silent.

"We will form our own country!"

"Victoria! Victoria! Victoria!"

A man dressed in rags steps forward and yells, "I nominate the Hero of Vicksburg, James Blood, for Vice President."

"Yes! Yes"

I look at James and he smiles and shakes his head.

The young woman in the pretty lilac dress steps forward "I nominate Ben Butler."

"Yes! Yes!"

"I have spoken to both men," I say, "and they will not accept."

The crowd chatters with multiple conversations going on at once. My supporters take turns suggesting other men for the spot in whispers both loud and soft while I clear my voice and take a deep breath. I know what I am about to say is easily the most controversial statement I have ever uttered.

"I nominate negro Frederick Douglass, because he took a bullet for the cause!"

A smattering of applause, a smattering of boos.

"We have done enough for the negros!" one man says.

"Negros can't govern," another man yells, "they only know chains."

"We need a white ticket!" a woman says.

"Negros are stupid," another woman yells.

"Spotted Tail! We need an Indian," another man says.

"Susan B. Anthony! Our Moses!" a woman yells.

"All fine choices," I say, "but let me tell you the truth about our Moses. In my time of darkness, I turned to Madam Moses for safe harbor and do you know her response?"

"No! No!"

"She…" I begin and then the hall goes into complete darkness. Moses, unnoticed by me and my supporters, somehow cut off the gas to the lights. The crowd becomes loud, nervous. Broken, angry souls in darkness: the perfect conditions for a riot. James helps me off the stage and I yell, "Follow the sound of my voice! I am the light and the way!"

The crowd follows me out peacefully into the street. One older man starts singing in the street:

> *Yes! Victoria we've selected*
> *For our chosen head:*
> *With Fred Douglas on the ticket.*
> *We will raise the dead.*
> *Then around them let us rally,*
> *Without fear or dread,*
> *And we will put the despots*
> *In their little bed.*

ΑΩ

James, Tennessee, I, and the children reach the newspaper offices for another hard landing on a dusty floor when we see William Vanderbilt working like a little rat in the dark, padlocking the doors. James walks up to him and the two men exchange words, some pleasant, some not.

"Father will no longer allow Mrs. Woodhull to use this office. I have already locked up the brokerage firm," William says.

Tennessee steps in between the two men, and not bothering to flirt with William, she just asks "why?"

"Political differences," William says.

"Your father supports my candidacy," I say.

"But he doesn't support your Marxism," William says with some astonishment in his voice.

I nod, not knowing what to say. William walks away and Zulu tugs at my sleeve.

"Where do we go now?" Zulu asks.

"Marx," Tennessee says.

AΩ

We all take carriages to see the bearded German. Friedrich Sorge has been kicked out of three countries for fighting with the revolutionaries. He then came to New York and founded the New York Communist Club, adopting the principle that "every doctrine not founded on the perception of concrete objects" should be rejected. The club's goal was to end slavery. Once slavery was ended, so was the club. He is now considered the leading proponent of Marxism, although he didn't have the guts to publish *The Communist Manifesto*, I did.

I ask everyone to stay behind in the carriages and I walk briskly to Sorge's door and knock. And knock. And knock. I then start yelling. The door finally opens.

Forty-two, Sorge looks fifty, with tiny spectacles on his face and a salt-and-pepper beard and sideburns. He is in his dressing gown.

"Mrs. Woodhull," Sorge says, with more than a bit of annoyance in his voice, "it is late and improper for you to…"

"I need a place to stay. A place for all my family."

"Do you not have a home?" he asks.

"I have been driven from it."

"Perhaps you can find a poor house. Perhaps you have other friends. Perhaps the whores will take you in. But you cannot stay here," Sorge says. The German bastard starts to close the door on me. On me! I put my foot in between the door and the frame so he cannot.

"I printed *The Communist Manifesto* at a great personal expense," I say. "I formed Section 12 of the International Workingmen's Association singlehandedly. I brought thousands of spiritualists and suffragists into the fold."

Sorge sighs, nods, rolls his eyes, and puts his finger up, indicating for me to wait. So I wait. He comes back with a candle in his hand and a letter. I recognize the stationery immediately. Marx. I have received enough letters from Marx, letters of encouragement, to know his paper collection. "*Victoria Woodhull is a banker's woman, a free lover, and a general humbug,*" he begins. "*She brings us only riff-raff that is place hunting. Her talk of free love and female suffrage is folly. Women should help men seek their own emancipation from the capitalists rather than seek their own suffrage. We cannot support amateurs who assert themselves into this movement to seek utopian folly.*" Sorge smiles broadly and folds the letter, obviously elated that Marx has kicked me out.

I move close to Sorge and say, "You tell Marx that I will ruin any chance of socialism sprouting in this country."

I blow out Sorge's candle.

31

OUTCAST

Tennessee directs the carriage to Harlem and a tense anxiety hangs over all of us. We all know that we're in desperate, desperate straits if we have to rely on the kindness of the Harlem negroes. Now I'm begging my former servant for a floor to sleep on like a penniless bum. And the irony is that I have money, but it won't spend. No one, not even the whores, will take my greenbacks and house us, so afraid of Beecher and his self-righteous troglodytes they are. One dwelling proprietor, a short, bald, old man, told me that he would not do business with me, Boss Tweed, or any of the twelve horsemen of the apocalypse.

When Mabel first came to work with us, she lived in a tenement where she and her son had to share a water closet with eighteen other people. I gave her enough money, wages and otherwise, so they could move to a freestanding single family unit down the street. At least my spirit guide had the good foresight to be generous with Mabel, or I'd be sharing a water closet with one and a half dozen strangers too.

The carriage stops and Tennessee jumps out, motioning for me to wait. Watching her, I see her knock on the door and Mabel's son comes out. I am shocked when Tennessee's gestures tell me that she is intimately familiar with Thomas. Tennessee comes back and starts ushering everyone into Mabel's home. I tell James that I need to take care of some business, and he does not question me. I hold Tennessee back and pull her towards the carriage.

"You and Thomas," I say, more than ask.

Tennessee smiles slyly and says, "Variety is the spice of life."

I shake my head, not really knowing what Tennessee is implying, but certain in my knowing that I do not want to know. "Tennessee," I say, "intimacy with Thomas will only hurt our cause."

"Sister," she hisses, "if they are equally worthy in the eyes of God, then they are equally worthy in my bed."

"Tennessee," I begin.

"Sister," she hisses again, "do not tell me that you are becoming a lady, for I surely will have to disown you."

I start to argue with her but hold back after realizing she is right. I am having a Moses moment, a moment where political expediency trumps truth. "Quite right. I apologize. Share your affection with who you please, but tonight you are coming with me," I say.

"Why?" she asks.

"I refuse to be forced to walk down the steps to Hell while the self-righteous hypocrites are exalted into heaven."

"What are you going to do?" Tennessee asks.

"Drag them down to Hell with me."

ΑΩ

"Beecher is a liar!" The young newspaper lad screams, holding up his paper with the large headline "Beecher's Love Child" attracting a crowd. Tennessee and I watch the commotion from the broken out window.

"Beecher and Marx. You took out the right and the left in one issue," Tennessee says, "and I took out Luther."

I nod, knowing that Tennessee is proud that she was finally able to expose Luther Challis's debauchery at the French Ball all those years ago. I see from the reaction of the crowd that we will need to print more copies. Tennessee gets closer to me, resting her tired head on my shoulder. We have been up all night. Watching the crowd form around the newspaper boy is our reward. This will be our biggest windfall since Black Friday.

"Why did you not hit Moses? Expose her for the varietist she is?"

I kiss Tennessee on the head and wrap my arm around her back. "Because without Susan, there would be no me."

AΩ

"Nine thousand, nine thousand one hundred, nine thousand two hundred," Tennessee counts when the carriage hits a bump in the road and we're jolted. I quickly secure my money in my purse and I sit on top of it. The cash cannot escape. As I sit on the money, Tennessee and I both burst into laughter, the first laughs I've had for days.

"Who knew that ruining a man would be so profitable?" Tennessee asks, drinking from her flask, surrounded by stacks and stacks of newspapers. We are taking them to the newspaper boys in the far corners of the city, as they have not had the honor of spreading the scandal yet. But my first step will be the newspaper boy who sells right in front of Beecher's church.

"Victoria! Victoria!" I peek out the window and see James running after me. I knock on the ceiling for Thomas to stop. I open the door and I can see the corner of Beecher's church down the street. James climbs aboard and sits next to Tennessee on a stack of newspapers so he is directly in front of me. He grabs me by the shoulders and roughly pulls me to him.

"What is the first thing I taught you?" James asks with an intensity I have not seen before, except in our lovemaking.

I respond with a blank look. James releases me and holds up the newspaper and points to my name.

"When committing a crime, never leave your calling card," he says and then throws the newspaper down in disgust.

"Crime?" I ask.

"Are you intent on allowing your enemies to destroy you?" James asks.

"What?" I ask. I still do not understand.

"Comstock issued an arrest warrant," James says.

"For Beecher?" Tennessee asks, as confused as I am.

"No, Tennie," James snaps. "For you, for me, for Victoria. All of us."

"Beecher is the one who fucked her," Tennessee says.

"On what grounds?" I ask.

"Obscenity, indecency, libel. I don't know. Take your pick," James says.

James grabs my shoulders again and starts softly shaking me, "Victoria, listen to me. Let's take the money we made today and leave. We can have a new life. A fresh start. We can be happy."

"Happiness doesn't come from running," I say, thinking back to the times Father moved us from town to town.

"Vicky, I beg…" James gets on his knees in the carriage. His hands move down my shoulders to my hands.

"I've spent my life running. No more running, James. There comes a time when one must stand and fight."

James drops my hand and sits back on the newspapers. "If you won't run," James says, "then hide. I'll turn myself in. Hide as long as you can."

I shake my head. "No, no. You had nothing to do with this. I'll turn myself in."

James cups my face and puts his forehead on mine and whispers, "Vicky, I've never met a stronger woman, but the Tombs would break a man with ten times your strength."

"She has a speech tonight," Tennessee says.

"Then she will miss it," James says harshly, not moving.

I place my hands on James and lean in to kiss him. I then whisper in his ear, "Forgive me, but I cannot cower."

James grabs me by the arms and squeezes, hard. "Victoria!"

"James," I say, wriggling out of his arms, "I must walk this path."

James swears and leaves the carriage.

ΑΩ

"Who is that?" Tennessee asks as we hide in the bushes across the street from the house of Moses. The door opens and Anna and Susan walk out. Neither of them look happy, but then they never do. They truly are, as one newsman calls them, the vinegar virgins. Without the virgin.

"Anna Dickinson," I say.

"So there is a human uglier than Ben Butler. I had wondered. Susan could do better, even unsexed and all in black," Tennessee says.

"She is a whore traitor who deserves to be shot and fed to the wolves," I say. "Grant and Greeley both wanted her endorsement and she sold out to the highest bidder. And when she campaigned for Greeley she said that women do not need to vote because we have enough lazy and careless voters already."

"Jesus," Tennessee says, "these ladies would do anything for money."

I stay silent as we wait for Susan and Anna to leave, but I can tell by their body language that Anna has been kicked out of the tribe. It should only be a matter of days before she is charming the Beast. The two vinegars leave and we cross the street quickly, walk to the back of the house, and I hoist Tennessee on my shoulders so she can open a window. Tennessee lands on the floor with a thud and then runs to the front door to open it for me. I walk inside, remembering the last time I was here. Tennessee, who has never been here before, walks through every room to survey the décor.

"Not bad for a Quaker place," Tennessee declares, "just boring."

I grab Tennessee's hand and lead her to the large bathtub. "You stay here," I say, "and if Susan threatens you, use blackmail."

Tennessee nods and follows me out into Susan's bedroom, "What about you?" she asks.

I open the wardrobe and change into one of Susan's black dresses. I then take her shawl, and grab her extra pair of spectacles.

ΑΩ

Brave young men protecting the inexplicably fragile world from me are guarding the doors. There must be a baker's dozen of these naïve, sincere fools. I pass by undetected. My disguise serves me well. I walk into the packed auditorium, my biggest audience yet. Everyone in town has shown up to see if I will show my face. I see Theodore pacing up and down the stage. I catch his eye and give him a wink. He is taken aback. He rubs his eyes and checks his vision and then gives me a touching smile.

The crowd starts chanting, "Victoria! Victoria!"

Theodore jumps on stage while I make my way towards him. Loudly and distinctly speaking in his calming baritone voice, Theodore says, "It may be that she is a fanatic; it may be that I am a fool; but before high heaven, I would rather be both fanatic and fool in one than to be such a coward to deny a woman the right of free speech."

I take center stage and I have my back to the audience. Theodore moves to behind the curtains. The audience murmurs. Some praise me. Some damn me.

"Is it true?" one man shouts, "A free lover?"

I turn around and toss aside Susan's coat and throw her spectacles down and I yell as if my existence depends on the clarity and strength of my words, "Yes! I am a free lover. I have an inalienable, constitutional, and natural right to love whom I may, to love as long or as short a period as I can, to change that love every day as I please!"

Applause. The young police boys rush the stage, knocking me down in their eagerness to arrest me. One of the boys then picks me up while another one puts me in handcuffs.

I shout loudly to the audience, "You better take these off or you will only make me more powerful."

I hold up my hands and show the audience the irons shackling my wrists. Quiet. Awe. Applause competes with shouts of "For shame! For shame!"

ΑΩ

"What charge?" I ask as I am manhandled and hustled into a carriage where Tennessee is waiting.

"Obscenity," the officer spits out before slamming the carriage door on us.

"Where are your handcuffs?" I ask.

"I told Officer Handsome that if I run away, then I'll let him catch me," Tennessee says, smiling, and reaching for her flask that is still hidden under her skirt. Tennessee's demeanor is no different than if she were at a dinner party. I want to slap her. She leans back to take a swig and then discovers that it is empty. She shakes her head and puts it back under her skirt.

"Why didn't you blackmail Moses?" I ask.

"I did," she says, "or I threatened too. She told me that no one would believe a whore's word against Moses."

I look out the window and I curse Susan. I curse the world.

"Mabel is taking care of the children," Tennessee says, "and James has been arrested too."

"They have done it," I say. "They have taken down the triad." I curse myself. James was right. I should have taken the money and run, but that would only be a temporary, illusionary, panacea, for I cannot escape who I am. Put me in any city, and I would eventually end up in the same spot, both hated and loved.

The carriage pulls up to the corner of Ludlow and Broome Streets, to the federal prison. I am elated that I will be here in the Ludlow Street Jail, a debtor prison, instead of the Tombs. Not only are the accommodations fit for humans, but the debtors are my people. They will not harm a communist.

The policemen motion for Tennessee to get out of the carriage first. She does so and is immediately met with friendliness, some jokes, and a slap on her backside. No one requests for me to get out of the carriage. Four big hands reach in and pull me out as if I am sack of potatoes. No jokes are made. Two officers take each one of my arms and drag me through the front door, and we fall at the end of the procession line. In front of me Tennessee is making wild gestures with her hands, whispering naughty words to her soon-to-be-jailers and showing off her ankles. James is right, it makes one's head spin to think how quickly she will get out of this predicament.

AΩ

We are paraded down the row of cells and the shouts of "Victoria! Victoria!" by the debtors, prostitutes, and new immigrants begin before I even reach the second cell. The men remove their hats and stop smoking. The women bow to me. I nod and smile my appreciation at these tokens of respect. The cell door opens to an eight-foot by four-foot plain, concrete room with a concrete bench. Despite Tennessee's chumminess with the jailers, she is pushed in the cell first. She turns around and blows the policemen kisses, and the policemen wink in response. The policemen then turn silent, remove my handcuffs and shove me in the cell with such force that I am propelled against the concrete bench and I bang my knee. In pain, I take a seat and look around.

"Why are you so calm?" I ask Tennessee.

"A shining knight will come and bail us out," Tennessee says, "within a few hours."

"And how can you be certain?" I ask.

"Because I know men. And I know that in all our travels and associations we have charmed men whose hearts cry out at the thought of us in captivity. And at least one of those can afford the bail money."

AΩ

Our shining knight shows up in plaid pants, a purple silk shirt, and lavender gloves. He says loudly to the policemen as they are leading him to our cell, "This may be libel, but it is not obscenity. I am indignant, indignant that two women should be treated this way for merely publishing a rumor."

"Mr. Train?" I ask, looking up at his frantic expression. I have not seen him since he campaigned with Susan for the vote years ago. Since then he was in an Irish jail for being a Fenian, one who is dedicated to an independent Ireland through armed revolution. Beyond the letters from jail that were published in Susan's *The Revolution*, Train also wrote an essay about it and called it, "Everything I Do, I Do for Love."

The policeman unlocks the cell. Train walks in, removes his hat to reveal his dark curls framing his chiseled features, and bows to us, "Mrs. Woodhull, Miss Claflin." He then takes a seat on the concrete bench between the two of us and says, "I am going to get you out of this." He then takes a piece of charcoal out of his pocket and writes on the newly washed wall:

They are not free lovers, but love to be free
And are ready to die on a martyr's tree
In fighting down Christian bigotry

Tennessee laughs so hard she snorts. I'm in such a state of bewilderment that I just stare at this man.

"Mr. Train, forgive me for the crudeness of my words, but I thought you were my rival," I say.

"And why is that?" Train asks.

"You nominated yourself for presidency after I announced. You formed the Train Ligue after I formed the Victoria League, and you have always supported Miss Anthony," I say.

"It is true, I nominated myself, but we both knew that neither one of us would beat Grant. You know the people, Mrs. Woodhull," Train says. "They love to be humbugged. It is what ails our democracy. I possess tremendous power over audiences. So long as I could reach them with my voice, or talk with them or shake hands with them, I could hold them; but the moment they got out of my reach they got away from me, and slipped back again to the sway of the political bosses."

"And Miss Anthony?" I ask.

"Miss Anthony and I have been friends for a number of years. As for you, I have been watching you carefully like an angel in this mist. I doubted your sincerity when you came from Wall Street, then you allied yourself with that thieving, negro-loving Ben Butler. Why should we release the negro from his chains when the whites are still in chains? The whole war was for greed. The Butler-Grant thieves wanted to rob from the South. The Irish, the women, they have all had a worse fate. But then you published Marx… I guess I'm a heathen, lunatic, communist…" Train holds up his hands before saying, "I guess want I'm saying is that I am a man who fights for principle, not for personalities. And what you printed is in the Bible and it is not obscene and I will fight for your right to free speech until I am no longer able," Train says.

"We do not have a lawyer," Tennessee says, wasting no time in trying to negotiate her freedom, "and I am afraid bail will be high."

Train slaps his knee and says, "My lawyer is coming. And no worries on bail. You know I'm rich. Besides, I charged voters to hear me. Mrs. Woodhull should have done the same. Why I made $90,000 in admission charges. Despite being the only candidate to charge at political events, I spoke to more people and had greater audiences to listen to me than any other speaker during the nasty campaign."

"What should we do in the meantime?" I ask. "We may be here for hours before a hearing, even days."

"Listen to me now. I have never committed a crime, cheated a human being, or told a lie but I have been imprisoned in every sort of jail man has devised. And I have learned to use prisons well. They have been schools to me, where I have reflected and learned more about myself—a man's own self is the best object of any one's study. I have also made jails the source of fruitful ideas, and from them have launched many of my most startling and useful projects and innovations including erasers and canned salmon," Train says. He then takes the charcoal out of his pocket and writes on the opposite wall:

Stone walls do not a prison make.
Nor iron bars a cage; Minds innocent and quiet
Take that for a hermitage.

32

The Tombs

"No, Victoria, no!" James says, grabbing me by the shoulders in front of the judge in a little courtroom off the Ludlow Street Jail. The three of us were brought together to learn that one of us must stay in The Tombs. Even if we can make bail, only two of us can go home. The judge thinks all three of us together—"an unholy alliance" he calls us—will be a flight risk. The judge tells us that bail is eight thousand dollars. More than murderers have to pay. Ludlow is overcrowded with the poor, so the Tombs it is. James just got out of the Tombs for Ludlow was too crowded by the time the police found him. Train was arranging bail for Tennessee and myself when I instructed Train that it should be Tennessee and James who are free.

"You take care of the children," I say.

"Take the bail and leave. Leave at once. I demand it," James says.

"I cannot, I will not," I say.

"Victoria, goddamn it, woman! Be reasonable. Jail may not seem wholly uncomfortable at present, but you will be in the Tombs with rapists and murderers. Reformers have been trying to get that Egyptian eyesore condemned for the past twenty years. Not a dry cell in the whole place. No mattresses, raw filth, small cells, no light. The tombs would break twenty Victorias," James pleads.

"If there is one thing I know about myself, it is that I am survivor," I say.

"You do not know what desperate men do, and the Tombs have nothing but desperation. I have seen learned men become savages. Killed them, I've had to, with nothing but my hands and my smarts. I have spent days lying in filth next to corpses. I have endured the cold, the wet, the uncertain. Whatever you have endured in your past, as considerable as it might be," James says, "it wasn't this." James leans in to whisper, "I have no certainty that I will emerge from the Tombs, but I am certain that I am more likely to than you."

I kiss James on the cheek and take his hands into my own. His hands are shaking, sweaty, while mine are calm and dry. "James," I say, "I must travel this path, both for reasons that are in clarity and for reasons shrouded in shadows. My conscience would not allow me to walk and breathe freedom while you are in captivity for my actions. And our revolution needs a martyr, for social justice can only be achieved when people's hearts and minds change and they only change when they feel deep empathy for the victim of injustice. A few days of jail for me could mean the advancement of women's rights by decades." I lean in and whisper in James's ear, "This is my fate. I accept it with open arms."

I step back and James has tears streaming down his face as he shakes his head either in anger, or sorrow, or disbelief, or perhaps all three. Two policemen pull me back and James screams, "No!" James pulls on the policemen and he rears his fist back, about to punch the first one, and Train gets in the middle and stops James.

"It will only be for a few days," I say, "society will not allow me to be locked up for long, love. Have faith, James."

James shakes his head and pulls back his fist as if he is going to try to fight again.

"Calm down, man," Train says, patting him on the shoulder. "We will fix this. I promise. I promise."

Tennessee taps the policeman on the shoulder and flashes a smile and he lets go of me. Tennessee gives me a hug and whispers in my ear, "Humping, bumping Jesus, Victoria. I don't know what the hell you are doing." She lets me go and then says, "Remember when I told you that you were just like father?" I nod. "I was wrong," she says.

AΩ

New York Sun:
*A few days will bring the fact to light; if Mrs.
Woodhull be a falsifier let the withering contempt
of outraged humanity be unsparingly heaped upon
her; but if the Reverend Henry Ward Beecher be
guilty, let the devil's scorpion lash be applied to his
naked back and he be whipped out of society. We
wait developments.*

It is morning. I was granted a one-night stay at the Ludlow
jail before being transferred to the Tombs. I look outside and see
what could be my final resting place or my moment of triumph.
The New York City Halls of Justice and House of Detention
earned its name for it looks like a tomb awaiting the body of
King Tut with its portico and four columns. In 1842, Charles
Dickens in his *American Notes* asked, "What is this dismal
fronted pile of bastard Egyptian, like an enchanter's palace in a
melodrama?"

I walk in the bastard Egyptian and the smell tells me that
this is not a place where people triumph often, it may well be
my final resting place. I think of those characters who have gone
before me. Dickens is not the only man of prominence to notice
this bastard Egyptian. Herman Melville was fond of the Tombs
as well, using it as a setting for his stories.

Bartleby, a character in one Melville story, is sent to the
Tombs, and when he is told to eat he says, "I would prefer not
to." He starves to death in the courtyard of the Tombs. Upon
finding Bartleby's body in the jail courtyard, the narrator cries,
"Ah Bartleby! Ah Humanity!"

This story is widely interpreted as Bartleby being so
overwrought that he cannot work up the will to live. These
interpreters, the great demystifiers of literature, are wrong
and if they had spent one day in the Tombs they would have
understood. The food is sickening in color, texture, smell, taste,
and is offensive to the spirit. Bartleby was saving his dignity by

not eating this slop. I can take a few days of hunger in a peaceful silence, but if this keeps up I might end up choking someone to death for an apple.

Before Bartleby, there was Melville's *Pierre*. The details are murky, but Pierre was evidently a free lover for he was married to his sister and in love with another lady named Lucy. Through a series of wrong turns, he ends up in the Tombs and all three of them are together when Lucy dies of shock and Pierre and his sister kill themselves with poison. Three corpses in the Tombs.

That was Melville's attempt at romance.

I'm starting to wonder if I am a character in a Melville story, destined to death in the Tombs. Perhaps Melville is my unseen master, it is he who controls my actions. I wish he would have put me on a boat to fight a whale instead. But, alas, poor Ahab! I fear I would cut his other leg off.

I would gut Moby Dick.

AΩ

Day two and I am already cursing Henry David Thoreau. I thought I could spare his memory of my ire at least until day three. The pompous bastard made civil disobedience look too easy. He spends one night in jail, has a woman bail him out, and then sets himself up as a celebrated martyr for life. Will anyone applaud my time in jail? My sacrifices? No. They will spit on me. They will call me wicked. They will call me a whore. For I am not a man.

Thoreau was comfortable in jail. He wasn't in this bastard Egyptian swamp. In a town full of engineers we build a jail on top of a pond and then wonder why it is always wet. And New Yorkers are the smartest people on Earth? I have two inches of standing water in my cell. At least I hope it's water. Open sewers run past my cell, bringing tons of human excrement and smell. I cannot stand up in my cell, for it is too short. I do have a concrete bench. No light. No change of clothes. No bed. And it is a challenge to distinguish between the food and human excrement.

I am allowed out of my cell for one hour per day. They call it exercise, but it's just marching up and down the hall of the jail for an hour. Ministers come every day. The Catholic priest is here on Sunday and Tuesday mornings. The Episcopalian priest is here on Sunday and Tuesday afternoons. The Methodists get Mondays. The Jews get Wednesdays. The Presbyterians get Thursdays. The Baptists get Fridays. The Puritans get Saturdays. I told the warden that I'm a spiritualist so she sends them all to me.

I let them all in, I do need people to argue with. I need to stay mentally sharp for the court hearings. Father Paul is the first. He is a kindly, older man who radiates serenity. He walks in my jail cell and does some sort of blessing with beads and talk of the Virgin Mary. He takes a seat on the concrete bench. He has cloth sacks around his shoes to try to protect them from the foul-smelling water in my cell.

"Sister Victoria," Father Paul asks, "do you love your enemies?"

"Love your enemies?" I ask. "Well, that's the last thing you say to a woman in the Tombs. How am I supposed to have the will to get up in the morning, to fight, to live? I will have no will left if I sit in here in love. Look at Jesus. He loved his enemies and then he let them crucify him. "

"That is not the lesson of the crucifixion," Father Paul says.

"Perhaps not the intended lesson," I say, "but it is a lesson there is no doubt. Jesus lost the will! He did not see his revolution through. If he had, I would not be standing here, for we would all be loving each other. And if my enemies loved me, then I would have rights. Love your enemies. What nonsense. Maybe my enemies need to love me. Maybe the holier-than-thou needs to start loving me. He, after all, makes his dollars from preaching this nonsense."

Father Paul removes his spectacles and says sternly, "The Gospel is not nonsense."

"If you love, then you do not fight, if you do not fight, there is no revolution, if there is no revolution then we all sit here in chains. No sir, I will not sit here in chains loving my enemies. I will wrap these chains around the beasts of hypocrisy and prejudice and cut off all breath. And if you want to help then tell my enemies to love me."

Father Paul shakes his head, mumbles some prayer, and leaves.

ΑΩ

"You have been in a fight," I say, touching the bruises on James's cheeks and eyes. James backs up as if the pain was still fresh. I inch closer to him in response and place my hands on his shoulders. Days and days have gone by when I have had little solace save the people of God who come by and argue. And now James is here.

"What is it," I ask, wanting to know why he abandoned me these many days.

James grabs my left hand and puts it to his lips. He then embraces me tightly, kissing me on my crown, my forehead, and finally my lips.

"No love in the Tombs!" the fat and greasy inmate Maggie, who is the cell across from mine, screams. I hear the loud steps of the warden, and I push James away and sit down on the concrete bench to put more space between us.

"No free lovin' in here," the warden, a big hunk of an Irish maiden with brown matted curls stuck to her head, says to us between the bars. James nods to her. She walks away, just out of sight, not out of earshot.

"I have been avoiding you," James says, "staying away until the bruises go down. For you have enough to worry with, being here… you need to keep your strength up…"

"Tell me," I say.

"Victoria… we can discuss at a later time…" James begins.

"Tell me."

James sighs and shakes his head slowly. He then takes a seat next to me on the concrete bench. "They destroyed our printing presses," James says, "with an axe. Seized our newspaper office. Took over our business accounts."

"Who?" I ask.

"The government, Victoria, the government. They intend that we do not print one word ever again."

James grabs my hand and I drop it and jump up, "What fresh tyranny is this?" I ask. "The seizure of public property even before guilt or innocence has been determined?"

"I tried to stop them," James says, "fought five men." He touches his bruises and says, "They won."

"We cannot beat them physically, they outnumber us," I concede. "We must beat them in court."

"I'm afraid our anti-tyranny budget is being dwindled in hopes of getting you out of here, love," James says, gently.

I nod and say nothing, for there is no need to argue the point. But one day I will sue, and if this country is a just one, I will win. I sit back down and kiss James on the cheek.

"I may be in chains," I say, "and I feel no restriction, because the real chain is the spiritual one between us and it will never be broken. Your love gives me strength."

James and I sneak one kiss and then I wipe a tear from his cheek. James whispers is my ear, "You are my life, my beginning, my ending, my alpha and omega."

James gives me one light embrace before the warden yells, "Time's up!"

ΑΩ

To the Editors of the *Herald*:

Sick in body, sick in mind, sick at heart, I write these lines to ask if, because I am a woman, I am to have no justice, no fair play, no chance through the press to reach public opinion. How can anybody know for what I am accused, arrested, imprisoned, unless the public are allowed to see the alleged obscenity? If the paper is suppressed and I charged with crime, in what way can I substantiate the truth, when the judge before whom I only appear as witness, constitutes himself as plaintiff, prosecuting attorney, judge, jury, and witness? When has it ever been known in this land of so-called religious freedom and civil liberty, that pulpit, press, and people tremble before a cowardly public opinion? Is it not astonishing that all Christian law and civilization seem to be scared out of their senses at having a poor woman locked up in jail? Suppose, Mr. Editor, that some enemies of yours should throw you into a jail cell for an article, suppress the Herald, arrest your printers, prosecute your publisher, shut up your business office, close all the avenues of press and lecture hall against your honorable defense? Would not every land ring with outrage? "Oh liberty," said Madam Roland, when the French capital was shaking the conscience of Europe, "what things are done in thy name!"

Sincerely yours,
Victoria Woodhull, Cell 11

AΩ

I somehow smell the lavender gloves moments before they are wrapped around the bars of my cell.

"I've thrown my lot in with yours, " George Francis Train says, proud of himself. "They will have to release you now." He motions for the warden to let him in, and she does. He bows down to her and tips his hat, and the Irish maiden giggles. Train comes in my cell and takes a piece of charcoal out of his pocket and makes seven marks on the wall, one for each day that I have been here. He then moves to another wall and starts writing.

"What did you do?" I ask.

"I started my own paper," Train says, shaking his head from left to right while talking, "the *Train Ligue*, and I reprinted all the filthy versions of the Bible, Song of Solomon and such, all the verses that use the same language as you did." Train then starts laughing, a high-pitched frenzy sort of laugh, followed by a rhythmic slapping of the knees, while keeping his back to me, intent on writing out a couplet or two.

I place my body between his charcoal and the wall, touching him lightly on his bended shoulder. "You are their enemy," I say. "You are their enemy because you are successful, the people love you, and you do not walk the line. You call yourself a heathen, a lunatic, a socialist, a suffragist. You are a Copperhead, a Fenian, a threat. They will destroy you. They would have done it years ago but they did not have any legal pretense, and now you have given them one. You must stop your printing at once."

Train stands up as tall as he is able to without hitting his head, and for the first time in all our encounters, he looks me in the eye. "Howe sets murderers free. I'm sure he can set a rich man free who does nothing more than print the Bible. The case will be dismissed before it is tried."

"You give your enemies too much credit. For them to allow you to print those words, means they have to allow me, and they will not throw their lot in with Mrs. Satan. They will follow your reason," I say, "and it will not mean freedom for me, it will mean imprisonment for you."

Train bends back down and continues to write on the wall. "I do not believe," he says, "that any court in the land would face the danger of trying to convict a man of publishing obscenity for quoting from the standard book on the morality read through Christendom."

I take a seat on the concrete bench and begin shivering and crying. I hate to think of this man in the Tombs, especially on my account. Train, oblivious to my emotion, finishes his writing and stands up. He motions for the Irish maiden to open the door. He tips his hat to me and squeezes my hand through his charcoal-stained lavender glove in what he thinks is a comforting gesture, but I find no comfort. He then whispers to me "all will be well." He leaves and I can hear him entertaining the maiden warden on the way out. They both laugh heartily and their sing-song Irish voices carry down the dismal corridor.

I turn to the wall and read what Train has written:

> *Stand ye calm and resolute,*
> *Like a forest close and mute,*
> *With folded arms and looks which are*
> *Weapons of unvanquished war.*
>
> *And if then the tyrants dare,*
> *Let them ride among you there;*
> *Slash, and stab, and maim and hew;*
> *What they like, that let them do.*
>
> *With folded arms and steady eyes,*
> *And little fear, and less surprise,*
> *Look upon them as they slay,*
> *Till their rage has died away:*
>
> *Then they will return with shame,*
> *To the place from which they came,*
> *And the blood thus shed will speak*
> *In hot blushes on their cheek:*
>
> *Rise, like lions after slumber*
> *In vanquishable number!*
> *Shake your chains to earth dew*
> *Which in sleep had fallen you:*
> *Ye are many—they are few!*

AΩ

"Greeley dead?" I ask Theodore Tilton, who looks as nervous as a slave at auction. Tilton with his back to the jail bars takes out his bright white, stiff handkerchief and wipes his brow. I motion for him to take a seat next to me on the concrete bench and he shakes his head in declination.

"What a coward to die in the midst of defeat," I say.

"Victoria!" Theodore admonishes.

Fat and greasy Maggie has been listening the entire time as she does to all of my conversations as entertainment is so scarce, and bellows out, "Well the poor bugger's wife died."

"Yes, Maggie," I say to the old redhead, "I know Greeley's wife died, but he didn't have to go join her. Look at me, I'm in the tombs! Do you see my laying down and dying? "

"Truth it be," Maggie says.

I get off the bench and walk to Theodore, grabbing his arm so he will look at me and not the filthy water I'm walking in, and say "Defeat is the precise moment when you must gather your courage and fight even if it is only to anger your enemies."

"Grant was at the funeral," Theodore says.

"And I'm sure he was sobbing just as Pontius Pilate sobbed for Christ while they were driving the nails through his hands," I say.

"Grant did not kill Greeley," Theodore says.

"Unseen forces," I say, "they are out to get all of us. Every non-conformer or every conformer with one non-conforming thought, they will wipe us out." I look at Theodore and I place my hand on his cheek, forcing him to look at me, "You should leave the country. You are the enemy now, too."

Tilton sighs and grabs me, kissing me long and slow, as if we were great lovers doomed, saying goodbye for the last time. I break away, astonished at the depth of his passion.

"Leave with me," Theodore says. "I'll get you out of here, I'll find a way."

"I will never leave James. And, despite all of this, I could never leave this country. America holds the promise of revolution. And…" I say before taking a deep breath and grabbing Theodore's hand, "I'm seeing this case through, whether it means freedom or execution."

"Victoria," Theodore says, "I have always been the first in line to admire your spirit, but you may have passed into madness."

"Mad!" I say. I consider this for a moment and I shake my head. "When my light is extinguished and I say no more than 'yes please' and 'thank you sir,' that is when I have gone mad."

"And what is this business about blackmail," Theodore asks.

"Blackmail?" I ask.

"Tit for tat, very fine women are outraged and…"

"Oh that," I say, "I concluded to shut the mouths of a clique of loose and loud-tongued women who were continually stabbing me… and making me a fiend incarnate of the people. I grouped the clique together in an article, which I sent each member. The filthy fountains suddenly ceased to vomit forth their slime and I have had no occasion to publish the articles, but if it still arises I shall not hesitate to do so."

Theodore shakes his head sadly, kisses me on the forehead, and knocks on the bars for the jail matron to open the cell.

"I have to protect myself," I say. "You were the one who told me to go after Henry. You understand this."

Tilton does not say anything, he only lets out a sigh.

"Who did you vote for?" I ask Theodore, placing my hand on his elbow.

"Greeley," Theodore says, holding his head down out of embarrassment. "I'm sorry Victoria, I could not throw away my vote, and getting Grant out was more important than making you a footnote of history."

"Theodore," I say, nearly sneering, "you'll make a fine man one day."

Tilton looks at me, my insult cutting at his core. He opens the unlocked cage and starts to leave. I swallow my fury long enough to spit out, somewhat sympathetically. "As it turns out, either vote was for the walking dead."

AΩ

"Your clothes. Mine," fat Maggie says, interrupting my spirited discussion with Napoleon on Josephine. I look at the pile of clothes she is pointing to. The dress that I was arrested in, along with Susan's cloak and spectacles, lay folded on one edge of my concrete bench. James brought me a change of clothes when the children visited. We had a terrible fight that day. James did not want Zulu to be exposed to the Tombs, but I thought it important to see the sacrifices others are making for her generation. In his anger, he left before I could change into my fresh clothes and give James my filthy ones.

"It occurs to me," I say, "that perhaps my dress size is not your dress size."

"You thinks I don't know me own body?" Maggie says while pointing through the bars at me. "The cloak is what I'm after. Spectacles too."

"They do not belong to me," I say, running my hand over Moses's coat, the one I disguised myself in, was arrested in.

"Stole 'em?" Maggie asks.

"It is my every intention to return these to the rightful owner…" I begin.

"Stole a man's spectacles you did," Maggie laughs. "You are a cold fish, Missy, a cold fish."

"Woman's," I say, "these belong to a woman."

Maggie laughs even harder, "A woman? Stole from an old spinster, ye did."

"Spinster?" I ask.

"She never get a man in those clothes," Maggie says. "Your clothes are woman, but those, those are the black cloud o' death they are. No man wants to be next to the black cloud o' death, does he?"

I shrug and turn my back, trying to initiate contact with Napoleon again. He only wants to talk about Josephine, but I need to know about his exile to Saint Helena. He tells me it was as damp there as it is here. Dear Napoleon is worried about my health. He tells me that his supporters thought it was the journey from coronation to exile that killed him, but this is not true. It was the dampness.

"Still mine," Maggie says once again, interrupting my conversation with the Emperor. I turn around and look at Maggie, really look at her, searching for some kind of soul light. All I can see are fat, pudgy arms pointing at me through the bars.

"Return stolen goods?" Maggie says, laughing. "Right back here, she will, spinster will send you back here."

I consider this and I tell Maggie that she will understand, even though I am not entirely convinced of this myself.

"Understand? Not a damn thing, Missy, or they wouldn't be spinsters, would they now?" Maggie asks.

"Why do you need them so?" I ask.

"Getting out," Maggie says. "Me man paid my debts. But November and no coat. The darkness in here, it's done somethin'... somethin' to me eyes."

I nod. Maggie needs the coat and spectacles more than Susan.

ΑΩ

My Dearest Victoria:

I shall not be able to find time from my public duties to take part in the trial of your case... I cannot believe that in... the persecution of yourself and sister for sending obscene literature through the mails, in the Courts of the Unites States, there is the slightest need of my services or my counsel, I feel as certain as I can of any question, upon the construction of the statute, that the action of the United States Prosecuting Attorney was based wholly upon a misconstruction and misconception of that statute... The statute was meant to cover, and does cover, sending that class of lithographs, prints, engravings, licentious books and other matters which are published by bad men for the purpose of the corruption of the youth, through the United States mail... To test it, suppose on your trial the indictment should set out the words which you are alleged to have sent, and then the District Attorney should send a copy of that indictment through the mail to his assistant, and the words should be held to be obscene writing, then he would have transmitted the same obscene writing which you had and would be liable to a like condemnation. If I were your counsel I should advise you to make no further defense but mere matter of law. I do not believe that a legal wrong can be done you in the behalf before any learned and intelligent judge.

Sincerely,
Benjamin F. Butler
United States Congress

AΩ

"Are you on a hunger strike?" William Howe asks. The dandy lawyer is dressed in a bright orange waistcoat and wears large jeweled rings. On his third marriage, Howe is just outside the circle of respectable society. Howe is known for his flamboyant courtroom theatrics. He once summed up an entire case in two hours on his knees in front of the jury. The defendant was acquitted. He is the favorite attorney of Butler, Train, and the whores. How the whores, Butler, and Train can all agree that this man is the best attorney in all of New York escapes me, but I suppose those are the only people in this town who see people for who they are. Train hired Howe for me since the state has seized my "ill-gotten gains." Butler was second in line to hire him, but Howe told him that his retainer was already paid.

"You look terrible," Howe continues, kindly, taking a seat next to me. He picks up my arm and holds it up, "Skin and bone, madam. Women should have some meat on them." Howe opens his bag and hands me an apple, "Skeletons cannot lead revolutions." I say nothing. Howe shakes his head and then pulls out a newspaper. "You received the letter from Butler?" he asks. I nod. Howe hands me the newspaper. "Butler paid for it to be reprinted in every major newspaper from here to Albany, determined to produce a favorable judge and jury for you." Howe laughs. "That conniving blowhard has his moments, he does." Howe laughs again. And still, I say nothing. "You know," Howe says, "that I have represented all sorts of vile creatures, men who rob orphans, women who stab their own children, men who beat and murder their wives in the most heinous of ways, and yet none of them have produced the amount of newsprint that you have. Nor have any of them produced the split in the public as you have. The papers have referred to you as the renegade queen, a saint, Joan of Arc, a whore, Mrs. Satan, and a scorpion from hell, sometimes all in the same paragraph. The people, they either love you or hate you. You elicit no moderate sentiment; it's either canonization or damnation."

I give a slight nod, not knowing what to say. How am I to explain why the truth ties men's souls in knots? Loud noises in the cell across from mine catch our attention. Maggie left a few days ago, and the cell is being worked on. It looks like they are trying to make it dry. A bed with a real mattress is being moved in. A bowl of fresh fruit is set out on the concrete bench. I stand up and yell through the prison bars to the matron, "Who's coming?"

"A lady," she says, "a real lady. Here soon."

William Howe shakes his head in disbelief, "I am on my third marriage, and you have had one and half marriages and yet they treat you five times as worse than anyone else... of course, I did not take on the Protestant God. And now you have Comstock after you... the little self-righteous prick. But we followed him, we did. He bought twenty copies of your paper and mailed them out himself so the state could charge you with sending obscenity through the mail. The wily little bastard. Puritans like that will ruin this country."

I grab Howe's hand and squeeze it so hard that his giant ruby makes an impression on my palm. "Can you prove this?" I ask, seeing hope in my case for the first time.

"If I have to," Howe says, "but I know men like Comstock. Once they swear an oath to God in morning's light, then they tell the truth despite all the evil they had done the night before."

"What about Train?" I ask, "He was going to reprint Bible verses…"

"Reprint he did, in jail he is, across the courtyard," Howe says, shaking his head. "All sorts of people have offered to bail him out and yet he refuses, he wants to set legal precedent by forcing this to a trial."

"You will get him out," I say, half asking.

"I will, but I do not know at what price. The Copperhead has more powerful enemies than you do. They are more silent than yours but more deadly. And he does not have any of the support among the elite that you do," Howe says.

Before I can respond, two male prison guards walk to my cell and I know by this rare occurrence that something is wrong.

"Mr. Howe," the first guard, clearly panicked and sweaty, says, "your client has escaped."

"Which one?" Howe asks. I hope it is Train. I can just imagine Train talking his way out of jail and marching towards paradise.

"Sharkey," the second guard says. I immediately recognize the name, for William Sharkey was one of Tweed's men who killed a man over a gambling debt.

"How did he escape?" Howe asks.

"In a woman's cloak and glasses," the first guard says, "a spinster outfit. One of our boys says it looked like something Mrs. Woodhull had on when she was arrested."

I freeze, forcing my body and expressions to be a statue so as to not give anything away. Damn Maggie. I did not know giving her a coat would make me an accessory to breaking out a convict.

"Gentleman," Howe says with exaggerated exasperation in his voice, "every woman has a spinster outfit, even the whores down at the Tenderloin. I know because I have represented all of them at one point or another, and the outfit they wear for their court appearance is just as you described."

"And the spectacles?" the second guard asks.

Howe turns to me, "Mrs. Woodhull, do you wear spectacles?"

I shake my head.

"See, gentlemen, Mrs. Woodhull does not wear spectacles, not only according to her testimony, but I can tell you that I have never seen her with spectacles on nor in all the newspaper accounts I have read do they mention spectacles," Howe says. "Besides, Mrs. Woodhull has been here for seventeen days now and has had no possibility of being in the men's Tombs. And Mrs. Woodhull would have no interest in helping a murderer. She is in jail, unjustly at that, for her creative flourish, not her dastardly deeds."

The two guards look at each other, nod to Howe, and leave. Howe then looks at me with some suspicion and holds up his hand, saying, "I do not want to know."

Howe knocks on the cell bars to signal to the Irish maiden that he is ready to leave. As he waits, he picks up the apple core, tosses it in his bag, looks at me and says, "Eat. Whatever they give you. Eat. Even if it is monkey dung. Eat."

ΑΩ

Why am I here? In this tomb swamp? What role did variation or chance play? Or is it fate? Or is this completely my own doing? Is this the consequence of one misstep after another in the futile search for a new world?

"Blood of my blood," Napoleon says. "Do not ask why for only God knows. Just survive."

I lie on the bench, and close my eyes, and try to turn myself into a bird. If the Ohio Indians can do it, surely I can.

"Mama," Zulu says. I open my eyes to see Mabel standing with Zulu. I jump up and grab her hands through the cell while we wait for the guard to come with the keys.

"Mama?" Zulu says again before bursting into tears. Perhaps James was right, I think, perhaps Zulu should not see me this way. Not once in all of my jail time self-indulgent thinking did I think about how I must look, but now when I see myself through my daughter's eyes, I know I must look like a shell of who I am.

The door opens and I hold my precious daughter in my arms, I tremble with the joy and greatness of the moment. Mabel remains outside the cell to give us privacy but gives me a sincere smile before turning her back on us. I move to the bench and motion for Zulu to join me. I place my arm around her, kiss her on the head, and stroke her hair.

"How is your brother?" I ask.

"He misses you," Zulu says. "He paces nervously and cries all the time."

I nod, my soul sinking thinking about Byron suffering even more because of me.

"Why do you have to do this, Mama?" Zulu asks.

I kiss her on the forehead again, "I do not want any man or government to prevent you from living your life as you see fit. If you want to own property, if you want to be a lawyer, if you want to marry a man from a different country or race, if you want to be President, then you have that right. God gave you that right and no government can take that away. You see me in chains and filth now, but I am striking a fatal blow to tyranny."

"But Auntie Tennie did the same things and she is not in jail," Zulu asks.

"I asked Tennie to take care of you, James, and our business interests," I say.

"But I need you," Zulu says. "You are my mother."

"Yes, but I am also a symbol. And as a symbol for reform I must live through the consequences of this fight. This is the only way I know to move hearts and minds," I say, not sure I believe my own bravado.

"I fail to understand, Mama," Zulu says.

"And I am here so you never have to," I say, kissing Zulu on the cheek, holding her tight. Zulu then tells me all about how James was able to find a school that would take her, but that she has to go by a different name. At school she calls herself Emily Blood. They must travel quite a distance to school daily.

"Do you like your teacher?" I ask.

"Miss Helen is nice," Zulu says. "Although we argued. She was for Grant. And when I disagree, she tells me I will lose friends if I do not agree. She says a woman can be right or can be happy, but she cannot be both."

"Zulu!" I say, jumping up so quickly that I almost hit my head. "You have every right to express yourself just as any man. You do not hear men talking such nonsense. This is the kind of chatter that forms an invisible prison around our souls. You can be right and happy. And you will. I will see to it. Do you think anyone ever told Grant to remain quiet, that he could be right or happy, but not both. No, I do not suspect so."

Zulu nods and I sense that the strength of my emotion made her uneasy. I pull her to me and I hold her. After minutes in silence between us, Mabel motions that it is time for them to go. I kiss Zulu again and thank her for being a brave girl. We both cry and kiss again.

The guard opens the door and before Zulu leaves, she turns around, "Miss Anthony is a wanted woman too, Mama."

"What?" I ask. "Why?"

"Folks say she voted."

ΑΩ

Dearest Susan:

There is no time, now, to indulge in personal enmity. I have none toward anybody. I hear they intend to crush out, in your person, the Constitutional Question of Woman's right to suffrage, as they are attempting, in my person,

*to establish a precedent for the suppression of my
newspaper. As for me, I have a pretty large fight of
my own on hand, but, if you can, make use of me.*

Respectfully,
Victoria

ΑΩ

I am back in Washington, delivering my Memorial to
Congress. I am convinced that if I just add extra emotion, make
my voice sing-song like a sermon, then these men will listen to
reason. I begin reciting it, over and over, stopping to correct
myself or change intonation or change emphasis. I was born in
Ohio. I live in New York. I am a *citizen. I* am a citizen. I *am*
a citizen. I am *a* citizen. *I am a citizen. I am a citizen. I am a
citizen. I am a citizen. I am a citizen. I am a citizen. I am a citizen.*

"Shut up, missy!" the jail matron says. "You've been saying
that nonsense for seven hours, you have."

I get up off the floor, my entire dress drenched in water,
and take a seat on the concrete bench, still whispering "I am a
citizen." I run my fingers over the charcoal sentence on my wall,
"Rise like lions after slumber," smearing it. I worry for Train. The
men's side is worse: murderers, rapists, pedophiles. But he has
suffered in prisons around the world, surely this is a nice one by
comparison. I can't imagine the prison in Ireland even had a roof
as poor as those people are.

A door opens. Gasps. Applause. Maggie's cell, now dry and
newly furnished is open. And Moses walks in.

This sight of Moses is a new beginning for us. A new step
in the movement. I jump up, feeling the energy of a thousand
saints enter my soul, "How does it feel for the queen of half-
measures to boldly break the law?"

Susan looks up at me and a wave of shock mixed with pity
dances across her face, but her words betray nothing, merely
stating, "Glorious."

Euphoria overcomes me and I jump up and clap my hands together, "Hot damn, Moses!" I say. "Now that you are no longer a chaste virgin, we can join together and bring about a new world order. Think of how powerful we will be when united."

"I voted for Grant," Susan says.

"For Grant?" I question. Seeing a nod, I yell, "For Grant! If anything shows the inability of women to vote intelligently it is you. The Republican Party has done nothing worthy of the support of Women Suffragists. It advocates war, military despotism, and the perpetual spoilization of labor."

"Grant's wife is sympathetic to our cause," Susan says before whispering, "and I have it on her most sincere authority that she can work miracles in the bedroom."

I laugh, "So Grant's wife performing bedroom tricks in the name of suffrage is perfectly desirable and proper, but my sister flirting with the legislators is low and cunning? Your Quaker logic is folly. Grant is old and not amenable to change. You know this, and still you vote for him on some silly notion that a night in the bedroom will turn back hundreds of years of repression. You rebel, breaking the law to vote for the status quo. Congratulations."

"Seeing as how you are the first presidential candidate in history to spend election day in jail, I would say that I made a wise decision. Besides," Moses says, "poll workers were spitting on your votes, ripping them up, burning them, and throwing them in the latrine and laughing every moment. You could never win."

"Do you take me for a fool?" I ask. "Jesus Christ himself would not beat Grant. And a woman and a freed slave on a ticket had zero chance of beating anyone. Do you think I do not know this? It's not about winning, it's about fighting! It's about symbols! It's about unity! Unity! Unity!"

"Unity? Unity?" Susan asks. "How dare you speak to me about unity."

"In your heart, you know our aims are one," I say.

"Women must show that we are reasonable and can work within the current political structure, Mrs. Woodhull, and while I can assign many adjectives to you, reasonable is not one of them. If you were influenced by women spirits, either in the body or out of it, I might consent to be merely your sail hoister; but as it is you are owned and dominated by men spirits, and I spurn all of them." Susan says.

"I understand Train is the only man you have ever aligned yourself with. Of all the men you could choose, you pick a hated Copperhead. How well did your approach work, Aunt Susan? How many years have you labored for nothing?"

"Nothing? Because of me, our sisters in Wyoming and Utah have the vote. We must go state by state," Susan says.

"So you won the right for all four women who are married to the same man to vote in Utah. Quite an accomplishment. Maybe when they add two more women to their orgy, they can vote too. And state by state? Convince thirty-seven ever-changing groups of idiots to give us what is rightfully ours instead of one group of idiots," I say.

"I will not be lectured to by you. I have travelled thousands of miles, expended all of my money, endured every unkind word and unflattering description to fight the prolonged slavery of women. I know this cause, I live this cause, I breathe this cause. And I know how we will win. We will not win by epithets of free love, negro love, nor communism.   And we will not win quickly or hastily for then we would have won already. You demand too much too soon," Susan says.

"Moses is reasonable and Victoria is radical. And yet, we find ourselves in the same place. Jail."

"Quite right, Mrs. Woodhull, but I have a mattress," Susan says.

"Get comfortable," I say, pointing to the hash marks on my jail cell that show how long I have been here.

"They will listen to reason, I shall not be here long."

"Susan!" I say, more sternly than I had intended to. "Slavery, war, assassinations, denials of liberty, executions, and you still do not understand? Our government is not based on reason."

"Perhaps our government is based on fear, just like all of our actions. Do you know," Susan asks, "that Anna will no longer speak to me? Your threats of blackmail scared her off."

"You can do better," I say, "than a whore who betrayed your cause."

"Never speak to me of her. You are not fit to. Of all the great affections in my life, Anna was the dearest. Twenty-five years we have been friends," Susan says.

"Calm down, Susan," I say. "She will be back. Besides, the world is large and full of precious dickeys. You will find another."

"And where did my coat go?" Susan asks.

"What?" I ask, unsettled by the sudden change in discourse.

"I heard you dressed like me to elude the police," Susan says. " And I know you were in my house. And I'm missing a coat. Where is my coat?"

"You are delusional," I say, "no one could ever confuse the two of us, even in the same cloak."

"What about my spectacles?" Susan asks, "I only have two pair."

"I tried them on," I admit, "and I still did not see the world as you do."

The jail warden opens the cell and brings Susan a beautiful dish of meat and fresh vegetables and fruits. She immediately starts eating her baked apples. I'm handed the same unrecognizable smelly slop that I have refused to eat. I use my fork and hold my nose.

"What are you eating?" Susan asks.

"Monkey dung."

AΩ

Susan's trial is the next day, the bleeding hearts among the powers that be could not stomach the thought of so fine a lady spending another night in the Egyptian bastard. A day later, the rabbi brings me the *Sun*.

> *New York Sun:*
> *Miss Anthony was ordered to pay the sum of one-hundred dollars for violating the law in trying to cast a vote. Her response was: "I will not. I protest this high-handed outrage upon my citizen's rights... you have trampled under every foot every vital principle of government. My natural rights, my civil rights, my political rights, my judicial rights are ignored."*
> *The judge asked her to pay the fine a second time. Miss Anthony refused and asked to be imprisoned so that she may appeal. The judge told her that jail is no place for a fine lady and refused to remand her to prison.*

AΩ

My father is holding me down, his stained hands and dirty fingernails gripping me with a strength that I cannot match. His hands roughly fumble beneath my clothes as he squeezes my breasts. His drunken breath is in my mouth as he is stripping me, whispering, "You are the one I want." I fight back. I hit his head with mine. I scream "Save me, Demosthenes! Save me, Napoleon!" I'm running and my father is chasing me. I grab a knife that is hidden in the roots of a tree. I hide from my father. He runs towards me. I trip him, then I turn him over to face me and I jump on top of him. I take the knife and I stab him with all the power that I can. Blood oozes out of his chest, out of his heart, out of his mouth. He is gasping. I stab him over and over again until there is nothing left but blood.

I wake up on the cold concrete in a pool of raw sewage that has overflown from the trench outside my door due to the heavy rains. I sit up, covered in stench. My head is bleeding. I must have fallen off my concrete bed. I reach underneath my dress and tear a piece of my dress off to mop the blood off my head. I shiver and shake as I make my way back onto my bed of concrete in the dark. I use my dirty clothes as a blanket.

Napoleon is right. It isn't the exile that kills, it's the dampness.

AΩ

I'm lying on the floor, nearing the end of a multiple hour conversation with Napoleon, when the jail maiden opens the cage for James. I sense him before I see him, and I continue staring at the wall instead of him, for I can no longer face him. He walks in the jail and sets some fresh clothes on the bench. He gets on his knees and looks over me.

"Victoria," James says with a gasp as he bends in front of me and picks me up, sitting me upright. He picks up the bloodied cloth on the floor, "You have been bleeding." He holds my head up so he can get the most light to examine the wound on my forehead. I say a silent prayer of gratitude that he did not bring the children with him. I could not bear it.

"Who did this to you?" James asks in a demanding way.

"My father," I say.

James looks at me the same way he looks at beggars on the street who speak of salvation and damnation.

"They have broken you," James whispers before taking his place next to me and holding me. He rubs his hands through my hair and whispers promises that everything will be fine, everything will work out, we will be home soon.

"Napoleon will save me," I say. "He tells me I only need onions."

James holds me tighter and continues to whisper reassurances. He tells me that my trial date is set for tomorrow. After thirty-one days in the tombs, I will see a new room, a new building, new people. My supporters will be there. My detractors will be there.

"Howe has determined the best strategy for tomorrow is for you to remain silent," James says.

I whisper, trying to save my hoarse voice, "I will not sit idly by while some men try to rescue me from my own decisions. Decisions, by the way, which were true and just. I will expose the hypocrisy of the court, of the Constitution, of the tyrannical Christians, of..."

James jumps up, grabs me roughly by the shoulders, and whispers, "I will not hear it, Victoria! You will do as you're told. You will not steal time from your children. You will not steal time from me. And you will not continue to place yourself in harm's way for a posse of ingrates who have sold you down the river! For tomorrow, the only cause is you. The only cause is Victoria Woodhull and preserving your freedom. No revolution. No equality. Just you."

Taken aback by James's fury, I start shaking and crying. With the exception of our first meeting, I have never been afraid of James, but for the first time I see how this man could find the rage needed to kill.

"The revolution?" I whisper.

"It's over, Victoria. Over. Admit defeat. We were ahead of our time. If we were born fifty years later, then maybe we would have a chance, but we are at the wrong point in history," James says before kissing me on the forehead and whispering, "please accept this."

I nod to placate James, not accepting anything.

"You will stay silent tomorrow?" James says.

I nod.

"Say it," James says.

"On the graves of my dead sisters, I swear that I will not speak a word in court," I say.

James visibly relaxes and holds me in his arms.

Silence is my gift to you James, my gift to you.

33

JUDGMENT DAY

Three armed men pull me out of my cell before I have finished my morning monkey dung. I am wearing, or trying to wear, the clean dress that James brought me. But being a man, he forgot each of the five layers of underthings I need to make the dress fit to form. No drawers, no chemise, no corset, no corset cover, and no bustle. The lack of support combined with my immense weight loss leaves the dress hanging on me as if I am Zulu dressing up in my clothing. I console myself with the thought that my orphan look might garner sympathy.

The men walk me over the bridge of sighs, the enclosed overhead hallway that leaves from the Tombs to the court. I look to my left and I can see the gallows. The executioners are readying the noose. No doubt my enemies hope it is for the great Mrs. Satan.

The men, holding me in such a way that I can feel the bruises spring to my skin, finally shove me in the courtroom and my world becomes a circle. Reporters circle like sharks sniffing blood. They have discussions in front of me, wondering whether this thing in front of them could really be Victoria Woodhull. She looks so different. So frail. What did they do to her in jail? Was she on a hunger strike? Did they starve her? Did they beat her? Did the male guards have their way with her? Is Train in love with her? Where is Butler? Are Train and Butler free lovers too? As a consensus is not reached, the sharks then turn to me and ask these questions. I stay silent, for James. Only nodding at their first question, am I Victoria Woodhull. I will not deny who I am.

The reporters part and I can see more of the courtroom. It is another standing room only venue for Victoria Woodhull. As the reporters leave and more people can see me, there are audible gasps and cries. I dare say even my enemies are shocked at the implications of my appearance. My supporters start chanting, "Victoria! Victoria!" and my enemies stay silent.

William Howe is at the bench, already working the judge, swapping tall tales. Dressed in a white suit with a peach vest, he wears a large wooden cross around his neck. The suit must be custom made, for I cannot imagine a store in New York selling such colorful threads. I get close enough to Howe that I can hear him telling the judge, "So I said 'what shall we do for fun sweetheart, pretend that I'm big and you're tight?'"

The raucous laughter of the two men stops when I pull on Howe's jacket sleeve. He turns to me, obviously not knowing I am there. He nods to the judge and walks me over to the table in the courtroom, and he holds out a chair for me.

"James and Tennessee will be here momentarily," Howe says.

I nod.

"You do understand, Mrs. Woodhull, that you will not whisper, speak, yell, whistle, moan, sigh, testify, make any speeches, have any outbursts?" Howe asks.

I nod.

"And you only answer the judge's questions if I indicate you should and you give only the answer and nothing more?" Howe asks.

I nod.

"And no talking to reporters, regardless of how many scandalous implications they make?" Howe asks.

I nod.

"Mrs. Woodhull," Howe says with a broad grin. "Silence looks good on you. In fact, if I thought you could stay that way then I'd make you my fourth wife."

A commotion breaks out among the reporters and I do not even need to turn around to know it's Tennessee.

"Tennessee!" the reporter from the *Sun* yells. "This has been called the trial of the century."

"Well, darling," Tennessee says. "If something is worth doing, it is worth doing well."

"Miss Claflin!" the reporter from the *Herald* yells. "Why were you not in jail?"

"A mysterious benefactor paid my bail, and I tell you truthfully now it was more than murderers and more than Boss Tweed had to pay for stealing New York City!" Tennessee says.

"But your sister…" the reporter says.

"My sister," Tennessee says, "prefers martyrdom. As for me, I do not want the nails in my hands. I have beautiful, smooth hands. Want to feel?"

Tennessee continues to make her way down the aisle towards me, but I do not turn around. I can only hear her movements between the clatter of her shoes and rustling of her bustle. She finally walks in front of me, looks down and sharply inhales. I look up and manage a small smile.

"Miss Tennie C," a reporter yells over my head. "It is reported that you have slept with a negro, uttered blasphemy, and smoked bad cigars."

"That's ridiculous," Tennessee says. "Everyone knows cigars are sinful."

ΑΩ

James sits behind us, for there is not enough room at the defendant's table for all of us. He reaches through the railing and I reach back and we hold hands, neither one of us letting go.

"Why did you not come see me?" I whisper to Tennessee. The judge has already asked me my name. My speaking part for the day is over. My one line.

Tennessee looks down and shakes her head and whispers, "I wake and I weep for you. I sleep and I weep for you. I simply could not bear it, sister."

Anthony Comstock is called to the stands. James tells me that this slight young man was the biggest pain in the ass in the entire Union army, for Comstock would routinely go around and give lectures on the social and spiritual ills of swearing. I'd say a man facing certain death is allowed a few goddamns. Even more horrifying for Mr. Comstock was the literature in the Union camps that instructed men on how to masturbate. Not only were there instructions, but also drawings of naked women. Now while I find it odd and perhaps alarming that a man does not know his own penis well enough that he needs written instructions on how to touch it, I'd say that a man facing certain death is allowed a few orgasms.

But Comstock believes any sexual activity, whether alone or with ten whores leads to disease, death, and hell. He has even tried burning anatomy textbooks at the local college.

"Do I smell onions?" I lean over and ask Howe as Comstock is getting sworn in.

"It's my handkerchief," Howe says. "It contains the juice of a dozen raw onions in case I need to get on my knees and cry for you, my dear."

I nod. So that is what Napoleon meant about onions saving me.

Howe jumps up and approaches Comstock like a cat approaching a mouse.

"Please state your name for the record," William Howe says.

"It is Anthony Comstock, not Anthony J. Comstock, as the court and the newspapers indicate. I move to record that *J* is in no way part of my good name."

"And what is your profession, Mr. Comstock?"

"I am the Head of the New York Society for the Suppression of Vice," Mr. Comstock says, as if this is some great achievement.

"And please elucidate the court on what that means."

"I am a weeder in God's garden. I fight smut dealers," Comstock says taking extra pleasure and care when saying "smut."

"And who is your employer, Mr. Comstock?"

"I work for Jesus Christ, our Lord and Savior, and the YMCA," Mr. Comstock again speaks as if he is some great, noble creature.

"And why are you here today?"

"I charge Victoria Woodhull, Tennessee Claflin, and James Blood with obscenity," Comstock stands and points to us. "These free lovers are smut dealers who wish us all to sink to the levels of the beasts."

I start to stand up, but James, still holding my hand, quickly squeezes it hard, so hard it hurts. I nod so James can tell that I understand and sit firmly in my chair. I feel ill. It is against every fiber of want in my body to stay silent faced with such charges.

"What words did the accused use that you find objectionable?" Howe asks. I note that he is not reaching for his handkerchief yet, so things must still be going our way.

"If it please the court, I wish not to say it aloud out of concern for the youth," Comstock says, even though I do not see one face younger than twenty in the crowd.

"Your honor, if…" Howe shrugs and holds out his hands in an exaggerated gesture of helplessness.

"Mr. Comstock, I am afraid you must be explicit in your charge…" Judge Blatchford says before shaking his head, "as distasteful as it might be."

"A state of purity," Comstock says. "A state that I'm sure the defendants have never experienced."

Laughter breaks out in the courtroom with Tennessee laughing along. I turn red.

"Your honor," Howe implores.

"Mr. Comstock, answer the question with preciseness," the judge instructs.

"Virginity," Comstock says.

"Does not Shakespeare, the Bible, and Lord Byron use the same language?" Howe asks.

"Not in the same way, sir, no," Comstock says. "This use was intended to arouse lewd thoughts. The devil is using the newspaper to sow seeds for future harvest."

"And how was this material presented?" Howe asks.

"In the *Woodhull and Claflin* weekly newspaper," Comstock says before standing up and loudly stating, "a mouthpiece for free lovers, sinners, and anarchists."

"And you seek to prosecute under the 1872 Comstock Act?" Howe asks.

"That is correct."

"The Act regulates obscenity distributed through the mail," Howe says.

"That is correct," Comstock confirms.

"What proof, sir, do you have of any newspapers being sent through the mail?"

I hold my breath, knowing that Comstock himself sent the paper through the mail. Will he try to produce proof and say that it was we who placed the news in the post? Or will he, as Howe predicts, tell the truth being bound by oath to God.

Comstock says nothing, but looks down on the floor and shakes his head in defeat.

"Judge Blatchford," Howe says. "As the defendants were charged based on the misconstruction of federal code, I move the case be dismissed."

I hold my breath, James squeezes my hand.

The judge looks straight ahead and nods, "I am entirely satisfied that the prosecution cannot be maintained and the government can provide no evidence to support an indictment."

The courtroom erupts in wild applause with a smattering of jeers. Tennessee jumps up and claps, yelling "Woo hoo." James rushes over to thank Howe.

I hang my head and cry. No onions needed.

AΩ

James holds my hand as we lead a parade out of the courtroom and into a crowd of supporters and naysayers. Reporters, nearly crushed by my supporters, fight their way to me. Question after question is thrown my way and I stay silent. Finally, I ask James if I may say something before we get in the carriage. James nods and gives me a kiss on the cheek. Climbing up the carriage, I stand next to Thomas, the driver, and say, clearly and distinctly: "This case was not about Beecher or Tilton or the words I chose. This case was about the crucifixion of a prophet who shares the new gospel of equality and freedom. They may succeed in crushing me out, even to the loss of my life, but let me warn them and you that from the ashes of my body a thousand Victorias will spring to avenge my death by seizing the work laid down and carrying it forward to victory."

"Victoria! Victoria!" shout my people as I climb down.

"For shame, for shame," shout my detractors as I get in the carriage.

We drive off to shouts. Victoria! For shame. Victoria!

34

RESURRECTION

The moment I hold my two children again is a spiritual experience, a true rebirth. For these seconds it matters not that I have lost time, lost my money, lost my business, lost my home, and been reduced to relying on the kindness of negro servants. All that matters is that I have Zulu and Byron and they have me.

Mabel gives me a warm smile when she sees the look of peace on my face. James is close by. Tennessee is doing her best to flirt with Thomas, who has already had experience giving into her temptations.

"Thank you, Mabel," I say, knowing this woman has given me more than I can ever repay. Mabel nods and points to the blankets on the floor. I must look exhausted.

"I'm sorry…" Mabel starts, "for what you have been through."

I kiss Zulu and Byron on their heads and give them one more squeeze before letting go.

"Were there no prejudices to be overcome, the man or woman who dares fight for a truth might win an easy victory," I say before everything goes black. I try to stay on my feet but weakness overcomes me and I hear screams right before I hit the floor.

AΩ

"Do not speak. Do not move. Your life depends on you remaining quiet," a doctor whispers in my ear. I am vaguely aware of blood oozing from my mouth. Someone, perhaps James, wipes it up. In and out of consciousness, I smell the mustard plasters the doctor is applying to my thin, naked body, I feel the sheets around my feet, and I hear the bargaining that James is making with God. I go back to sleep.

I wake up and hear that "she" will be dead by morning. I hear Tennessee's sobs and oaths of love, and I hear James promising someone that he will not let me die, even if it means we live as hermits the rest of our lives.

Live like a hermit? There is no way in hell I'm living like a hermit. I open my eyes to protest and this one act causes all kinds of activity around me. James holds my head up and pours my own miracle elixir down my throat. A warm and tingly sensation floods my body from my head to my toes.

"No deal," I say.

James leans down and says, "What love? What is it, my darling?"

"Never a hermit," I say, pausing only to indicate that I need more elixir, which James quickly provides. "If you want to bargain with God," I say, "trade your life, not mine."

James smiles and gives me a little laugh. Tennessee grabs three shot glasses and fills them.

"To my sister," Tennessee says. "May she never be a hermit."

We all drink.

ΑΩ

"Victoria Woodhull Dies" is the headline in all the newspapers. I grab a robe, grab the *New York Sun*, and walk out of the house to where the reporters have gathered like flies on horse shit. I open the door to great gasps by reporters who start saying, "She's alive."

Reading from the *Sun*, I say, "The world is rid of one of the most remarkable, albeit terrible and dangerous women who ever lived."

I throw the newspaper down and yell, "Wrong."

AΩ

"Dangerous!" I say to my family, slamming the door, still fuming over my premature obituary. Is this how the world will remember me? Dangerous? "Inequality is dangerous. We must redouble our efforts."

James is next to me in an instant, placing his arms around me, "We almost lost you, love. You must rest. Leave the revolution to others, you have done your part."

"Quit?" I ask.

"Respectable people do it every day," James says. "Let someone else fight these battles. Tennessee can give speeches and…"

I squirm out of James's tight embrace. "Have you gone mad?" I ask. "They took our firm, destroyed printing presses, left us with insurmountable legal bills, and you want me to walk away?"

"Times occur when admitting defeat is more courageous than fighting," James says. Scrutinizing his handsome face, I can see that James is weary, sick, and worried about me. I end up in an embrace with him again and kiss him on the cheek.

"Do not fret for me, love," I say. "I can do anything as long as you are by my side." James kisses me on the forehead and looks into my eyes with some sort of odd expression that I had never seen before from him. Resignation.

AΩ

I will never be able to say what woke me up, but wake up I did. I sit up and count heads. Zulu, Byron, Tennessee, Mabel, Thomas… no James. I touch my right hand with my left hand and feel the moisture of a goodbye kiss. I jump out and run out of the house, in my nightgown, in the dark.

James is only seven paces ahead of me and I run to catch up. I wait until I am right behind him and ask, "You're leaving?"

James turns around, looking defeated but determined. He holds his hat and runs his fingers across the brim, looking down at it, unable to meet my gaze.

"At my most desperate hour?" I ask.

"Forgive me," James whispers.

"I can forgive my father," I spit out. "I can forgive Canning. I can forgive every enemy, but I cannot forgive you. I expect betrayal from everyone except you. Not you. Never you."

James finally meets my gaze and gives me a kind smile, "I cannot debate you, my love. We both know you are the winning orator. You have moved men's hearts at every turn…"

Crying, I take a step toward James and reach out, he takes a step backwards. "And I cannot move you to love me?" I ask.

In an instant I am in James's loving arms and he is kissing me passionately, tenderly. In between kisses I whisper, "You do love me, you do."

"My love for you is so deep that it passeth all understanding," James says. "You will always be my alpha and omega."

I kiss James on the cheek and grab his hand, trying to pull him back to Mabel's. His feet stand planted, immovable.

"A wise woman once told me that loving and living with are two different propositions," James says.

"Have you found someone else?" I ask.

"One minute with you is worth a lifetime in the embrace of another," James says.

"Why, James, why?" I sob. Am I not woman enough? Am I not pretty enough? Do I shine too bright? Am I too much? I want to ask but all I can get out between heaving sobs is "why?"

James holds me, makes soothing cooing noises and kisses my hair. "We are still under the same moon, the same sun, the same stars…"

"It is not enough" I say, taking deep breaths, trying to convince my body not to collapse.

"Look for my face in the crowd," James says. "I will be there."

"I cannot go on," I say. "I simply cannot go on without you. Nothing makes sense anymore…"

"Fear not," James says, "You will find a way, you always do. And we will find a way. We will find each other again in this life or the next."

I place my hand on my heart and whisper, "Our chain is unbroken." And James turns around and walks away. I wait until he is but a speck in the distance and I collapse on the ground, sobbing hysterically. I stay there for hours until Tennessee finds me and brings me back in.

35

REVELATION

Tennessee pours me a shot. I've sat unmoved at the window for three days, watching for any hopeful sign of James's return. Every white man who walks by brings me a large dose of hope followed by bitter disappointment when I realize the man is not my James.

"No account dastardly son-of-a-bitch," Tennessee says.

A knock at the door. Footsteps.

"I've been to every house of ill repute, every alley, every home of every known acquaintance looking for you two," Benjamin Butler says as he strides in and acts like he owns this home.

I continue to stare at the window, saying nothing. Butler gets on his knees and flashes his hand before my eyes.

"Are you ill?" Butler asks.

I say nothing.

"Disease or fatigue?" Butler asks.

"James... gone" I whisper, struggling for words "... abandoned."

Butler softly and gently pulls my chair back from the window and he gets on his knees in front of me, "Forgive my plain talk. It is of urgent necessity. You do not have the luxury to be low-spirited or doubtful or desponding."

I manage the energy to look Butler in the eyes. I even give him a bit of a smile. It is good to see an old friend.

"I devoted last night to your enemies, bungling in their malice as they are," Butler says.

"What have I done this time?" I ask, the first words I've spoken above a whisper since James left.

"Libel," Butler says as he gets off his knees and stands up. "The good minister will deny all that we know to be true."

I look at Tennessee. Tennessee mouths "fucker."

"I was in a state of despair, thinking of you in court again," Butler says. "But the morning brought rays of hope. Indeed, divine providence."

"Beecher killed himself?" Tennessee asks with inappropriate glee in her voice.

"No, no," Butler says. "Commodore Vanderbilt died."

Tennessee gasps and she starts crying. "How?" Tennessee asks between sobs. Butler shakes his head and hands her his monogrammed handkerchief. I stand up, putting my arm around Tennessee.

"I do not know, nor do I care," Butler says. "We have no time to dwell in sympathy for a man who was given riches beyond measure."

"William?" I ask, wondering how his son is doing.

"Set to inherit everything," Butler says. "Not allowing time for their father's body to grow cold, the siblings have announced they will contest the will."

"On what grounds?" I ask with some incredulousness in my voice.

"You." Butler says.

"Me?"

"Only a man of unsound mind would support you."

I shake my head, not believing what I am hearing.

"I predict William will bring pressure upon you not to testify," Butler says. "Indeed, he will likely offer you passage out of the country with a sizeable allowance."

"What should we do?" Tennessee asks.

"Take it," Butler says firmly.

"And leave?" Tennessee asks. "Leave the fight?"

"Victoria," Butler says, "may you and I speak in private?"

I nod. Tennessee walks outside.

"Victoria," Butler says, "life with people like you and me cannot roll on like a long, calm, quiet summer's day. We face the storms, the melancholy of autumn, and we fight for the bright promises of spring. In all my military movements, I never met with disaster, but I did retreat. You, my dear, you must retreat."

I stand directly before Butler. "I have sacrificed too much to leave now. Not until we have won."

"Who will take care of Zulu and Byron when you are in jail? Who will pay your bills?" Butler asks, pacing the floor. "You are penniless. My pockets are only so deep, love. Vanderbilt is gone. Train is in the Tombs, likely declared to be a lunatic. And the communists have turned their backs on you, and even if they hadn't—communists are a poor lot, aren't they?"

"I will find a way," I say. "I always do."

"Your enemies will not hound only you my dear. They will come after James."

"James?" I ask.

"Yes, as editor and part owner of the press, he will be legally liable… but if you two leave they have no witnesses against James."

"James could run… start anew."

"He could," Butler says. "Would he, or would he stay behind for you? Can you imagine him in the Tombs for weeks, months, years?"

The thought of James in the Tombs, paying the price for my impulsive actions, reduces me to tears. Butler looks for his handkerchief to give me and then realizes that Tennessee is still clutching to it outside, drying her eyes over Vanderbilt. Without his handkerchief, Butler instead tries to comfort me with a clumsy embrace.

"I will go," I whisper in Butler's ear, "For James. For James."

"You must know of my reverence for you," Butler says, before releasing me and grabbing my hand. "I will not let you drop the flag. I will pick it up and carry it with me into my great political battle. Once I win the governor's race, I will advance female emancipation. This is my solemn vow."

I drop Butler's hand, "Any association with me will harm your campaign."

Benjamin gives me a nod.

"I will go," I say, finding my loud voice. "Deny me at will. Call me a humbug, a liar, a whore. Just win. "

Butler nods, "When you speak to William, demand refuge in England."

"England? Women are allowed even fewer accommodations…"

"You speak the language," Butler says, "you will change minds."

Butler starts walking towards the door, "In due time, you may be able to return. If my journey from Beast to candidate for Governor is any indication…"

"Yes," I say, "but you are a man. Men are forgiven all sorts of sins."

Butler opens the door, "Requesting your leave is a sin I may never forgive of myself."

Benjamin Butler gives me a bow and leaves.

AΩ

"I have hundreds of beautiful letters from him expressing his hopes for my candidacy," I tell William Vanderbilt, who is physically and mentally struggling sitting in the cramped kitchen of a negro house. Tennessee is next to me. An enormous nude Venus is staring at us. Mabel and Thomas are spying on us from the kitchen doorway, their mouths open.

"You have letters?" William asks.

"How kind for him to will me my favorite portrait," Tennessee says. "Your father was virile for his age. Night, after night, well…"

Tennessee pours William more tea, "… he fucked me like a stallion. I'd be happy to testify."

William chokes on his tea, coughing.

"Sugar?" Tennessee asks.

AΩ

Tennessee, my children, myself, and a small army of Vanderbilt servants walk towards the *Oceanic*, the finest of the passenger ships. I'll hand it to the Vanderbilts, when it comes to getting rid of dangerous women, they spare no expense. We even have six staterooms to ourselves, but I doubt that six staterooms is enough space to hold my grief for the loss of my man, the loss of my country.

As we get closer, I feel a hand on the excess fabric of my new stiff, white, fashionable dress pulling me back. I turn around and I am face to face with James. Although it has merely been months, James is a bit thinner, and a bit older than when we departed, but no less handsome. My heart leaps at the sight that I have longed to see every moment of every day since we said goodbye.

"Hello," I say, not knowing what to say despite practicing multiple versions of heartfelt soliloquies days in and days out. I look over my shoulder and see Tennessee nod. She takes the children and the servants towards the ship while I stay behind.

"I know not... I mean... I find myself unsure..." I begin clumsily.

"I read of your departure in the papers," James says, giving me a small smile. "I had to say goodbye."

"Goodbye?" I ask. James gives me a small nod, and I sigh, looking at my feet to catch my breath. He will not fight for us.

"Do something for me when you get to England," James says.

"Anything," I say.

"Be happy."

"If you are not by my side, I cannot," I say.

James takes two steps forward and tucks my stray hair behind my ear. "My alpha and omega," James says as he takes me in his arms and gives me a long kiss full of yearning and promises. He releases me and I stumble backwards a step before James catches me in his arms.

"Last call," the boat conductor yells, "all aboard."

Now that I am steady on my feet, James lets go. The boat whistle blows, signaling it is time to pull away from the dock.

He looks down and whispers, "You must go."

"I cannot believe," I say, my eyes welling up with tears, "that this is the last time I will see you."

"One day you will look up," James says, reaching out to wipe a tear from my cheek, "and you will see my face among the crowd."

I turn around and slowly walk up the ramp to the boat and join my family on the observation deck. I look down and catch one more glimpse of James. He has his hand on his heart. I instantly place my hand on my heart. The departing whistle blows and I turn around and face England, my cheeks wet with tears.

AΩ

"Victoria," Tennessee says in a mock British accent while pausing her brisk steps to brush lint off her fetching gray dress, "if you truly care about future generations, then you would teach these women how to cook and these men how to fuck."

"Tennessee," I say, embarrassed by her loud public vulgarity, "we discussed at length that in England you must at least pretend you are a lady." Tennessee rolls her eyes and gives me a naughty smile as we continue on our journey to St. James Hall. I've been here for weeks and I still find myself looking up as I am walking, trying to take into my mind every detail of the majestic London buildings.

"Last evening I dined with Richard," Tennessee says, "and his mother made toad-in-the hole. This particular recipe specifies that one must find three rotten, smelly sausages, undercook them, and then stuff them into mealy, bland, dense putrid batter. I tell you now I never missed Dan Tucker's onion soup as acutely as I did when I put the toad's head into my mouth. Despite this insult to food everywhere, I was on my best behavior. I really was, that is until old Lady Wragg told me that I am in danger of becoming an ape leader."

"A what?" I ask, while carefully trying to navigate my steps over the side of several large piles of horse manure.

"An ape leader," Tennessee repeats. These Brits think that a woman who ignores the Biblical imperative of being fruitful and multiplying goes straight to Hell, and is then forced by Satan to be the leader of the apes."

Stunned, I stop in the middle of our street crossing and Tennessee has to pull me along so a carriage does not crash in to me. "Tennessee," I say, "that is the largest, foulest load of rubbish I have heard in all my years."

Tennessee prods me along, hand on my elbow, and whispers into my ear, "Don't worry, dear sister. I told Old Lady Wragg that I would rather lead the apes for eternity than spend one more night teaching her son how to poke his toad into my hole."

"Tennessee! You did not," I say.

Tennessee straightens up and stops whispering, "I have never had to repeat, 'that is not it' so many times. He even tried my navel."

"Did you really say that?" I ask again.

"My navel!" Tennessee repeats with exaggerated gravitas, as if a deadly sin has been committed. I try to stifle a laugh, but cannot. Tennessee smiles at my laughter and hands me my speech as we walk into the St. James Hall. Like me, this hall has mixed reviews. It hosted Charles Dickens right before he died and the hall has been stage to some amazing musical symphonies. But the proprietors of the hall allow constant performances of the Christy Minstrels (also known as the blackface minstrels) with their off-color jokes, vulgar melodies, and rhythmic drumbeats to be within earshot as symphonic performances, which turns off the lovers of Bach and every other proper Englishman. For this week, Bach has been moved to another night and my speech will be within earshot of the blackface performers.

"I made notes in the margins, you must emphasize the moral argument over the constitutional one," Tennessee says.

"Why?" I ask, engrossed in our regal surroundings.

"We are in the land of kings now, Victoria. Divine right and all that rubbish, no Constitution…"

"Yes, yes," I say, alarmed at my absent mindedness. "It is as if my body is here in London and my mind and soul are elsewhere."

Tennessee smiles, squeezes my shoulder, and kisses me on the cheek before taking her seat in the front row. I spend a few minutes behind the curtain, reading a modified version of the speech I have given many times. I then open the curtains myself and walk onto stage alone, for there is no one to introduce me. I take the stage and speak louder than I ever have before for brass instruments, drums, and the faint echoes of slapstick comedy are competing for my audience's attention.

These men, and the audience is only men, are not the riff-raff free thinkers I am accustomed too, but establishment, regal men all dressed in their finest suits. From the looks on their faces, more than half of them showed up expecting Bach. I look at all these polite, staid men and think how different this land is than the land of my alpha. My ancestors ran away from this country just so they would be free to speak in tongues, amens, and hallelujahs while writhing to the melodic pleas to Jesus. Carnal sins twisting and turning, mixing with the Lord's promise of eternity demonstrated in a public frenzy would never occur here. These passionless people have never had to remake their country into something new, for they are happy to remain unchanged, never moving. And yet, here I am, product of spirit and earth, speaking before the royal subjects asking them to accept me, not only accept me but to give me the rights they afford their men. And if they do, it will be the biggest change this country has ever seen. But how can they worship one Victoria with gold and diamonds and deny this Victoria the opportunity to earn bread? The eyes of the audience betray nothing, looking neither pleased nor perturbed at my pleadings. Most are statues with a few brave non-conformists pausing their pose to check the time on their pocket watches. "In closing," I say, "I plead for the intellectual emancipation and the redemption of womanhood from sexual slavery—social evils can only be eliminated by making your daughters the peers of your sons." The tepid applause begins, coinciding with echoes of laughter and trumpets from the other stage. I raise my gaze and search the thinning crowd for a familiar face, desperately seeking the one that I ache for. My alpha, my omega.

AΩ

Bibliography

Barnhart, Robert K. *The Barnhart Concise Dictionary of Etymology*. New York: HarperCollins Publishers, 1995.

Butler, Benjamin F. *Autobiography and Personal Reminiscences of Major-General Benjamin F. Butler: Butler's Book: A Review of His Legal, Political, and Military Career*. Vol. 1-5. Boston: A.M. Thayer & Co., 1892.

Butler, Benjamin F. *Correspondence of Gen. Benjamin F. Butler*. Big Byte Books, 2014.

Christian Union, New York, various issues 1870-1873.

Cincinnati Daily Press, various issues 1860-1862.

Cook, Tennessee Claflin. *Constitutional Equality a Right of Woman, or, A Consideration of the Various Relations Which She Sustains as a Necessary Part of the Body of Society and Humanity, with Her Duties to Herself Together with a Review of the Constitution of the United States*. New York: Woodhull, Claflin & Co., 1871.

Evening Star, Washington, D.C., various issues 1870-1873.

Foner, Eric. *Reconstruction: America's Unfinished Revolution, 1863-1877*. Updated ed. New York: Harper Perennial Modern Classics, 2014.

Gabriel, Mary. *Notorious Victoria: The Life of Victoria Woodhull, Uncensored*. Chapel Hill: Algonquin Books of Chapel Hill, 1998.

Gallman, J. Matthew. *America's Joan of Arc: The Life of Anna Elizabeth Dickinson*. New York: Oxford University Press, 2006.

Gentleman's Companion, New York, various issues 1867-1868.

Goldsmith, Barbara. *Other Powers: The Age of Suffrage, Spiritualism, and the Scandalous Victoria Woodhull.* New York: Harper Perennial, 1999.

Gordon, John Steele. *The Scarlet Woman of Wall Street: Jay Gould, Jim Fisk, Cornelius Vanderbilt, the Erie Railway Wars, and the Birth of Wall Street.* New York: Weidenfeld & Nicolson, 1988.

Griffith, Elisabeth. *In Her Own Right: The Life of Elizabeth Cady Stanton.* New York: Oxford University Press, 1984.

Harper, Ida Husted. *The Life and Work of Susan B. Anthony (Volume 1 of 2) - Including Public Addresses, Her Own Letters and Many From Her - Contemporaries During Fifty Years.* Vol. 1. Qontro Classic Books, 2010.

Harper's Weekly, New York, January 31, 1863 and November 25, 1871.

Humanitarian, New York, various issues 1892.

Kruse, Timothy. *The Yankee International Marxism and the American Reform Tradition, 1848-1876.* Chapel Hill: University of North Carolina Press, 1998.

Lutz, Alma. *Susan B. Anthony: Rebel, Crusader, Humanitarian.* CreateSpace Independent Publishing Platform, 2014.

MacPherson, Myra. *The Scarlet Sisters: Sex, Suffrage, and Scandal in the Gilded Age.* New York: Twelve, 2014.

New York Herald, various issues 1870-1873.

New York Tribune, various issues 1863-1873.

Nolan, Dick. *Benjamin Franklin Butler: The Damnedest Yankee.* Novato, CA: Presidio, 1991.

Ottawa Republican, various issues 1863-1864.

Revolution, New York, various issues 1868-1872.

Saavedra, Miguel De Cervantes. *Don Quixote*. New York: Penguin Books, 2003.

Sachs, Emanie N., and Carrie Chapman Catt. *"The Terrible Siren": Victoria Woodhull (1838-1927)*. New York: Harper & Brothers Publishers, 1928.

Seitz, Don C. *The Dreadful Decade (1869-1879); Detailing Some Places in the History of the United States from Reconstruction to Resumption*. Indianapolis: Bobbs-Merrill, 1926.

Shaplen, Robert. *Free Love and Heavenly Sinners: the Story of the Great Henry Ward Beecher Scandal*. New York: Knopf, 1954.

Shelley, Percy Bysshe. "The Mask of Anarchy." 1819. Accessed November 16, 2015. http://www.poetsgraves.co.uk/Classic Poems/Shelley/the_mask_of_anarchy.htm.

Sherr, Lynn, and Susan B. Anthony. *Failure Is Impossible: Susan B. Anthony in Her Own Words*. New York: Times Books, 1995.

Stanton, Elizabeth Cady. *History of Woman Suffrage, Volume I*. Project Gutenberg, 2009.

Stanton, Elizabeth Cady. *The Woman's Bible*. CreateSpace Independent Publishing Platform, 2010.

Stern, Madeleine Bettina. *The Pantarch: A Biography of Stephan Pearl Andrews*. Austin, TX: University of Texas Press, 1968.

Stiles, T.J. *The First Tycoon: The Epic Life of Cornelius Vanderbilt*. New York: Alfred A. Knopf, 2009.

Stowe, Harriet Beecher. *My Wife and I*. CreateSpace Independent Publishing Platform, 2015.

Stuart, Nancy Rubin. *The Reluctant Spiritualist: The Life of Maggie Fox*. Orlando, FL: Harcourt, 2005.

Tilton, Theodore. "Victoria C. Woodhull, A Biographical Sketch," *The Golden Age*, tract no. 3. New York: 1871.

Train, George Francis. *My Life in Many States and in Foreign Lands*. CreateSpace Independent Publishing Platform, 2015.

Train, George Francis, and John Wesley Nichols. *The Man of Destiny. Presidential Campaign, 1872. The Most Remarkable Book of Speeches in the World*. New York, 1872.

Trent, James W. *Inventing the Feeble Mind: A History of Mental Retardation in the United States*. Berkeley: University of California Press, 1994.

Underhill, Lois Beachy. *The Woman Who Ran for President: The Many Lives of Victoria Woodhull*. Bridgehampton, N.Y.: Bridge Works, 1995.

Weisberg, Barbara. *Talking to the Dead: Kate and Maggie Fox and the Rise of Spiritualism*. San Francisco: HarperOne, 2005.

Whitman, Walt. *Leaves of Grass: The Original 1855 Edition*. Mineola, NY: Dover Publications, 2007.

Woodhull & Claflin's Weekly, New York, various issues 1870-1873.

Woodhull, Victoria C. *The Origin, Tendencies and Principles of Government; or, A Review of the Rise and Fall of Nations from Early Historic Time to the Present: With Special Considerations Regarding the Future of the United States as the Representative Government of the World*. New York: Woodhull, Claflin & Co., 1871.

Woodhull, Victoria C., and Cari M. Carpenter. *Selected Writings of Victoria Woodhull: Suffrage, Free Love, and Eugenics.* Lincoln, NE: University of Nebraska Press, 2010.

AUTHOR'S NOTE

It can take years to recognize a visionary; it can take longer to appreciate the deep sacrifices made in a desperate desire to construct a new world.

Victoria, one of the most written-about women during her lifetime, had enemies who tore down her accomplishments with false accusations and innuendo and had friends who wrote her out of history altogether. For advocating "radical" positions including liberal divorce laws, the criminalization of marital rape, woman's political and economic equality, and the eight-hour workday, she lost nearly everything. Victoria spent her fortune on legal bills, saw her newspaper go out of business, had her property confiscated by the government, lost the love of her life, and was forced into exile, away from the country of her birth.

Victoria's life is open to interpretation, and I have taken the sympathetic view. After reading so many news articles from her time period and biographies whose sentiments range from neutral to judgmental, I wanted Victoria to finally have a voice of her own—a voice apart from what is left from her own writings and speeches. The desire to give Victoria her own voice is why I chose to write this novel in first person, from Victoria's view.

The way Susan B. Anthony is portrayed may shock some readers (it shocked my mother). In terms of her sexuality, we have letters that indicate she shared her bed with women, women she affectionately referred to as "my nieces." Her relationships with Anna Dickinson and with other women are well documented through Susan's letters and diaries. For example, in one letter, Susan wrote, "*I shall go to Chicago and visit my new lover—dear Mrs. Gross—en route to Kansas. So with new hope and new life.*" Susan never married and made several disparaging comments throughout her life about marriage, including, "*I think any female would rather live and die an old maid,*" and, "*I never felt I could give up my life of freedom to become a man's housekeeper.*"

When I was young, if a girl married poor, she became a pet and a doll. Just think, had I married at twenty, I would have been a drudge or a doll for fifty-five years. Think of it!"

Readers might also be shocked that Susan B. Anthony is not as angelic as history has painted her. It is important to keep in mind that this novel was written from Victoria's viewpoint, and she and Victoria were at odds, despite brief moments of an intense friendship. And Susan made mistakes that stemmed from both her resentment at her friends pushing for the enfranchisement of African-Americans at the expense of women, and her jealousy for the new generation of reformers. Susan's mistakes do not, in my opinion, diminish the sacrifices that she too made for future generations. They do, however, need to be considered when wondering why it took the United States so long to grant women the right to vote. The Nineteenth Amendment, the Anthony Amendment, which gave women the right to vote, was debated annually for forty years before it passed, mirroring the time Moses spent in the desert.

Susan had such animosity towards Victoria that when Susan was tasked with writing the 5,700-page tome *History of Woman Suffrage*, Victoria was not mentioned once. Despite being the first female stockbroker, the first woman to testify in front of Congress, and the first woman to run for President, Victoria is not in these pages. Anthony's glaring omission of Victoria explains why most of us did not learn of Victoria when growing up; the textbook authors rely on Anthony's version of events. As someone once wrote (we know not whether it was Machiavelli or Churchill), "History is written by the victors." Although in researching this time period, I fail to see who the victor clearly was in the late 1800s, I can see from the Susan B. Anthony coin on my desk that Anthony is the victor in terms of historical record.

While this is a work of *fiction*, many of the events are true. While Victoria and Tennessee did not leave diaries, we have letters, newspaper columns both by them and about them, speeches, interviews, and court documents to use to piece their story together. Having said this, Victoria and Tennessee were fast and loose with the truth, seeking to promote their cause by nearly any means necessary, and they were not above lying to see their mission through. For example, Tennessee did lie on occasion about studying law, even though we know not how this could have happened in that day and age. Other witnesses also disagree about how to interpret events. For example, everyone seems to be in agreement that Canning Woodhull was a morphine addict and alcoholic. Some witnesses claim that Victoria was so cruel to Canning that "she drove him to it." Victoria's often repeated claims that Canning spent all his money on drugs and whores have been questioned by others who were alive at the time, but Canning himself never came out and refuted Victoria's claims. This could be because the claims were true, or it could be because Canning and Victoria remained on friendly terms and Victoria's tales of woe, whether true or false, would serve her cause. Nearly all of Victoria's biographers believe Canning did spend his nights with prostitutes, so that is the view that I choose as well; although, we can never really know. I also do not know the true extent of Tennessee's promiscuity. In various biographies, her contemporaries have claimed the following: she was a prostitute at a young age, she suffered from a venereal disease that left her sterile, she gave Commodore Vanderbilt a venereal disease, she was heard telling Vanderbilt that she slept with five hundred men, she flirted with African-American men (one African-American regiment made her their colonel), and that she often talked in vulgarities. All the newspaper articles refer to her "indecencies" and reference her sexuality in some way, whether it was the way she wore shirts, her mannish haircut, or her flirtatious ways. In court testimony, Tennessee did say that Victoria and James "saved" her from a horrid life.

In addition to the writings we have by Victoria and Tennessee, we have letters and diaries from Susan B. Anthony, Elizabeth Cady Stanton, Isabella Beecher Hooker, Benjamin Butler, and George Francis Train. The diaries and letters from Susan B. Anthony and Elizabeth Cady Stanton were very useful in illuminating their opposing views on Victoria and her radical ideas. Anthony wrote that she was never so hurt as when Elizabeth Cady Stanton supported Victoria. Elizabeth and Victoria remained friends throughout Victoria's life. Benjamin Butler, curiously, does not mention Victoria in his autobiography at all, nor does he mention suffrage. I believe this is because the cause was unpopular and Butler was trying to cement his image for history. His letters and autobiography, however, do provide fascinating glimpses into how he perceived The Civil War, his fellow Congress members, and his family. George Francis Train left a slim autobiography in which he describes having invented everything from erasers to canned salmon, and also describes his involvement with Victoria Woodhull. He paid dearly for his support of Victoria, for it led the government to confiscating his money and property and declaring him a lunatic.

The character we probably know the least about in terms of motivation is James Blood. We have the *Harper's Weekly* article described in the novel, which details James Blood's bravery; we have the Tilton campaign biography of Victoria, which mentions James; and we have the Emanie Sachs biography, *The Terrible Siren*, which interviewed James's contemporaries. A few biographers conclude that James wrote most of Victoria's speeches and newspaper articles. When confronted with this assertion during his lifetime, James denied it, saying that no one was more capable than his wife. I side with James on this question, not only because I take the sympathetic view of Victoria, but also because she started a journal in England and gave speeches for decades when she was no longer with James, and her later writings and speeches are constructed similarly to her earlier ones. After reading everything I could about James Blood from his contemporaries and in newspaper articles, I can only come to the conclusion that James was motivated by a deep love and desire for Victoria. James believed in their shared causes, but he believed in Victoria more. James's later life will be explored in an upcoming book.

In addition to reviewing the sources mentioned previously, I also spent hours reading newspaper articles from that time period. Many of them were so colorful that they are included verbatim in this book. I want to express my deep appreciation to the American taxpayers for making it possible to do this while still in my pajamas, for all of them were found on the Library of Congress website *Chronicling America*. The website does not have all the issues from the time period, but many are available. I hope that this project continues and is completed, for it is an amazing resource for anyone who is interested in history and how events were reported during the dawn of the newspaper age.

As with any work of historical fiction, there are events and people I have left out. I did not continue to write until Victoria's death. That is because I see a clear break between who Victoria was in America and who she becomes in England. My next book will focus on who she becomes in England. Readers will be pleased to know that she remains feisty and independent. I also did not devote any time to the court proceedings of the Beecher-Tilton affair. This was a difficult decision, but since this was written from Victoria's point of view and Victoria was not in court during these proceedings, I did not see an elegant, engaging way to do it. She will discuss the court proceedings and the fallout briefly in the next book. For those of you who cannot wait, Beecher denies everything, Mrs. Tilton confesses, Beecher is exonerated and Mrs. Tilton has to live in shame for the rest of her life as Theodore abandons her and his children and moves to France. So it was the typical story of a woman paying for everyone's sins.

I also left out Stephen Pearl Andrews, the editor of the *Woodhull and Claflin's Weekly*. Radical abolitionist, remarkable linguist, devoted socialist, and founder of the social theory Pantarchy—a combination of the philosophy of Universology and Anarchy—Andrews no doubt influenced Victoria by contributing to her thought. In fact, according to some census data, Andrews lived with Victoria and James for a period of time. A few scholars give Andrews the sole credit for publishing *The*

Communist Manifesto, and I find this to be unfair. First, Victoria had a correspondence with Karl Marx and attended several meetings of the International Workingmen's Association herself. In fact, some scholars believe the split between Woodhull and Marx over women's rights is the reason that Communism never took hold in America (leave it to a Vanderbilt protégé to end Communism before it starts!). Second, Victoria was owner of the paper and decided what was to be published. The same scholars who claim that she did not really publish *The Communist Manifesto* also claim that she is solely responsible for printing the Beecher scandal article. In terms of her publishing activities, Victoria either deserves all of the credit or none. With our limited knowledge of the inner workings of the newspaper, we cannot simply choose which articles we believe she had a hand in and which she didn't (if any). Therefore, I give her all the credit for everything published, whether wise in hindsight or not.

I also left out the continued involvement of Victoria's worthless family. Her parents, siblings, and their families continued to follow Victoria from place to place, taking her money and emotionally abusing her. Anna "Roxy" Claflin claimed that James Blood routinely tried to kill her, but James, Tennessee, and Victoria denied this and he was found innocent in court. Roxy Claflin also tried to blackmail Commodore Vanderbilt. Victoria's sister, Utica, would follow her from speech to speech to yell out profanity and opposing arguments. All of this caused Victoria great embarrassment. Utica died due to her addiction to morphine, but it was rumored that she died of venereal disease. Whether to protect Utica or protect her family from embarrassment, Victoria declared that she had personally witnessed Utica's autopsy and that her vagina was "free from disease."

A few men have said that they had affairs with Victoria (including Theodore Tilton). I did not include this innuendo or gossip either. One of the men, Joseph Treat, who was a friend of Victoria's, wrote a damning article stating that both Victoria and her mother were prostitutes and ran a brothel. This article was only refuted by Victoria, her friends having deserted her at the time, and influenced countless retellings of Victoria's life.

In addition to what I have left out, there are some events that I changed or guessed at. With the dialogue, I tried to include bits and pieces of the characters' own writings, but I, of course, do not really know the specifics of any conversation with any certainty. How Benjamin Butler and Victoria Woodhull initially met, for example, is unclear. Victoria recorded that she went to Benjamin Butler in the night and asked him to open the Congressional committee for her. Butler was really asked by a reporter if it was true that Victoria offered a glimpse of her body in exchange and Butler did reply, "Half-truths kill." We do not know, of course, what the precise discussion was that night. We do know that both Susan and Ben were, in fact, in love with Anna Dickinson at this time. And in what evidence we have of Butler helping and supporting women, we do not see any evidence that he worked closely with Susan B. Anthony.

I changed how and when Victoria and James Blood met. They met in St. Louis in 1866; he came to see Victoria for a reading, and he was still married at the time. Victoria has said that they were married on the spot by the "powers of the air." James got a divorce, and she and James travelled the Midwest performing psychic readings under the name "Madame Harvey." They then moved to New York.

I also compressed Victoria's multiple jail sentences into one. She did indeed spend more than a month in jail. Most of it was in the Ludlow Street Jail rather than the Tombs, but she also spent some time in the Tombs. Victoria did refuse bail at first, but then she was released for one charge, arrested for another, and so forth. This went on for several months.

The ending, when Victoria is sent to England, is placed right after the end of her court date. In fact, there were multiple hearings. She also went to France for a bit of time, came back, and tried to resurrect her paper and rehabilitate herself over a period of about four years. Then Vanderbilt died and she was asked to leave (and richly rewarded for doing so) and start a new life in England. I plan to explore her British life, which is equally fascinating, in the next book that I devote to Victoria.

I hope you enjoyed Victoria's story. If you have any questions or need a source for any particular piece, feel free to email me at eva@rebellioustimes.com. You can also find me on Goodreads, Facebook, and Twitter. Thank you!

Acknowledgements

My hands trace the gold embossed letters on the two *M* volumes of *The World Book Encyclopedia*. I flip through the second one, read about Myanmar, and place it back on the shelf in our small home library. I then pick up the *WXYZ* volume and open it to the entry on Victoria Woodhull. Reading the brief two paragraphs, the words "first female presidential candidate" jump out at me. I run with the encyclopedia in my hand to my father, a political science professor of two decades, and show it to him. He had never heard of her. I then take the book into the other room and interrupt my feminist mother, who told me bedtime stories of Susan B. Anthony when I was young, and have her read it. She has never heard of her.

That was two decades ago, and I have been fascinated with Victoria Woodhull ever since. Her story also makes me question what events and people are in our history books and why. More importantly, why are events and people left out? Once I started researching Victoria in earnest, I realized how little I know (and most Americans know) about the time period of Reconstruction. We seem to be taught about Lincoln's assassination, then the teacher and the books mumble something about failures, and then we're in to World War 1. But I contend that Reconstruction was a glorious and captivating period in American history: brave people were grappling with new realities and trying to rebuild this country into a new and better version of what it had been. Reformers fighting for women, emancipated slaves, and immigrants were not always successful, but they were finding a voice and using it.

All of this is a way of saying that I want to thank the makers of *The World Book Encyclopedia*, wherever they may be, for giving Victoria her two paragraphs. It saddens me that people today will not be flipping through a set of encyclopedias, making new discoveries. I also want to thank my parents, who gave me their interest in history, politics, and feminism. Their political debates taught me that both sides can simultaneously be right and wrong. And their habit of reading the same books and discussing them over dinner also gave me a love for the written word.

As I mention in the Author's Note, I want to thank the American taxpayer. It is with taxes that the Library of Congress (http://chroniclingamerica.loc.gov) was able to digitize so many newspapers from Victoria's time. I also want to thank the International Association for the Preservation of Spiritualist and Occult Periodicals (www.iasop.com) for digitizing many issues of *Woodhull and Claflin's Weekly*. And I want to thank all the researchers who came before me; you can find their books in the bibliography. One book in particular, *The Yankee International: Marxism and the American Reform Tradition, 1848-1876*, by Timothy Messer-Kruse, was essential in my understanding of Victoria's relationship with Marxist ideology. This enthralling account should be read by anyone interested in American political parties and ideology.

I want to thank my editors Amanda Boyle and Sam Clapp for their corrections, questions, and suggestions. Their insight and recommendations have been invaluable. Fellow author Mara Jacobs took a day out of her schedule to walk me through the publishing process, and for that I will be forever grateful. Thanks also to Alan Clements, who worked with me over a period of months on the cover design. His professionalism and talent helped carry me through the last mile. I also want to thank Liz Peryam and Cheryl Cohen for catching errors.

A special debt of gratitude is owed to my family. My husband took over many day-to-day tasks so I could continue to sit at the keyboard. And he never complains when my muse wakes me up at 4:30 am with promises of caffeine and inspiration. My husband is my biggest cheerleader, and I would not be able to face a blank screen without his loving support.

Finally, I thank Victoria, Susan, Elizabeth, Isabella, and all of the reformers who made sacrifices so I could live this life.

318

ABOUT THE AUTHOR

Raised by a conservative political science professor and a liberal women's rights advocate, little Eva grew up on a steady diet of political analyses, social commentary and media critiques. Dinner table discussions analyzed the state of the union. Bedtime stories highlighted famous feminists. Even the tooth fairy left Susan B. Anthony dollars.

One fateful day before anyone had heard of Google, Eva cozied up with the WXYZ volume of the *World Book Encyclopedia* and discovered two paragraphs about Victoria Woodhull. When she realized neither of her highly educated parents had ever heard of the first woman to run for president, Eva became entranced with Victoria Woodhull and the other renegades, rebels and fighters erased from the history books.

She spent years researching the Reconstruction, becoming immersed in the stories of extraordinary citizens fighting for - and against - a brave new world. Eva's first book, *The Renegade Queen*, explores the forgotten trailblazer Victoria Woodhull and her rivalry with fellow feminist Susan B. Anthony.

Eva grew up in Tennessee and earned her B.A. in Political Science from Indiana's DePauw University. She still lives in Indiana, where you'll find her reading about history, enjoying a classic movie, or packing for her next trip.

She loves to hear from readers. Drop Eva a line at eva@rebellioustimes.com.

THANK YOU

Thank you for reading *The Renegade Queen*. I hope you enjoyed it. Would you like to know when my next book is available? You can sign up for my e-mail newsletter at www.rebellioustimes.com. Follow me at twitter at @evaflyn or like my Facebook page (Eva Flynn). Reviews help other readers find books. I appreciate all reviews, whether positive or negative. Thank you.

42273485R00183

Made in the USA
Middletown, DE
06 April 2017